TO BE HUMAN

Macaire O'Grady

*For Mamale, who looks at the impossible
and rolls up her sleeves.*

PROLOGUE

"Nobody can go back and start a new beginning, but anyone can start today and make a new ending."

-Maria Robinson

What do you want to be when you grow up?

This has to be the most harrowing and convoluted question that life has to offer. No, but seriously. I'm convinced it's a trap, created by adults in order to lure the dreams of young children into a minefield of reality.

Okay, bear with me here. I'll explain my reasoning.

I've seen this phenomenon more times than I care to admit, and it never fails to boggle my mind. Especially when a poor, oblivious child is expected to give a serious answer. I mean, really, besides professional thumb-sucker or miniature hellion, how else is a toddler supposed to answer The Question?

My mother has always been quick to inform me that, at age 47 with two children, a happy marriage, and a perfectly crazy household, she still hasn't figured it out. This being said, she was more than happy to encourage me to just be myself, and to become whatever my little heart desired.

"Be happy," she always said, *"if you're happy I could care less what you're doing. Just make sure it's legal."*

It was then with that state of mind that I confronted The Question years later in my second grade classroom.

"Maria? What do you want to be when you grow up?"

With as much confidence as an eight year old can muster up, I firmly answered, *"I wanna be a vampire!"*

Hey, at least I get points for creativity.

At the time, my answer could be quickly overlooked, ignored, forgotten; because, really, with the girl to my right wanting to be a unicorn and the boy to my left eating paste like it was the stuff of life, I wasn't very out of the ordinary.

Go figure, back then, I was the normal one.

Now? Not so much.

The only reason for that is because other kids have their hopes and dreams squashed and conformed and their imaginations run dry by the time they make it to high school. No one wants to be a princess, racecar driver, or the President Freshman year. Oh no, the Board of Education has meticulously taken care of that.

By the time I entered high school, I don't think my answer would have been the same as it was in that second grade classroom, but the dream I had sparked an interest, which became a hobby, and then degenerated into an obsession.

So, to put it plainly, say hello to the brand named *vampire freak* of her high school.

I would always find myself thinking after hearing it spit in my face, seeing it written all over my books, and knowing the words were in the glares of my classmates:

Sure, you guys all thought it was the bomb when we were tiny tots. It's really romantic and sexy when you read about it in Twilight, *but, when I say it, it becomes the work of the devil.*

Life is so unfair.

Now, even more years later, I tell my friends about this and the rest of my hellish high school experience and they laugh and laugh, and laugh some more until they forcibly drag me out of the house and take me hunting to take my mind off of it

Uh-huh, you read it right.

Hunting.

It should go without saying that my new friends aren't exactly that normal either, because I'm not talking about furry little animals.

I'll take this from the top; my name is Maria and this is my messed-up, screwy, overturned life in a nutshell.

I was born and raised in the humble and oh so lovable city of Rochester, New York, a magical and diverse land of various, busy towns, delicious, third-generation bakeries and delis, and an accent that's so mangled it can only be called Rochesterian. It's a pretty sweet place to grow up, filled with history, culture, and some of the best food New York can throw out there. It's the place that managed to give me my fun-loving, New Yorker attitude with a supreme love of sarcasm and a thorough understanding of the proper use of the wordless, middle finger.

But that only goes so far when it comes to high school, especially if most of my comforting, sarcastic commentary stays locked in the noggin.

Remember that little question I was talking about earlier? It succeeded in completely destroying any normal, social life I might have had in those "glory days." And that cute, little name I was given? After a while, it might as well have become a label on my forehead; I receded into myself so much I *became* that person: the loner loser who got straight A's and spent lunch reading all of the fiction the library had to offer.

In other words, I had eight friend-free hours five times of week. The epitome of *not fun*.

It was only after I got off the motorized, yellow monstrosity that I could hang out with my best friend in the entire world.

Kate.

From the first day I ever met her, Kate and I clicked right away. It was an almost instant friendship, and this friendship was solidified after she answered The Question.

"*Um…a werewolf? What else?*"

Love that kid.

If only she went to my high school, then life would just be dandy, but Kate's home-schooled due to fact that her foster home is in the boonies. I try not to bring it up too much; any mention of the fact she's a foster kid only seems to make her good moods go downhill.

Completely understandable.

She's never been the only person of interest in my story of life, though. I somehow managed to find someone else who was crazy enough to be my friend. In a situation that's far too embarrassing to put into words (I'll put it this way; it involves a big tree, uncontrollable goggling, and an incredibly dramatic fall), I came face to face for the first time with Daimon.

Even after a highly degrading first encounter – which I, oh so suavely, ran away from – he talked to me like a normal human being, something I didn't get from kids my age too often. In the months following, we grew closer and closer, and, by some form of miracle, Daimon became my boyfriend.

I'm still reeling with shock myself.

It was only because of these two wondrous personalities that I made it through three years of high school. It's also thanks to them that it was only three years that I had to endure.

Think all of this is strange enough? Well, you ain't seen nothing yet.

Welcome ladies, gentlemen, and others, this is the part where my life becomes messed-up, screwy, and overturned.

PART I:

TO WISH CAREFULLY

CHAPTER ONE

"A true friend is someone who thinks that you are a good egg even though he knows that you are slightly cracked"

-Bernard Meltzer

Now the beginning of this oh-so-beauteous tale actually takes place in a less-than-beauteous situation.

The setting: My quaint, little house, or, to be more accurate, my bedroom.

The plot: The wonderful, brave and inspiring heroine has been woken from her deep slumber by a continuous, persistent – *annoying-as-hell* – noise.

The antagonist: whoever owns the finger pushing the doorbell.

Mondays are the work of the devil, I thought bitterly from under the pillow I was attempting to smother myself with.

But then, by some miracle, the ringing doorbell suddenly stopped, and the house fell silent once more. Sighing in relief, I sank back down into my soft sheets and prepared to fall asleep once more, but, before it was even remotely possible, a thought hit me.

There was only one person who would have dared to wake me up so early during my vacation week, and she would never give up after only five minutes of effort.

As if that was her cue, the window to the right of my bed – with a conveniently placed trellis paired with a broken lock – opened up marginally enough for a loud voice to yell in, "Wake up, sleepyhead! The sun's all up and shiny; come and admire it with your best friend and a warm smile on your face!"

A well-aimed projectile to her face was my only response.

Feeling secure once more, I convinced myself to worry about her perilous fall later. It was sleepy time and I was tired, but, never being one to just *take a hint*, the doorbell returned to its ringing spree.

Great. She survived. Hooray.

Spitting out expletives that would make a sailor's hair turn gray, I violently rolled out of bed and stomped across my room.

A dirty pair of shorts, conveniently located in a ball on the floor, was added to my gigantic pajama shirt, and, combing my hair back into a nicely gnarled ponytail with my fingers, I completed my own adaptation of morning fashion.

I didn't even bother looking out the mirror on my way out; it was bound to be unpleasant.

In a manner remarkably similar to an enraged toddler, I trudged down the stairs and across the foyer, stopping in front of the door to grab the doorknob, twist it harshly, and throw open the door to one of the only people brave enough to wake me up this early in the morning.

As she opened her mouth to say something overly-cheerful and completely unappreciated on my part, I grabbed her by the front of her shirt and hauled her up to eye level to place her even with my best I'm-going-to-kill-you-painfully glare.

"Give me one good reason I shouldn't break the finger that's connected to the doorbell and feed it to the Dachshund next door," I snarled.

Kate, who had become a little cross-eyed trying to maintain my gaze, seemed to be, amazingly, unaffected by my threat and IGTKYP Glare.

What the–

"Because I have hot coffee from Dunkin Donuts to offer up to the princess of darkness," she chirped happily.

Oh…so that's why.

I narrowed my eyes and shifted my gaze to the ground next to her feet where, low and behold, two styrofoam cups sat on the ground, complete with choirs of angels and halos in my mind's eye.

After a moment of deliberation, I released Kate from my hold, grabbed one of the cups, and retreated back into the house, making a beeline for the kitchen where it could be properly appreciated.

I'm what some people call an easily tamed morning monster.

Kate trudged in after me, not bothering to wait for an invite, closing the door behind her and taking off her shoes just as she always did before joining me in the kitchen. She was in her usual getup today: cozy, flannel shirt with a heavily broken in leather jacket left unzipped over the top, a pair of jeans that gave distressed a whole new meaning, ratty, muddy sneakers that had seen better days...maybe three years ago, and her precious canvas messenger bag with a pretty moon design emblazoned on it.

Minding her curly, chestnut hair that got tangled in absolutely everything it could, she pulled the strap of her bag over her head, set it against the wall of the kitchen, walked over to the nearby cabinet to grab some snackage, and then meandered on over to where I was sitting in a chair cradling my coffee to me closely.

"I can see the time alone in the house is already having a tremendous impact on you," she said dryly as she turned the chair next to me around and sat in it backwards. "Do you feel the urge to throw a large, unsupervised keg party yet?"

I took a sip of my coffee, wincing when it burned my tongue. "Party of two, already happening," I informed her.

"Good point. You had breakfast yet?" When I shook my head, she threw a granola bar she had scavenged on the table in front of me. I proceeded to attack the breakfast bar with the ferocity of a rabid wolf. "Where is everyone anyway? I'm positive you've told me a gazillion times, but I've already forgotten."

It was hard talking around a large mouthful of chewy granola, but I managed it. "Seamus had a camp for 'gifted' children this week. My parentals went with him."

So, I have this little brother, Seamus. He's two and a half years younger than me, and he just happens to be the perfect child. He gets straight A's, he's athletic, he's popular...

He's *normal*.

And, as much as I love the twerp that I'd help to raise, it's really kind of annoying being the problem child all the time. Camps like this aren't a rarity in this household, neither are awards ceremonies, championship games, and grand social events. I'll give you a hint; none of them are for me either.

My current train of thought was abandoned when I noticed Kate watching me carefully over the top of her coffee. Her bright silver eyes stared unflinchingly into my blue ones. "You've got that look on your face again, Ria. Stop thinking like that."

"Thinking like what? That I love coffee? Because I like it a bunch," I bluffed taking a swig.

"Mhmm..." She was unconvinced, but didn't push the issue any further.

"So, is there any particular reason you've decided to wake me up, or am I really going to have to break your finger once I finish my coffee," I asked, trying to change the subject.

Her eyes brightened, and I knew she had moved on. "Oh yeah. The parents are gone; the sibling has gone with them. You are a free woman, which means you need to join me in the terrorizing of innocents; preferably at the movie theater!"

"Kate...we do that when my parents *are* here."

"Yeah, but it feels cooler when they're gone," she reasoned. "Besides, there's a good, new horror movie showing!" Without warning, she was suddenly standing on top of her chair, gesturing enthusiastically and occasionally sloshing coffee onto the pristine floor as she exclaimed, *"The Dark Side of the Moon*, the tale of all creatures who scare the bananas out of people, paired with blood and gore in one girl-shrieking, hair-raising movie!"

She looked towards me hopefully, waiting for an excited and joyous reaction. So, not one to disappoint, I slid my gaze to the floor and casually remarked, "You're going to have to clean that up."

She wilted visibly. "That's all I get?"

"I thought *Dark Side of the Moon* was a Pink Floyd album?"

Setting her coffee on the table and hopping off the chair, she made her way to the sink to retrieve some paper towels. "I give up. You're unmoved."

Laughing, I took some of her paper towels and helped her with the mess, "I'm game. What time is the movie?"

Wasn't it unusual for a horror movie to have such an early showing? Or any movie for that matter? But Kate wouldn't have woken me up so early unless–

Cheerfully, she answered, "Seven o'clock tonight."

Oh, no. Oh, *hell* no.

The IGTKYP Glare was back as I struggled to contain my now-murderous thoughts. Kate took note of the sudden turn of events, and fled towards the other side of the kitchen to her bag as I began to descend upon her with the fury of hell at my back. Frantically, she rifled through the bag as I drew closer looking up periodically with a hilariously frightened look on her face.

"I could have slept for *hours*?! And you woke me up to tell me I have to wait *all day* for this movie?" My voice was quickly discovering new octaves, and it only seemed to be scaring Kate that much more.

One hand was now reached out towards me, ready to protect herself should it come to that. The other hand had found whatever it was she was searching so desperately for, and, as she pulled it out of her bag, she yelled up at me, "Holy crap! Take a chill pill! I didn't come empty handed!"

In the space between us, she had a box set of DVDs I quickly identified as the greatest horror movies ever made held up in front of her like some sort of makeshift sacrificial offering.

Hope lit up her face as my anger gave way to excitement, and she continued valiantly, "I even come with super-duper buttered popcorn and rot-your-teeth candy! It'll be like we're spending all day at the movie theater!"

Rather than pouncing on her and beating her as I had originally intended, I crushed in her a big, bear hug. "Kate, you rock!"

I'm probably bipolar at this time of day. So, sue me.

Without wasting any more of our precious time together, we immediately got to work converting my family's living room into our personal media entertainment center. In other words, we threw all the cushions and pillows we could get a hold of onto the floor, and filled the space surrounding our thrones with various kinds of junk food. I got to work setting up the technological side of things, and, before we knew it, we were ready to commence the day o' horror.

We spent the entirety of that day in the couch potato position, eyes riveted to the screen. During lulls in the plot, we added our own, personalized commentary. When someone died an excruciating and overly-dramatic death, we cheered and laughed, and at the end of the movie when the two obviously-destined costars decided to make out for five minutes, we covered each other's eyes howling, *"EW COOTIES"* like we were five years old again.

It went by quickly, though, just like it always does, and, before we knew it, we had to begin our trek to the movie theater. It was close enough that we would feel like fatties driving. So, instead, we walked through the town arm-in-arm, our usual fashion, striking up innocent conversation along the way, AKA, the endless vampires vs. werewolves debate.

"Who the hell *doesn't* want to become a bigass wolf and be the fearsome hunter of the supernatural world?"

"Yeah, but who cares about all that when you have the perks of remaining in a versatile and *damn* good looking form with all the perks of said hunter."

"Oh please, a vampire doesn't have half the available arsenal of a wolf!"

"Uh-huh. Sure. 'Look at me! I'm a fearsome, killer wolf, *fear my super fleas*'!"

Even she let out a snort of laughter at that. "Oh, come on; like you wouldn't enjoy being a werewolf."

"Well that just goes without saying," I informed her wryly. "It also goes without saying that I would enjoy being a vampire even more."

Much to my amusement, she groaned in frustration. "I'm never going to win with you, am I?"

"Not likely."

Shaking her head in disbelief, she wondered aloud, "Now how am I supposed to survive all week with you?"

I sent her a sideways glance. "You won't have to. I have prior engagements planned for certain days."

Taken by surprise at my words, she actually stopped in the middle of the sidewalk and turned to me, a wordless question in her expression, but she seemed to figure it out soon enough.

In a moment, her face became bitter. "Prince Charming," she growled between clenched teeth. "Should have guessed he'd strike first."

She seemed to have formed a very opinionated knowledge of Daimon for not having met him yet. "Now, just relax, Kate. You two are perfectly capable of sharing my time diplomatically for the next week."

She sighed heartily. "I'm perfectly capable of that. I just wished that somehow, deep, deep, deep, way, *way* deep inside that black hole of a heart of yours, you would remember and honor the strong friendship we share and refuse your precious man-candy to help me disturb the peace for a whole week," she accused while shaking her head sadly.

I stared at her open-mouthed and amazed. She smiled, "I knew you would see it like that." She said triumphantly as we resumed walking.

"No, that's not it, Kate. You managed to say a whole, intelligent thought without my help or a dictionary," I placed a hand over my heart, and wiped an imaginary tear from my eye. "I'm so proud."

Maybe, in the future, it would be wiser to wait to insult her when she's not attached to my arm.

After a few blocks of silence, she tightened her grip on my elbow. "Hey, Ria?"

"Yeah?"

She hesitated for a moment, deliberating. A flashing red warning sign went wild in my head. Kate thinking was never a good sign.

"What do you think of werewolves, like, honestly and completely serious?"

That managed to throw me for a loop; she was usually never serious about...well, anything really, but especially about things like this. "I suppose they're pretty cool. I'd like the thought of having a choice to become something completely different, even if it is as a big, hairy dog."

"Better than being human," she said with a dry smile.

"Anything is," I snorted, "But that's not it. They're like...the good guys of the bad guy world, all heroic and junk. It's really kinda noble once you think about it, but, on the flip side, everything you hear about werewolves makes them sound like tortured souls, torn between being a monster and acting as a human. It's hard to imagine the pain they would go through for just being what they are."

Warning! Warning! I am officially taking this question way too seriously.

Not interested in getting into a psychoanalysis of mythical canine shapeshifters, I turned to Kate to make a witty remark to alleviate the conversation from all seriousness, only to see a bitter grimace covering her face.

Unfortunately, I knew that look. It was the same look she got whenever she talked about her foster parents, her past, or her real family.

It was her grim face, and it never failed to make me nervous.

"Yo," I said, rapping on the side of her head with my knuckles, "Anyone home?"

I had succeeded in knocking her out of her pensive state. "Sorry," she apologized quietly, "Thinking again."

"Well stop doing that," I chided lightly. "You're going to overwork something in there, and then you won't be able to fully appreciate the cinematic adventure we're embarking on!"

Her grimace became a small smile, and she allowed me to pull her along faster when I informed her that the previews were at stake. There was no more serious talk for the rest of the night and Kate really seemed to enjoy the movie, but I couldn't help but notice that, when she thought I wasn't looking, she allowed that thinking face to appear once more.

I didn't question it, but I resolved to keep a watchful eye on her for the rest of the week. There was something wrong with her, and I would definitely find out what it was.

Chapter Two

*"In the silence of night I have often wished for just a few words of love
from one man, rather than the applause of thousands of people."*

-Judy Garland

After threatening Kate with a drastically shortened lifespan
and one less finger to boot the night before, I had prepared myself
for a far less *interesting* morning the next day, but, alas, it was never
meant to be.

At least it wasn't the doorbell again.

Resting comfortably on the pillow next to my snoozing face,
ready should an emergency arise in my sleep, sat my over-loved
iPhone; the very same iPhone that chose that very moment to begin
blaring my overzealous 'Sexy and I Know It' ringtone directly in my
ear.

The ensuing moments were spent with me frantically trying
to untangle myself from the sheets that had constricted me
somewhere between the surprised flip off the bed and the crash
landing on the floor. Quickly giving up on that front, I reached up
towards my pillow and searched with my fingers for the infuriating
little communication device.

"Yo," I managed sleepily once the phone was by my ear and
connected.

The amused chuckle at the other end certainly sped up the
waking up process. I'd know that chortling anywhere. "Good
morning, Maria," Daimon greeted warmly. "Perhaps I called a little
too early?"

"Nah," I responded while continuing to wage war against
the uncooperative sheets, "I was just finishing up the morning
workout when you called."

Another amused chortle. "Oh, really?"

"Oh yeah, five mile run," I bluffed with a smile. "Decided to take it easy today; I *am* on vacation after all."

"Good idea," he drawled, completely unconvinced. "Maybe now you won't be too tired to join me this evening for a little rendezvous?"

Be still my beatin' heart. I attempted (cough FAILED cough) to pull off a noncommittal response. "Well, I don't know. There are plenty of people who wish time with my esteemed presence today, but I'll see what I can do."

"I'm honored."

"What time?"

"Let's go with six o'clock," he responded smoothly. "Maybe by then you'll have bested your bedhead."

Maybe by then I'll have bested my sheets, I thought before finally resolving to burn them for their delinquency before he got here.

"Hey. Workout hair, remember?"

"Right, workout hair."

"I'll see you at six then, oh ye of little faith."

Chortle number three. "Goodbye, Maria."

There were a few unhurried moments that followed with me lying on my back on the floor with a crazy grin on my face just thanking whatever heavenly being was bored the day Daimon and I met.

That was until I realized I had minimal time to go best my bedhead.

And the sheets.

Damn.

At precisely six o'clock, not a minute more or less, the doorbell rang, and I bolted from my sentinel post by the door to greet Daimon by practically mowing him over with an enthusiastic hug. From my position, I could feel his chest rumbling with laughter as he wrapped his arms around me in return.

"Hello to you too," he greeted fondly. "I can see your five mile run didn't tire you out in the slightest."

"Well, it's been a rather boring and uneventful day," I told him while pulling away enough to look up at his face. It really had been, too. Kate had informed me yesterday that she wouldn't be able to wake me up ridiculously early or even hang out today, for all of her complaining about Daimon stealing me away. She apparently had some "business" to take care of.

He was still smiling warmly down at me, "Well, we'll just have to do something about that, won't we?"

"My knight in shining armor," I laughed while turning to grab my jacket. "What did you have planned exactly?"

Confiscating the jacket from my grip to help me put it on, he answered, "A lovely walk down Memory Lane with the girl who, quite literally, fell onto it."

"You're hilarious, really. I only dream of being the comedic genius you are someday."

When the jacket was secure, he turned and held out a gentlemanly elbow for me. "Mademoiselle?"

Excuse me while I pick myself up from the puddle of girlish goo I've become.

Rather than voicing that potentially embarrassing thought out loud, I simply laughed at his antics and took the elbow that was offered me. I followed along as he led me away from the house and down the street, talking animatedly the whole way. Daimon and Kate were two of the only people I could maintain any sort of conversation with without stammering like crazy or wanting to murder. There was just something about them that made me feel very comfortable in their presence, very *safe*, a rare feeling for me when with another person in my age group.

It wasn't long until we reached the park down the street from my house. *So this was what he meant by Memory Lane*, I recalled while fighting determinedly against a blush. It didn't work; Daimon noticed the rosy pink covering my cheeks and chortled again.

Arrogant jerk, bringing me to the place where we first met then laughing at my embarrassment.

Taking it a step further, he decided it was necessary to stop by a certain tree and casually observe it for an extended period of time. That was about the time I decided it was completely okay to forgo maturity.

Discretely tip-toing behind him, he was completely unprepared for my sweatshirt attack. Taking the ends of his hood in my grip, I pulled it over his face and then pulled the threads tight.

Middle school trolling at its finest.

He recovered quickly, though, and the look on his face was enough to make me squeak and run away. He gave chase, and, knowing I didn't have a prayer of outrunning him, I monkeyed my way up the infernal tree.

He stood at its trunk watching me, not even the slightest bit out of breath (compared to me who was already dying).

"Are you going to fall off now for my amusement?"

I couldn't even muster up the energy for fake anger; I was loling way too much. Instead, I lay back against the tree and looked down at him, daring him to act with just one look.

Crossing his arms over his chest, he called up, "This is quite the balcony you've found yourself, Juliet."

Warning: you are about to witness an overly excessive and nerdy amount of *Romeo and Juliet* references.

"Is it too much for you, good pilgrim?"

A warm smile lit up his face as he reached up with a single hand. "Dear saint, will you not give me the honor of taking your hand?"

There was really no hope of refusing a request like that. Lazily letting my hand fall from the branch, I reached out towards him and allowed our fingers to brush.

And like any good Romeo, he was not content with just that.

Entwining our fingers, he used the new grip to pull down. My heart was beating frantically as I felt myself slipping from the branch. Closing my eyes, I began to will away everything I owned while holding back a scream.

This is the end. I can see this epitaph on my grave: *"Lovesick loser killed by a Shakespeare reference. Let this be a warning to all romantics out there."*

"Maria," he teased lightly. "You can open your eyes now."

I did so, one at a time, only to find that he had somehow managed to catch me. Super Daimon held me in his arms, and before I could even work to comprehend how he had done the impossible, he started walking somewhere.

"Daimon, what on earth are you doing?" My voice was all breathless, like I had been sucker punched in the rib cage.

He raised one elegant eyebrow and replied blandly, "Carrying you. I thought that should be obvious."

I rolled my eyes at him and his powers of observation, "Ha ha, that's funny, but can you put me down now?"

"I *could*, but why deny myself an indulgence?"

"Daimon! I'm too heavy! Put me down!" I argued without any real force.

He stopped and looked down at me. "That was clearly an insult directed at either you or me. In both cases my answer is still no."

I sighed, admitting defeat, and contented myself in using his shoulder as a pillow as he continued walking. Truth be told, I was quite comfortable right where I was. It was completely dark now, and I could barely see anything in the night.

"Where are we going?" I asked lazily.

"You'll see. Be patient," he berated lightly.

"You and your theatrics."

It seemed like only moments later that I felt his warm breath at my ear. "Maria, wake up."

"Huh? Five more minutes."

He chuckled, sending a puff of air to my neck and shivers down my spine, which, of course, he felt and smiled softly at. "Maria, open your eyes. Look."

I gave in with a heartfelt sigh, opening my eyes to something I really did *not* expect. "Daimon…"

There were, in fact, no words for a situation like this.

I knew we couldn't have possibly left the park, but I had seen the this place from top to bottom many times; taken walks down its paths since I was a little girl; angered the ducks that lingered in the pond more times than I cared to remember; seen every rock, tree, and blade of grass there was to be seen here, so this couldn't be in my park. This enchanted grassy knoll, shadowed by a tall, somber willow tree with a view of the night sky that simply took my breath away, could in no way be the park of my childhood. There was no possible chance. Zip. Nada. No way Jose.

I was so enraptured by the scene I had been carried into (quite literally) that I barely registered the fact that Daimon seemed to find my dumbfounded look endlessly amusing. I silently resolved to torture him later for making me showcase my femininity in such an embarrassing fashion.

"What do you think?"

Like he didn't already know the answer to that.

Turning to look up at him, I gave him my honest opinion, no sarcasm included, something that was, indeed, rare for someone like me.

"I couldn't be happier, Romeo."

We decided to settle ourselves down at the base of the tree with Daimon leaning against the trunk and me using him as a rather nice cushion. I ended up with my back against his chest with his chin on my shoulder as he wrapped both arms around my waist.

I turned my head and looked at him, determined to commit this moment to memory more than I had with any other with him. I noted his half-lidded eyes, two bright and beautiful emeralds, shining almost unnaturally with contentment and happiness; his brown-blonde hair falling over his forehead, looking like it was streaked with sunshine; his skin, paler than even my own, shone almost as brightly as his gaze did in the moonlight; and his lips, stretched in an unbelievably warm smile directed right at little ole me.

The way his lips brushed against my forehead provided a perfect seal for the memory.

"Maria," he whispered in my ear. "Look."

Confused, I turned and followed the path his gaze had taken, only to gasp in surprise when I saw the shooting stars flashing across the night sky.

I could have cried at how perfect the moment was.

"Make a wish, Maria," he whispered into my hair.

As ridiculous as it sounds, I closed my eyes and squeezed his hands, wishing like a child because that was how he made me feel, carefree and blissfully happy. When I was with him, there was no unhappiness or evil that could touch me.

Content with my wish, I opened my eyes and made a hum of satisfaction.

"What did you wish for?" he asked curiously.

I smiled and shook my head, "You know I can't tell you. That would make the wish all screwy!"

It was then that he whipped out his secret weapon, The Voice, a persuasive, soft tone that made my heart pound and could get me to tell him anything he wanted to know. "Tell me, Maria. What did you wish for?"

I sighed, I couldn't fight the power of The Voice, and he knew it, but maybe I could cheat. "Well I was *going* to wish I was with the most *perfect* person in the *entire* world..." I bit my lip, hoping he would buy it.

"Excellent answer, but try again."

I sighed. "I wished that I could live in one of my favorite stories, in a different world, a place where there's magic or mythical creatures. I don't want a cookie cutter life, I want excitement and adventure, and I don't want to just read about it; I want to live it."

He didn't respond to this. He merely rested his head in the crook of my neck and began rocking me side to side slowly.

His pensive silence told me he was deep in thought. I knew from experience that if I didn't say something, he could stay like that forever.

"Don't think you're off the hook, mister," I warned. "What did you wish for?"

"Well I was *going* to wish I was with the most *perfect* person in the *entire* world..." he joked, making me laugh lightly. "I wished that tomorrow would go even better than today?"

"Oh? And what did you have planned for tomorrow that could possibly be any better than this?"

The tip of his nose traced down my neck in the softest of caresses. "Now I can't tell you *that*," he chided. "That would ruin the surprise."

"How long will it have been? By tomorrow, I mean."

"Isn't the girl always supposed to remember that," he joked. "Tomorrow will be six months since I began courting you."

The smile that came to my face was filled with nothing but joy and warmth spread through my veins. I wondered vaguely if I had ever been so happy in my entire life. Doubted it.

"That's a good wish," I finally whispered.

"How about yours?" he wondered aloud so quietly I had to strain to hear his voice. "Are you sure you would want something like that? It might not be as fun as you think. Those stories you read have much more darkness than you'll ever find in the real world."

"Then I'd just make it my job to find the light and prove you wrong."

I could practically feel the smile hovering around his lips. "If anyone could do such an impossible thing, it would be you, Maria. I have no doubt."

I was so caught in my own thoughts, I almost didn't hear what he said. Was it selfish of me to wish for a new life? To be perfectly happy and healthy and still find myself wanting more?

"Someday," I whispered, almost to myself, "I'll reach a place in my life when I'll sit beneath the shooting stars and be so happy that I wouldn't even want a wish to change it."

The arms at my waist held me even closer. "I will do my best to help your wish come true."

"Well," I stated happily. "This a good start."

"What is?"

"You sitting beside me."

He laughed again at my utter hilariousness and I turned my head in time to see him smile before placing the softest of kisses on my lips.

"I love you." He said sincerely, making my heart flutter wildly as he rested his forehead against mine.

"Ditto." He laughed and kissed me again.

CHAPTER THREE

"When we honestly ask ourselves which person in our lives means the most to us, we often find that it is those who, instead of giving advice, solutions, or cures, have chosen rather to share our pain and touch our wounds with a warm and tender hand. The friend who can be silent with us in a moment of despair or confusion, who can stay with us in an hour of grief and bereavement, who can tolerate not knowing, not curing, not healing and face with us the reality of our powerlessness, that is a friend who cares."

-Henri J.M. Nouwen

I woke the next day to the blissful sound of sweet, sweet silence all around me.

Sitting up cautiously in my bed, I strained to hear anything, be it persistent doorbells, maniacal friends, or blaring phones, but, miraculously, there was nothing, absolutely *nothing*. The birds were chirping, the sun was shining, and I was ready and set to go and have a fantastic and wonderful day–

Then it hit me; just like it always does.

"Son of a gun!" I cursed heartily.

Whenever my mornings start out as peaceful and trouble-free as this one had, that meant the rest of the day was just preparing to take a nosedive into hell.

No joke. *Every time*. Take the last few days, for instance. Shitty mornings, *fantastic* days.

Coincidence? I think not.

Just as I started thinking like that, though, an eerie and inexplicable feeling washed over me. There was nothing to explain it, but suddenly I just knew that something was *wrong*.

It was one of those weirdass gut feelings; if my mother was here she would call it my developing "Mom instincts" with my "ovaries working overtime," the same thing she got when either my brother or I was about to do something really, *really* stupid - an instinct that was well-honed, I assure you.

Multiply that by ten and that's what I was feeling.

Goosebumps rose on my arms and I tried to rub them away instantly. There was nothing wrong, I tried to convince myself. I had talked to the fam the night before after I got home and they were just dandy at nerd camp; Daimon seemed fine last night during our date under the stars (a thought that I recalled with a warm smile); and Kate...

Shit.

I had even *noticed* she'd seemed weird when we hung out two days ago, and then that "business" she had to take care of yesterday...

The sound of the doorbell pulled me out of my disturbed thoughts, and I rushed over to my other, not-broken window that was on the front wall of the house. Throwing it open, I hung precariously out of it to get a glimpse of who was at the front door. The breath that had been trapped in my lungs escaped when I saw it was Kate's form slouching by my front door. She noticed me in the window, and I sent her a smile when she turned to look up at me.

"You know where the key is," I called down to her. "Come inside and wait while I get dressed. I promise I won't even take that long."

I frowned as she turned away from me wordlessly to pull out the key my family kept (in an overly cliché manner) under the potted plant by the door. Usually, she would have at least answered me with some form of snappy comeback, but all I got today was silence?

Paranoia, I chided myself immediately as I retreated inside and shut my window. *She's probably fine; I shouldn't get all worked up over a stupid feeling.*

I quickly went to my closet and pulled out my favorite pair of butter-soft jeans and, with a wry grin, my Pink Floyd "Dark Side of the Moon" t-shirt. Doing the quick standard bathroom run, I brushed, flossed, combed, scrubbed, then ran out of my room and down the stairs, jumping off the last four steps and making a beeline for my living room where Kate was probably sitting waiting for me. I was now completely determined to dispel any sort of worried thoughts and bizarre feelings in order to have another great day with my best friend.

But as I rounded the corner, the bright smile I had ready on my face for her fell instantaneously only to be replaced in full force by goosebumps.

Okay feelings. I will never doubt you again.

She was in the corner of my living room, sitting in the chair farthest away from the doorway, more somber and grim than I had ever seen her before in my life. As I froze in the doorway, her gaze slid over towards me from atop her laced fingers, and my breath caught in my lungs. Her eyes, normally so bright in their unique silvery color that they looked like stars, now were as hardened as steel.

I don't like this; I don't like this one little bit. There might as well be sketchy mood music playing right now.

Staying true to my character, I tried to dispel the tension with a joke. "Take your shoes off, kid. Why don't you stay a while?"

"I'm leaving," she answered coldly.

Maybe a part of mind registered her words, maybe that was chill that crawled up my spine to the base of my neck, but the rest of me refused to even see it yet. "So, were you just pining to see my face or something?"

"Maria." That made me freeze. Kate never used my full name, not since the day we first met. "I'm leaving this place. Forever. I'm not coming back."

I tried my hardest to push it away even as a deep cold spread through my veins like ice replacing all of the warm feelings that had been accumulating over the past few days.

Leaving?

And in that one moment, I felt more alone than I had in a long time. Like I was just another girl getting shoved around in a busy high school hallway; someone who had no one care what they thought, or had to say, someone who might as well have been invisible to the rest of the world.

The person I had been before I had met Kate;

Before Kate had saved me.

And then suddenly the coldness was swept away by fiery anger. I was angry. Angry at how she thought she could just walk into my house and act like I was of absolutely no importance to her, like there was no semblance of friendship existing between us. Angry at how she thought she could put that *mask* on her face and just push me aside like chump change.

"Care to elaborate on that?" I asked; my voice deadly quiet.

Obviously, she didn't expect that. Her eyes widened just a smidgen before narrowing once again.

"I'm not permitted to say anything to *you*," she said coldly.

I couldn't help it, I did one of those really nice angry snort-laugh things. "Excuse me? Who the hell do you think you are? I mean, you look like my best friend, but last I checked she wasn't a bitchasaurus. So, if you have something to say to me, I suggest you rethink how you word it."

I watched as, right before my eyes, her tough girl disguise shattered and a haunted and miserable expression took its place. It was then I noticed how her eyes were red-rimmed, as if she had just finished bawling, and the deep, purple marks scored into the skin beneath them, as if she hadn't slept in a week.

Realizing her farce had failed, she held her face in her hands and shook her head back and forth, "I can't...I can't do this," she whispered painfully. "Not to you."

Without a moment's hesitation I hurried over to kneel in front of her seated form. Slowly, I pulled her hands away from her eyes, caught her gaze in mine, and *held* it, *refusing* to let go. "Then don't. Now, we're going to try this again, and this time you're going to be civil about it," I said softly, with only a hint of steel. "You're leaving?"

She nodded sadly, biting her lower lip.

"And whoever is making you leave told you can't tell me anything?"

"Or anyone," she corrected quietly. "They–"

I saw her hesitation, and the fact she couldn't tell *me*, her best friend, informed me that someone had her on way too tight a leash. That made me angry. No, *beyond* angry.

"Kate," I assured her. "You can tell me *anything*. You know that right? Whatever's goin' down, whoever's holding the ropes, it doesn't matter. I'm your best friend, no matter what, and I would do anything for you, no questions asked."

Her eyes were wide with wonderment. "Do you mean it? Do you really, really mean it?"

"Of course I mean it, you dork," I said, acting affronted. "When have I ever said anything I didn't mean?"

"Never," she smiled blearily.

"Exactamento, my friend." I squeezed her hands tightly between my own. "I will never abandon you, Kate. Whatever you're facing, we're gonna face it together, and we're going to get through it."

She stilled, and her eyes looked over my expression, as if testing the depth of my sincerity. I hope she saw a helluva lot of sincerity there too because I meant every word of it. I saw as she mulled over something in her mind and hesitated for a moment until she finally asked, "Even if it meant coming with me?"

I probably should have expected that one. But I didn't, and the not-quite-a request hit me like a ton of bricks.

Leave?

"Okay, so maybe the 'no questions asked' part was a bit of a stretch," I murmured.

Her tightened grip on our joined hands made me look up at her now determined face. "I wouldn't expect it either," she said seriously. "I'm going to ask too much of something from you, Ria, and maybe later I'll hate myself for it or regret it, but, for now, I'm going to be selfish. Because...I know I wouldn't have even bothered coming here today if I wasn't going to at least try."

"Then would you kindly spit it out? Please? Before I die from a suspense overdose?"

I'd hoped for a little lip twitch, or some other sign that she wasn't afraid, but instead she opened and closed her mouth like a fish out of water before ripping her hands from mine. Jumping to her feet, she stepped a few feet away and stood with her back facing me.

"I wish it were only that easy," she whispered, sounding pained again. "But I don't if I can."

What was so awful that she couldn't even tell me about it? "Kate, if you're worried I won't believe you, or that I'll tell someone, I promise I–"

"I'm not afraid you'll spill the beans, Ria," she said with a sadness that took my breath away. "I'm afraid you won't be able to look me in the eye like you do, if you knew the truth."

"There is little to nothing you could ever say that could make me do that to you, Kate," I vowed soberly.

She shook her head. "You don't get it Ria, because I haven't told you anything yet. Though, it's a miracle you haven't even suspected it." Reaching up towards her face, I watched as she pulled something out of each eye. Her contacts? "I am a *monster*, Ria, but I refuse to be too cowardly to admit it to you anymore."

There was something I wanted to say, some words I wanted to spit out, but it was all forgotten the instant Kate turned around to face me and I came face to face for the first time with the full force of her eyes.

"Ria, I'm a werewolf."

If I thought that her eyes were like distant stars before, now they were brighter than the light of a full moon. Not only that, but the large, human pupils I had been used to seeing were now catlike slits that gave her eye a completely otherworldly look. I felt pinned in place by the mesmerizing effect they had. It was almost enough to distract me from the words she spoke.

Almost.

Maybe I should have run away screaming; maybe I should have started quoting Bible passages and Hail Mary's at her; maybe I should have started laughing and then asked her to tell me the real truth, but I couldn't. Kate was still looking deeply into my eyes, and all I could think about was how I had to prove her wrong. She thought she was a monster.

I sure as hell didn't.

So, with the classic single raised eyebrow that conveys more than words ever could, I told her, "Kate, you could have told me anything short of a mass-murderer, and I wouldn't think anything less of you. All you've succeeded in doing is improving my opinion of werewolves in general." I couldn't help but laugh at her flabbergasted look. "You're my best friend. You're a good and caring person; I might not have been here if not for you. Admitting to me that you're a fuzzy, evil-vanquishing shape-shifter isn't going to make me see you as a monster. No matter how badly you want to get rid of me, I make friends for life."

By now, I could catch the sheen of tears she refused to cry shining in her eyes. She took two steps and fell on her knees in front of me, reaching for my hands as desperately as I reached for hers and held tight with a grip that made my joints creak.

"I could never want to get rid of you," she declared softly. "Not when you're the most decent human being I've ever had the privilege of knowing."

"Me? Decent? Yeah, right. Who are you kidding," I joked.

There was a smile on her face as she shook her head. "You'll never realize just how amazing you are, will you, Ria?"

"Hopefully not, I'm bad enough as it is."

And then she was hugging me, so tightly I could barely breathe, laughing softly next to my ear, and I couldn't do anything but reciprocate and laugh in return.

Maybe someday you'll realize just how amazing you are, Kate.

CHAPTER FOUR

"A true friend unbosoms freely, advises justly, assists readily, adventures boldly, takes all patiently, defends courageously, and continues a friend unchangeably."

-William Penn

Once our gushy, emotional moment was finished, Kate moved to sit next to me on the floor with both of our backs leaning against the front of the chair and our shoulders pressed together. She sat ramrod straight, Indian-style staring distantly at the floor; I watched her out of the corner of my eyes with my knees tucked close to my chest. Soon enough, she would sort out her chaotic thoughts, and I'd be waiting in the wings to hear what she had to say.

She was uneasy, that much was obvious. Her hands were twisting and intertwining together in her lap, betraying just how nervous she felt, despite my promise. She had already admitted her big secret; I couldn't imagine what she had anything that was more earth-shattering than that.

Deciding enough was enough, I reached out and took one of her hands into my own forcing it away from the other one. She gripped it like a lifeline without turning to face me.

"Maybe you should start from the beginning," I suggested patiently. "Like, explaining the reason you're hear consorting amongst insignificant and weak humans in the first place."

The corner of her mouth twitched upwards. "You're hardly insignificant," she retorted, "and, truth be told, *they* don't even know about you."

"*They*?" I questioned skeptically. "Care to be a little more cryptic? I might actually catch on to what you mean."

"The ones who sent me here," she clarified offhandedly. "I came here on a standard reconnaissance assignment, scoping out the area for...the enemy."

I felt my eyes narrow. "There you go being all cryptic again. Who the hell are *they*? Animal, vegetable, mineral? And what do mean the–"

And then, suddenly, I understood what Kate was implying. Playing it cool, I dropped her hand and jumped to my feet in surprise, spluttering one incoherent question after another.

"Ria? Breathing is necessary for basic human function," she reminded me.

I managed one deep breath before asking, "So, if you're a werewolf, then you're enemy is...*there are vampires here*?!"

"Congratulations, you've made a connection a five year old child is capable of. I will have to remember to give you a gold star later for your brilliance."

"*Are you serious*?!"

"About the gold star? No. Sorry, for the letdown."

"NO! Not about the stupid, gold star!" I took a deep breath, calming myself. "Are there really vampires around here? They're really *real*?"

Again the wordless, single, raised eyebrow comes into play. "Have you really so little faith in your precious hellspawn?"

"No! It's just, yesterday I was only wishing that there was a world like this within my reach" Literally. "and today it's suddenly here right before my eyes. Maybe my wish came true?"

She smiled sharply, "I can't exactly sympathize. It would be my biggest dream come true if they didn't exist, if you catch my drift."

"Okay," I affirmed, still way more excited about all of this than I should have been. "So codename: '*they*' sent you to check out the vampires in the immediate area, and that's how you ended up here."

"Yes," she nodded.

"And now...?" I couldn't really guess what was even happening now.

She sighed. "Up until now I've just been working for *them* as their lackey, but now I'm the appropriate age to begin formal training, and *they* know I'm more valuable to them as a soldier than an errand girl."

As soon as she said that, it felt like hundreds of butterflies were playing *kamikaze* in my stomach again. "So, you don't have a choice. You have to go."

"Yeah," she whispered. "It's what I've been waiting for practically my entire life. Every wolf does. I just...I didn't expect to meet you and become your friend, and..." she trailed off. "Now, I don't really know what I want."

"It's your choice," I told her quietly. "It's your life, your decision. In the end it's what you want that matters."

"But it's not," she argued, slowly beginning to stand up. "Because now I'm making it your choice; I want you to come with me, Ria. I want you to abandon this empty life that has nothing worth offering you to come follow me, and become part of a world you only dreamed about joining."

In my astonishment, I actually took a step back from her. The universe had to be playing tricks on me; had it been only yesterday I had wished for such a chance? Was it really Kate who was holding open a door I had never seen before?

Could it even be possible?

"Kate, I'm *human*. Straight up, normal, average, completely, run-of-the-mill, *human*. I can't follow where you're going, no matter how much I want to. It's just not possible."

She was standing up straight now, watching me with a calculative eye that was becoming annoyingly recognizable. It was like she was staring at me in a Petri dish, and it was also the look she got every time she was about to drop a bombshell on me.

"And if there was a way?"

Yup, there it is. The proverbial bombshell.

"Is there?" I asked breathlessly.

I didn't know what to make of the serious look she leveled me with. "If there was, would you come with me? Could you take that inner strength I've seen and use it in tandem with the werewolf curse? Could you become the first human to successfully complete the rigorous training needed to become a soldier for *them*?"

"Who, Kate," I demanded, beyond the point of impatience. "Who is it you're talking about?"

Her shoulders tensed tightly under her flannel shirt, and I saw her hand clench the back of a chair she was standing next to so hard her knuckles became white.

"*Them*," she ground out. "*The Council*."

I gave it some time to soak in, but then I just couldn't help myself. "Well, that sounds wonderfully cliché and everything, but that means nothing to me unless a provided explanation is given."

Her head whipped around to face me so quickly I was surprised she didn't have whiplash. "The Council," she repeated, talking as though she had a bad taste in her mouth. "The people I live to serve and will continue to serve until my dying day; one of the most feared names in the supernatural world; and the primary leadership behind a quarter of the world's werewolves."

"That sounds serious."

"Yeah, it's pretty damn serious."

A moment of silence followed in which I attempted to grasp the magnitude of what she had told me, and failed miserably opting instead to take a different avenue of conversation.

"So," I ventured hesitantly, "if I were to say yes?"

"If you were to say yes," she explained smoothly, a distinct flicker of hope lighting up her expression for a moment. "I would Change you into a werewolf, and you would follow me back to the main headquarters and training facility. From there, we would plead your case to the Council, and, with any luck and their *explicit* permission, you would spend the next two years training with me and other werewolves our age in order to become fully-fledged soldiers under the Council's banner."

I absorbed this as calmly as I possibly could, closing my eyes and burying my face in my hands as visions of such a future played out like a movie in my head. I saw Kate and me; I saw us becoming two badass werewolves subduing evil and saving the world together complete with bad visual effects and cheesy, heroic lines, and it looked incredibly cool and wonderful and perfect and brilliant–

But then I saw my parents' faces: warm and loving, taking care of me even if they couldn't fully understand me; teaching me as well as they could; and telling me that they loved me *so much*, and would no matter what happened.

I saw Seamus' face: from his baby years, looking trustingly up from the safety of his crib and reaching out to me, his older sister, for love and protection; I saw his current much more pubescent face, which held the same trusting expression, albeit in a much more subtle, "manlier" form.

I saw Daimon's face: I saw love that went above and beyond the average teenage fling pouring out of every part of him; I felt his warmth seep into my bones and chase away all of my doubt and anger as he whispered the most magical words I'd ever heard in my ear and gave them enough meaning for my heart to start doing gymnastics in my chest.

"*I love you…*"

And that was when the eyes began leaking. I was so torn apart, and *so damn confused* that I didn't know what to think anymore.

Hell, I didn't even know what I was *supposed* to think anymore because the line that normally separated the morally correct things from the outrageously obvious temptations – a line I normally took great comfort in blatantly ignoring – was suddenly nowhere to be found.

It seemed the good old conscious was on vacation again. Useless thing.

Tears poured down my cheeks sluggishly as I pulled my hands away from my eyes in order to clench them into fists at my sides. Kate's expression told me that she wanted to come over and hug me and scare all of my big, bad fears away, but she and I both knew she couldn't.

"I...I don't know, Kate!" I practically yelled out. "I don't know anymore! I want to go with you; I don't want you to leave me and I don't want to be stuck here, but I can't leave them behind! I love you, but I love them too! Mom and Dad, Seamus, and Daimon..."

"Don't you deserve to be happy?"

My now sufficiently watery gaze met hers head-on. "What?"

"Don't you deserve to be happy," she repeated rather slowly, as if my IQ had lowered hundreds of points and I'd started sprouting blonde hair.

"I...I am happy," I mentally punched myself in the face as the statement came out sounding more like an unsure question.

"Are you really?" she asked quietly, with an edge that made it sink it deep. "It makes you happy to pretend to be someone you're not in order to please your parents' expectations? Does it make you happy to have a brother who loves you, but wishes you were different so he could maintain his 'image' while still being related to you?"

"Stop," I pleaded weakly.

But she didn't. "Does it make you happy knowing that you love one boy with all the love in your big heart, but can't be sure he loves you so much when he's too perfect to be real?"

"Please stop," I tried again, ever more weakly this time. She was ripping me apart from my deepest fears and doubts, and I could feel myself tearing inside.

"Does *it make you happy* that you'll be stuck in this boring human life forever, never getting a chance to taste that excitement you've always dreamed of having just because it never happens to the people who actually *believe* it's possible?"

"Shut *up!*" I shrieked. I wanted to hold my hands over my ears in the childish way of trying to prevent myself from hearing anymore of what she was saying.

"No," she said quietly. "It scares you more than anything, doesn't it? That you'll be trapped living a boring, average life forever. That, no matter how many people you love, no matter how many people love you back, you'll never get a taste of that excitement you've always wanted to experience, and you'll always be stuck in this little box of conformity that's been put around you, where there's no space left for you to just be Ria."

Here's the thing that about the "person who knows you best." It's freaking awesome when you're having a bad day and you just need to sit down with him/her and a tub of cookie dough to rant, but during heated arguments, they have more ammo against you then should even be considered *fair*.

"So, what do you want me to do, Kate?" I whispered brokenly. "Do you want me to leave behind everything I've ever known to follow you into this dangerous and life-threatening world? Do you want me to just pack up my bags and go without another word to my family, leaving them high and dry? What exactly do you *expect* from me?"

She continued to watch me from across the room, not daring to approach me when I was this upset, but, despite all of her harsh truths and cutting words...she looked as sad and confused as I did. She wrapped her arms tightly around her stomach, as if shielding herself from something. "I know, Ria. I'm expecting so much from you, and I'm saying things that hurt, and just kinda being an all-around bitch, but...I'd be willing to do *whatever it takes* to get you to stay with me."

For a moment, I was convinced she would start crying just as I had, but, instead, she simply closed her eyes and began breathing deeply. She did not start talking again until she had a firm grasp on her emotions. "I don't know what I'm ever going to do without you," she whispered so quietly I wasn't sure I was even supposed to hear it.

When I didn't respond - because, at this point, I was pretty close to being emotionally spent for the day - she took a step towards me. "I live in such a dark world, Ria; where things that should be beautiful are wasted; where things that should be cherished are thrown away for the sake of power and strength, but around you, it's different.

"You're like a breath of fresh air for me, Ria. It's unbelievable just how forgiving and...*good* you are."

"I'm not perfect, Kate," I reminded her, despite being flattered by her words. I was no St. Ria.

"No, maybe not, but you're already doing a lot better than I am," she argued, and, suddenly, a smile lit up her face and a breathy laugh escaped her mouth. "I feel *good* when I'm with you Ria. You probably won't believe this, but I've done some pretty terrible things in my life, things I can't bring myself to confess to just yet, but, when I met you, I had a clean slate, and I turned out to be an okay person.

"I have to go back, Ria, but the werewolf Kate that works for the Council isn't the same girl you know here. I'm scared, I'm scared that when I go back there, I'll become that girl again, and that's not who I want to be. I want to be the girl that's Ria's best friend, that listens to her conscience, that hasn't done anything unforgiveable to anyone.

It seemed that, in that one instant, everything fell into place in my head. The clouds cleared and there it was: my answer. Maybe it wasn't a question of the right or the wrong choice anymore. Maybe it was just a question of where I was needed most.

And Kate, standing in front of me bravely holding back her tears and speaking words straight from her heart, looked like she needed me now more than ever.

Here was the universe giving me the chance I wanted, the escape I needed from a cookie cutter life, and, hey, who was I to spurn a gracious offering from the universe?

"Well," I said almost conversationally, "looks like you need a personality cheerleader then, huh?"

She seemed confused by my ambiguous answer; I had to keep myself from smiling. After being confused as hell for the past half hour, I felt she deserved a little vagueness in return.

"What...What do you mean?" she asked timidly, like I was going to pull one hell of a joke on her or something.

I just gave her one of those looks in return. "What I mean is that you better start planning what you're going to tell these 'Council' people when you arrive with me in tow."

Suddenly, I found myself with an armful of teenage werewolf girl as Kate launched herself across the room - an impressive distance, might I add - towards me, gripping me with a strength that threatened the safety of my ribcage.

"Kate, as you may or may not have mentioned before, breathing is necessary for basic human function," I reminded her kindly even though I returned her hug wholeheartedly.

"Thank you," she whispered blearily into my shoulder. "Thank you for not leaving me."

A smile formed on my face, "Thank you for taking me with you."

Thank you for being my friend.

Chapter Five

"I have been impressed with the urgency of doing. Knowing is not enough; we must apply. Being willing is not enough; we must do."

-Leonardo da Vinci

I was ready to reach for a crowbar by the time Kate finally let go of me and returned to the rather pressing task at hand. She didn't want to let me out of her sight. Honestly, what was she expecting? Me whipping out some advanced magic trick to make like Houdini right before her eyes?

Unfortunately, that wasn't likely to happen.

She towed me up to my room and grabbed what she deemed my "ragged, threadbare, dragged through hell and back" backpack - which is *so* was not; it was just....over-loved - and proceeded to pull out random pieces of clothing from my closet. This included: various pairs of ratty jeans, some t-shirts, and a pair of scruffy boots (that were actually *made* for walking).

As I watched her pack what she deemed appropriate and necessary for the road ahead of me, I mulled over a few pressing thoughts.

1. How was I supposed to become a werewolf between now and the impending Council meeting?

2. Would *they* even let me train with Kate?

3. How was my family supposed to take this?

4. Daimon. Daimon. Daimon. <3

The heart was actually there in my thoughts, slightly obnoxious, but definitely necessary.

But these thoughts needed to be taken care of in order; I felt the first was the most pressing, and it sounded like a good place to start.

"Hey, Kate?"

"Yeah," she answered distantly while using her entire body weight to shove what looked like a book into my bag.

A book that could now be considered nonfiction. Chyeah.

Focus, Ria. F-O-C-U-S.

But wait. How does someone go about asking a question like this? 'Hey there, I'm still a puny, insignificant mortal over here. Is this fact going to change anytime soon?'

Time for the direct approach.

"When were you planning on…um, Changing me?"

Kate's reaction was immediate; the hands forcibly shoving crap into my bag froze in midair and looked as if they were trembling a little bit. For a moment, her eyes glazed over and she turned to face me. Her fear was almost tangible, and it was enough to make me afraid too.

"That's right," she murmured. "I almost forgot. We should…we should get that over with."

Detachedly, she put my bag on the floor, and, by the look on her face, it was easy to see she was in Lala Land.

"Come on," she called. Somehow she'd already made it to the door and was walking down the stairs. I scrambled to follow behind her, nearly tripping over the oversized bag in the process.

Kate stopped in the middle of the foyer at the bottom of the stairs. In the midday light, the space was bright and seemed more spacious than ever. The gentle clapping of Kate's boot heels against the wood floor echoed eerily, making the space seem even bigger. When she reached the very middle of the room, she stopped without turning around to face me.

"I'm…I'm going to Change, Ria, and then I'll have to…bite you," she said quietly, uncertainly.

Processing…processing…

"Wow. That's *really* anticlimactic," I told her jokingly, despite the fact my heart rate had just doubled. "You'd think there'd be some magic junk to add to it."

"Well there is, but I think explaining it is a little beyond my mental capacity at the current moment."

I completely understood, seeing as I seemed to be in the same frame of mind right about now. "Are there any side effects I should have to worry about? Anything you haven't told me yet?"

"I...I don't really know," she said shakily, not looking me in the eye. "I've never Changed a human before."

Great. Now I'd made her nervous. "Well then, we'll just figure this one out together."

"You know you don't have to do this."

Whoa. Didn't see that one coming. "What? What are you talking about?"

She still didn't turn to face me, but her voice carried over the large space. "It's nice that you can put on a brave face, even at a time like this, but I can tell you're afraid. It's perfectly normal. So, if you want to back down...I understand."

"Listen, Kate, I don't want a get out of jail free card," I told her, exasperated with this sudden turn of events. "I made my choice, and here I am. So, buck up because I'm not giving up."

She didn't say anything in response, but I noticed the tension in her shoulders lessened slightly, only a little bit, though.

"Get ready then."

That was the only warning I got.

It wasn't the creepy skin-ripping, monster-emerging nastiness that all of the movies have. It was much more subtle than that; I barely even noticed it at first, but, then, I *felt* it. It was like the air around us had become supercharged with lightning. The skin on my arms became covered in goosebumps and the back of my neck was tingling like crazy.

But that was all soon forgotten when Kate started to really Change.

Her eyes closed as her limbs began to stretch and change. They extended to points where they could be called anything but human, sprouting thick waves of wavy, chestnut hair, and then her face did the same. Her whole body grew, until she was no longer standing in front of me, two-legged and completely human, but rather on four massive legs as a fully transformed werewolf.

There was nothing recognizable about her, including the newly-changed jaw lined with a row of dangerous-looking, steak knife-reminiscent teeth.

The teeth she was going to have to use to Change me.

And then, she opened her eyes, which were still wonderfully, astonishingly silver. For 1.3 seconds, I could breathe a sigh of relief, taking comfort in being able to recognize something of Kate in this giant wolf.

But after those 1.3 seconds, something began to change. Her eyes took on an unnatural gleam, and then suddenly the clear whites of her eyes became shadowed with inky, black darkness. Within the span of a blink, her whole eye, barring the gleaming silver iris, was a shiny onyx color.

It seemed impossible that she could so thoroughly change herself when the whole process took only a few seconds, but the Kate I had known and loved as my best friend was no longer identifiable. Instead, I was left with this creature of fantasy in front of me.

I could hear my pulse beating heavily, separating each second from the next as I stood frozen in front of her. My mind was screaming in protest because what it was seeing defied every law of nature out there; it was close to making me sick, but, despite all of this, I wasn't afraid. I couldn't be afraid; because Kate was standing there in front of me, still as a statue, and I knew that she saw herself as a monster.

If I freaked out now, it would only solidify that thought.

So, I ignored every rational part of my brain attempting to comprehend this, pushed away all the fear that froze me in place, and forced myself to see Kate in this wolf in front of me, my best friend, and someone whom I never passed up the opportunity to prove wrong.

The first step forward was by far the hardest. When she didn't move, it got easier. When I stood less than a few feet away from her, I lifted one of my hands and reached towards her.

The hair was softer than I imagined, closer to human hair I had spent many a night braiding than dog fur. It was warm, and covered with something that made my fingers tingle. I tangled my fingers in it and traced my gaze over the features of her new face making myself memorize them, until I met her large silver eye.

The silver eye stared back at me, and I almost forgot *what* I was looking at, remembering *who* it was instead. I saw Kate for a split second, the human one, and it was enough to make me smile, a genuine, warm smile, that showed her I was not afraid. It was only then, that I saw her eye soften in understanding.

"Still not a monster," I whispered, "still Kate."

A whine escaped her lips and she nudged my right arm with her cold nose. I looked at it for a moment trying to grasp what she was trying to say. It didn't take long for the light bulb to go off and I started to roll up the sleeve of my shirt. I stopped when it had reached my shoulder and tucked it in tightly so it wouldn't roll off.

"So help me God, if you get *any* blood on my 'Dark Side of the Moon' shirt…"

The threat was less help than usual in bolstering my failing courage. My breathing was quickening, for all that I tried to calm it. I couldn't back out now. I couldn't be afraid, but I was. I was so scared of those sharp teeth that my legs were shaking. I was never good with pain, the very thought of it made my body break out in a cold sweat and my stomach tighten with terror.

Kate saw I was afraid. I wasn't exactly hiding it, but I didn't want her thinking it was because of her. "Kate," I told her quickly, my voice cracking slightly as the panic set it. I pushed it down and continued, "I'm not afraid of you, and I never will be, but I am scared; I'm terrified of getting hurt. I want you to know that, okay? And no, I'm still not backing out."

Her gaze was soft and understanding and it warmed my heart to see that our bond, our friendship, was so strong that it passed through any physical barrier that stood in our way, made me feel all warm and fuzzy inside. It was enough warmth, that even the icy tendrils of fear pulling me inside were pushed back a little bit.

Silently selling my soul, I held out my arm to her, baring the smooth, pale, and unmarred skin to her deadly jaws. She hesitated for a moment, and then shifted slightly; I saw the smooth muscle ripple under her heavy coat. She had moved so that her shoulder was now in front of me with her head facing the inside of my outstretched arm. I was confused; I didn't know what she was trying to tell me. She made an impatient movement with her right leg and suddenly I got it. I reached out to her and gripped the thick hair of her large shoulder tightly, preparing myself. I closed my eyes and turned my head away, hoping I wouldn't see.

"Just do it," I ordered tightly.

There was nothing in the world that could have prepared me for the pain. As her teeth tore through my arm like butter, I screamed to high heaven. It tore through the air even as I tried muffling the noise. In amongst the dizzying, nauseating pain, I could feel something else. It ran through my veins up from my arm into the rest of my body; when it hit my chest, it felt like my heart had to pump twice as hard as usual. I had this crazy feeling that if I looked down I could see it beating out of my chest with effort.

By the time she released me, I was gulping down air as deeply as I could. Was I hyperventilating? Not cool. Only my grip on Kate's shoulder kept me on my feet. When she shifted back, her shoulder was still under my hand, but, without the massive wolf body to hold me up, my legs gave way quickly. Kate followed me down, kneeling in front of me and prying my fingers off of her so she could run to the kitchen next door.

Only then did I look down at my arm to inspect the damage. It was hard to see through bleary eyes – when in the hell had I started *crying?* – but a few heavy blinks later it was fully visible. Her teeth were so big that only six of them managed to make a dent in my arm. The punctures were lined up in a row and high enough on my arm that I could easily cover them with a t-shirt sleeve. Thanks to my undying love of gory vampire movies, I wasn't exactly the squeamish type, but this was friggin' *nasty*.

But, never fear, no blood found its way to the Dark Side of the Moon t-shirt.

Kate was soon back with me, a load of medical supplies in tow. Though her movements were unhurried and smooth, her anxiety was clearly threatening a hostile takeover.

"How are you feeling?" she asked with splashing some alcohol on a towel.

Even in excruciating pain and feeling as if my heart was jack hammering my ribcage, I managed one of my classic 'Really? *Really?'* expressions. "Yeah, I'm floating on cloud 9 Kate. You should really try this sometime."

"Well, sarcasm means you're going to make a full recovery."

"Regardless, this patient would really appreciate being bandaged up sooner rather than later."

And that's when she put the alcohol to my arm, and I was *thisclose* to screaming out loud again. "Actually," Kate began, seemingly oblivious to my pain. "I was really, *really* impressed. You didn't faint. That's tough."

"Am I getting an award for effort later?" I gritted out through my teeth.

"Well if you're going to be testy about it," she quipped, tying off the last of the bandage and packing up the supplies. "I'm going to clean up the blood from the floor. I think it would be best if you just chilled out for a while. Blood loss can hit you harder than you think; so do not run around like an idiot."

She was just lucky my arm was incapacitated.

"When it gets dark we'll head out for the train station."

That caught my attention. "Train station? That's how we're getting out of here?"

She nodded, then shrugged. "Flying gives me the willies, and I'm too much of a lazy ass to drive all the way there."

I smiled, managing - for once in my life - to hold back a sarcastic remark to that. It was harder than I thought it would be to push myself off the floor to stand up. My vision swam a little, and I think someone turned the room upside down when I wasn't paying attention, but I managed it.

I tried my hardest not to look at the floor, at the bloodstain Kate was now cleaning up; I kept the smile on my face and walked away towards the stairs. When I had my foot on the first step, I stopped, but I didn't turn around to look at her. I called loud enough that she could hear me. "Kate?" Feeling her stillness behind me, I went on quickly. "Thank you. I know you don't think you're doing me any favors, but thank you."

Then I walked away without hearing her answer.

Chapter Six

"People so seldom say I love you And then it's either too late or love goes. So when I tell you I love you, It doesn't mean I know you'll never go, Only that I wish you didn't have to."

-Jalal Ad-Din Rumi

Waking up from the groggy sleep I had fallen into was like surfacing from very deep water, slow and kinda hazy. It was, however, helped along by the fact that my right arm might have felt better if it was being amputated. I had so brilliantly decided mid-sleep to roll over onto it, and was now paying the price.

With a hiss of pain, I pulled my arm out from under me and shimmied my legs over to the side of my bed. On my feet, it took at least ten seconds of patient mental counting for the spots to disappear from the edge of my vision. A quick glance to the bedside clock told me I had slept for at least a few hours and still had a few more until Kate and I were even thinking of leaving.

Great. What was I supposed to do for a few *hours*? My stuff was all packed. I was now thoroughly infected with werewolf-ness. Was there anything else...?

And suddenly, I felt my throat constrict as my breath caught. There *was* something I still had to do.

I had to say goodbye.

It may have seemed pointless to the average individual when there was really no one *home* to say goodbye to, but...I'm not exactly normal, and, believe it or not, it was *not* so incredibly easy for me just to pack up my bags and bid home a fond farewell.

My steps were heavy and slow as I shuffled from my room to the hallway. Distantly, I heard the buzz of a TV on downstairs and figured Kate was just amusing herself until it was time to go. I continued walking. By the time I reached Seamus' room, I had started shaking again, but I meandered on past that to the door at the very end of the hall.

I placed my hand on the aged wood, and some of those shakes quieted. Instant relief. With a small smile set in place, I turned the knob and walked inside.

My parents' room carries with it their presence, as does any other place they've explicitly forbidden entrance to – some creepy parent power, I'm convinced. As a kid, I wasn't allowed in here for fear that I would break one of the many picture frames, pull the lamp cords, swing from the ceiling fan, or whatever shenanigans my parents expected me to get into.

But now, much older and hardly any more mature, the room was comfortingly familiar. The solid, navy walls made the space cozy, and the wood floor gave it warmth. I traced my gaze over every inch of the space, committing it to memory. I walked around the room, letting my hand drag across the things that came in its path: my mother's large wooden armoire, my father's tall dresser, and, finally, the ornate, mirrored dressing table.

It wasn't used for its conventional purpose; instead, it looked as if it would give out under the weight of the many, many pictures that called it home. They were in every kind of picture frame imaginable – including plenty of crappy noodle-covered first grade art projects – and some pictures were even tucked into the side of the mirror. I couldn't help the sad smile that flickered to my face as I looked over so many happy memories. Most of the pictures were of Seamus and me during the younger years, when every parent feels the obsessive need to document every moment of their child's life. The others were more spread out over time, but each one made the ache building in my heart heavier and heavier.

There was one that really caught my attention; I'd nearly forgotten we had it. The memory was an extra-special one. We'd been attempting (*failing*) the dreaded Christmas card shots – which my mother needed to have done *perfectly*. However, with the cast of characters she had to deal with, it was quite the challenge and usually only succeeded via threats or bribery. This particular shot had been the last of a slew of failures. My mom sat on a chair in the middle, composed and smiling in the appropriate manner.

The rest of us? Not so much.

Seamus was on the far left behind her crossing his eyes and looking as mental as possible. I was in the middle next to him, with my hands on my mom's shoulders and making a creeper-ish expression that had me laughing even now, years later. My dad, on my other side, looked extraordinarily normal and deceptively innocent until you noticed the pair of bunny ears sprouting from behind Mom's head.

Upon seeing the picture, my mother proceeded to, how to put it nicely, blow a gasket or two, and while the rest of us were ROTFL-ing, she sought immediately retaliation.

She made it our Christmas card. We still get jokes made about it. Success.

I didn't notice the first tear that fell from my eye, or the second, but, when the sobs began to build up deep in my chest, I didn't even try to hold them back. They tore through me one by one, betraying the pain that was beginning to tear me up from the inside out.

I took two steps away from the table and laid myself down on top of the neatly-made bed, curling up in a ball and smothering my crying in one of the pillows. I felt so small and alone in that one moment, just mulling over the knowledge that I would probably never see my family ever again. If only I'd known that when they'd left; if only I'd known that when I'd called them last night. I needed them now more than ever.

I closed my eyes and tried to imagine them there with me; just like I was a kid again, coming into my parents' room after being convinced there was a boogie man in my closet. I would be huddled to my dad's chest (because nothing bad could ever reach me there) with his arms around me, and my mom would be there combing her fingers through my hair, rubbing my back, and whispering soothing words in my ears, words that would chase all of my fears away.

Sometimes, Seamus would come in, having been woken up next door, and stare up at me in my parents' bed offering me his favorite stuffed animal to sleep with. Later in the night, he would always come into my room and climb under the covers with me. When he had nightmares, I always did the same.

Just imagining it gave me the same comforting effect. My breathing slowed and calmed and the sobs soon died away until there were only tears falling silently down my face. It was only when I'd calmed that I pushed myself off of the bed and away from that warmth. With heavy feet, I walked to their master bathroom to wash the tears from my face.

I hadn't seen my reflection since earlier that morning, before Kate had Changed me. As I washed my face with cold water, I took note of the differences already there.

My skin was paler than usual, almost sickly looking. I tried to bring back color to it as I scrubbed, but to no avail. There was a sheen to my eyes that was not there before, similar to the unnatural gleam Kate's eyes had taken on when she'd Transformed in front of me, but that could have been my overactive imagination at work again. It was hard to see anything behind the red puffiness they had adapted.

Seeing that, I suddenly felt like a big crybaby. I made my choice; I knew what I was getting into. It was beyond time to suck it up and take it like a girl because, no matter how many tears I cried, I wasn't going to see my family again. I had no desire to involve them in the world I was launching myself into; I would very much prefer it that they stay clueless and blind to the things that go bump in the night.

On the other hand, I was pretty sure that the people in the new world I was about to enter wouldn't appreciate me crying hysterically over every little thing either.

I thought of Kate, then. She had just endured a fair share of the same emotional trauma that I had just experienced, and she had done it without shedding a single tear, whereas I had closely resembled a waterfall.

It was high time I started following her example.

So, that's it then, I thought firmly. *There's no more room for tears where I'm going. They won't help solve anything anyway. Crying to Mommy and Daddy isn't going to help me get through intense werewolf training. So, it's time to stop needing to hold somebody's hand every time the going gets tough! This is Ria, new and improved, ready to get going!*

Feeling optimistic over my self-given pep talk, I dried my face and marched out of the bathroom. Out of the pot and into the fire was the best way to test my results. Seeing everything made my throat tighten a little, but there was no more urge to find a pillow and sob uncontrollably.

Progress!

My eyes stopped on the "picture table" again, though. Could I be selfish one more time, really quickly? Treading back over, I picked up the picture in the very front, the Christmas card picture I was looking at before.

Just one memento then, I thought as I pried the photo from its frame and looked at again.

"Goodbye," I whispered to the faces in the picture. Then, taking a deep breath, I carefully folded it in half and slipped it into the back pocket of my jeans.

Mission Accomplished.

Chapter Seven

"We cannot change our past…we cannot change the fact that people will act in a certain way. We cannot change the inevitable. The only thing we can do is play on the one string we have, and that is our attitude."
-Charles Swindoll

Just as I was finished tucking the picture away, Kate burst unexpectedly through the doorway. Turning sharply towards her, I immediately took note of her frightened expression and some exasperated part of me wondered what *else* could possibly go wrong today.

"Kate?" I asked worriedly, coming towards her to grip her shoulders lightly. "What is it? What's wrong?"

"Ria….Daimon is here."

Silly me, it can *always* get worse.

My heart stopped beating, I swear it did, but anything I was about to say, be it blasphemies, expletives, or otherwise, was interrupted by the all too familiar sound of the doorbell. Kate and I locked eyes, a moment of wordless communication and quiet panic passing between us.

"What should I do?"

"Go lay down in your room," she told me firmly, already ushering me out the door and down the hall. "I'll tell him that you're sick and he shouldn't stay long. Lord knows you already look sick enough."

That was definitely true, as much as I hated to admit it.

I was already dive-bombing into my bed as Kate ran down the stairs and answered the door. I was too far away to hear what was being said – where were these new werewolf powers when I needed them? – but it wasn't long before I heard the soft tread of footsteps coming up the stairs.

I took deep breaths and tried to control my heartbeat, hurriedly throwing on a sweatshirt lying on the floor near my bed to cover up the bandage completely. I could only imagine how that conversation would end.

"Where did I get this boo boo? Oh, I just tripped...into the jaws of my best friend who is actually a werewolf in the hopes that I might become one too because I'm leaving with her tonight in order to endure years of intense werewolf training. Well, bye!"

Oh boy.

By the time the door creaked open slightly, I was lying peacefully in bed under my abominable sheets attempting to calm my building heart attack.

"Maria," God did his voice really have to be so perfect, even at a time like this?

"Hey there," I croaked, my voice still rough from the extensive sobbing I had just finished.

He came to my side of the bed and pulled over a chair to sit beside me. Brushing the hair away from my face, he laid a soft kiss on my forehead in greeting before pulling away to look me in the eye.

"Isn't this just my luck," I told him.

His smiled was soft and it made my throat tighten in pain. "How are you feeling?"

Well, currently my heart is being broken into a million and two pieces, but I'd rather not tell you why. Time for the standard answer. "I'm fine." I tried smiling, but it felt too sad, even to me. "I'm sorry."

"You're sorry for getting sick?" He snickered quietly.

I leveled him with as severe a look as I could manage. "I'm sorry for getting sick and ruining your plans."

His thumb brushed softly across my hand. "Maria, you can hardly control when you don't feel well, and you can hardly expect me to be upset with you because of it."

He must have seen something akin to amazement and appreciation in my expression. The hand not holding mine found its way to my face where it cupped my cheek softly. His smile turned fond. "One day of plans hardly matters. All that does matter is that you are here with me today," he said, gently tracing his thumb across my cheekbone. "As it is, I plan on sharing many, many more anniversaries with you in the future."

It was then I that I decided that karma was in fact the biggest and most vindictive bitch I'd ever come across in my entire life, and that was *really* saying something.

"Thank you," I whispered, truly touched. I tried my hardest not to think about it or about everything that I was going to have to throw away because of one little choice that I had made, but of course a slideshow of images raced through my mind.

His eyes lit up as his smile grew. "Anytime, Maria."

I saw no trace of annoyance or dishonesty in his expression. It was always the same with him; he spoke what he thought and it was always the truth. Which made his whispered avowal that much more heartbreaking.

"What did I ever do to deserve someone as great as you?"

Whoops. How did that leave the noggin?

His face pinched together, and worry spread across his features. "Maria, are you all right?"

I couldn't make the right words come out, and, luckily, I didn't need to. At that moment, Kate's voice cut across the tense air of the room.

"Sorry to interrupt," she said in a way that didn't sound sorry *at all*. "I just wanted to make sure you were all right up here."

Was that my imagination, or did Daimon actually scowl at Kate? It was only for a millisecond, though; he was smiling now, but I knew him well enough to see that it was forced. "Maria is fine, Katherine. We were just talking."

Teehee. He calls her Katherine.

Katherine narrowed her eyes slightly, sharp smile set firmly in place, just like his. "It's probably best for Ria if she gets some more sleep. It'll only help her heal faster."

If his hand wasn't holding mine, I would have never felt the sudden tenseness that overcame Daimon at her words.

"You are right. If you will give us a moment, I will say my goodbyes to Maria."

Kate looked very self-satisfied as she nodded and walked out of the room. It was actually starting to make me a tad bit irritated.

Daimon's soft sigh brought me back from my thoughts, though, and, with the sad, strained look on his face, it finally hit me.

These would be our last moments together.

If he thought my spastic, renewed grip on his hand was strange, he made no comment.

The frustration that was making the corners of his eyes pinch relaxed and an easy, natural smile spread across his lips. "I'll give you your present now before your warden comes back and kicks me out your window," he joked lightly.

"You. Did not. Have to get me anything."

It was always the same with him. I insist. He ignores. I get shiny pretty thing. He gets crappy, homemade failure.

"Of course I did anyway though," he said, unperturbed as he reached into his pocket and pulled out a long red box that might as well have had "expensive, overpriced jewelry" written along the side.

I watched wordlessly, though, as he gently opened the box for me to see the treasure inside.

"Daimon..." I lost my breath just looking at it.

His smile grew as he tugged the delicate chain from the box and held the silver locket up to my eye level. "Do you like it?" he asked quietly.

The chain was so thin and pretty I was afraid it would break at my touch, but it seemed to be strong enough to hold the small heart-shaped locket.

I watched, still not able to speak, as Daimon opened it neatly and showed me the inside where a D and an M were engraved on either side of the heart in a swirly, Edwardian script.

It was only when he shut it again that I saw the shooting star etched onto the front of it.

"It's so perfect," I finally choked out, looking up into his eyes, moved beyond belief at the warm look I found there.

Commit this moment to memory too, Ria. This is how you will always remember him.

His fingers were cool and deft as they latched the necklace to my throat. I touched the silver lightly, reverently. Before I could stop myself, I shot up from my reclined position to wrap my arms around his neck and hug him tightly to me. The pain in my arm became more bearable when his arms wound just as tightly around my waist.

"I love you, Maria," he said softly, but with conviction I could never doubt, in my ear.

I fought past the lump that was forming in my throat long enough to choke out, "I love you too."

That was how Kate found me a while later; legs pulled tightly to my chest, with one arm holding them there, and my other hand softly fingering the cool metal of the locket.

"Hey," she called softly to me, "it's time, Ria."

It was strange at just how numb I felt as I strapped my backpack, and followed behind Kate, choosing to ignore the line of worried glances that she kept sending back to me. It wasn't until we were out the door and halfway across the yard that I stopped, only for a moment, and looked back over my shoulder.

The house of my childhood, the place where I'd grown up, my safe house, stood alone in my vision. Countless memories played at once across my line of sight, but they were broken by the call from behind me.

"Ria?"

I had to protect those memories. I had to protect this place and the people that would continue to live here.

With any luck, they would never have to see me again.

"Promise me something, Kate?"

A hesitant pause. "Yeah?"

"I don't want them to ever be involved in any of this." I didn't bother specifying that I was talking about my family. She knew; I knew she did. "Promise me they'll stay safe. No, swear it."

"I swear to you, Ria, I will watch over your family and keep them away from anything evil that comes their way."

And, with that, I turned away and followed her into the night.

Goodbye everyone. Wish me luck.

I'll miss you.

CHAPTER EIGHT

"Don't be afraid of your fears. They're not there to scare you. They're there to let you know something is worth it."

-C. JoyBell C.

The excitement of the train ride had little effect on my uncharacteristically pensive attitude. I sat with my forehead pressed against the cool glass of the window most of the trip, watching as miles and miles of land continued to separate me from home.

Kate sat similarly, and, to anyone else, it would have seemed like she was deep in thought too, but, as stated once or twice before, I'm her best friend and I could tell that if the silence stretched on any longer, Kate was going to start screaming.

Hey, it's part of the job description.

Her shoulders were too tense, for one, and the way she was tapping her fingers against her twitching leg and glancing in a not-so-subtle manner towards me every minute was beginning to make me just a tad bit exasperated.

Finally, with a deep sigh that made her eyes snap immediately in my direction, I came out of my shell of sulking. "You know," I told her quietly, still looking out the window. "If you don't ask whatever it is you're dying to ask, you'll never find out."

When she didn't respond, I turned my gaze to meet hers. She looked really torn about something, and maybe a little like she was in pain. Before I could ask her what was wrong, she closed her eyes and took a deep breath. When she opened them, she was calm and collected again, all fidgeting came to a screeching halt, and the mildly panicked look in her eyes was gone.

"While we have time alone," she began. "I think it would be best if I tell you some of the important intricacies of werewolf society….*before* we arrive."

She didn't ask her question. I wasn't so oblivious that I didn't notice that, but I chose not to comment. She would ask eventually.

"That's probably a really good idea," I told her, turning to face her completely and tucking my legs to sit Indian style on the seat. "Teach me the ways of werewolves, furry one!"

It was in this moment Kate seemed to realize she had a challenge on her hands, but, valiant as ever, she began her lecture.

"Now, werewolf society, as you will no doubt quickly discover, is based completely off of three things: your family, your strength, and your pack. We'll start with the family.

"Over the centuries, the werewolves of this region have been separated into twelve clans. There is no definitive ranking of the clans, but each one has special talents or strengths it's known for. The strongest member or leader of each clan serves as a member of the Council, and represents the best interest of the clan as a whole."

"Hold up," I interrupted, leveling her with a skeptical gaze. "I'm getting a serious 'old, white men ruling the world' vibe here. Are all of them old?"

She hesitated, "They're…. well-aged."

I'll take that as a yes.

"Uh-huh, and are all of them white males, perchance?"

Another pause, "There's not a lot of diversity in this region anyway."

Oh, I am *good*.

Seeing my smug look, her eyes immediately narrowed. "Most of the werewolves who live in this part of the US immigrated from Europe centuries ago. There's lots more supernatural activity there than here, but this is where a lot more of the fighting takes place. There they try and handle it 'civilly'."

"That fact changes nothing," I told her haughtily. "But you said most…?"

She nodded; happy for a change of subject, I assumed. "When the wolves first came to the New World, they formed an alliance with the Native American tribes already living here. We've been close with them ever since." She smirked, "They're like the unofficial thirteenth clan."

"What did the alliance entail, exactly?"

"The werewolves who came to this region would protect the Native Americans from the vampires who got off of the same ships, and, in return, some of the strongest of the Native American men were Changed."

"But the tribes aren't represented on the Council," I argued, not fully understanding.

"No, but the standing Chief serves to represent the Native American wolves and advises the Council in certain matters."

Based on the tough set of her mouth, and the grimace that shadowed her face for a moment, Kate seemed to think the whole thing was just as ridiculous as I did.

"*Anyway*," she continued. "The only way you can really earn a name for yourself in society is by your strength, which is measured during your training and in your time with your pack out in the field. It can be based off of your skill, your smarts, or even the strength of your Gift."

"When did we start getting presents?" I asked quickly.

"Will you quit interrupting me," she snarled. "You'll never find out *anything* at this rate!"

"Well so*rry*! You can't just keep springing this stuff on me and not expect me to get a teensy weensy bit lost!"

Kate sighed deeply in a way that made me want to knock her over the head. "A *Gift* is a special bonus that comes with being a werewolf. A heightened sense, a healing power....it could be anything. Every family has one."

"And what about me? Don't I get a present?"

"Your *Gift* will present itself as your training progresses. There has never been a single werewolf without one before, don't worry."

And, simply because she said not to worry, I didn't. Kate had yet to lead me astray (not counting this entire expedition).

"Tell me more about this Council," I asked, suddenly curious.

Kate sat up straighter in her chair, face serious, but regarding me almost warily, as if surprised I had brought up the subject at all.

"The Council basically rules and regulates every aspect of the werewolves in this region of the world," she said evenly. "They monitor training and organize the packs when training is finished. Then, they delegate certain strategists and generals to deploy certain packs on missions and patrols based on various specialties and whatnot."

Her words made me wonder more about what she wasn't telling me than what she was. It made me wonder what kind of fear and respect these men commanded that Kate's eyes glazed over and her hands tightened on her armrests to keep from shaking. The more I heard, the more interested I was to meet these people...wolves in the flesh.

This should probably tell you a thing or two about my insanity level.

"When we arrive at the main compound I will have to introduce you to the Council before anything else." Kate leveled me with the most serious face I had ever seen her direct at me before in my *life* and there had been a lot of those lately. "Ria, this is very, *very* important. The Council doesn't take very kindly to humans in general, and they don't have any idea that I've Changed you yet. You need to prove to them that you can do this, and that you won't be afraid."

A thought suddenly hit me at her worried tone. "Kate, are you going to get into major trouble for doing this? For Changing me?"

She shrugged in a nonchalant manner that made my eyes narrow automatically. "Don't worry about me; we'll just have to see what their reaction is to you."

That's a completely obvious "Yes Ria, I am going to get put into time out for this."

But, before I could open my mouth to yell at her she was talking again, this time about training, telling me all of the wonderful things I had to look forward to for the next few years of my life.

That is, if I managed to receive the Council's approval.

The train eventually made it to our destination (late, of course), and, from there, a chauffeur took us in a really swanky car to the main compound. Throughout this ride, I was even more unbearably impatient than I had been on the train. Halfway through the trip, Kate had whipped around and made it perfectly clear that if I sporadically tapped my fingers *one more time* she was going to leave me *alone* to deal with the Council.

It was at this point that I remained so perfectly still and tense that Kate, in turn, began rhythmically beating her head against the glass of her window.

Thankfully, before any permanent damage was done, we arrived at our destination.

I felt like a kid in the world's biggest candy shop as I gaped, mouth hanging wide open as I surveyed the grounds around us. I vaguely registered Kate's soft laughter behind me, but quite frankly couldn't gather enough focus to hit her for it.

The entire place was *enormous*, and I had an inkling that I hadn't seen half of it yet.

We wound our way along a long, gravel driveway that lead to an extravagant, white marble building that looked older than dirt, but well-maintained. It reminded me of Capitol Hill, or maybe even a City Hall, only on a much more grandiose scale.

With great, white pillars framing the massive three-story structure, it looked as formidable as the name that was boldly displayed on its front.

Eastern Quadrant
1537 AD

Behind the main building were various other buildings varying in design, style, as well as age. Some were clearly gigantic gyms, others were dormitory-looking, and then there was one, the closest one to the Council Building, that very nearly rivaled it in size. It was undoubtedly an arena. I almost didn't want to know what sorts of events were held in it.

The driver pulled the car around the circular end of the driveway, right up to the Council Building. A sense of numbness seemed to overcome me as I stepped out of the car, and, for the first time, it really hit me: I was going to have to sell my case to a bunch of haughty, old men with a thing against humans who would then control every single part of my life until the time they stepped down.

Fan-freaking-tastic.

How did I ever manage to get myself caught in situations like this?

One second, I was frozen in place in front of the building, heart pounding and mind racing; the next, Kate had my shoulders firmly in her hands as she turned me to face her, pulling me out from my mildly-panicked state.

"Ria, I will not let anything bad happen to you," she said firmly in a tone that sounded like a promise. "No matter what they say to insult you, degrade you, or reprimand me, they can't change two very important things."

"And what are those things, Kate?" Was that my voice shaking? Crap.

"For one, you've already been Changed, and, no matter what they do or how much they wish it, they can't Change you back."

"And the other thing?"

A warm smile spread across her face as she let go of my shoulders and folded me into a very warm and comforting hug. "You're *you*, Ria. You don't even understand your own worth yet. They would be crazy not to see how valuable you could be to them."

I suddenly found myself very, very happy that I had Kate as my friend. Practically glowing from her hard-earned praise, I buried my head into her shoulder, hiding the smile that had spread from her face to mine. Too soon, she let me go to take my elbow as per usual and lead me up the steps to the Council Building.

And I realized then that I wasn't afraid anymore. Because she was right for the most part, I had nothing to worry about, and no matter what they said to me...

She would still be standing beside me.

CHAPTER NINE

"Before I knew you, I thought brave was not being afraid. You've taught me that bravery is being terrified and doing it anyway."

-Laurell K Hamilton

About halfway up the steps, I realized that I had no absolutely no idea as to what I was really expecting to be on the other side of that main door. Maybe a bunch of hairy people walking around barking at each other, wolves lurking in random dark corners just waiting to be bothered, a "Beware of dog sign"?

What I did know was that I didn't expect the normal reception room that came with any office building I'd been to.

It had a hushed sort of air, filled with the sound of typing, quiet chatter, and rustling paper. The few people who walked by were dressed neatly and ignored us completely in order to do whatever work they had to do.

This could quite possibly be considered the biggest letdown of my life.

Without pause, Kate made her way around various people with me in tow towards the front desk.

Seated behind that desk was a small, redheaded woman wearing a headset and typing away busily on the computer she was staring dazedly at. After a few seconds of that, she leaned back in her chair contentedly and pulled out a nail file from her drawer to have at her perfectly manicured nails.

Yep. This *was* just like any office I've ever been too.

The woman, who I assumed was the head secretary here, had wild, red hair, tightly, but naturally, curled sticking out from all over her head. Her heavily-framed glasses sat halfway down her nose, accentuating her heart-shaped face and high cheekbones. She was middle-aged and wasn't extraordinarily thin, but neither was she robust, which took me by surprise. I assumed all everyone here would be perfectly in shape, all the time.

Was this woman not a werewolf?

She looked up from her nails as we approached, obviously peeved at having her cuticle time interrupted, but when she got a better look at Kate, that all changed. Her face suddenly lit up and, with a happy cry, she dropped her forgotten nail file and stood, reaching out to take Kate's face in her hands and pepper it with kisses.

It was at this point that I bit my lower lip to keep from laughing.

"Oh my goodness, sweetheart! I haven't seen you in ages! I missed you so much!" Kate's dismayed expression was funny enough, but, when the woman pulled away to suddenly smack her lightly upside the head and glare fiercely with her hands resting on her hips, I nearly fell over laughing.

"Where in the seven hells have you been?" she scolded, but as Kate opened her mouth to give some sort of an explanation, the woman suddenly held up one her hands. "Wait! On second thought, I don't want to know what kind of dirty work the Council has you doing running amongst humans."

Heaving a great sigh, she plopped back down onto her comfy desk chair and picked her nail file once more. As she resumed her work, she finally looked up at me over the rim of her glasses.

"And who might this be?"

Kate wrapped her arm tightly around my shoulders. "Aunt Rose, this is my best friend in the whole, wide world Maria. Maria, Aunt Rose." Kate's voice suddenly turned quiet with an edge that made me nervous. "She's a little present for the Council."

Somehow, I didn't like the sound of that.

I could see where Kate learned how raise a single eyebrow so well. "Is this a surprise party or am I bringing the piñata?" Rose asked dryly.

Kate's smirk was so evil that I had no doubt she was enjoying this experience far too much to be considered healthy for me. "Everyone could use a good surprise every once in a while."

"Mm-hmm." Rose was obviously unconvinced. "Those men need something, but it's not a surprise. I hope you're ready for the consequences of this little stunt, kiddo."

"Oh, but Aunt Rose," Kate said quietly, leaning over the desk. "This gift is non-returnable."

Rose just stared open-mouthed at her for a moment before looking at me, then back at Kate questioningly. "You...her," was all she could spit out. Kate nodded, never changing her absolutely wicked look. Seeing Rose's look of utter disbelief, I had the most wonderful mental image of Kate getting the scolding of a lifetime. Not only that, but I was going to be here to witness it.

That is, until Rose took that moment to cautiously scan the immediate vicinity before leaning forward to give Kate a fist bump. "You, my lovely little niece," she cackled happily. "Are going *straight* to hell."

Aw hell. Now I know they're related, I thought miserably. *There's absolutely no hope for me.*

Once she and Kate had finished their bouts of evil laughter, Rose turned towards me and smiled in a way that reminded me of my mother's smile.

Don't think about that now, I scolded myself as a sudden wave of homesickness washed over me.

"Best of luck to you, Maria," she said warmly. "You'll be fine with Kate, don't you worry."

I returned her smile as best as I could. "Thanks."

I noticed Kate roll her eyes at my quiet, subdued tone, and was grateful she didn't make any unnecessary comments. She seemed to understand how hard it was for me to come out of my shell.

After all, she had to deal with it herself once before.

"What room are they gathered in today, Rose? The formal one?" Kate chirped happily. Seeing Rose seemed to have lightened her mood.

Rose quickly shuffled through some papers on her desk until she found the one she needed. "Uh, yup. They're all ready and waiting for you." When she put the paper down, Rose settled a serious look on the both of us that only looked a little anxious. "Be careful," she warned.

"Don't you know I'm always careful, Aunt Rose," she shot back as she began to lead us away from the desk to the hallway behind.

Rose's skeptical snort did not ease my fears in the slightest.

Despite my best efforts, I felt the dread that had been containable up until this moment begin to rise. Sweat slicked my palms even as I rubbed them nervously against my jeans, and by now I was sure my heartbeat was loud enough for the whole world to hear.

After all, Kate seemed to hear it well enough.

Her firm tug on my sleeve in the crook of her elbow managed to catch my attention. "Hey you, don't be a chicken *now*. You've been so good!"

I tried taking a deep breath, really I did, but I just couldn't seem to get enough air into my lungs, which, certainly did *not* help with the heartbeat problem.

Just as we were going to turn a corner, Kate pulled me to a stop and turned me to face her. "Ria, how many times do I have to say it? I will not let anything bad happen to you. Ever."

"It's not just me I'm worried about, Kate," I told her frankly.

A cocky smirk crossed her face, and I wasn't sure I liked it. It wasn't a good look for her. "I'm worth way too much to them to be punished, Ria. No worries."

"If you say so." Can you tell I'm unconvinced? Because I pretty much am.

"All right," she said excitedly. "Into the wolves' den!"

Those being the final words said, Kate straightened herself and marched around the corner, naturally expecting me to follow behind. When I did, I found myself faced with quite the intimidating sight.

Protected by two guards who looked like they ate nails with their Fruit Loops in the morning, stood the largest and most elaborate pair of doors I had seen in my entire life. They were easily over ten feet tall and made of a dark, aged wood that I could clearly smell, even from a small distance away.

But that was hardly the most impressive part

Across the center of the doors was an extensive and intricate carving: twelve wolves, six on each door, all of them howling upwards towards an ivory moon that was set in the wood above them. The detail of the carving was so realistic that it could have been a painting; I had the almost-overwhelming urge to reach out and run my fingers along it, but restrained myself from acting like a curious three year old child.

As I moved to stand beside Kate, a quick peek out of the corner of my eye told me that she had schooled her expression back to "serious Kate." I followed her lead, attempting to make my face as blank as I could. The two guards made no move, merely shifting their gaze to look down at us in a rather condescending manner.

"The Council is expecting us." The firm, regal tone next to me booked for no argument. "Open the doors."

Surprisingly, they didn't hesitate to follow her order, turning around to push the heavy doors open with an echoing creak that made me wonder just how heavy they really were. Without any sign of nervousness, Kate held her head high and walked right into the now-open room with me right on her tail.

Into the wolves' den...

It was even more of an effort now to keep my jaw from practically breaking off in pure awe.

I should have suspected the lavish style of the doors would hint at just what was inside. The room we were entering was straight out of a history textbook, or even a European palace.

The first step was the only one that echoed, but it was enough to give me chills. The entire room – floor, ceiling, walls – was constructed of pristine, white marble that looked very expensive and very pompous. To each side of us, lining the walls, were single rows of colossal statues raised on a high pedestal.

Each of those statues was of a great, howling wolf.

At the other end of the room, hanging high above us on the wall, was a large, gilded picture frame - decorated with the same sense of exquisite detail as the entrance - of a size I'd never seen before. However, the subject within that frame was not a picture of an ancient battle or another great wolf figure.

It was just a list of traits and characteristics written in very elegant - very *old* - script:

Selfless. Strong. Empathetic. Persistent. Trustworthy. Respectful. Reliable. Honest. Serene. Open-minded. Confident. Self-disciplined.

The words sparked my curiosity; I wanted to know what they meant, but it would have to wait until later. Much later.

I had other things to think about now.

The second step I took was muffled by a long, blood-red carpet that ran the length of the room up to the focal point at the very end. Situated just below the large picture frame and raised on a dais was a long table made from the same dark wood as the door and with seats for twelve.

And there they sat, looking just as I had pictured them. Twelve old men, with grey-streaked hair, aged faces, and stern expressions. The amount of arrogance and self-importance they were oozing almost made me roll my eyes.

Which, I would have done, had I not been so immobilized by fear.

Sure, they were old and looked as though they could have been hiding walkers behind their chairs, but there was an air of danger around them that was damn-near suffocating me. I was a fly on the wall, pinned to the spot by just their gazes. Each pair of eyes was a physical weight as they examined me up and down with distaste.

I hate being the center of attention, I thought desperately, forcing myself not to fidget and just endure it for as long as I could.

The back of Kate's head suddenly entered my line of vision as she stepped slightly in front of me and shielded me from their gaze. Their attention simultaneously shifted to her, and, suddenly, I could breathe again.

The doors were sealed behind us with a final, resounding slam that made the situation that much more terrifying.

"Honored Council members," Kate began humbly. "I apologize for being so late. I was detained."

I watched as a subtle power play took place at the table, with every member glancing towards the central figure seated in the exact middle, in the place of honor. The chair he sat in was taller than all the others, meaning this guy was head honcho. His gaze, however, remained firmly on Kate, never acknowledging the others. Just when I thought the silence would never end, he sat back completely in his chair and raised his chin slightly.

His voice was deep and powerful enough to make me feel like my bones were reverberating from the sound. It was a voice that demanded respect. I had this frightening image that it could bring me to my knees if I wasn't careful.

"You have a story to share with us, Kari. I suggest you start from the beginning."

Kate nodded slowly. "I will be sure to. Thank you...Grandfather."

CHAPTER TEN

"There is a woman at the beginning of all great things."
-Alphonse de Lamartine

I had never, *ever* in my life been more confused than I was now (and this is coming from the girl who took a semester and a half of calculus. I *know* lost).

First of all, did Kari = Kate? And little miss *Kari* couldn't tell me that the leader of the entire Council just so happened to be her grandfather?

Can you tell that being left out of the loop is one of my biggest pet peeves?

"The Council originally sent me into the city of Rochester, New York in order to validate the rumors of heightened vampire activity in the area," Kate said calmly. "After months of dead ends, I was called home to begin training. However, with the help of one of the locals, I was able to find the vampire of interest."

I couldn't help but feel like I was playing the part of Random Local #1 in this story.

The Council Head's head tilted slightly to the side, exactly like a dog does when it's confused. "Nothing in this story gives me reason to believe you should have found it acceptable to bring home a stray."

The displeasure in his tone was unmistakable. I very nearly winced at the insult, but Kate was firm. She probably had plenty of experience dealing with these guys.

"Grandfather, you know I would not have done so unless I found it absolutely necessary, and I am well aware of the ramifications of my choice, but, after the help that she gave me, it would have been dishonorable to leave her to the vampires we discovered. She needed my protection, and I couldn't give it to her from here."

It was a deadly game these two were playing in front of me; The Council Head trying to get past Kate's defense, and Kate just barely holding her ground.

I wondered vaguely where I belonged on the game board.

When his eyes narrowed slightly, I could practically see him making his next move.

"Really," he drawled casually. "So, this is the reason you saw fit to Change her without the Council's permission as well? And do not lie to me; I can already smell her blood changing from here."

Um. Ew. *Stop* smelling me from across the room, *please*.

"I saw fit to Change her because she has already proven herself to be of value to the Council. Her intelligence, her loyalty, and her strength are all aspects that the Council searches for in its soldiers. The knowledge she possesses of our world is impressive, and her courage is more worthy of a wolf than a human. I saw in her someone that the Council would find invaluable.

"I am also well aware of the increase in vampire activity that has taken place in the past few years. You are going to need all of the help you can find in the times to come. Better to start with someone whom you know will prove her worth."

The tension was thick between the two adversaries as they stared each other down from opposite ends of the room. An impasse was generated between them, neither one wanting to give way to the other. I felt my palms grew clammy, and kept them firmly fisted at my sides, fighting the urge to rub them against my jeans, but then the Council Head's eyes landed on me, and all bets were off.

His gaze tore through me without any visible effort, to the point where there was nothing left in the room but us two. Shining silver eyes, just a shade darker than Kate's familiar ones, pierced me so deeply I felt as though he was in my head, rummaging through whatever thoughts were of interest before tossing them aside one by one. I had the faint thought that I might actually start screaming.

And it was that thought that got me to buck up. I told Kate (Kari?) that I would do my best and not be afraid. So, sneaking a big, soothing breath, I schooled my deer-in-the-headlights expression into one that was calm and collected, and forced myself to meet his gaze head on.

If he was surprised by my sudden bout of courage, it didn't show at all, but the silence hanging in the air around us seemed to lighten just a bit, and I had a feeling that I had done something right.

"Very well," the Council Head finally conceded. "We, the Council, will allow your companion..."

"Maria," I answered, speaking firmly.

He paused, as if surprised that I could speak at all. "We will allow Maria to participate in the same training as the other pups, under surveillance, of course."

In any other situation I would have dropped to my knees professing my great relief to the heavens, but, seeing as I have *some* brainpower, I kept my gaze locked on the Council Head's never-wavering one, fighting the urge to smirk at our little victory over the resident butthead.

As if sensing my insubordinate thoughts, the Council Head smirked in a manner that was unsettling enough to raise the little hairs on my arms.

"With any luck, she will make it farther than the other humans who have tread this same path," he drawled casually.

Kate's hand was firm on my shoulder as she, too, looked him in the eye and murmured, "Don't worry, honored Elder. She will."

After some intense negotiations (coughs THREATS cough), Kate and I secured a double room on the top floor of the first-year dorms. I contained myself for as long as possible, but, when the door to our room shut, I immediately began assaulting Kate with the nearest possible pillow.

"You have less than thirty seconds to reveal all previously withheld information, Kate slash Kari," I ordered between vicious whacks from my feathery weapon of doom.

"If you stop assaulting me, I could clearly tell you what is going on!" She yelled out at me between pillow slaps.

After one last hit, I decided to take her advice and cease fire. "You have five and a half minutes starting now. Use them wisely."

She shot me an exasperated glance and shoved me off of her before collecting herself and starting her explanation.

"I didn't tell you everything for two reasons: one, there really wasn't any time, and, two, because I didn't want the Council thinking I had gone and spilled their deepest, darkest secrets to you already. If you acted surprised, you were safe."

"Okay, I understand that, but why keep the basics away from me. Like, your grandfather for example....*Kari*?"

She wrinkled her nose in a slightly disgusted and very childish manner. "I never liked that name. It's Norse, like my family, but can be translated into Katherine. Thus, we have Kate."

I held the pillow up threateningly. "You are neglecting the most important question. Grandpa sits in the biggest chair, sweetheart.??"

This time, her face sobered up completely until I could see frown lines that were far too old her for her face. "I wasn't kidding about the heightened activity of vampires. Their numbers seem to be increasing exponentially. I think they're getting ready to try and wipe us out. The Council seems to agree with this, and thus granted emergency wartime powers to the strongest member of the Council, my grandfather."

Hadn't these people ever seen *Star Wars* before? Wartime powers never end well. On second thought, *they never end at all.*

She seemed to understand my thought process. "There's nothing anyone can do about it now. We can only hope that this war ends soon, and he relinquishes the power when the time comes."

Yeah, and maybe my ears will grow to the point where I can fly and people will call me Dumbo. Good luck with that.

My now-amusing thought processes were interrupted when I noticed Kate holding her face in her hands and the slight trembling that was quickly overtaking her body. Dropping the pillow, I moved to kneel in front of her and pull her hands away from her eyes. Making sure her troubled gaze met mine, I told her as sincerely as I could, "I am, and will forever be, grateful for what you have done for me today, Kate. That I promise you."

Her returned smile held the same gratefulness I was feeling. "God, I hope so, 'cause I'm never going to let you forget this either."

Kate soon had some "important business" she needed to accomplish. So, she told me to twiddle my thumbs until she got back.

Naturally, my response was a pillow to her face.

After five minutes in the room alone, though, I was quickly bored of staring at the wall. I left the building to explore the gigundous campus that I would have to memorize within the span of a few days (yeah, hint hint: it wasn't going to happen). Funnily enough, I managed to locate something akin to one of those big map stand things that you find in a mall. Ten minutes of my time was spent trying to ingrain that picture in my head.

As I was looking at it, though, I suddenly heard what sounded like a wolf's howl coming from somewhere behind me. I wheeled around automatically, looking for any sort of howling werewolf, but didn't see anything. Curiosity peaked, I followed the sound, running across the campus past the buildings and occasional person, straining my ears for a repeated sound until I reached a patch of woods. Disappointment ran through me. *I missed it*, I realized, *I must have run past whoever it was, but what wolf would be running around a busy campus?*

I smacked my forehead at the thought. *Duh Ria, maybe a* werewolf, *going to a* werewolf training school, *you sure catch on quick.*

But, to my great surprise, it rang through the air again, and I realized it was coming from *inside* the woods.

Some nagging part deep inside of me (like my common sense maybe?) was telling me this was stupid. I didn't know who the hell was running through the woods as a wolf, and I had no business with them, but, of course, I ignored it and walked forward anyway, keeping my eyes and ears peeled for any huge wolves running around.

Ria, you're going to get yourself killed. *Walking around looking for a wolf, when you're not even completely Changed yet? You're going to be dog chow!*

I squashed the annoying voice down into my mind when I heard people talking, *people*, not wolves. Quietly, I wove around the trees and bushes following the voices. What I found was…interesting to say the least.

First of all, I saw the creepy Council people and that had me crouching behind a bush praying to God that they didn't hear or see me. After a few minutes of me silently making my will, I realized no one had killed me yet, and was filled with some hope. I looked up past the bush and saw the Council again with head honcho numero uno himself standing in the front, and talking with a woman. She caught my eye immediately.

She was an old Native American woman. Her dark toned skin was weather-beaten and wrinkled, and her hair was a deep, raven black threaded with silvery gray. She stood over a dark, carved wooden staff with bones and beads hanging off knotted strings attached to it. Every time she shifted, they would move and make soft clinking noises. She was wearing what I assumed was traditional Native Why is that American garb, with many several beaded necklaces and a small, brightly-colored bad hanging at her hip.

I couldn't hear what they were discussing across the clearing, but looking past her made all hopes of getting away unnoticed halt abruptly in their tracks.

Behind her was a gathering of formidable wolves. They were all in a straight line, standing tall and looking pretty freaking scary. All of them were large and strong, with eyes that seemed like endless black holes. Their fur colors were different running from a pure black that matched their eyes, to a dark chocolate brown. There was only one wolf that was really different from the rest. His fur was so black it looked like it was dyed with the shadows of the woods, but there were streaks of fiery red every so often.

Nice hair man, I thought and giggled a little bit.

This actually ended up being a *very* dumb thing to do, because the awesome-haired wolf looked up from the conversation and *straight* at me. I automatically covered my mouth with one hand, and held very still behind the bush, hoping that he would look away.

But he didn't. He shifted on his feet, and I thought he was going to blow my cover, and, I couldn't let that happen.

I shook my head and hands in front of me in the universal *"stop it, stop it, stop it!"* expression.

He stilled, and stood there a few endless moments before he bobbed his head slightly at me in agreement. When I relaxed enough to breathe again, I mouthed a quick, "thank you" to the cool-haired wolf, and looked back at the Council.

They weren't there anymore.

I craned my neck every which way, searching the whole clearing for the Council or the woman; I could see the old farts walking away from me and literally sagged with relief.

But where did the woman-?

"You have much to learn if you wish to sneak up on us, little wolf."

I couldn't help myself, I shrieked, jumped halfway out of my skin, and attempted to wheel around to face the threat.

I ended up falling back into the bush with a strangled scream.

What an entrance, that took skill.

When I managed to right myself, I saw the old woman leaning on her staff before me with a single eyebrow raised at my outburst. I could feel my face burning with embarrassment. So, I quickly ducked my head and let my bangs cover my blush. I did look up through my hair just in time to see her cock her head at me, like a dog. That was becoming quite the commonality around here.

"What is your name, little wolf," she asked me coolly.

The woman's voice was old and rough, filled with self-assurance. *A storytelling voice,* I told myself. *It's a voice that people find themselves wanting to listen to.*

"Maria," I answered demurely, not looking her in the eye.

She was obviously not impressed. "You are a quiet one," she noticed, "I am old, little wolf; my hearing is not as it once was. You are going to have to speak louder."

I heeded her request, gathering my courage and speaking a little louder, closer to my normal voice. "Maria."

She shook her head. "Perhaps you are unintelligent rather than quiet, if you cannot even follow my directions."

Okay. Way to just piss me off. "My *name* is *Maria.*"

She simply stared at me for a moment, before nodding her head and smiling conspiratorially. "Good, I knew you had voice in their somewhere. It was hiding with your courage."

Say *what?*

I gaped at her, open-mouthed, trying to comprehend what the old (and maybe senile) woman was thinking.

Well, she broke a record for getting me to talk normally in the shortest amount of time, the sneaky jerk. But there was still something that confused me: if I still had Changing human blood flowing through my veins, then how did she know I was a wolf?

I asked her, "Are you a wolf too?"

She snorted, she actually *snorted* at me. "Do not be foolish, that was past my time," She answered simply.

Simply enough to successfully confuse me even more. "What do you mean after your time? I'm pretty sure werewolves have been around longer than you."

She stared at me, searching my confusion with her deep, onyx eyes. "Have you lived under a rock your whole life?"

I stiffened. "No, I just don't know anything about the history yet."

She understood my words immediately, her eyes widened and her nostrils flared as she leaned forward on her staff closer to me. "You are an outsider," she breathed.

I nodded slightly. I saw the moment her face changed and became evaluating, trying to understand why poor, little human me was now running around with the wolves.

Her long, bony fingers tapped her staff lightly as she thought. Now that I was closer, I saw the different runes and animals carved onto its rough surface.

I also felt the power contained within the staff; the ground around it seemed to hum with life. I found myself wanting to reach out and trace my fingers over the darkened surface, and feel every ridge and carefully made cut. I wanted to feel the power at my fingertips, and have it tell me its story.

"You like my staff, don't you, little wolf?"

My trance was immediately broken. "Yes, it's very beautiful. Did you make it yourself?"

She shook her head and stared down at it, holding the large knot at the top in the palm of her hand. "It is an heirloom, passed down from leader to leader of my tribe," she explained, returning her gaze to me. "I am the Chief."

I could believe it. Something about her just seemed so right for the job, her age gave her wisdom, her voice was hypnotic, drawing me to hang on every word and listen to it,

And if I do say so myself, she has a *wonderful* sense of sarcasm.

"And you," she continued thoughtfully, "Will make life around here very interesting, I think."

Glad to see that makes *somebody* happy.

Deciding that sitting on the ground and hiding behind the bushes was now just plain stupid, I got to my feet in a very ungraceful manner and wiped the dirt from my ass.

The Chief woman just kept staring at me, as if her searching glance could unravel my darkest secrets.

I was starting to believe they could.

Then, she suddenly looked to her left at something; I followed her gaze, but saw nothing in the woods. Without a word, she turned and started walking in that direction, and, when she noticed I was just dumbly watching her, she looked over her shoulder and called, "Come, little wolf, we will go on a walk. I have much to ask you."

Without question, I walked after her, jogging a little to catch up and walk by her side. She was a head shorter than me, but for some reason, her presence seemed so much taller. She used her staff for support, but didn't rely heavily on it.

How did someone who walked with a freaking staff move so fast anyway?

"So," she began. "You are new to this, very, *very* new to this sort of life. You are excited for it to begin?"

Knowing that every word I said was going to be heavily evaluated, I thought carefully before I answered. "I am. I wouldn't have chosen this if I would regret it later. I know every day will be something new, a new experience, person, tradition, and I'm ready for that. It's something my old life never had."

"Tell me, about this old life of yours. What was it like?"

Break out the violin and play me some tragic music for the full effect please.

I sighed deeply and ran a hand through my hair before I noticed the old woman was chuckling slightly at me. "What," I asked.

"That bad, eh?" she smiled.

I laughed too. "Not so much bad, I mean, not compared to other people. Just, lonely, I guess; very lonely and…quiet."

"You surprise me; I would have thought your life to be loud and exciting."

There's that sarcasm again.

I laughed again at her antics, finding them refreshing after a day of pure nail-biting, head-banging, Council-induced stress.

"No, books aren't very good for a two-sided conversation," I told her, "and mine weren't any good at attracting people to talk to."

"Ah, I see."

The path broke through the woods and out into the open. The bright sun blinded my eyes for a moment, until they adjusted and I saw where she had brought me.

The area was a giant rocky outcrop. It sat on the backside of the property the school was on: I could see my dorm building around a half of a mile away. The sun shone brightly here on the green grass. The rocks ranged from all shapes and sizes, scattered randomly across the area. The part of the place closest to the school was one large cliff that looked over the rest of it. Overall, it was very beautiful.

Well this is one hell *of a good thinking spot.*

The woman went and lowered herself onto one of the medium-sized rocks. I sat to her side on the ground resting my back against another rock. I took a deep breath of the fresh, clean air around me and sighed, already feeling so much calmer.

That darn woman must have had a kick out of just watching me because she laughed at me again. "You look like you carry the weight of the world on your shoulders, little wolf."

"I feel like it sometimes," I drawled.

"You are too young to know what it feels like. You shouldn't *have* to know what it feels like."

I breathed a laugh. "That doesn't mean I don't."

"Hmm," she agreed, "tell me this then: why did you choose this life? Your old one must have been much safer, much less stressful, books cannot bring much danger to a person."

I felt a smile pull at my lips, and ducked my head so she wouldn't see it. "It was for a friend, and for myself."

"Oh! So you do have a friend, you liar! One who speaks better than books, I hope?"

Depends on the book. "She is my very best friend; she has been for almost two years. I was going to lose her and be lonely again, and, if she left, she would have been lonely too. I couldn't let that happen. So, I packed my things and joined her."

"Just like that?" The Chief pressed, "You left your whole life behind for her?"

"Yeah, just like that."

She considered this for a moment before saying, "Then she is lucky to have such a friend, little wolf, very lucky indeed. Who is the special friend of yours?"

Before I even had the chance to speak, I heard her calling my name. "Ria! Ria, where are you?"

I turned and looked over the rock to see Kate turning around in circles and looking every which way for me.

The woman spoke behind me, "She heard you talk about her. Your friendship must be strong."

"Yeah, it is." I smiled. I stood up and waved my hands yelling, "Yo! You with the weird face and the annoying voice! You calling me?"

She turned in my direction and, first of all, casually gave me a stiff middle finger before she started jogging in my direction.

"Perhaps I was mistaken," the woman drawled amusedly.

I turned and smiled at her. "What? Don't all friends talk like that?"

Her smile was bright against her dusky skin, "Go to your friend, little wolf. I shall see you again soon."

I nodded. "I look forward to it, Chief uh…"

She raised her chin, setting her face in a smooth expression, eyes twinkling with mischief, and looking every part the proud Chief she was. "I grow weary of overused titles, little wolf. You will refer to me only as…Grandmother." She must have noticed my surprise and seen I was about to argue; she held up her hand. "I insist upon it, little wolf. Now go, your friend calls to you. Go."

I felt a smile pulling at the edges of my mouth, and let it spread. "Whatever you say….Grandmother."

CHAPTER ELEVEN

"Blessed are they who have the gift of making friends, for it is one of God's best gifts. It involves many things, but above all, the power of going out of one's self, and appreciating whatever is noble and loving in another."
-Thomas Hughes

Kate and I spent the next few days trying to get me acclimated to the campus and introducing me to all the teachers that we could find before classes started. There were some friendly faces, some who were excited to bring some "diversity" to their classes, as they put it; those were the academics for the most part. The fitness and fight trainers regarded me with expressions that conveyed their clear annoyance at my lack of experience.

Well, pardon me for my lack of time spent in alleyways or juvie, I should have known that someday it would come in handy when I was saving the world one vampire at a time. My bad.

My schedule consisted of physical training, combat training (which started off one gender, then split into coed classes), first aid, history, Transformation, paranormal creatures, and magic, which I was extremely excited to find out was accessible to a werewolf. I'm still really upset it will be lacking a wand though.

The night before the training started was the hardest. I could barely eat the dinner Kate brought up to the room and talking was at a bare minimum. I was mostly just trying to function normally without dissolving into a pit of insanity and uncertainty.

After a while, Kate stopped trying to communicate with me. She simply moved to sit on the bed beside me, and let me rest my forehead on her shoulder as my body was overcome by nervous shaking.

When that had run its course, she tucked me under the covers and sat by my bedside, holding my hand until I drifted into a dreamless sleep.

There are many ways I liked to be woken up early for school: my mother combing my hair softly between her fingers, my dad coming in every five minutes for a half an hour telling me to get up, even my ringtone has its moments. All of these methods are acceptable before noon, and any others would be met with violence, including the one Kate was using.

Beating me over the head repeatedly with a pillow was *not* acceptable, by *any* stretch of the imagination.

This is what caused me to, quite literally, *attack* Kate.

Lunging out of my bed, I caught her midsection and knocked her surprised form to the floor. I tore the pillow from her hands and proceeded to wail on her snapping out profanity-laced threats, explaining exactly *how* I was to be woken up in the morning.

"Holy crap, you raving harpy," she howled. "Calm down! Have mercy!"

When I felt she'd sufficiently learned her lesson, I left her with the pillow to cling to as I retreated to our bathroom and followed my normal morning routine with the full knowledge that she would be emotionally scarred by this experience.

When I came out of the bathroom, she was right where I left her, except she had managed to pull herself into a fetal position, holding the pillow tightly to chest and staring as if seeing me for the first time.

"I have no doubt that you will be just fine having your fight training in the morning, Ria. Your sheer violence will make up for your lack of experience."

My glare informed her I was going to hold a grudge for her incompetence, and she beat a speedy retreat into the bathroom.

She learns fast.

Looking over to the bed, I noticed that, between her beating and the fetal position, Kate had taken the time to lay out my clothes for the day. I saw that the jeans were ones I had brought with me. Stretchy and worn, they were ready for just about anything. The plain, black t-shirt, however, was new, along with the leather boots that were sitting on the floor at the foot of the bed. Putting on the unfamiliar clothes made me feel like a different person, but when the jeans took their regular place over my arse, I suddenly felt more comfortable.

Kate chose that moment to come out of the bathroom and examine my progress. Satisfied that I could manage to tie my own shoes, she quickly sat me on the floor so that she could sit behind me on the bed and French braid my hair (apparently, opponents were not above pulling hair to win matches. Catfight much? Or…dog…were….fight?).

When she was finished with that, she pulled out our two backpacks and put our gym clothes and textbooks in there. Handing one to me, she let me throw it over my shoulder before putting her arm around me and walking out of the room.

Downstairs on the ground floor of the building, there was a giant mess hall and kitchen. Everyone ate breakfast there before departing to their classes. Seeing as I was not yet conscious, Kate pulled two trays through the line and deposited large masses of fruit and various other healthy bits that didn't look fit for consumption (they obviously lacked both sugar and chocolate. What the hell). Last time I ever let her do that.

She chose a seat by the large bay of windows, and I couldn't help but observe that there was no ball of fire in the sky yet.

"Kate, what time is it?"

"Six."

I swore between bites.

The cafeteria was quieter than I expected it to be, indicating there were those who, like me, considered it a punishment to get up this early.

The noise level began to rise, though, as more students blearily shuffled their way through the line. Some of those bleary souls even looked like they were heading towards....our table? I stiffened immediately, ready to flee at first notice.

When a piece of pineapple hit my head, I turned to see a scowling Kate. "Would you calm down? Anyone who messes with you here has to go through me first. So, *chillax*."

I was going to make some snide comment about her middle school level vocabulary when there was suddenly a foreign presence invading the seating space directly in front of me. "Well, look who finally decided to show up! Long time no see, Captain!"

They did some complicated handshake thing that takes skill I obviously don't seem to possess. I looked up only to start when the figure in front of me could have passed for the Iron Giant. He was *huge*. Not like...obese. He was just ridiculously tall, but his face was warm and open, so my spidey senses told me he could be trusted.

Never doubt the spidey sense.

"Sorry, Austin. I've been rounding up some more troops," Kate explained, tilting her head not so subtly in my direction.

Turning to me, his smile grew even wider, and he held his hand out to me. However, instead of taking my hand like I was used to, he held my forearm, a custom Kate had let me in on a few days ago. I returned the squeeze and quickly released his arm.

"Nice to meet you; I'm Austin."

"Hi...I'm Maria," I responded meekly. Damn it.

Kate just rolled her eyes. "Don't worry Austin, it's not you. Her mother just told her not to talk to strangers."

"Ah, she's from one of the outer families then," he assumed, taking a sip of his water bottle.

Kate shook her head and waited until he set his water bottle down before she leaned forward and whispered, "She's an outsider."

Austin proceeded to spew water across the table: my first dodge of the day.

His expression was now incredulous. "You're *human*?"

I attempted to sink into my chair and just disappear. "Not anymore," I muttered.

He looked at Kate and smirked evilly; I was beginning to think it was a werewolf thing. "You are *so* bad."

She shrugged and began eating her food again, looking deceptively innocent.

Before anything else could be said, someone else came over and planted himself next to Austin. "So it begins, ladies. All of our free will is gone as of today."

"Good morning to you too Vincent," snorted Austin. "Stop scaring the new girl."

As he was getting ready to take another bite of his food, Austin suddenly looked at Vincent's face, then back to mine. He did this multiple times before anyone spoke.

"Would you like some assistance there, Austin?" Kate drawled.

He looked at Kate and pointed to the two of us. "Are they distantly related or something?"

I looked up, baffled, just as Vincent did, but quickly found why Austin was asking such a question. Vincent looked as if he could be my twin. He had the same pale, ivory-toned skin and wavy black hair as I did. His eyes were blue, but more of a dark sapphire to my bright, icy blue. He didn't wear glasses, but his facial structure was similar to mine. He didn't have Austin's bulky muscles, but rather a tall, lean frame.

Trippy, man...

"I don't *think* so," he said, examining me like I was him. "Are you from my clan?"

"No," Kate answered for me. "She's not from around here."

Vincent turned towards me with confusion written all over his face, and then suddenly looked at Kate, practically bouncing in his seat. "Kate, is this the human girl you brought back?" He looked at me. "Did she really Change you out there? Where's your scar? Do your parents know? Have you-"

Austin whacked the new guy on the back of his head so hard he almost did a face plant into his food. "Shut your face, dipstick. Can't you see she's shy?"

Vincent snarled up at Austin. "Can't you see I'm curious?"

"How did you even know she was human?"

Vincent rolled his eyes at him. "Nobody has their head in the clouds constantly like you do, idiot. *Everyone's* talking about it."

I really did sink into my seat. *I want to go back to bed; I didn't sign up for talking to people.*

The two noticed my pain-stricken expression and immediately started reassuring me. "Don't worry, people think it's cool! You got chosen to come here by Kate!"

Austin nodded in agreement. "If Kate chose you then you must be good."

"Well *I* don't see what's so special about her."

Oh, for the love of God, I can't believe I would want *to go back to being ignored and insignificant.*

Turning slowly in my seat, I saw the haughty, conceited voice came from the end of our table in the form of the tall, blonde, and obviously arrogant bimbo.

She stood with her chin so high it was a miracle she could level us with her degrading gaze. Her eyes settled on each person at the table for a moment, until they landed on me and narrowed, but that wasn't what threw me.

In the light of the sunrise in the window behind us, I saw familiar silver eyes.

"Desiree," came Kate's cold voice behind me.

"Cousin, what is the meaning of this lie you have been telling? You could not have possibly picked *this* out in your travels." She lifted her top lip in disgust when she acknowledged me. "Just look at her. She's barely able to say a word, and whether she's shy or just plain stupid, it doesn't matter, she won't last long. I'd give her a month before she cracks under the pressure, maybe even less than that."

Out of the corner of my eye, I saw Kate stayed calm and collected, placing her emotionless mask over her face to hide her fury. She hid it well; I caught it only when I saw that her hand was on the table in a white-knuckled fist. To my great surprise, Austin and Vincent shot up from their seats and glared at Desiree, lips peeled back from their teeth in loathing and rage.

"Lay off the new girl, you egotistical witch," Vincent ground out. "She's done nothing that could have possibly upset you."

Her eyes left me only to send Vincent a scathing glare. "Shut up, puppy. You forget your place."

"As you forget yours, Desiree," Austin's voice was more controlled but no less frightening. "You have no right to accuse Kate of lying to the Council and everyone else or to insult her friend in such a way."

Desiree's chin tilted even higher. "I have *every* right to express my opinion on the matter. I believe she has taken one of the members of the outer family and brought her in, giving her this guise to make her more popular. The Council would not punish their *pet* for such a lie." She turned to me and gave the most vicious glare I have ever had directed at me in my life. "But you can't fool me. You have no way to prove your outrageous story. Kari probably took pity on such a slow, bashful, ugly-"

It was only then that Kate's temper snapped. She stood up from her seat so fast her chair fell over behind her. As she reached across the table, I allowed her to haul me up by my right arm.

Kate was *livid*; her eyes were made of solid ice as they stared straight at Desiree, and her voice was so cold I thought it would freeze the air between us.

"Ria, show her your mark."

The whole cafeteria was eerily silent; I could practically feel everyone's gaze on me as I took my left hand and unwrapped the fresh bandage I had just put on that morning. It was slow; my hand shook against my will. Finally, as the last tie was undone, the ghastly injury was revealed.

I heard the two boys hiss in sympathy, but my attention was focused on Kate and Desiree.

Upon seeing the mark her teeth had left behind, Kate's eyes softened slightly in what seemed like pure misery, but immediately hardened when she looked back up at Desiree. I toughened myself up before looking back at her. To my surprise, she seemed completely unmoved. I saw her eyes examine it up and down. Her face showed no remorse and no compassion whatsoever.

"Is this enough for you, Desiree?" Kate hissed as she released my arm.

Silver clashed with silver like two steel blades as Desiree came to her own defense. "She may have been human, but it changes nothing." Turning to me, she narrowed her eyes even further and spat, "It just makes you an uneducated weakling who won't even last as long as someone from the outer families would."

"Don't worry new girl, one of her cronies must have forgotten to make a proper sacrifice to her this morning."

Turning sharply on her heal with murder written in every inch of her face, she turned to face a smaller blonde girl younger than her, closer to our age. The girl was staring impishly back at Desiree, brown eyes alight with mischief.

Desiree was seething beneath her proper speech and haughty disposition. I watched carefully as, while she must have been raging on the inside, she never lost control of her temper, but rather channeled into harsh words and ruthless insults. I had to give her credit, she had the potential to be the most heartless, cold-blooded, and supercilious bitch I had ever seen or heard in all my life, and that was saying something.

Props to you, I think you've just won bitch of the year.

"Don't presume you can make such comments to me, Cindy." She spoke slowly and her tone was almost as icy as Kate's, almost. "I no longer associate myself with you."

"I'm happy to hear it." Cindy seemed impervious to any of Desiree's abusive comments. "Now go have your hissy-fit somewhere else. It's too early, and the new girl hasn't even made a dent in her breakfast yet."

Without another word, Desiree sent one more scathing look my way before turning on her heal and stalking off. Looking awfully proud of herself, Cindy took the empty seat next to me, sat down, and proceeded to begin munching on her breakfast as if all was good and well in the world.

It broke the spell of silence that had settled across the cafeteria, but now there were frequent glances in our direction followed by murmured comments.

I tried not to think about everyone looking at me as I sat down again, but it was near-impossible.

Everyone took their seats after me without a word. Austin and Vincent began to dig into their food in earnest, and Kate faced the window with her eyes closed, trying to get a hold on her temper, I assumed.

Once she finished her bite of food, Cindy looked at me with a friendly smile on her face. "Hey, new girl, don't worry about Desiree, she's just got a stick up where the sun don't shine." She held out her hand to me and ended up gripping my forearm just as Austin had. "I'm Cindy, a former buddy of hers, but don't worry, I'm clean now."

I managed a small smile and a nod. "Thank you," I mumbled.

She seemed puzzled for some reason. "Thank you for what? I didn't do anything."

I swallowed the lump in my throat and forced my voice out, louder and surer this time. "Thank you for sticking up for me, to Desiree, I mean." I turned to Austin and Vincent. "To both of you too, thank you."

"She speaks!" Vincent threw up his arms and spoke to the sky. "Hallelujah!"

This time, when Austin hit him, he really did do a face-plant in his food.

Cindy let out a series of some sort of squealing-giggling noise I assumed was a laugh.

Kate, who had her mind taken off her anger when I started to speak, saw this and started guffawing, almost snarfing her eggs.

I bit my lip hard, but, to my dismay, some restrained snorts began coming out.

When Vincent lifted his head out of the mess, I lost control and promptly began laughing my ass off. It was un-ladylike, loud, and I assumed very unattractive, but, good God, did I need it.

"So what's your name, new girl? I can't call you that forever," Cindy asked in a bubbly attitude I was beginning to think she exuded all the time.

"Maria," I was speaking normally now, almost as loud as I did with Kate.

"Maria, huh," Austin okayed. "Hey Kate, what was that you called her?"

"Ria," she said around a mouthful of food. I kicked her under the table and she winced.

"Don't talk with your mouth full, fatty. Didn't your mother teach you that's bad manners?" I scolded her.

Kate rolled her eyes at me. "No you didn't, Mother."

I smirked and noticed the others were staring, surprised.

"Is that what she sounds like all the time? Cause I could totally dig that."

Cindy and Austin kicked Vincent together.

"Welcome to the werewolf world, Ria," Cindy said kindly as Vincent and Austin started yelling at each other. She stared at my face for a few moments, silently mulling over something. "How in the world could she even think to call you ugly? She may know how to put on pounds of makeup, but your blank canvas is much prettier."

I practically spit out my drink all over Austin. "You don't have to lie to get on my good side, Cindy," I told her jokingly.

She almost looked affronted, and I quickly backtracked, wondering if I had already insulted her after only a few minutes of being in her acquaintance.

"That won't do," she said simply. "12pm this Saturday. My room. I'll prove it to you."

Everyone at the table rolled their eyes, but I thought on for a moment, or, more importantly, thought about what Desiree had said.

I had spent my whole life being that awkward, mousy girl in the corner, not giving a damn about makeup or clothing, but I was beginning to feel like a fresh start deserves a fresh look.

This could be just what I needed to complete my transformation.

"All right," I agreed, much to everyone's surprise. "I'd like that."

Cindy squealed and attached herself to my side. "Just you wait, Ria. We'll make Desiree eat her own words. We'll start with your hair and fix your glasses and introduce you to makeup and..."

I stopped listening and casually managed to detach her so I could eat my food without being handicapped. She released her death grip on me to help me redo my bandage so that I could eat. I noticed Kate looking my way. She was smiling at me, a genuine, warm smile that made me smile back at her. I knew what she was thinking immediately.

Way to go, Ria.

I was totes thinking the same thing

CHAPTER TWELVE

"I do not pray for a lighter load, but for a stronger back."
-Phillips Brooks

After leaving the cafeteria, we made our way to gym, where the girls were split from the boys into two separate classes; something I was *very* grateful for. Our teacher, a short, stocky woman who looked like she could pick me up and break me in half over her knee, sent us to change in the locker rooms. She was one of the few teachers I hadn't officially met yet, so I was more than content to hold off on that encounter for as long as possible.

Kate led me through the large room, looking at the different locker numbers as she passed them. She stopped at #114, and opened it to reveal a fully stocked locker with a mirror, towels, deodorant, extra shirt and pants, a brush, and, to my relief, a bottle of Ibuprofen.

"God bless Aunt Rose," Kate whispered reverently.

"Amen to that."

I was hurrying to fit the shirt over my head when I heard Kate ask with unnecessary enthusiasm, "So, are you excited for your first day of gym class?"

"Oh, I am *bubbling* with excitement, Kate. Can't you tell? Even more so now that I know that only the *girls* will be laughing at me." I pulled the tank top down as far as I could, but, even stretched to its farthest, it would only reach just past my belly button. "This is degrading," I whined.

"Just feel lucky we're both *in* gym class. Less than twenty years ago, girls wouldn't even be here."

My head shot up so fast I thought I heard my neck crack. "What?" I demanded.

She looked at me, confused. "I thought you would have guessed by now." She leaned closer to me and lowered her voice. "Women have only recently been allowed to fight as wolves. Their training used to just be history and magic. No fighting at all."

I swallowed this for a moment. Now the Chief's words to me made sense.

"Do not be foolish, that was past my time."

Knowing Kate would not appreciate me voicing my views, I restrained them to my thoughts.

Curse those stupid, sexist, egotistical, self-centered, chauvinistic, bigoted men who rule the world with an iron fist. They're everywhere!

Kate looked at me curiously. "At least you're showing an ounce of restraint."

I gave her a look.

To this, she rolled her eyes and shut our locker. "Come on, we should remind Ms. Johnson the human is in her class...*before* she tries to make an example of you."

I felt my heart rate triple and tried to come up with an excuse worthy of stalling.

"Uh...um, I refuse to leave this locker room until I have a satisfactory shirt!" I announced.

Nice.

Her eyes narrowed. "What's wrong with the shirt?"

"Half my freaking stomach is showing, that's what's wrong!" I gestured wildly with my arms. "And I don't have abs like you do! Mine are protected by an ample layer of fat!"

"Don't worry; we'll get rid of it."

"I wasn't referring to *that* problem!"

She rolled her eyes and turned to walk out the door. "Well you better start working on that problem before our class joins the boys next year."

Whoops. Did not think of that.

Making a quick sign of the cross, I followed Kate back into the gym, silently cursing to myself.

We were the first ones finished dressing; the gym was empty except for the fierce she-man who was laying out a few mats. She looked up at us when we walked in.

Her face was stern, it didn't change as she nodded at Kate and said, "Good to finally see you in my class, Kari. It seems like Rowan has been out of here for years. I was wondering if you would ever show up."

Kate used her sharp smirk. "I would've come years ago if they had let me, Ms. Johnson."

"Hmph, I sure you would've." Her eyes caught sight of me and narrowed. "Who's this?"

Kate pulled me out from behind her and rooted me in place with an arm around my shoulders. "This is my friend Maria, ma'am, remember? I'm sure you've heard *loads* about her already."

Ms. Johnson's eyes lit up with curiosity as I saw them flicker between my face and my bandaged arm. "You know the gossip around this place; who couldn't have heard about it?"

I thought about Austin and had to hide a smile.

I had no trouble hiding it when her firm eyes returned to me. "All right, human. Don't think that I'm going to give you a break just because you're new to this."

I wouldn't *dream* of it. No one else has.

"I expect you will be working *twice* as hard as Kari here to come to par with your fellow classmates; you will need to if you want to survive."

I thought about Desiree once more, her taunting words and cutting remarks, and came to a determined resolution. You know what? I was going to prove her wrong. I was going to prove *everyone* here wrong. It was at that moment I decided that I wasn't just going to be the scrawny human who actually managed to become a wolf because her friend had family in high places. No, I was going to be part of the *best*. I was going to fight *twice* as hard. I would make Kate proud as I fought *by her side*, because I was sure that Kate would end up on top.

"Don't worry, Ms. Johnson," I told her firmly. I felt Kate looking at me in surprise. "I will."

I wish I had had half the strength of my words. By the time we walked out of first aid and back to the locker room, I thought I would never fully regain use of my arms...or legs...or body...

Well, at least the first medical seminar wasn't on *me*.

"Hand me that bottle of ibuprofen, or there'll be hell to pay," I warned.

The weirdest thing happened: when Kate threw the bottle at my head, I *growled* at her. It was a low, dangerous sound that came from deep in my chest, and it was something I had never done before.

Kate looked up from the locker to meet my shocked face. "Well, *that's* new."

With a hand at my throat, I felt my pulse speeding. "Please tell me that's normal, and if it isn't please lie to me."

Kate didn't *look* that worried. She shrugged noncommittally. "I wouldn't be worried about it. It just means you're Changing faster than we thought. The faster you do, the faster you'll gain strength to catch up. No worries."

I thought about her words, and quickly realized she was right. With this advantage, I wouldn't have to worry about being called out for being a "weak and stupid human."

A pile of clothes thrown in my face brought me back to earth, and I realized I had another class I still had to go to.

"Hurry and get dressed," Kate told me, reading my mind *again*. "Rowan said that this teacher hates it when students are late, and you haven't even met her yet."

"Rowan?" I asked, remembering it was the same name that Ms. Johnson had mentioned.

Without looking up from the inside of the locker, she answered, "My brother."

When I fully recovered from my shock, I managed to pull my jeans and t-shirt back on and followed Kate out the door at a brisk sprint.

The building was farther away than I thought it would be, only adding to our panicked pace. However, in a manner I imagine would be absolutely epic in slow-motion, we leapt through the door just as the bell rang.

Huffing and puffing, we high-fived each other before we heard a drawling voice.

"You were almost late for my lesson, little wolf."

You have *got* to be kidding me.

Turning, I saw the Chief standing just behind us, leaning on her ancient, carved staff, just like I left her.

Apparently, you weren't kidding me.

Kate was already in full-out apologetic mode, sprouting out excuses and promises not to let it happen again and elbowing me in a not-so-subtle cue to follow her example. Before I could even express my opinion on her behavior, the Chief intervened.

"There is no need to grovel," she told Kate gruffly. "You are the granddaughter of the Council Head. Act like it."

Tight-lipped and strangely meek, Kate firmly nodded her head once.

"Besides," her tone lightened until it was amused as she slanted her eyes towards me, "you were dragging around a rambunctious human, were you not?"

Not bothering to fight the smirk on my lips, I found myself responding in the same tone, "Rambunctious is my middle name, Grandmother."

A series of uncontrolled gasps and goggles erupted around the classroom. Looking over at Kate, I saw that she was prepared to forgo the Chief's admonishment and begin apologizing all over again. Well, either that or hit me.

A soft, husky chuckle brought my attention back to the Chief, who was now smiling fondly and looking at me in a way that made me feel like she was seeing someone else in my stead. "And I am beginning to think that 'Mischief' is mine, little wolf. Go ahead and take the last two places." With a gleam in her eye she addressed the rest of our gob-smacked class, "And the rest of you stand up. We begin *now*."

With a great sigh, I plopped myself down in the seat beside Cindy at lunch and dropped my head to the table in an ungraceful heap. After a few seconds, someone started poking my head.

"I don't *think* she died," Cindy assured the others.

"At least she didn't hit her food on the way down," Austin joked as he and Vincent took the seats across from me, "and yes she's still breathing."

"It looks like someone's been chewed up and spit back out." Vincent noticed gleefully. He too poked my head. "How was your first morning of werewolf daycare, Ria?"

I could only manage a murmured grunt as my answer.

"Come again?"

The grunting was more insistent.

"Rough day?"

That voice I didn't recognize; it was a boy's low voice, deeper and huskier than Austin's or Vincent's.

I looked up from my comfortable patch of table and into familiar eyes.

Awesome-haired wolf! You retained your majestic mane of uniquely colored locks in human form! That just totally made my day!

There was no doubt in my mind that it was the wolf I had seen with the Council and Grandmother.

Remembering that he had totally saved my butt from getting in trouble with the Council people, I smiled warmly at him. "Just a little bit," I replied.

"Can I sit here?"

I nodded, and he took the seat next to me without a word. I looked up at Kate, who was giving me the "WTF" look again. I still hadn't explained the whole "Grandmother" thing to her yet.

Everyone else at our table seemed to be in the same state of shock.

"So, Carter," Austin asked just a tad bit awkwardly, "what brings you to our humble table?"

Carter looked up at Austin. As they spoke, I observed him more closely. His tanned face was serious, unemotional, seemingly moved by nothing. He didn't joke around like Vincent and Austin. His eyes were black and depthless, hypnotizing if I looked for too long. He was tall and built with muscles that could only be gained through years of hard work; I would guess he was around six feet tall.

My favorite trait, though, was his hair.

It was long and shaggy, curling around his ear and falling over his face, just over his eyes; black as midnight, but with occasional highlights of flaming red. It looked natural.

Speaking of hair… "Oh, Ria, your braid is coming out. You must have had more fun in training then the rest of us. Here, let me fix it for you."

Without asking me, Cindy pulled out the tie from my hair and began to unravel it from the French braid Kate had put in that morning. I began eating my lunch, enjoying the feel of her playing with the long, tangled strands. With deft fingers and obvious skill, she quickly and neatly contained my mass of thick, black hair into another French braid.

"I can't wait until I get my hands on your hair," she mused. "Does this weekend sound good to you? I can hardly wait any longer."

It took me a moment to register what she was talking about: *the makeover, duh.…*

"Um, sure, I don't think I have anything planned for this weekend." I looked over at Kate. "Secretary," I called to her. She looked up at me, amused. "What have we going on this weekend?"

"Oh, my lady, numerous parties and joyous social gatherings, all of which demand your esteemed presence," she cried happily.

"Hm, cancel everything," I commanded her. "I need my makeover done effective immediately. Everyone else will just have to make do without me."

"Yes ma'am, of course."

Cindy, Kate, and I laughed at our own silly stupidity and looked over at the boys to see what had become of their conversation, but they were all gaping at us as if we had sprouted three heads.

"What?" Kate demanded.

Vincent just shook his head. "Girls," as if that was the explanation for everything on our side of the table.

The other two boys nodded in somber agreement.

Amused, all of us girls looked at each other again. "Boys," Kate drawled.

And then we all lost ourselves in a fit of laughter that had the table next to us staring.

With a great sigh of relief, I fell onto my bed; exhausted and finally finished with my first demanding day.

I feel like I had been trampled on by a herd of wild rhinos. Maybe Austin too.

Kate stood by her bed watching me with amusement written all over her face.

"If I wasn't so tired I'd be on that side of the room wiping that smirk off your face, you bitch."

She laughed and sat down on my bed beside me. "So, you survived. That's longer than some people thought you would last."

"Joy and rainbows and fluffy freaking bunnies," I maturely responded.

"I'm glad that makes you so happy." To that I replied with a snort. "So, you think you can do this?" she asked me seriously.

I looked up at her worried face. "Don't get your hopes up. I'm not quitting anytime soon. You're going to have to share a bathroom with me for a *long* time."

Her smile was relieved and thankful. "I'm so happy." I couldn't tell if she was sarcastic or not. She got up from her spot on my bed and stood in the middle of our itty bitty room facing me. "Now, we just have to work on those muscles of yours."

I groaned and pulled the pillow over my head. "Ms. Johnson works me hard enough. I don't think I can do anymore."

"That's the spirit!" she called, heaving the pillow off of me and tossing it to the other side of the room. "Come on Ria," she encouraged softly, making my eyes narrow in suspicion. "Don't you want to make Desiree eat her words?"

I hauled myself off the mattress with surprising speed and agility. "Bring on the painkillers and water bottles," I growled again, the rumbling sound almost comforting. Kate looked on approvingly. "That *witch* is going to regret she ever doubted me."

Kate slapped me on the back. "Alright tiger, let's begin the torture, and while we're at it, you can explain where 'Grandmother' and Carter came from."

Dear God, what have I signed up for?

CHAPTER THIRTEEN

"Our deepest fear is not that we are inadequate. Our deepest fear is that we are powerful beyond measure. It is our light, not our darkness, that frightens us most. We ask ourselves, 'who am I to be brilliant, gorgeous, talented, and famous?' Actually, who are you not to be?"
- Maryanne Williamson

I can't begin to comprehend how that first week of my new life passed by so quickly. Before I knew it, it was the weekend.

Most students regard their weekend with a sense of happiness and freedom knowing that it's their time to do whatever they want and not have to worry about school (or…training in my case). How did I start my first weekend?

With Kate dragging me down the hall towards Cindy's lair of all things evil and cosmopolitan.

Can you tell I'm having second (smarter) thoughts about this whole makeover business? Now, if only I could get Kate to see the light too.

"Ria, you were the genius who decided to say yes to Cindy. Think of yourself as bound to that promise for life. Come hell or high water you are getting that makeover."

"Kate! Think for a second! What if she doesn't want to waste her time anymore, huh? Or what if I end up looking horrible? It'll scar her for life and she'll never be able to move on and accomplish anything! We should just proactively turn around before we single-handedly ruin Cindy's life!"

But as I was pivoted to take off at full tilt, Kate quickly closed in on the door of doom and pounded her fist against it with the force of a small sledgehammer.

Moving to face me again with a sharp grin firmly in place, she boasted, "Well, no going back now."

"...I never liked you anyway."

Before anything else could be said, Cindy opened her door and inspected it for a second, as if to make sure it was still whole. The look she gave Kate was a strange mix of admiration and incredulity.

"Nice knock. Very sophisticated."

With a snort, she shoved me towards the door and turned to walk back down the hallway. "I'll be back to pick you up in a few hours, honey! Play nice!"

Before I could even think to respond that, she was gone and I was yanked back into the room, the door shutting behind me with a decisive *click*.

Cindy was a little ray of sunshine. Hands on hips with a smile so wide and white it was blinding me, she asked, "Are you ready to embark on a journey of discovering your inner beauty?"

An unenthusiastic finger twirl was all I could muster up in response.

Pouting, she led me over to her bed and sat me down at the edge of it. The sheets and comforter were a hot pink color that went against everything I stood for, and there were way too many fluffy stuffed animals covering it to be considered normal. As I shifted away from one that was getting too close, I accidentally hit another which squeaked in an indignant manner that made me question just how inanimate it was.

Cindy had merrily skipped away to go retrieve her torture devices, and as she returned with bags of varying shapes and sizes, a sense of impending doom came over me. She laid them out on the remaining space of the bed, arranging tools and makeup and God only knows what else.

I felt faintly like a patient watching her doctor arrange her scalpels for a coming surgery.

I was good for a few minutes, sitting by and watching quietly (silenced by fear, I think), but then she pulled out some unrecognizable tool that looked *dangerous*.

"Whoa! Hello! What in the hell is that?" I pointed a shaky finger in its general direction.

She followed my pointed finger and rolled her eyes. "Calm down, Ria. It's for your eyelashes."

"To do *what*?"

"Curl them," she explained patiently, continuing to arrange her torture devices.

I was still perplexed. "Why the hell would you want to *curl* them?"

She rolled her eyes again and deposited two pink bath towels in my lap, not taking care to notice when I nearly shoved them off on principle. "Now, go wash your hair. It needs to be wet when I cut it."

My hands went convulsively to my hair as I leaned away from her. "You are *not* cutting my hair. It's taken *years* to grow this out. Not an *inch* is leaving it."

She grabbed my shoulders and looked me fiercely in the eye. "I am not cutting it short. Relax. It looks good long, but it needs a trim and a few layers. Your bangs could use some work too. They're covering half of your pretty face." She pulled off my glasses, and shooed me into the bathroom. "Do you know how to put in contacts?"

I felt my brows furrow. "Well, yeah. I have some, but I never wear them."

"Don't worry," she assured me. "I got more for you. Kate told me your prescription."

Damn you, Kate. I will get even.

She began pulling the door shut behind me. "Now, hurry up so we can get started." She looked me up and down and the pout returned to her face. "This could take a while."

And with that she shut the door, sealing my fate.

I was most definitely not a happy camper, and I was most definitely never agreeing to anything like this ever again.

Especially if Kate thought it was a good idea.

I winced every time I heard the *shink* of the scissors slicing off a piece of hair, but Cindy seemed immune to my suffering. She had been happily narrating this whole adventure, explaining all of the ins and outs of the beautified world she was trying to introduce me to. I tuned out sometimes, but, when she decided to bring up a new, different conversation, I froze in my seat.

"So, you lasted your first week! You've surprised a lot of people, you know? I know a lot of people gave you a hard time when you first came here, Desiree especially, but I think you're really brave to have made it past that!"

"I'm not brave." The whispered words slipped out of my mouth before I could stop them.

The scissors stopped for a moment, and I looked up in the mirror on the dressing table in front of us to meet her puzzled gaze.

"Why on earth would you think that?"

I hesitated for a moment, reluctant to change any good opinion she had of me, but I didn't want any phony friends. I refused to put up any fake pretenses. "It wasn't bravery that got me here. I was selfish and selfish and Kate was desperate and persuasive. That's the basic gist of it," I informed her.

"I don't think that's true-"

I cut her off, knowing that false praise would only make me feel worse about myself. "You don't know the half of it."

I thought for sure she would go on and ignore me, or maybe even kick me out of her room altogether.

But she didn't.

Setting the scissors down on the table, she turned my chair around and pulled up one of her own so that she could sit in front of me. Suddenly, the bubbly, fashionista whom I had been stuck with for the better part of the day became an unfamiliar, serious, and much more mature girl that I had never met before.

Settling her elbows on her knees, she rested her chin on her folded hands and leveled me with a glance that told me just how serious she was.

"So, tell me," she said simply. "Make me understand."

I didn't need any further encouragement. I mean, don't get me wrong, Kate would always and forever be my best friend, and I could always, *always* talk to her, but having someone else to talk to wouldn't be so bad either, you know?

So, I told her everything. I told her about my old life, my family, Daimon, school, Kate. I explained how Kate had spilled the beans and how I convinced her to bring me along for the ride. With a weak tremble in my voice, I relayed my last meeting with Daimon and showed her the locket that I always kept on me. Then, I finished off with my first terrifying meeting with the Council, and the words that Kate's grandfather had spoken to me.

She was silent the entire time, her attention never wavering from my story. I couldn't help but feel nervous by the end of my explanation. Maybe it was better to leave things the way they were before and just have her believe that I was actually someone worth mentioning.

She seemed to understand when I was done with my tale. Sitting up from her assumed position she asked, "Is that everything?"

I nodded weakly. She took that as her cue to launch herself out from her chair and nearly barrel me over with a hug.

Cindy was barely taller than me sitting down, so her head came to rest perfectly on my shoulder. I didn't even have time to react when she started speaking to me.

"You silly, stupid girl," she admonished in a fierce whisper. Were those *tears* on my shoulder? "You are the bravest, most loyal friend I have met in my entire life."

Did she really not get it? "Cindy, I *ran away from home*. That's like, the least brave thing anyone can do."

Pulling away from my shoulder, I could see that there really were tears falling down her face. "Running away from home for your own selfish reasons is cowardly. Ria, you came here, changed what you are, and rode blindly into the unknown for the sake of a friend! *That's* why you are brave. Very few people could do that." She seemed to understand my questioning look; she shook her head. "I would most definitely not be able to do that. No way."

Sitting down in her own chair, she leaned back and folded her legs Indian-style. "At least, I'd have to be able to take my older sister with me. I couldn't do anything without her."

As she looked away from me, a small, happy smile slowly overcame her features and her expression became strangely nostalgic.

Following her gaze, I saw a picture on her nightstand of herself riding piggyback on someone who could have been her twin, only slightly taller.

I swallowed past a lump in my throat to answer. "Seamus doesn't need me. He's perfect on his own."

"Well, of course he is! He had an older sister like you to raise him!"

I shook my head. "No, I didn't have to do anything. I think he just came that way."

Cindy's laugh was like small, tinkling bells, light and airy and so, so...Cindy. "I hate to break it to you, sweetheart, but people aren't born perfect. They have to work at it." How could someone so tiny and unthreatening have such a penetrating stare? Her eyes seemed to pick up every little nuance on my face. "Do you miss him?"

I wanted to say no. I wanted to say that I was fine out here on my own and that I knew he would be fine without me. I wanted to say that I was okay with the thought of never seeing him again.

But my mouth and my brain seemed to be on two separate levels.

Sadly, I nodded to Cindy, whose gaze had turned pitying. "I do. It's only starting to hit me how much I'm going to miss in his life. I'll never see him graduate. I'll never be able to harass his girlfriend ever again. I'll miss him growing up and getting married. I'll never become the aunt that sneaks his kids way too much candy. I know he's going to accomplish great things, but I'm going to miss every one of them."

Cindy, bless her, had more tears welling up in her bright, chocolate brown eyes and was covering with her mouth with her hands.

"I...I couldn't even imagine what you're going through." She paused for a moment, brows furrowing in deep thought that I knew better than to interrupt. Coming to a decision, she reached out to hold my hands between her own. She leaned towards me and quieted her voice to a whisper as if there was someone in the room she didn't want hearing us.

"Listen, Ria. I'm going to promise you something. If I accomplish anything in my life, it'll be for you to see your brother one more time."

Ignoring the overwhelming shock that was obviously all over my face, she squeezed my hands and reiterated. "I swear, Ria. You *will* get to see Seamus again and you *will* get to properly say goodbye."

I took this as my cue to launch myself out of my chair and attack her with a hug.

She was laughing again, that tinkling sound reaching my ears, and I discovered that I was laughing too. "I'm pretty sure that this involves breaking a few of the Council's rules, and I shouldn't encourage that," I whispered, "but thank you, all the same."

Her carefree smile tensed for a moment at the mention of the Council, and I could have sworn her eyes looked around the room for the barest of moments, but her cheerful atmosphere was back before I could even think more about it.

"Hey, that's what friends are for right?"

I couldn't do much more than nod in agreement, almost overcome.

"Now," she stated firmly, pulling away from our hug and wiping the tear streaks beneath her eyes, "we have a job to finish, and we have to keep chugging along here." Winking conspiratorially, she added, "We're meeting everyone for dinner, and you know what Vincent will be like if he finds out you kept him hungry for even five minutes."

Smiling for the first time since I had entered this hallowed place of cosmo girls, I turned back towards the mirror and handed Cindy her pair of scissors.

"Let's get this show on the road."

An unimportant number of hours later, we were walking downstairs to meet the others for a night out on the town. Cindy had bought me a new outfit to wear, and (thank the good Lord) there was no pink involved whatsoever.

She seemed disappointed by such a fact until I plainly informed her that if she had bought me anything pink I probably would have held it under a hair dryer until it burst into flames, thrown the ashes out the window, and gone to dinner naked.

That changed her perspective a little bit.

For the billionth time that day, I reached up to itch my nose, only to growl when Cindy smacked my hand away.

"Oh, stop that. Don't want you messing up your make up now, do we?"

I hate it when she had a point.

Excitement and nervousness rolled in my stomach as she hid me around the corner from the main entrance hall and told me to wait. How would everyone react? Laughing, pointing, snide remarks? I was prepared for anything.

I knew the instant they all saw Cindy because even I could hear Vincent's whiny bellows as he slowly died of hunger.

"You are such a drama queen," she scolded. I could just imagine her staring down Vincent, hands on hips as he cowered behind someone else. "Have you forgotten why we're all here in the first place?"

"Then bring her out already so I can be fed!"

Her gusty sigh made me giggle quietly from around the corner. "You'll never learn. Anyway!" Okay. Giggling was dead. Now I was nervous again. "Presenting the new and improved Ria! Please, come on down!"

Taking a deep breath and centering my mojo, I took that fated step out into the open and did not dare to look up until I was next to Cindy and her small arm was placed reassuringly around my waist.

The first I noticed was Austin, who was sitting in a one of the comfy chairs in the middle of the room. He was reclining so far back that the chair was on two legs, but, as I looked up, he actually lost balance in his chair and fell backwards, taking him and the open-mouthed Vincent (who was standing up and leaning on the back of the chair behind him) to the floor.

Carter, I noticed, was slightly away from the rest of the group, leaning against one of the walls with a foot propped up. His only reaction was to widen his eyes a little and look me over up and down, which made me blush in *extreme* embarrassment.

Kate was frozen where she stood, eyes wide, mouth open, searching for what to say (be it sarcastic, genuine, or gibberish, I assume). Finally, she stomped over to me and took my face in her hands turning it this way and that, looking at my eyes my nose my mouth, my hair, my lips, my skin....everywhere on my new face.

She turned my head to the side, and I saw her eyes narrow. "I didn't know you had your ears pierced."

Of all of the things you could have said, I thought about rolling my eyes for a nanosecond, but settled on smiling brightly at her instead showing off my newly whitened teeth.

That was only part of the package deal though.

My unruly and obnoxious hair was now straightened, cleaned, and smoothed with so many products my head was most likely a fire hazard. I hadn't noticed how dark it was before, but the dark brown I had known my whole life could now be mistaken for black hair.

I also took pride in the fact that my face was now as smooth as a baby's bottom and lightly covered in various bits of makeup. My eyes (which were the only part I had liked about my face before) were now free of glasses and accentuated with eyeliner. They looked almost as if they were glowing they were so bright and blue.

All in all, I looked like a completely different person.

And Kate chose to remark on the two silver hoops that adorned each ear.

Typical.

She returned my smile with a ruffle of my hair, and together we turned our attention back to the fallen pair, which was quite amusing.

Austin was just now righting himself and Vincent was moaning in his spot beneath the chair about how fat Austin was.

"Maybe we should just leave him here to starve," Kate suggested brightly.

The newly-mobile Vincent only flashed her a wolfish grin and came up behind Kate and me, putting his arms around both of us. "We'll see ya later fatty, my two hot dates and I are heading out to the club."

After sharing a look of mutual exasperation, Kate and I elbowed him simultaneously, took each other's arms, and skipped out the door, ignoring his cries of pain and everyone else's laughter behind us.

The cool breeze blew my hair out of my face and sent chills racking through my body. Moonlight was the only thing that guided my way as I walked away from my building down a path that was steadily becoming more and more familiar to me. It was not a long way from my dorm room, thankfully. Therefore, it was an ideal spot for me to go and think.

I wasn't afraid of the height or the rocks as I sat on the edge of the large cliff. I wasn't so clumsy that I would fall over the edge, hopefully.

Letting my legs hang over the rock, I rested my elbows on my knees and my head in my hands. I closed my eyes, allowing the tranquility of the area to fill me, and attempted to forget my first hectic week of training in exchange for some peace of mind.

It was working. My breathing became deep and even, my mind went blank, and the strong beat of my heart was steady and slow.

I could hear everything around me as I blended in with nature, including the rustling of grass that signaled someone was gradually coming closer.

"You have mastered meditation already, little wolf."

"Grandmother," I greeted, allowing a small smile spread on my face.

She didn't sit next to me, but she came to my side and stood looking out at the place she had brought me to. The weight of her presence settled over me, and I sat up, turning to face her.

"You have spent a week here, and yet you live to tell the tale, little wolf. I am most impressed." It was then she seemed to notice my drastic change in appearance. Her eyes widened and she smiled. "And you do it with a new face, how interesting."

I ignored her last comment. "Why does everyone seem so surprised that I haven't died or run away yet?" I asked exasperated.

Her eyes cut to me. "You would not be the first of your kind to do so."

I wasn't surprised; Kate's grandfather had said as much, but Kate wouldn't go any further on the subject, no matter how much I had bugged her about it. Maybe the Chief would tell me more?

Before I could even open my mouth, she looked away and told me, "That is something you are not ready to hear about, I'm afraid. Later. We will have that conversation later."

Damn woman reads my thoughts now too.

Knowing that was as good as I was going to get with this woman, I didn't argue the point. "Don't think I'm going to forget about it either, Grandmother." The title still felt foreign on my tongue. I felt my mouth wrinkle up.

The Chief laughed at my expression. "You will grow accustomed to it, little wolf. I promise."

"You still won't tell me why I you want me to call you that though, will you?"

"Not now," she answered cryptically.

I sighed, and let my head fall back on my hands like before. "Then what *can* you tell me now?"

"You are going to have a test Monday."

"But I hate Monday tests!!"

My cry of frustration echoed across the entire clearing, along with her husky laughter.

Chapter Fourteen

"All truths are easy to understand once they are discovered; the point is to discover them."

-Galileo Galiliei

Naturally, the first month of training didn't include Black Ops sweeps of the Vamps secret lair or remakes of ancient werewolf battles. Disappointed?

Baby steps, people. Baby steps.

First, we started off with the building blocks of what made wolves powerful. Like magic.

Which is so freaking awesome that we can use. Had I known this a few years ago, I might have just picked werewolf over vampire from the get go. Alas, I was just forced to see the light a little later.

Now, let me elaborate on this a little bit because this whole aspect of werewolfism really threw me for a loop at first. Werewolves don't come preprogramed with magic; we're not witches. Without getting into all the intricate histories, werewolves were created to counterbalance creatures like vampires, berserkers, and all sorts of crazy monsters that shouldn't exist. In effect, we fight the things that go against nature, and, thus, have nature on our side.

Very few people realize the intrinsic magic that nature is filled to the brim with, and that's just fine with us. We use it to our advantage. That being said, we're not the only magical creatures who have access to it, we just have the strongest claim to it; so, it comes easier to us.

Anywho. Magic. Cool stuff. Really excited to learn about it.

Every day, I came to class ready and waiting to learn something new, and when I actually accomplished something (like lighting a candle from across the room? Chyeah.) I nearly wet myself with excitement.

Grandmother spent weeks coaching us on all the nuances of magic. We were a part of nature, she told us, sometimes more beast that (wo)man, and it was from nature that we drew our power.

However, can you say *roadblock*? At this point, I was definitely more woman than beast. I hadn't even practiced transforming yet. Hadn't even had it come to mind.

(Barring the times that I woke up nearly screaming in a cold sweat from nightmares of a red eyed monster with long, blackish-brown hair and surprisingly *in*human behavior).

So, I sat in class and listened and *focused* with every iota of my attention span, hoping to pick it up easily through sheer willpower. Not so easy.

Each passing day, I grew more frustrated with the fact that everyone else was running circles around me as I struggled just to keep up. Even with a little extra help from Grandmother during my extracurricular, time I was still just barely passing the minimum requirements.

Not only that, but when I turned to an especially adept group of friends seeking help, I found myself facing a strangely silent lunch table. WTF.

I tried not to judge though, I honestly tried. Maybe there was some secret werewolf code of rules about not giving advice, or answering questions, or being in anyway helpful to friends.

Or maybe after a particularly frustrating day of Gifts class everything would just have to come to a head, and I would have to just tell it like it was.

At the end of that particular class, Kate and I were waiting patiently for the bell to ring so we could go to lunch. She seemed to notice I was wearing my angry face.

By now she knew the drill: do *not* try to talk to Ria when she's wearing the angry face; it will not be pleasant and it might even end up painful.

She held her curiosity well, staying by my side, but not speaking to me, for the remainder of class. The bell rang fifteen minutes later, and she went to get our stuff with me following behind her with all the menace of a shadow wraith. All the same, she hooked her arm through mine as we made our way to the cafeteria where everyone was eagerly waiting for us, talking animatedly with one another.

Well, everyone but Carter who was just talking like he normally does. Minimally.

My tray made a very dramatic slam on the table as I sat in the isolated emo corner, determined to cool off before I tried talking to anyone. I took the bread roll I had picked up in line and proceeded to tear it apart for no apparent reason.

Conversation stopped at the other end of the table, and all eyes were on me, but I ignored them and continued to dismember my little roll. I tried to imagine it was Desiree, but that did little to help. Suddenly, the mutilated roll was plucked from my fingertips and placed on the table. When I tried to pick it up again, a large, warm hand wrapped around mine. I recognized the dusky skin immediately.

His eyes were dark and serious, always saying more than he ever did, like now, for instance. Long, silent stare translation: cut it out *and/or* what's wrong.

I sighed. "Gifts class," I told him, as if that explained everything. Obviously, it didn't. He continued to stare blankly at me, his eyes still blatantly curious. I was really close to shifting away uncomfortably in my seat. "I don't really know. I just don't get why I can't seem to do anything right, or why every spell is a battle to learn."

His eyes narrowed then, saying he understood what I was trying to say.

"What kind of problems," he asked quietly.

"Carter..." Austin was the one that spoke, but I got the feeling that the warning was coming from everyone.

"I won't tell her," he told them simply, over his shoulder.

"Why?" I snapped. "Why won't anyone tell me anything?" I sent a glare at every one of them. My frustration bursting at the seams, I was so close to completely losing my temper. Unwontedly, the image of the red-eyed monster flashed in my thoughts, and then vanished just as quickly.

Kate looked sympathetic, but I didn't buy it. *She doesn't get it. None of them get it. They played together as puppies, and I'm not even a full-blooded wolf yet. There is no way they understand what I'm going through.*

"Ria," she began in a tone that was really grating my nerves. It was as if she were trying to explain something to an idiot or a petulant child. "Tradition dictates–"

"That you can Change a human anytime you feel like it? That you can go against the Council's best interests? Or is it you're supposed to hide what can help your friends from losing their sanity? That makes perfect sense! Why didn't I see it before?" I snarled at her. "Screw it if you can't tell how to pass Gifts! Maybe some other kinds of advice would have been better; there are other things I expected to hear about by now. Things you have been purposefully keeping from me, and that's not fair."

"Ria–"

There it was again. That *stupid, patronizing* tone. As long as she insisted on talking to me like that, I would not sit around and listen.

I ripped my hand out of Carter's tightened grip, stood up from the table and walked away from them without looking back.

There was only one place where I could really calm down enough to think straight. So, that was the place I headed to first. Seated on the edge of the cliff, I tucked my knees to my chest and hid my face in them. My nails had dug into my calves and were only starting to relax after what must have been a half an hour of quiet meditation. I tried to clear my head and forget about all the evil thoughts hovering at the edge of my mind, but they flew around and prodded incessantly like obnoxious mosquitoes.

I was so deep in my get calm zone, that I didn't even notice the figure approaching me until it spoke.

"What do you want to know about first?"

Lifting my head slowly from my knees, I pulled myself out of the daze that the deep breathing had locked me in and spared him a glance over my shoulder.

"Aren't you afraid the Council will spank you if you tell me anything?"

Impervious to the bite in my tone, Vincent shrugged casually and took a seat next to me. He let his legs hang over the edge and swung them around fearlessly, resting his hands on the edge next to them and leaning forward slightly.

"This is quite the spot you found yourself here," he remarked, looking out at the scenery around us. "Do you come here a lot?"

Diplomatic evasion. Nice.

I sighed. "Yeah, it's just so peaceful. It's like a little bubble of landscape that's disconnected from the rest of the world. It's a place where I can calm down enough to think."

I looked over and saw that he was watching me from the corner of his eye. Even caught, he didn't look away. "You're right, you know," he said very quietly.

I sucked in a deep breath. "Right about what exactly?"

Surprisingly, the normally quirky and jokester Vincent scowled slightly, an expression I had only seen on his face when I first met Desiree. "This keeping you in the dark thing is unfair to you. After all the shit you've been through already, you've been as patient as a saint and yet you're still blind and deaf out here."

This point of view was certainly new to me.

Suddenly, the smile was back on his face. Vincent turned towards me and sat Indian-style, rubbing his hands together like we were about to get down to business.

"Okay, since you can't make a decision on your own." Here he paused, recovering from my blow to his head. "Woman! I am trying to assist you! Now, unless you insist on assaulting me some more we'll start with magic 101 first."

He reached out and damn near lifted me off of the ground before turning me to face him. Then, he held his hands out on his lap waiting for me to reach for him rather than just taking mine on his own. I've discovered that Vincent is surprisingly sensitive to those around him, despite the fact that he acts like a moron most of the time. He's just very subtle about it, like now.

Hesitantly, I reached out and placed my hands on his, to which he answered with a reassuring squeeze.

"Now, lesson one begins," he said lightly. Closing his eyes, he took a deep breath and fell silent (which was odd, for him at least). After a few moments, I was getting uncomfortable with the silence, and was about to ask him what he was doing, when I felt it. The tingling feeling was almost unnoticeable at first, like pins and needles in my fingertips, but as time passed, it grew more insistent. Even as it grew stronger, though, it never made it past my fingers.

"Let it in, Ria." I almost jumped at the sound of Vincent's voice. Looking up, I saw that his eyes were still closed, and he was still relaxed. "This will help you understand, but you have to allow it in."

"How do I do that?"

"You're going to have to trust me."

He opened his eyes then and entrusted me to a hopeful expression. My heart melted at the sight of it. Vincent was being subtle again. There was a plea behind his request.

He was asking me to trust him like I would any friend.

"Okay," I whispered. "I trust you."

I didn't realize how tensed he was until he had heard my words. His shoulders sagged and his lips quirked in a lazy smile that I couldn't help but return. Slowly, he shifted our hands so that our fingers laced together. I shut my eyes just as he did and relaxed back into the calm place I had found just a few minutes ago.

It was like a dam had burst as the tickling sensation rushed past the barrier my anxiety had set up and followed the path I had made with my mind. Without meaning to, my eyes flew open, and I gasped in surprise. I saw that all of the little hairs on my arms were standing on end.

I could barely use words to describe what I was feeling. It was magic, I knew that, but it was coming right from Vincent. That I didn't get. It felt primal and wild, and yet it was tempered somewhat, like he had complete control of it, so I wasn't scared. It was almost....soothing in a way. As it fluctuated under my skin, I felt revitalized and energetic. Like I had just chugged one of the 5-hour energy things (PS. Never do that. You go from like two hours of being high on life to a 16 hour nap. Fail).

Soon enough, it began receding. I got the feeling that Vincent was pulling it back into his body somehow. Calmly, I sat and waited until I knew it was completely gone before looking back up at Vincent.

I was surprised to see him regarding me with a calm, expectant expression. It was borderline nervous if you ask me. Was he worried about what he had just shown me?

"What," I started before realizing my voice was dry and quiet. Swallowing hard against the lump I didn't know was in my throat, I tried again. "What was that exactly?"

He smiled shyly. "That was…me. It's also why the rest of us have such an advantage over you."

"Okay Sparknotes, can I have the full novel and not the summary please?"

My sarcasm seemed to dissolve whatever tension lingered, though the reference was lost on him. "Each of our werewolf clans has developed and specialized their own specific brand of magic for hundreds of years. Different bits of knowledge and hidden secrets have been passed down from generation to generation in the hopes that the next will be stronger than the last."

That is so cheating, I thought morosely. Where can I get my own clan?

"So, what's so specialized about that?" I asked, confused.

"Each clan over the years has separated into their own sort of specialty. My clan, for instance, is known for their ability to heal people.

"You see, Ria, what you learn in Gifts is that magic comes from nature, which is true, but each person also has their own capabilities and strengths to add to the whole process. I can do little things like light a candle, but I can't kick down a tree like Austin can because that's not how I'm preset. My powerful magic lies in my clan's ability to heal other werewolves."

"How do you do that?" I asked him, fascinated with this new concept.

He seemed happy enough to preen. "What happens is, well, it's hard to explain, but it's like I use my own energy to seek out problems in other people. Like, what I just did; I could tell you were overtired and frustrated. So, I gave you energy and eased the stress."

"Can you do anything else?"

"Oh yeah, my clan works in the hospitals healing broken bones and fixing up the wear and tear that comes with active duty. The worse the injury, the more energy it takes out of us to heal, but it's worth it in the end."

"That is just too damn cool," I admitted. "What can the other clans do?"

He first told me about the super strength Austin's clan boasted, which also included a freaking hilarious childhood story. Apparently, Austin and Vincent have been friends forever (surprise, surprise), and got into as much mischief back then as they do now (again, surprised? Not). One day, Vincent had stolen a doll from Austin's younger sister and climbed a tree up to the branches she was too short to reach. In the end, the toddler had gotten so angry that she ripped the tree right out from its roots (which made a *very* surprised Vincent fall to the ground), and, then, proceeded to swing the tree at him until he relinquished her precious toy.

I have never wanted to meet someone more in my entire life.

Cindy's skills were centered in the area of locating people (slash vampires). Her family was fondly referred to as the 'Navigators'. They could track anyone and then determine the strength of their opponent, which in the case of vampires, would be entirely dependent on their age. The older the scarier.

Vincent wasn't so sure about Carter. The tribes tended to keep hush hush about what they could and couldn't do, but rumors spoke louder than facts. People said that they had the ability to talk to other animals, while others said that they "wind whispered" whatever the hell that meant.

However, Kate was the greatest shocker out of everyone, and the biggest worry too.

This chick could read minds.

Well, not exactly, because that would be weird and frightening and I would probably strive never to think anything around her ever again. Kate came from a family of telepaths. In other words, she could open up her thoughts to other people or set up "mind conversations" (as Vincent so aptly put it) between multiple peoples' heads. That's impressive.

But as Vincent rambled on, I couldn't help but shiver in fear remembering the Council Head. The thought of him rummaging through my thoughts, and being capable of God knows what else, was making me sprout grey hair.

I almost didn't want to hear anymore.

"So, what about humans?" I asked him.

He froze; I felt it through our still-intertwined fingers. "What about humans?"

"Have they ever been known to have a specific power? How many of them actually became wolves in the first place? And why are there no more humans left here?"

Vincent's grip tightened until it was almost painful. Was he really shaking? "I–I can't tell you that." In an attempt to calm him, I ran my thumbs soothingly over the backs of his hands. His gaze met mine again, and his hands loosened a tad. "I'm sorry, Ria. I really am, but there are things I am literally forbidden to talk about here."

"Forbidden?" The word left a bad taste in my mouth. "Really?"

He nodded. His teeth were tightly clenched, enough so that his words had to be forced out between them. "As you can probably imagine, their loyalties didn't exactly last long, and the Council never forgives or forgets a betrayal. Ever."

I thought about that for a moment. Was that what everyone was expecting from me too? Was I just another human who was going to run away?

A slight pressure on my hands was enough to bring my attention back to Vincent who was staring at me apologetically. Turning up his watch he said, "Lunch is almost over, we better start heading to our afternoon classes."

He moved to get up, but I pulled him back down to my level. When he looked confused, I let go of his hands and reached out my arms to wrap around his neck.

"Thank you, Vincent. You're a good friend," I told him honestly.

Chuckling slightly, he reached out and squeezed me in return. "Just lookin' out for you, Ria. You're funny enough to keep around, and you don't even smell like a nasty human anymore."

I pinched his shoulder and laughed when he jumped. Pulling away, we pulled each other up and walked to class with our arms over each other's shoulders.

"Hey," he said just as we were getting close. "Don't you think it's time you started calling me Vince? Vincent makes me feel…ancient."

Smirking up at him, I replied, "I could call you Vince, or maybe V-man." At his incredulous face, I tried again. "The Vinster? V? Oh, oh VT! Then you can be like 'VT phone home'. It's ingenious!"

Instead of answering in a dignified manner Vincent threw me over his shoulder and stated, "This conversation is over. Never mention any of those names in front of me or anyone else ever again, or I'll have a full psychoanalysis drawn up for you, and we both know that won't end well."

"Whatever you say, Vince."

A decidedly happier aura surrounded me when I came back to my spot later that night.

I had sat by Vince at dinner and spent the entire time joking with him. A social barrier I didn't realize existed between us had come crumbling down, and he had somehow wormed his way into my good graces, the sneak.

Tonight, I lay sprawled out across the ground instead of hunched in a little ball of anger. The world was good as gold, and I was happy where I was. Hallelujah.

After chilling out in Happyland for some time, a familiar presence made her appearance.

"Hello Grandmother," I greeted warmly, tilting my head so that she was in my line of vision, albeit upside down.

She paused, looking down at me. Whenever she does that, I picture a pitcher (whoa say that five times fast) at the windup. Only she's preparing herself to throw out some sarcastic comment rather than a ball. Well, at least hopefully because I am not prepared for anything flying towards me at the present moment.

Very calmly, she asked me, "You are under some sort of influence, little wolf?"

I will never know how she does that with such a straight face.

I really don't know what was so funny about it, but the smoothly delivered comment had me literally ROTFL-ing.

If I was standing up I would have doubled over with laughter, but, seeing as I was still lying on the ground, I simply laughed so hard tears of mirth spilled from my eyes. Grandmother noticed this and was stunned for a moment, before she smiled warmly down at me.

"You were not like this when you left my class, quite the opposite. Something has made my little wolf incredibly happy," she noted; with a gleam in her eye she added, "or some*one*, perhaps?"

That was enough to calm me down again. Wiping away the happy tears, I sat up and turned to face her. "Now why would you think that?" I asked her with a smile of my own.

"A little bird told me you were looking to find what happened to your human predecessors."

Attention snagged. "I never pegged Vincent as a tattler."

Smirking, she took her place at a rock that was tall enough for her to sit on and that had a place for her to lean her staff against.

"Trust me, little wolf, tattling was far from his mind. I am not bound by the same codes of silence that young Vincent is. What he sought from me was help for *you*."

Turning my head sharply to face her, I asked dazedly, "He asked you to tell me what he couldn't?" At her nod, I found myself flabbergasted. "But why?"

"Why not," she returned wittily. "Are you surprised to find that you have made friends here, little wolf?"

"The concept is, I admit, a bit new to me."

"I am happy to tell you get used to it. Now, the real question here is why you did not come to me first with such questions. Surely you know this is a sensitive topic?"

"I already have," I reminded her, bristling slightly at her admonishment. "I've gone to everyone I trust now and no one will tell me anything! What's the big hubbub about it anyway? Why can't you tell me?"

Her voice cut across my rant effortlessly. "I couldn't tell you before because you weren't ready to hear it. You were new, fragile. If I added any more pressure to you, little wolf, you would have broken. After that you have not asked me to tell you." She smiled. "I have kept you far too busy."

Still as sneaky as ever; when am I ever going to know this woman's full agenda?

"And now?" I wondered curiously.

Her gaze shifted away from me to look up at the moon lighting the scene below us. Her expression became calm and pensive, and she looked every bit the wise Chief I knew her to be.

"Now you are ready," she told me quietly.

I looked out too, trying to find whatever she had fixated her attention on so fully while asking, "What happened to the humans before me, Grandmother?"

"Many different things."

I almost considered jumping off the cliff in aggravation when she paused, leaving me to think that was all she was going to tell me, but, moments later, she continued, "The ones taken as children were better adapted, but too immature. They were lost in foolish accidents and their own mistakes. Older ones were not suited for such a grueling life; they lost themselves to their own misery or insanity. After seeing so many failed attempts to integrate humans into our society, the Council ceased any efforts to bring humans in."

To my surprise, her story was not done yet. "Then, around ten or so years ago, the Council was willing to bring in another human to try again; they hand-picked someone, a female, to everyone's great surprise." Feminist mentality dictated that this was enough to make my eye twitch. "They housed her, put her through training with others her own age, and let her become part of a pack to serve them fully. For the first time ever, a human had managed to become a full-blooded wolf in service to the Council."

"What happened to her?" I asked nervously, not liking where this story might go next.

Amazingly, Grandmother sighed deeply at my question. "She betrayed the Council," she said dejectedly, "joined a vampire coven set against them, and renounced her allegiance."

We were silent for a moment, Grandmother immersed in dejection and sadness, while I was thinking about what kind of person would do that. Since arriving at the campus, paranormal creatures had been something I studied on a daily basis. I was seeing vampires for what they truly were: heartless and selfish murderers; monsters who were too cowardly to face death, and who stole life from others to escape from it. I found that I couldn't idolize creatures like that anymore. Taking my thoughts back to the present, I vaguely realized something. Quietly, I reminded Grandmother, "You never really answered my question."

She sighed again. "No one knows. She ran off with the coven and was never seen or heard from again. Her name is now forbidden to be spoken by those who serve the Council, and Changing a human became punishable by death."

My whole body went cold. Death? Kate could have died changing me and taking me with her? She risked her life and her future so that I could leave my past behind?

There was no question as to why she hadn't gotten in trouble. She was the Council's errand girl, not to mention the Council Head's granddaughter. She was too important to kill, as callous as that sounded. She had known that, or assumed it at least, and took the plunge.

I was going to smack that idiot the first chance I got.

"That's why everyone's so nervous about me," I realized out loud, "why everyone was so curious to find out what I was like…"

She finally turned to me then, and I caught a flash of sadness rippling through the deep, black depths of her gaze. A sudden train of thought hit me.

Did she know the girl? Did she befriend her like me; take her under her wing?

Grandmother shut her eyes and tilted her head back, taking a deep breath before opening them again. "Such talk ruins the happiness you have gained today. Do you have any other questions, little wolf?"

"Yes, actually. Vince told me about the powers of the clans." Her eyes turned sharply to mine and zeroed in, I recognized this as the face she would make when I did something to surprise her. "I was wondering if humans were known for any kind of power like that, or if I'm just stuck without any magic of my own."

"Due to a lack of successful humans to look towards, it is unknown as to whether everyone shares a power. However, the one we can look to was able to utilize different traits a wolf has while still in her human body, claws, speed, and such."

"Really?" I breathed, looking down at my hands. "That's amazing!"

"Hmm," she agreed. After a beat of silence, she plucked her staff back into her grip and stood to face me.

"There is one more thing I have left to share with you, little wolf." Reaching into her jacket, she fumbled around for a moment before pulling out a parchment that looked even older than *her*.

Crooking her fingers, she gingerly placed the paper in my hands as I moved to stand in front of her.

"What is this?" I asked, holding it like it would disintegrate if I gripped too hard.

"I've been keeping this for someone like you," she told me wearily, to my surprise. "Everyone else is breaking their silence today, I might as well too. It's ancient knowledge, a spell of sorts, maybe the last copy of it too. I want you to memorize it...and then burn it. I shudder to think what would happen if it was found in your hands."

I was slightly scared now, but also flattered at the obvious trust that this required. "I don't understand."

"Read it in private," she bid me. "You will understand then. This is best in your hands, little wolf. If there is anyone who will benefit from this spell and use it wisely, it is you. Use it only when all else fails."

Without another word, she began to walk away. I was used to such abrupt departures by now, but tonight I had one last question for her.

"Grandmother?" I called.

I heard her footsteps stop. "Yes?"

I hesitated, wondering if it was something I could ask, but decided she wouldn't care if it wasn't. "What was her name?"

She didn't move or speak. I didn't turn to face her. We stayed like that, with me waiting anxiously and her thinking carefully. "Alessandra," she said finally, walking away from me again. "Good night, little wolf."

"Yeah," I whispered, "good night."

The dormitories were already winding down for the night when I made it to our door. Bundling the ancient scroll carefully in my pocket, I laid my hand on the door and prayed that I would gain forgiveness.

We hadn't spoken at dinner. I didn't know what to say, what I *could* say. Now that I knew the truth, it was going to be even harder to get the right words out.

That little shit had risked everything to bring me here, more than I could have even imagined. If that didn't prove her worthiness as a friend, I didn't know what ever could.

And I had bitched her out earlier today in front of all of our friends and the general public too.

Just as I considered fleeing to Cindy's room for the night to wallow in my own guilt, the door opened under my hand and Kate stood in front of me.

She wouldn't look directly at me, but rather at the floor quietly for a few moments before saying, "I figured you might want to sleep in your own bed rather than in the hall tonight."

Turning around, she went to go back into the room, but then I found my courage and reached out to hug her tightly to me.

"I'msorryI'msorryI'msorryI'msorryI'msorryI'msorry—"

"Whoa, breathe, Ria." I caught her gaze then, and she seemed to realize something. "Who's the big mouth?"

"Grandmoth–the Chief," I admitted.

"Well, I don't want to hear a word about it," she warned, hugging me back. "We both did what we had to do."

I nodded into her shoulder. "Kay."

After a few moments, though, she put both of her hands on my shoulders and set me a step away from her. Taking a deep breath she said quietly, "I'm sorry for what I said earlier. That was completely not cool of me to do."

"Kate..."

"Don't! Just wait." She let her arms rest at her sides and finally looked me in the eye. "Everyone helped you today at lunch, as quietly as they tried to do it; I heard them giving you tips of the trade and spilling family secrets. Now, it's my turn."

We did a lot of talking that night, like we hadn't in a really long time. When it was late enough that we couldn't keep our eyes open, we finally lumbered into our respective beds and hit the hay.

As Kate went to turn out the light, though, she paused and looked at me. "Hey Ria?"

"Yeah," I answered sleepily.

"For the love of God, don't ever tell the Chief I called her a big mouth."

Hours later, in the dead of night, I would unravel the scroll under the safety of my sheets. The words on the scroll made me gasp aloud in shock, enough so that I had to check and make sure I didn't wake Kate up. As soon as I was sure I had it memorized, I pulled on my cloak over my pajamas and ran outside to burn it and bury the pieces.

When I was safe and happy in my bed once more, I pondered the reasons Grandmother would have given me such a spell and the possibilities it created.

Sleep completely eluded me that night.

CHAPTER FIFTEEN

"The wings of angels are often found on the backs of the least likely people."

-Eric Honeycutt

I figured after all of my question and interrogation the night before, Grandmother would spend the class exploring our own individual "specialties."

Move over, Kate. Who's the psychic one now?

It turned out to be exactly what we did that day. I was partnered up with Kate, and we worked together to take my power out for a test drive.

In other words, sitting on opposite sides of the room, Kate held up a book and set up a connection between our noggins. I proceeded to stun myself by enhancing my own vision to read the words to her...in my head.

Needless to say, after a while I was feeling like I belonged in the looney bin, talking to voices in my head, something that Kate found endlessly amusing.

I relayed the entire experience to Vincent at lunch, and he responded by proudly clapping me on the back and taking full credit.

After the excitement the morning had brought, sitting through my Paranormal Creatures lecture was just not cutting it.
Sliding my eyes to Carter, who was sitting right next to me, I wondered vaguely if I could coerce him into a subtle game of hangman.

Yeah. Not likely.

Instead, I just unobtrusively observed him out of the corner of my eyes. For someone who came across as a tad bit unapproachable, or at the very least a lone wolf, he had integrated well with our little group of misfits. He didn't talk much, but you could always sense the weight of his opinion; he was by no means an open book or anything, but it was just kind of obvious when he weighed in on something. A little shake of the head, the raising of an eyebrow, the narrowing of eyes, that was all it took.

My eye traveled upwards, and rested on the trait which had first brought my attention to him. To this day, I still hadn't figured out whether his red streaks were natural or not. They couldn't possibly be, and yet I had a hard time picturing Carter dying his hair every few months.

Just the thought of Carter with a box of do-it-yourself hair dye made me snort. Being in the middle of class, I covered it up with a cough, but Carter was anything but fooled. Without so much as a glance, he wrote something in the margin of his notebook and carefully slid it to where I could see it.

You're staring.

I would have rolled my eyes at Captain Obvious, but, seeing as he was looking towards the front of the classroom, it would have been completely lost on him. With a smile, I realized this was as close as I was going to get to hangman with this kid. Reaching for my notebook, I wrote my own message.

Maybe there's a booger on your face. Ever think of that?

I swear to God I saw his lip twitch. I don't care what anyone says, I'm calling that a smile.

Is there reason my face is more interesting than your grade?

Jeezum. I sometimes forget this guy is actually capable of complete sentences.

I was wondering about your hair, actually.
What about it?
Is it naturally awesome? Or can I purchase it in a box?
Lip. Twitch. It must be the end of days here, people.
What do you think?

Those written words were giving off a rather patronizing air for just any old sentence.

If I was so sure than I wouldn't be asking. Duh.

He paused for a moment, possibly debating my sanity, a rather normal occurrence for me. Finally, he wrote.

Natural.

Well, then. Mystery solved.

I goggled quickly for another moment before realizing I wanted the last word.

You think I could find it in a box anyway?

I saw him shake his head out of my peripheral vision, but it was more of a shake of disbelief than a negatory. So, I dreamed.

After class was over (we were not caught. Oh yeah), Carter followed his usual routine of gathering his books, standing up from his seat, and waiting for me with limitless patience.

The first time he did this, I thought I was in his way or had the leg of my chair crushing his foot in place, but instead he was waiting to escort me to our next class we had together.

It goes without saying that this took me weeks to get used to. Maybe even beyond that.

After a while, though, when I did grow more at ease around him, I noticed that I would see him more often than I expected throughout the day. During random passing periods, he would show up at my side, lead me to class (not saying a word the entire time, mind you), and then be on his merry way.

Flattered as I was to have obtained a stalker my first month of werewolf school, it began to feel a little stifling after a while. When he tried to follow me to The Spot after a particularly trying day, I confronted him.

"Just what do you think you're doing, Carter?" I snarled, feeling a little more than wolfish at the moment.

Unmoved, he crossed his arms over his chest and centered his unwavering stare on me. Understanding it was too much to ask him to talk to me, I growled and moved to poke him in the chest.

"Listen, dude, walking me to class is nice and cheery and wonderful, but I do not need a constant bodyguard watching over me. I really don't. So, unless you come up with a *really good* excuse, you can take a leave of absence."

He was still staring, and it was still disconcerting. Finally, after a long, tense moment, he gave his answer.

"You need to be watched."

I had the sudden urge to beat my head repeatedly against one of the nearby trees. Pinching the bridge of my nose and taking deep yoga breaths, I tried again.

"Yes, thank you. We've already established that much. The intent behind that reason, however, remains unclear."

Silent but deadly strikes again. After a good five minutes of silence, I finally threw up my arms and stormed off.

The next day, I walked to my classes alone, and despite all of my anger and confusion, I found myself missing his stoic presence that had become so like my own shadow. This went on for a week before anything climactic happened. No, I didn't go running back to him sobbing and begging for him to continue to haunt me. Don't even think like that.

Nope. Before that could happen, I met up with Desiree in the hallway.

I tried to avoid confrontation. I really did, but then she had to go open her mouth and sprout obnoxious noises from it. People, we're lucky I didn't just strangle her (no one would have complained if I did, probably). She hounded me relentlessly on how she was amazed I was still here and sane, and made some really bitchy comment about how Kate probably had everything to do with that. Then, she said some other stuff that makes me too PO'd to repeat.

I'm thinking Desiree was expecting the coward that first showed up on this campus, but I was about to introduce her to the changed woman I was.

My comeback included something about the mysterious nature of her birth and maybe a thing or two about her mother. You know, keeping it classy.

Too bad she didn't appreciate its beauty. Come to think of it, she didn't really appreciate it at all. You see, the tricky part in all of this was that she brought her little cronies with her.

So, Ria may or may not have gotten the beating of a lifetime. I was so outnumbered, though. That's my story, and I'm sticking to it. After Desiree was satisfied with my state of disrepair, she turned up her nose and walked away.

Bitch.

This was how Carter found me a few minutes later.

As he knelt down next to me, I smiled up at him. "Were your 'Ria senses' tingling?"

With a snort that was somehow dignified, Carter reached out and lifted me up and onto his back. Barely registering what was going on, I let him carry me to the infirmary and put me down on one of the beds. The nurse saw us and ran to get some supplies, and Carter, seeing that I was alive and in good hands, turned to leave.

Somehow, I was brave enough to reach out and grab his sleeve.

When he looked down at me, my gaze settled on the ground and I shifted uncomfortably. "Stay. Please." I was sure that he was going to leave me and that I had thoroughly made an idiot of myself.

So, when the scrape of a chair against the floor reached my ears, I couldn't help but start and look up disbelievingly to see Carter settling himself next to my bed, sleeve still firmly in my grasp. I sent him a small smile as a thank you.

The nurse came back to bandage me up as best as she could and clean the blood off of my face. She gave me medicine that would take the edge off the pain, but I would have to stay in bed for a little while.

Sighing as she left the room, I leaned my head back and finally gave into the heavy guilt settled over my heart. "I'm sorry," I said quietly.

Silence. It was light, but enough to set my teeth on edge with frustration.

Soon, though, I heard him sigh.

"I was trying to keep you safe."

Well, hello there spoken word. Nice to meet you.

"Yeah, and I was the idiot who couldn't understand that Desiree was still lurking around somewhere."

But Carter shook his head. "I wasn't protecting you from her."

"Then who were you protecting me from?"

He was quiet again for such a long moment I was sure that he wasn't going to answer me. Resigned, I sat back and closed my eyes, until I heard the whisper come from his chair.

"Yourself."

Sitting up straight, I couldn't find the words to the questions I wanted to ask. He seemed to understand this because he started in on his explanation.

"You're doing well, but there's still much you don't know about," he said completely composed. "You're still in danger of losing yourself."

"Losing myself? What are you talking about?"

He was staring at the hand still attached to his sleeve, enough so that I contemplated letting go. However, a few seconds later, he removed it from his person and turned my hand over in his, observing it closing. "Your powers are controlled by natural-born instincts. You are the balance between two animals. One side is dictated by logical thought, taught to act rationally and to control emotions. The other side, untamed and wild, is a beast, a beast that, should you ever lose yourself to your more unrestrained emotions, would reveal itself, and wreak havoc to anything that stood in your path, friend or foe."

In my mind were visions of the red-eyed Ria from my nightmares massacring the townsfolk. I couldn't hold back the shiver of apprehension at the thought. To my surprise, though, he wasn't done.

"When a werewolf is pushed to their emotional limits, they change into something else entirely. They become a creature known as a wendigo."

The name sounded familiar; I flicked through all of the knowledge my love of fiction had brought me, and recalled the name from a Stephen King novel. "I've heard of that," I told him quietly, "a creature that used to be a whose heart turns to ice and who snacks on humans."

He nodded. "That is the description from the legends, but it's not likely that they actually turn cannibalistic. They just kill anything that stands in their way."

"That sounds awful," I whispered. "How can someone free themselves from that?"

My blood froze as Carter shook his head. "You can't. No one has before, and it's an ancient law that wendigos are immediately executed."

"So no one has even tried to help them," I asked incredulously.

"People have tried and failed more times than can be counted, and in the process, those affected have destroyed everything and everyone they once cherished without regard to their emotions."

Silence took its place between us again. I tried absorbing everything he had just told me, and failed miserably.

"So, you were protecting me from becoming a wendigo?" Somehow, I was still confused.

Again, he shook his head. "Not just that, humans are known for having a hard time adjusting to their new instincts and darker emotions. Insanity was a common cause of death for them." He looked away from me then. "I was protecting you from losing yourself, and who you really are, and all I succeeded in doing was making you angrier."

Do my ears deceive me? Was that an apology I just heard?

I held his hand tightly and waited to speak until he turned back towards me. "I can hardly be angry with you for trying to protect me. If I had known that from the beginning I would have tied you to my side." I treated him to a warm smile. "You're a very calming presence to have around, you know that? I feel safe around you."

His normally expressionless face softened the slightest bit. "When I first met you, I could smell you were human. I was curious. I had never met a human before, and I wanted to see how long you would last." He seemed to wince at his own callousness. I squeezed his hand to let him know I wasn't offended. "I don't know when I stopped observing and started caring, but I never want to see that happen to you."

Knowing that Carter wasn't the touchy-feely hugging kind of person, I entangled his fingers with mine and held tight.

"I'm glad I'm your friend, Carter."

After that, Carter started following me around again, and, this time, I always greeted him with a smile.

"Ria. Are you coming?"

Startled out my thoughts, I smiled apologetically at him. "Got lost in the noggin again, sorry about that."

He shrugged, completely indifferent to my spaciness. It was understandable. We were on our way to Transformation, and today was the big day I had been waiting for. Time to like, actually Transform.

I struggled to breathe in and out in a normal fashion the whole way there.

A gentle bump against my shoulder made me direct my gaze up to the looming bodyguard I was so familiar with.

"You will be fine," he said serenely. "You're ready for this."

And suddenly I felt as though I was, just because he said so.

The Transformation room was more like the size of a humungous gym. A lot of our classmates were inside, including the rest of our groupies. However, today, I noticed that there were more unfamiliar figures here as well. Older wolves, teachers, and miscellaneous others (including Aunt Rose who saw me and waved so enthusiastically that she actually hit someone next to her. Completely unconcerned, she blew me a kiss too) were crowded around waiting for class to start. The sight of our teacher, Ms. Langley, talking to Grandmother made me smile. She must have come to keep an eye on me.

When the bell finally rang, the students arranged themselves in a cluster in front of all of the adults. Getting everyone in order, Mrs. Langley explained that she would be assigning every student a pair of proctors to watch over him or her. In turn, they would give us advice on how to make the process smoother and easier. When she was sure everyone understood what was happening, she began calling out the names. Barely containing my anxiety, I waited (im)patiently for her to call me.

"Maria," I could have cried with relief. "You will go with-"

She was cut off by the sound of the doors being thrown open. We all turned and, once we got over our shock, hurriedly stood at attention when the Council Head, in all his glory, strolled into the room. I felt Kate stiffen minutely beside me and gently bumped her hand with mine. She didn't look over at me, but her head inclined just slightly.

Mrs. Langley walked around us and bowed to the Council Head, the picture of respect. "Honorable Council Head, what may I help you with?"

He didn't answer her right away, but rather looked around the room, making students squirm uncomfortably where they stood and adults avert their gaze.

It seemed strange to me that this room of people, who had been lively and talkative not 30 seconds ago, was all petrified with fear that bordered on awe.

Just what kind of hold did this man have over these people?

When his gaze landed on Kate and me, I'm proud to say we stood firm and stared right back at him, refusing to be intimidated.

He answered Mrs. Langley's question in a tone that made me grind my teeth in anger. She wasn't dirt, so why did he insist on treating her like it? "Has the human been assigned a group yet?"

I dug my fingernails into the palms of my hands so hard I almost drew blood. The audacity of that man is going to be his downfall.

Calm down, Ria, I thought to myself. You don't want to do this in front of him. This is what he wants.

Mrs. Langley's voice sounded a bit more strained when she spoke again, surprising me. "No, I have not assigned *Maria* to a supervisor yet, sir. I was planning on letting the Chief take her by herself." If he wasn't standing there, I would have breathed a sigh of relief, but I knew that the big-headed ass was going to ruin my day.

My assumptions were correct. He raised his chin in a very Desiree-ish fashion and said, "That is unacceptable. The Chief is not a wolf, should the human lose control of herself she would be unable to defend herself."

Everyone standing around me sucked in a sharp breath, and leaned away a little. For one dangerous moment I saw the world in a hazy red as fury swelled within me. I almost took a step forward towards the pompous ass, but a firm hand – most likely Carter's – fisted in my shirt behind me, holding me in place. There was so much rage building within me that my whole body was shaking.

I clenched my eyes shut and forcibly pushed the anger down, not away, but down enough so that I could think on my own. When I looked back into his steel gray eyes, they were shining with victory.

That son of a female dog.

Mrs. Langley seemed to have my back on this one, something that I would have to thank her for later. "Honorable Councilman, I assure you, I see Maria every day. If I ever thought there was the slightest chance she may be a source of danger to those around her, then I would have sent for you immediately."

I waited for her to point out the special grandmother/daughter relationship we shared, but was pleasantly surprised when she didn't; the whole world knew about it, but still, I was so relieved. Mr. Council butt's mission to make my life miserable did *not* need a push in that direction.

"Nonetheless," he continued to argue. "The safety of the Chief is a priority to all of us here. I shall personally oversee the human's first transformation, alongside the Chief."

Aren't you old enough to be dead yet? Just lie down and go to hell like the nasty, evil being you are.

Mrs. Langley bowed again to the Head of her Council, "I cannot go against your wishes, sir. You may do as you believe what is the best choice." I couldn't help but notice how reluctant the words seemed coming out of her mouth, and if I saw it, he must have as well. Luckily for her, he wasn't paying much attention.

"Maria, if you would." He held out an arm, gesturing towards the section of the room we were to practice in, and, like a good little wolf, I bowed and walked where he had indicated.

The Chief was standing there waiting with a stern grimace I had grown to recognize as her "Chief face." I had only ever seen her wear it three times. Strangely enough, each of those three times had been when she was talking to a member of the Council.

Hmm. How peculiar.

I felt the presence of Kate's grandfather behind me, along with the weight of everyone's stares on my back. As discreetly as I could, I took a deep breath and turned to face the Grandmother and the Councilman. Grandmother waited in a relaxed position with both hands rested on her staff; she was not worried I would hurt her, and, for that, I was more grateful then I had ever been in my life.

Kate's grandfather waited with his arms crossed over his chest and his feet shoulder-length apart, deceptively calm. I saw his muscles were tensed and ready.

The most powerful werewolf of the Council...I restrained a shiver at the thought. There was no telling just how strong he really was. If he even thought I was losing control, he would have the authority to contain me, with or without force.

I really hope he won't need to. I sent a quick prayer with the thought; I wasn't taking any chances today.

We waited in silence for a few minutes while the rest of my classmates were assigned groups. Everyone was to Change at the same time. While we were getting all settled, I noticed more Councilmen come to observe our class. They didn't oversee any students, merely stood by the wall and watched us...me.

No pressure Ria, no pressure at all.

143

When Mrs. Langley was done, she turned from her group to face the rest of her students and the proctors. "You may begin," she called.

The rush of energy that filled the room was amazing. Made of the most basic and primal power, it made goosebumps break out along my arms and all of my hair to stand on end. I closed my eyes and pulled some of that energy out of the air and wrapped it around me, let it fill me, let it change me.

Opening my eyes I saw the world in a shadowed tint. For a moment I was confused as to why nothing was happening to me. I had done everything right. I had gone through every step Mrs. Langley taught us and followed them word for word. So why was nothing happening?

Those thoughts ended as the most excruciating pain I had felt in my entire life burst out across my entire body. I cried out and screamed until my voice broke, but that did nothing to stop it. It felt like every part of me was being shattered, then put back together in a way that was just *wrong*. My bones were broken then shifted into new positions, all of my muscles were pulled and stretched along my new limbs and all of my insides were modified and relocated.

That wasn't even the worse part.

More strength poured into me then I was used to. Darker, more sinister power ran through me, invading my thoughts and ideas. It made me see and wish for things that caused my human side to recoil in revulsion and incredulity. It was almost too much to bear.

The pain lasted for no more than two minutes, but it seemed to my hurting body like years. It didn't leave all at once. No, that would have been way too easy. Slowly, it receded from me, from the tips of my toes, up my legs, through my stomach and arms until, finally, it reached my pounding head. I lay broken and aching on the hard ground, gasping for breath. I pulled my hands to my head, so they could block out the sounds coming from around me – they weren't helping the headache – but no fingers combed through my hair.

By some miracle, I managed to open my heavy eyelids, and look over to where my hand should have been, but resting in its place was a gigantic paw complete with razor sharp claws extended off of each tip. The other arm was the same, I had to check.

Holy shit, Batman. I was a wolf.

Gathering my remaining strength in my legs (all four of them?), I tried to force myself up, but was too weak.

There was a light touch at the top of my head. Blearily, I looked up to see Grandmother standing over me, her face composed. The only way I could tell she was worried was the tightness I saw around her eyes.

"Rest for a moment, little wolf. The weakness will pass, but you must let yourself rest." Her fingers gently smoothed the hair between my ears. "You did very well." The note of pride in her voice was unmistakable.

I tried very hard to listen to her advice, but a second presence close by made it impossible to relax any further. I could see the Council Head from my angle; he was looking at me as if I had pleasantly surprised him.

I wasn't sure if that was a good or a bad thing.

So, though my strength was leaving me enough that my eyes slid shut again, I could not find it in me to relax while he was nearby and I was so vulnerable. My instincts would not let me.

Suddenly, a quiet, high pitch whine reached my ears, but I was too tired to open my eyes again. Instead, I just listened.

I heard Grandmother first. "Do not worry for your friend, she is fine." A pause. "Perhaps you should go back to your instructors?"

A low growl quickly dismissed that thought as the wolf came close enough that I could feel its heat. I forced myself to open my eyelids just as the wolf was lowering itself next to me. I tried to see who it was, but the only thing that covered my vision was black fur. So, not really knowing how I did it, I lifted my head weakly and turned it slightly to meet a familiar face.

Deep black eyes stared down at me in a face covered with ebony fur and (natural) fiery red streaks. Immediately, I identified the wolf as Carter. Without any rhyme or reason, I suddenly felt more at ease just having him next to me. I could tell he noticed me looking at him; a calming, rumbling sound that wasn't quite a growl came from his chest and he lay his head over mine, gently forcing me to lay back down, to rest.

With my head resting against my paws and Carter's reassuring presence (warm at my side and over my head), I would feel safe sleeping in front of the Devil himself.

Which wasn't exactly that far off.

Soon after, others came, and despite their radically altered appearances, I recognized all of them. One by one, my friends came to rest around me, each one offering support and reassurances. A warmth I couldn't identify filled my chest as I thanked all my lucky stars that I had found these people, and that they had become my friends.

Nudging my nose further into Carter's coat, I was especially thankful for my silent protector.

CHAPTER SIXTEEN

"I do not believe that the accident of birth makes people sisters and brothers. It makes them siblings. Gives them mutuality of parentage. Sisterhood and brotherhood are conditions people have to work at. It's a serious matter. You compromise, you give, you take, you stand firm, and you're relentless"

-Maya Angelou

After that first try, we practiced shifting every day in that class. Luckily, it got easier each time, and there was never the same ungodly amount of pain (which as I was told later was actually really normal. Um, thanks for the warning.).

Someone also mentioned to me later, in passing, that it was amazing I actually managed to Transform on my first try. Needless to say, that poor passerby was cornered and interrogated until I learned that previous humans had usually spent months just trying to do the initial Transformation.

Okay. So maybe it was a good thing no one had told me this before. The mental meltdown beforehand would have been cataclysmic, to put it lightly. Carter would have had to drag me to that classroom kicking and screaming, the poor thing.

But I am not thinking about that. I did it. It happened. I'm moving on and looking forward to the future.

And the future I was looking at included not getting my ass kicked by the enemy in front of me.

Kate and I stood next to each other, hands resting on our knees, panting and exhausted.

"Come on, Kate," I encouraged her, wiping the sweat from my brow. "We got this."

"Ria," she gasped between heavy breaths. "It's useless. Maybe we should just-"

I rounded on her. *"Don't* even think like that, Kate! We can do this!"

She deliberated this for a moment, before nodding. "One more try."

I clapped her on the back as she stood up straight and took to my attacking position. "Ready?"

Her face was serious, prepared. "Ready," she growled.

"One," I began.

"Two." Her eye twitched in her deep concentration.

"Three," we chorused together.

I took my leap on top of the enemy, pressing down with all of my weight and muscle. She rushed forward and bound it as fast as she could, leaving no chance of escape. It took a few minutes of struggling, but, in the end, the match was ours. Elated, I jumped down to give her a high five. Radiating pride and victory, we turned to face our work together.

"It's all packed and ready to go!" She laughed happily.

I turned and smirked at her. "I told you we could fit all our stuff into one suitcase."

She rolled her eyes, and hauled it off her bed. "Only because you don't have that much stuff, and we're going to *my* house."

"Bubble burster."

Finally, after months and months of endless training, we were allowed to go home for a break. When I found out about this impromptu break, I questioned Kate about the funky scheduling of this whole adventure, and was surprised to find there was actually good reason involved.

This schedule has been the same since the beginning of werewolf time. Training starts as soon as winter breaks in order to ensure the longest period of good weather, and then a recess starts at the first snowfall. We'll come back and do training in the deep snow, but first we're heading out to Kate's family compound (seeing as I can't exactly go home for break).

At the thought, I absently ran my fingers over the picture in my back pocket, the one I had taken with me so long ago. Would they even recognize who I was anymore? I was so different in both body and mind. It was like being a completely new person.

Pulling myself out of my thoughts, I took one handle of the suitcase as Kate took the other. We walked out of our room and locked the door behind us.

There would be a driver waiting on the main road that led up to the Council building. He would take us straight to the house, where I would be finally be given the honor of meeting Kate's elusive family.

I hadn't heard much about them yet, except for her brother, whom every teacher seemed to adore.

Not one of them ever let Kate forget it either. She worked her ass off every day, but I could feel the pressure that was placed on her shoulders.

It was similar to the one I had from my own sibling.

The lobby was eerily empty, unlike its normal busy and loud atmosphere. Most of our building's occupants had already gone, leaving the whole place quiet and vacant. There was, however, one person waiting for us, or rather me, at the door. Kate looked over at me in understanding.

"Go and say goodbye," she told me, taking my side of the suitcase from my hand and hoisting the whole thing over her shoulder. "I'll wait for you by the car."

I nodded and she walked away. Taking one last look around the lobby, I made my way to the doors and pushed them open. Noticing my exit, she turned around and came to my side.

"You are leaving now, little wolf?" she asked me in her typical drawl.

I nodded. "Yes, we were just heading out now."

Her face was calculative, just as it normally was, looking over my expression. "You are excited to go and meet them?"

To show exactly how I felt to her prying eyes, I smiled. "I've been waiting years for this, Grandmother. I am more than excited."

She seemed to approve of this because she nodded and rested both hands on her staff in front of her, something she only did when conversations were about to end. "Then I hope you will enjoy yourself, little wolf. No loud parties though, Kari does not like them."

"I'll keep that in mind," I told her amusedly.

Smiling softly, she beckoned me forward. I obeyed, confused, until she bestowed a kiss on my forehead. It was the first time she had ever done so before. Goggle-eyed, I stepped back.

"I will see you soon, little wolf," she said as she turned and began walking away from me. "Your training has only just begun."

I remained rooted to the spot for a few moments, watching her retreating back go farther and farther away from me. When I couldn't see her anymore, I went and met up with Kate at the car. She never asked about the little meetings I had with Grandmother and I never told. It was something private, something personal to me, like her dealings with the Council.

Except, I'm pretty sure I didn't want to know anything about those.

As I walked to the car, various students, teachers, and officials greeted me and sent their well wishes for a good break. Not many people saw me as a dangerous human anymore, for which I was eternally grateful. As time passed, I even felt less human myself. My transformation was almost completely complete. My vision had sharpened naturally to the point where I didn't need contacts anymore and my pupils had shrunk into the catlike slits normal for a werewolf.

Physically, I could already feel the difference too. In my gym and fighting classes, I had more endurance and strength then the average human, even with Kate and Mrs. Johnson's merciless training. I also fought better, natural instincts rose inside my head during a fight telling me the best way to strike my opponent: something I had come to appreciate more often than not. We found out that silver didn't affect me yet, to my great relief. Soon, I wouldn't even be able to touch it without my skin burning.

I was praying Daimon's locket was made of white gold.

My thoughts broke as the car began to slow down and turn into a driveway.

All around us were rows of houses, looking the same for the most part. I saw people discreetly looking down from windows at us, curious to see the human they must have heard about. At the end of the driveway was another house, this one larger than the others.

Kate caught me looking at it. "Though we are all related here, the nuclear families still live in separate homes. Since our family is the ruling one, we have the largest house." She shrugged and looked away from me, back out the window. "I'm not often home anyway," she said so quietly I knew I wasn't supposed to hear it.

The car stopped in front of the house, where I saw four people waiting patiently for us. As I opened the door and stepped out, I recognized one right away.

"Kate! Maria! Did you *walk*? I've been waiting for years and my feet are tired as hell!"

Good, old Aunt Rose, ever the same.

The woman ran down the front steps towards us, managing to tangle us both up into a group hug. We humored her through the typical pinching of the cheeks and kisses.

While I was enduring my share, she held me by the shoulders and looked at me carefully up and down. "Oh, for the love of God, are they even *feeding* you there? You've certainly slimmed down, Maria."

"I've been working out," I informed her flatly.

She whacked me on the side of the head affectionately. "Smartass," she admonished with a smile.

Another woman came up beside Aunt Rose, and I had to do a double take as an older version of Kate hugged her daughter tightly.

"It's good to see you again, sweetheart." Her voice was deeper and softer then Kate's, filled with warmth and empty of sarcasm: a mother's voice.

At that moment, my heart ached for my mother's comforting tone so much that tears almost pricked at my eyes, but I clamped down on my emotions as I had been doing successfully for the past months and they left, unnoticed.

Mother and daughter turned to face me. "Mom," Kate began. "This is Maria, Ria, meet my mother, Sarah."

I reached out to grasp her forearm, but she immediately walked forward to enfold me in a warm hug. "I'm glad I'm finally meeting you, Maria," she breathed warmly. "I've been waiting for too long to meet Kari's best friend."

When she freed me from the warmth of her arms, I smiled at her. "Just as long as I've waited to meet her family."

I'm happy I'm not meeting gravestones.

A man came next to Sarah; he reached out his arm for mine and I gave it to him, firmly grasping his as I met his familiar silver eyes.

She has her father's eyes.

He was not as warm as his wife. *Mate*, I corrected myself firmly. I recognized his blank expression and crisp, formal tone. "It's a pleasure to meet you, Maria. My name is Samson."

I nodded politely, making my tone respectful. "The pleasure is all mine, sir."

As he returned the nod, I saw his eyes gleam with approval. My heart soared; I had made a good first impression.

All of a sudden, he turned his head back to the house and called, "Son, come down and greet our guest."

I felt my heart stop beating in my chest; I knew who he was talking to. The prodigy of Kate's family: number one son himself.

He didn't look like Kate; he took to his father more than his mother. His mask was carefully composed on his face and his eyes more like ice than silver as they stared coldly down at me. I pictured Desiree that first day we met, with her cold, grey eyes glaring balefully down her nose at me.

His expression was not far from that.

He stood between Kate and their father, still glaring, as he held out his arm.

I took it, steeling myself not to react when he clamped down hard enough to bruise. I simply returned the pressure full force.

"Maria," he greeted tonelessly.

I responded in the same manner. "Rowan."

Kate was watching our interaction curiously; I realized that before training, I might have run away from the situation, or ended up in a jittery fit, stumbling out an apology for even looking cross-eyed at him. Now, the glares had no effect on me; I only returned them with equal force.

He dropped my arm like it burned him, turned away from us, and went back into the house.

Sarah sighed deeply, and Samson glared at the door, disapproval shining in his eyes. Rose decided to make her feelings known out loud, "Little brat never liked company anyway."

I assumed they were used to her banters; they simply rolled their eyes at Rose and invited me into the house with them.

Dinner was quite the event that night. Kate's family (sans the angst-filled douche bag) was just as interested in knowing absolutely everything about me as I was about them.

Eventually, the conversation basically became swapping family stories (including some *fantastic* bits of blackmail from Kate's childhood) and sharing our interests. Even after dinner, I found myself sitting in the parlor with Kate's father talking about the intricacies of werewolf society and comparing it to human society.

He was surprised to find that they weren't so different.

Soon enough, though, the excitement of the day caught up with me. He noticed my heavy eyes and drooping shoulders and had Kate lead me upstairs to the room I would be staying in.

By the time I was in bed, though, I was wired from the day's experience. There were so many thoughts swarming around my mind that, eventually, I just got up and decided to walk down to the kitchen for a glass of water.

I ended getting way more than what I bargained for.

As I stood by the sink watching my glass fill, I heard a slight rustling of clothing behind me, warning me I wasn't alone.

Turning off the faucet, I casually turned to see the tall, lean figure of Rowan leaning against the doorframe between the kitchen and the dining room. I stared at him for a while, waiting for him to make any sort of point/warning/insult, but he did nothing. He seemed to be waiting for me to make some sort of move.

So, not one to disappoint, I took a deceptively calm sip of my water and leaned back against the counter, fully intent on waiting him out.It worked the way I wanted it to. Rowan' eyes narrowed into dangerous slits, and he removed his hand from its casual place in his pocket so he could cross his arms over his chest. He meant it to be threatening, but it was really anything but. In the privacy of my own thoughts, I was daring him to try something in his own house.

"What are you doing up this late?" Despite his own impatience, his voice was smooth and toneless.

I just barely restrained an instinctual reaction to the threat between his words. I didn't need all of my teachers to tell me that this guy could be dangerous if he wanted to be.

"Just gettin' a midnight snack, Rowan." I kept my tone light and neutral. "You can run along back to bed now."

"After you, human."

My grip tightened convulsively on my glass before I could help myself. Immediately, I regret the reaction when his eyes gleamed with amusement.

"I can hardly be known by that distinction anymore, Rowan. It's been awhile since I've been completely human."

Just like a dog, his head tilted to the side, considering me. "Once a human, always a human. You will never become one of us, not fully. Why don't you just run back to where you belong?"

"As you're new to my acquaintance, I'll try to explain it patiently once." Downing my drink, I placed it in the sink and leaned my hands back against the counter, deceptively calm, but ready to spring if he came at me. I looked back up at him and made my tone as pleasant as possible. "There is a reason I left the human world, and there are many reasons why I cannot go back. This is my home now, and nothing you, or anyone else for that matter, say will make me turn tail and run back. Are we completely clear?"

He was openly sneering at me now. "Kari was a fool to have brought you here. She *is* a fool for becoming friends with a *human*."

The way he spat Kate's name was enough for a spark of irritation to build up in me. "Your sister is free to make friends with whomever she pleases, Rowan; no matter how well you think you know them. It isn't your place to judge her for that."

Rowan bared his teeth slightly. "I care little for the machinations of my sibling. What I care about is her tarnishing the family name that she should be trying to improve."

I was taken aback at just callously he spoke about Kate. I thought about my own little brother, how I loved him so much (and still did). I would never talk about him that way, like he was a tool rather than a living, breathing person.

"Do you have any love for your little sister?" I asked him quietly, but sternly to inform him I was being entirely serious. "Don't you care about her life outside of your twisted family hierarchy?"

Something about my question made him relax again until he his face was stoic once more. "Siblings hardly need affection to aid one another in growing stronger."

Was this guy for real?

I couldn't hold back the disgust and astonishment from my face. "Have you ever thought that it might help her improve faster? That your approval and encouragement would work better than an extreme amount of pressure and derision? You should be there for your sister! That's what being a family really means!"

I should know, seeing as I don't have that anymore.

The silence was thick between us as he seemed to absorb my words. I couldn't wait to see what he had to say to that. Then, calmly as you please, he opened his mouth and serenely asked his own question.

"Do you have a younger sibling, human?"

I wasn't going to let the backtrack to "human" get to me. I wasn't going to give him that satisfaction. "Yes," I responded smoothly. "I have a younger brother."

He paused, and I didn't like the look on his face. It was the look I would expect from a hunter who has his prey right where he wants it.

"Where are you for him now?" I froze. "Do you think he still loves you after you left him behind? Do you think all of your love for him really matters now that you're gone?"

He didn't give me a chance to answer. Pleased with my shell-shocked silence, he turned about face and strolled out of the kitchen.

That night I saw Seamus' face in my dreams. I saw him crying and heard his angry words of hatred and abandonment.

The next morning I woke up tired with bags under my eyes. Rowan sat across from me at the breakfast table and I saw the ends of his lips quirk upwards at my bedraggled appearance.

Damn kid.

Three weeks with Kate's family made me as familiar with them as she had been with my parents, barring Rowan (that bag of douche), who usually wasn't at home. His pack was stationed in the area so he was still able to visit his family between his duties, but he didn't seem inclined to stay at home any more then was necessary.

His loss, I thought, as Kate and I ate our weight in her mother's cookies. Her recipe must have been created in a moment of divine intervention, and his mother must not have made any of these for him as a child; he would have turned out sweeter if he had eaten more.

As the picture of Kate and I force feeding Rowan cookies filled my head, Kate's parents walked into the kitchen.

"Feet off the table, girls," her father ordered without looking up at us.

Sarah had stopped in the doorway and took in the sight of us inhaling her cookies with amusement. "You better still have room for dinner after eating all of those."

"Oh, we do," Kate managed around a mouthful of what I assumed was two cookies at once.

Seeing as her feet were currently on the floor, I could send her a punishing kick under the table. Now that I had more strength, my kicks came with a lot more *oomph* in them, something Kate had only herself to blame for. "How many times do I have to tell you, fatty?"

She sighed and mocked me. "'No talking with your mouth full, you ungrateful child. No one likes see-food.'"

I nodded in approval and shoved another cookie in my mouth, looking up in time to see Sarah walking away from us into the kitchen, her shoulders moving slightly with laughter and her head shaking back and forth in disbelief.

Without meaning to, I had stumbled upon something extraordinary here. I found another family that was willing to take me in in an adoptive manner similar to what my family had done with Kate. I had thought I could separate myself from a family just by leaving my home, but instead I gained a new one.

It was a novel experience.

Suddenly, without warning, the front door of the house opened so hard it slammed on the wall behind it. Months of training kicked in as Kate and I leapt from our seats and joined Samson to stand in front of her mother, the only one of us four who had not been properly trained.

That was past her time.

It was not necessary, however, because it was Rowan who ran into the kitchen the next moment. A distinct note of panic hit me as I noticed that the composed, calm, and collected soldier I knew was replaced by a frightened child. His eyes were wide, wild, and filled with apprehension as they searched for us. Two spots of color rose high on his otherwise very pale face.

Something was very, *very* wrong.

When his searching eyes finally found us, he seemed to calm a bit. His toneless voice would not reveal any distress as he said, "Kari. Maria. You are to return to the training grounds immediately. The car is already here for you, your things will be sent to you later. Father, you are to come with me to do a run."

Sarah pushed past us and laid a hand on her son's shoulder. At twenty-one, he was more than a head taller than her, but, in some way, she seemed to tower over him. In her most soothing tone, she asked, "Rowan, honey, what's happened?"

His eyes darted between all of us frantically. "There's been an attack. A coven of vampires ambushed a pack unexpectedly."

Sarah's hands went to her mouth as she gasped softly. "How many?" his father asked gravely.

Rowan met his eyes. "Seven, there were no survivors, and they were all killed before backup had arrived."

Ice ran through my veins. Killing one werewolf was hard enough, but taking down an entire pack and making sure there were no survivors was unheard of. Especially with just a single coven.

This *was* very, very bad.

"They're calling all of the trainees back in early. Security is being tightened for the time being around the perimeter."

Kate and I took that as our cue and walked out of the kitchen, grabbing our jackets that hung over the backs of the chairs we were sitting in. Even in such a grave situation as this, we each snuck a few cookies in our pockets, as inconspicuously as possible of course. Following Rowan, we made our way down the hallway and out the door of the house.

Sarah saw us off as Samson went to prepare to make his run. She hugged us both as tightly as she could, in my ear she whispered, "Be careful." To Kate she whispered, "Stay safe." The fear and anxiety in her tone was almost heart-breaking.

She's worried she's going to end up like one of those seven mothers today, hearing news of her children becoming a number in an ambush.

I didn't blame her.

The car ride back seemed to take three times as long as the ride there. Tension thrummed in the air of the small space. At the same time, Kate and I reached for one another's hands and held on tightly.

Ten minutes later we were there, breaking out of the car before it had slid into a complete stop and running to our dorm building, where a mass of fellow classmates were steadily making their way in. I searched the crowd and found the familiar heads I was looking for. It helped that Austin was as noticeable as a flashing neon sign with his height and red hair. Pulling Kate with me, we ran in their direction.

The broad backs of Carter and Austin were facing us. When we called out to them, they turned around to reveal a Vince supporting a very distraught Cindy. I felt my steps stop abruptly.

"Oh, God…"

Hearing me, Cindy looked up through teary, bloodshot eyes filled with so much pain I actually staggered back a step. However, I soon found myself walking towards her again, and, without any prompting necessary, she flung herself at me and held on desperately, as if she would fall apart completely if someone wasn't there to hold her. I hugged her tightly, running fingers softly through her hair as she cried into my shoulder.

Looking up at Kate over Cindy's shoulder, I shared a look of helplessness with her. Austin cleared his throat.

"Her sister was caught in the raid," he spoke quietly. "Help didn't get to her pack in time."

A loud cry burst through Cindy's lips as she buried her head deeper into my shoulder. I noticed Kate was biting her lip, her eyes gleaming more so than normal. My throat tightened, but tears did not prick at my eyes.

Maybe I'd become immune to crying.

Or maybe I'd run out of tears.

Austin mistook my distress, and wrapped his large muscled arm around my shoulders comfortingly. I leaned towards him, grateful for his warmth; my body was still so cold. Nothing else was said; there was nothing we could say. There weren't any words that would bring comfort to her now.

No words would bring back her sister.

CHAPTER SEVENTEEN

"A Native American grandfather talking to his young grandson tells the boy he has two wolves inside of him struggling with each other. The first is the wolf of peace, love and kindness. The other wolf is fear, greed and hatred. 'Which wolf will win, grandfather?' asks the young boy. 'Whichever one I feed,' is the reply. "

-Native American Proverb

It would take time for Cindy to heal. The loss she had just experienced was one that she would never forget, and, though I couldn't fully understand it, I would be there to offer all the support I could to her.

The immediate days following our return, she clung to me like a lifeline, never letting me out of her sight.

She confided in me that she had told her sister of the promise she made me, and her sister had been so unbelievably proud of her for going to such lengths for a friend.

"I told her all about you," she confessed weakly. "She liked you already. She wanted to help me find your brother again and meet you herself." Biting her lower lip, she steeled herself against another onslaught of tears. I held her hand tightly, offering silent support. "I will see my promise through, and then I know she'll be proud of me."

Our little group of misfits did everything they could to support Cindy and bring back a sense of normalcy in her life. I knew that she would always carry that pain in her heart from her sister's death, but, in time, that pain would lessen and she could live normally again.

A few changes were put into motion when we got back, making that harder than it needed to be, though. For one, security was heightened around the grounds. A few packs were stationed on campus to protect the trainees.

Unfortunately, one of those packs contained Rowan, who was a frequent sight to us nowadays. I would catch glimpses of him out of the corner of my eye, or see him watching me as I walked between classes.

He was making a statement, one I did not appreciate.

Another change was the newly-integrated classes. The fight and physical training classes that had been separated based off of gender were now combined into a single class (which was hilarious, actually. The boys were stupid enough to assume that they had to go easy on us. I bet I don't need to tell you how that ended). Not only were the lessons combined, though, they were suddenly intensified. Fights were drawn out past first blood, and injuries were much more substantial.

It was hard for me, fighting class. I didn't like spending an entire period wailing on the people around me. I had lived and learned and spent time with these people for a year now. So, as I wheeled around to grab the arm that was bringing a fist dangerously close to my face, I broke the bone and threw the person to the ground, and suddenly found myself growing increasingly sick.

So, that's how I found myself leaving class early to go retch outside behind the building where no one could find me. Hopefully. Not so much.

Between bouts of nastiness, I vaguely registered a soothing warmth between my shoulder blades. Something soft (a towel?) lightly touched my temple, wiping away the sweat that was there. The warmth moved from my back until it was a solid weight on my shoulder.

Now, at this point, I was emotionally drained and downright embarrassed. A wolf shouldn't be weak and get sick every time they hurt someone. They should be strong and keep their ass in the fight until everyone is taken down.

So, I really didn't want to have to look up into the mocking face of someone who was probably going to berate me or laugh in my face for my moment of weakness.

Nonetheless, I *forced* myself to see who was next to me. A sigh of relief left my lips when I realized it was Austin staring down at me, not with contempt, but rather open kindness.

"Are you all right," he asked softly only showing a hint of concern. It was werewolf etiquette; he didn't want to imply that I was weak.

"Yeah, fine." I wiped my mouth on my shirt and moved to stand up, but I did it too quickly and nearly fell over again. Austin caught me easily.

"Whoa, take it easy. This is normal," he said lightly, guiding me to sit on the grass against the wall of the building.

Shame boiled in my chest. "Sorry," I whispered.

"Ria, it's okay, really." I saw his small smile of understanding. "I remember my first time, too."

That got my attention quickly. Snapping my head up to face him completely, I asked breathlessly, "Really?"

He nodded, and moved to sit next to me against the wall. He looked up into the sky and watched the clouds with a faraway look in his gaze.

Austin always looked so at peace, though, never ruffled, which was something really rare around here.

"My clan is known for its strength. So, as you can probably imagine, I've been fighting for a long time; for so long now that it seems second nature to me." Shifting his gaze downward, Austin lifted his hand and looked at it carefully. "Every second of every day, though, I have to remind myself to watch my strength. I almost killed Vincent sparring once. I punched him and his skull cracked in three different places. If he wasn't such a good healer…" It was as if he couldn't bring himself to finish the thought. "I didn't come out of my room for days I was so wracked with guilt. Vincent made it in through the window eventually, though. He knocked some sense into me."

That must be why he's just so naturally gentle. Being so careful everyday has to have an effect on a person's personality, especially with something as dangerous as super strength.

Turning slightly, he held up his hand in front of him. Hesitantly, I lifted mine and lightly placed it over his. His expression was so much more open than anyone else's around here. Austin wasn't afraid to share his emotions with the world. He smiled brightly, showing off a flash of white teeth as he intertwined our fingers and held my hand reassuringly. "I know this is hard, fighting your friends, but I promise it'll be easier out there, in the real world. If you can make it through this, you can fight anyone, anywhere."

I thought about that for a moment, trying to imagine what it would be like, but found that I couldn't.

"I don't think it will for me," I whispered pulling my knees towards my chest as tightly as I could, a protection.

I could feel his eyes on the side of my face, analyzing. "Then…then maybe that's a good thing. It should be this way, actually."

"What on earth do you mean? It's not a good thing if I can't pass Fighting 101."

Austin was thinking hard about something, I could tell by the way his grip slackened slightly. "People should be less willing to resort to violence. They should be more like you, sick at the thought of bringing harm to another person. I'm not saying everyone should be a pacifist, but there are plenty of people around here who assume the best way to get something done is through force and fighting. So stay just the way you are, Ria, and don't ever be ashamed of it."

Nodding, I could feel a smile pulling at the edges of my lips as I reached over to give him a one-armed hug. "Thanks, man. Let's get back to class."

He squeezed me back lightly. I wasn't worried for a second he would hurt me with his Hulk-like muscles. "Don't worry about it. Mom understands what you're going through."

I stiffened and pulled away to look him in the eye. "Wait a minute. Mrs. Johnson, tough as nails and deadly Mrs. Johnson, gave *birth* to you? You came from that woman's womb?"

"I thought you knew that," he confirmed, surprised by my lack of knowledge.

My eyes narrowed jokingly. "You people always assume that I came programmed with everything I'd need to know. I'm not the psychic in the group, remember?"

He laughed and helped me to stand with him. "Sorry, it's just…you're so good at this already. We forget that you haven't always been this way."

"Maybe that's a good thing, too."

Seeing him smile, I turned to walk back into the gym, expecting him to be hot on my heels. Suddenly, though, I met resistance in the form of his hand grasping my wrist.

"Ria?"

When I looked at him, he had that thinking face on again. "Yeah, Austin?"

"I…I don't like it either. Fighting."

It may not have seemed like it, but this was a huge admission for someone who came out of a family like Austin's. This was like a kid from a devout Catholic family coming home and proclaiming he was an atheist. Sure, the same could be said for pretty much every wolf, but it was worse for Austin who was faced with the pressure to become a perfect fighter.

I'm sensing a trend here with these kids.

I shifted his grip on my wrist so I held his hand again, "I know. It's okay that you don't."

His shy, hesitant smile told me I had said the right thing. Standing next to me, he draped a heavy arm over my shoulder and together we walked back inside just as class was ending. I didn't miss Austin's casual thumbs up to Mrs. (Mama) Johnson, but I was surprised to see her return it with a wink.

Miracles never cease.

Days flew by without any notice. They became weeks and months of complete and utter devotion to training, to achieving my full potential and strength. Winter and Spring came and went, and before I knew it, it was summer, which could only mean one thing.

That training was almost over.

By summer's end, the final tests would start, the packs would be made, and we would "graduate" and be sent out into the world as werewolves serving the Council.

As much as the thought of that gave me grey hair, I couldn't help but be filled with a sort of wild enthusiasm to just get out there and live the life I had spent nearly two years preparing for. It's enough to make any girl a little impatient. I mean, come on, if I was still human I would be in college already.

However, if I really wanted that freedom, I would have to live through the tests to make it there first.

I wish I was exaggerating.

The Trials, as the final exams are formally called (first of all, *really*? Were they trying to make it as ominous as possible?), are made up of three parts, and a trainee must pass each part before proceeding on.

The first of which is a test (like an actual exam); the written portion is a combination of everything we've learned in our classes and the speaking portion is given in front of a tribunal of all of our teachers. They give a real-life situation (be it a surprise attack, battle strategy, reconnaissance, etc. etc.), and the trainee is expected to explain the best way to handle it.

So far, everyone had passed the first part. Hooray. Hurrah.

Now it was time for the fighting to begin.

Trial two is a fight against another wolf, one that has already graduated from training. The idea behind this is that a trainee should be able to display his or her strength to be equal to that of another wolf. The trainee has to come out either the winner or the fight can end in a draw. Either way is safe.

However, the fight in Trial three is a fight for your life.

No, like literally.

In the third Trial, the Council releases a prisoner from the prison (jokingly called the Kennel), and offers them a change to relieve some pent up frustration. Needless to say, these guys have a lot to let loose, and have no qualms over slimming down the ranks early. This is the portion of the Trials in which trainees have been known to die before they can graduate; this is the portion that will make or break a werewolf.

And this is the portion that I find the most disgusting and barbaric. When Grandmother first explained it to me, I attacked the nearby terrain with all the wrath of a woman scorned. I then had to sit and listen while she talked about anger management counseling while she wove a healing spell over my broken hand.

All of these things I already knew about the test. So, standing here in with all of my classmates as a proctor bellowed out all of the finer details was, in essence, killing me. I knew I was ready to face this, whatever came my way, but to just sit here and *wait* was nearly unbearable. My fingers had just begun to play with the hem of my shirt, a nervous habit of mine, when a large hand closed over one of mine, stilling it. Being careful not to turn my head at all, I shifted my eyes up and to the right to send a grateful look to the tall figure standing next to me.

Carter gave no indication on his face that he had seen my look, but his hand squeezed again. I let it fall away from my shirt, and was positive he would let go (Carter wasn't exactly the *touchy-feely* kind of guy), but to my surprise he intertwined our fingers and held fast.

Maybe he needed the support as much as I did.

On my left, I noticed that Austin's tall form was growing tenser by the minute. I was surprised to find that I was deeply bothered by it. The Austin I knew shouldn't be worried over anything. He was calm, he was kind, and he was brave.

Following the status quo, I, too, reached my hand over to hold on to his, giving it a light squeeze before returning my full attention to the proctor.

Maybe listening to the instructions would be good before starting this Trial.

Unfortunately, after the excruciating wait for all of the directions to be finished (with nothing new for Ria to learn), there was another long wait while the proctors prepared the list of matches and waited for the arena to fill.

Oh, wait, I didn't mention that this is what the arena was used for? My bad. Yeah, there are hundreds of people watching these parts of the Trials like some twisted kind of football game.

Knowing that pacing was just going to make me lose my mojo, I sat my ass down and did some *serious* deep breathing exercises. A few people actually followed my lead. I could feel their footsteps come close, stop, and then hear them lower themselves to a seated position beside me. Some were twitchy and left after only a few minutes, but others stayed just as still and tranquil as I did.

Vincent's call nearly made me jump. "People, where do you think we are some kind of temple? *Look alive.* They're about to announce the first match."

His words had the same effect as lighting a fire under everyone's ass. Forgetting the efforts spent calming themselves, they scrambled up to the edge of the balcony where the trainees waited and watched. I opened my eyes, slowly blinking them to adjust to the light and stayed sitting where I was. A cursory look around me showed that Austin was at my immediate right, eyes still closed.

The crackle of a loudspeaker brought my attention back to the announcer. He began with the required rote. "As it has been for hundreds of years before us, we again come together to witness the results of the training of those who wish to serve. Trainees?"

"We are ready." Our monotone answer was lilted with fierce determination.

"Trial two begins. The lists of matches are being posted. Match one begins in ten minutes. Best of luck."

A few teachers came in and posted the lists across the room, whispering similar sentiments and giving last minute bits of advice before leaving quickly again. Students rushed with all the force of a mob to get to the list first. I sat and waited.

That is, until I could hear my name being spoken around the group.

Vincent was the first to look at me, his face ashen and his eyes wide. "Ria..."

"Who is it, Vince?" I didn't let my fear creep into my voice; wouldn't let it. "Who is it I'm up against?"

Everyone turned to look between Vince and I with an anticipation that made my hackles rise.

"Desiree," he whispered obediently, no traces of his usual sarcasm evident.

I closed my eyes and sucked in a deep breath. "Anyone tries to tell me that these matches are random and I'm calling them out." My chin fell to rest on my chest and a deep sigh escaped me. "Hell, if that bitch kills me before Trial three I'm going to haunt her ass for the rest of forever."

My attempt at humor fell horribly flat, even for me. I tried to laugh, but a hysterical breathy giggle came out instead. Maybe I wasn't as ready for this as I thought I would be...

But before any similar thought processes could be carried out, two warm hands on either side of my face lifted my head up from my fear and brought my gaze to meet blue-green eyes. Austin examined me, not at all fooled by my brave face, thinking of something to say. I could almost see his tumultuous thoughts in his eyes.

Taking a deep breath, he breathed the words so quietly that I, close as I was, had to strain to hear them.

"This match isn't a coincidence; it's fate. You will win, and then even Desiree will see how far the human has come." Carefully, he leaned forward ever more until his forehead rested against my own. "Today is not your day to die."

I wished I could have been half as sure as him.

I reached my hand up to hold one of his wrists; we stayed like that for what seemed like a lifetime, but it was over too soon. Austin pulled his head away as the others came forward and sat around me. There was a hand on my shoulder, a chin on my head, a head in my lap, a hand in mine, and an arm around my waist.

Whatever happened to me in this match, I knew that my friends would be with me. They would always have my back, and they would always believe in me.

A proctor came into the room and called me to follow him. Disentangling myself from various body parts of various people, I stood and followed him, not looking back over my shoulder once. I didn't want to see everyone's faces, or see what they were saying.

My steps were confident, my chin was raised, and my breathing even as I followed closely behind the proctor. I wasn't afraid anymore; I was ready. There would be no more waiting, and there was no reason to be anxious. I would win or I would lose, it was that simple,

But I was going to try my damndest to come out the winner.

He led me to the trainee's entrance to the arena, seven concrete steps leading up to a doorway.

"Whenever you are ready, trainee," he told me calmly.

Bolstering my courage, I took one more deep breath and climbed the steps that would lead me into the arena.

I had already entered the space once today when the directions were being read off. The long, rectangular room that reminded me of the stadium I had seen my only football game in, but, instead of cool grass, hard rock made up the floor, and, instead of stadium benches, spectators stood, except for the Council who sat at one end of the arena in tall chairs in their places of honor. I immediately caught sight of Rose and the rest of Kate's family. Her mother was holding tightly to Rose as her father had a gentle hand on his mate's back. He nodded at me silently, offering his encouragement as she blew me a kiss. I smiled up at them as my opponent walked into the arena to face me.

Her posture was absolutely exuding confidence and malicious intent, already being a bitch before the fight even started. The look on her face told me she wasn't even thinking of going easy, but I wouldn't let her get to me. I wasn't the shy, little girl she had met my first day here. I wasn't the same girl whom she had beaten black and blue while her minions held me down.

No. I had changed, and I was going to show her that. I was going to show her mistake when it came to messing with me, and I was sure she was going to regret it by the end of this fight.

This bitch was goin' *all the way* downtown.

As was customary, we both walked to the center of the space and turned to pay our respects to the Council by bowing deeply. Then, our monitor came out and ordered us to shake arms. Unsurprisingly, it turned into "let's see who breaks the other person's forearm first."

The monitor then sent us to opposite sides of the arena. When I reached my side, I fell into a standard crouch, as was expected. In that matter of heartbeats before the match began, I brushed the locket with lingering fingers and prayed for the strength to come out of this alive.

And then it began.

She gave me no time to think. With all the fury of hell at her back, she came at me. She punched and kicked, and I blocked her each time, staying on the defensive, but not giving her an inch. She took it the wrong way and used the chance to mock me. "What's wrong, little human? Can't fight back?"

Well, actions speak louder than words.

I narrowed my eyes and grabbed her wrist on her next punch rather than just blocking it. Harnessing the momentum she had used, I set my feet apart and threw her over my hip behind me.

A chorus of cheers erupted from the section I knew my friends were watching from, and pride filled me for a moment before I clamped down on my emotions and forced myself to focus once more.

Apparently, Desiree didn't like my last move much. She looked up at me from her spot on the ground with hate *burning* in her silver eyes. She lunged at me with surprising speed, acting more on instinct rather than smarts, and I simply fell back with her, kicking my feet into her stomach and sending her away once more. This time, however, she landed on her feet and didn't pause for a second. Instead, she Transformed into a wolf and leapt for me before I had a chance to Transform too.

The force from her hit threw me farther than I had managed to throw her, and I most certainly *did not* land on my feet. I'd only managed to twist enough to avoid her teeth and claws. My head hit the floor with a force that made the room spin, but I couldn't give up this opportunity she had thrown at (or rather with) me. I Transformed too, and then the fight began in earnest.

This was a fight of the most animalistic nature, with neither of us holding back, and with her not at all averse to using cheap shots. Her last hit managed to throw me against one of the stone walls hard enough for a hairline crack to appear in it, and for me to change back into human form as all of us did when we had sustained extensive injuries.

This is so not looking so good, I ignored the thought. I wasn't giving up now. I *couldn't*!

But there was no time to think in a fight like this. A human-shaped Desiree appeared right next to me and fisted her hand in my hair in order to throw me again. I hit the stone floor ungracefully and fought to get to my hands and knees.

But it wasn't fast enough. She was already there, kicking my stomach and pushing me to my back once more with all the wind knocked out of me. I managed to look at her standing at my feet, blinking past the sweat dripping into my eyes. Her expression was cold, yet still displaying signs of her pleasure.

Sadistic little freak.

"You see where you belong now, little human? Do you see how truly weak you are now," she mocked. "Stay down on the ground, where you belong. This world holds no place for you."

Grinding my teeth together, I just barely managed to contain my fury from exploding. While traces of an angry red invaded my vision, I glared up at her with more hate than I had felt for anyone before in my life. The surprise on her face was just short of hilarious.

"I am only going to tell you this once, you *ignorant little bitch.*" Her eyes narrowed dangerously, but I continued on, "I am not a human anymore. So, just shut up and get out of my way!"

With that I lunged at her, calling on my inner magic to return her favor with interest, throw her against a wall, and use the speed to immediately follow up the hit with an uppercut punch that sent her into the air. My final kick carried more force than a hurricane as my foot made contact with her sternum and forced her through the air until she hit a nearby wall. The crack she made was nowhere near hairline. After a second of weightlessness, she dropped to the ground like a dead bug.

She didn't get up.

My anger and strength fell away from me immediately, and I nearly fell to my knees, but I reminded myself that I had just won my first match and that would look really anticlimactic. The monitor walked away from Desiree as people carried her off the field and came to me, holding my arm in the air and proclaiming me the winner of the match.

Thunderous applause rose from the entire stadium and my heart swelled with pride. It was enough to bring a weary smile to my face. Kate's mother was wiping tears away from her eyes, and I saw, for the first time, a full-blown smile on her father's face as Aunt Rose paraded around him attempting to get people to do the wave in their section.

But it was my friends who made me happiest. Kate was standing precariously on the rail, fist pumping enthusiastically with Carter spotting behind her, a look of happy exasperation on his face. Vince was hooting and hollering at the top of his lungs various yells of pride intermingled with profanities. Finally, Cindy was seated atop Austin's shoulders, applauding happily with a smile so wide I could see it from here, and Austin?

While holding Cindy's legs in place, he sent me a happy wink that proved he was related to his mother.

His was, by far, the most heartwarming gesture.

CHAPTER EIGHTEEN

*"Strength is itself victory. In weakness and cowardice there is no
happiness. When you wage a struggle, you might win or you might lose.
But regardless of the short-term outcome, the very fact of your continuing
to struggle is proof of your victory as a human being."*

-Daisaku Ikeda

We were allowed a day between the two Trials to rest up and heal whatever injuries we had managed to get. It was a day of respite, relaxation, and preparation for the next task we had to face. How did I spend my day of freedom?

In the hospital.

No, don't get all worried about me; I wasn't hurt any more than a minor concussion and major, super, heavy bruising. It was Kate. She was the only one in our circle of friends who didn't pass her second Trial. Surprised? Yeah, we were too.

Then again, when your brother is a total asshole prodigy, you would sustain a few hefty injuries too. It didn't help that she didn't fight to her full strength. I mean, come on, could she really be expected to when facing off against her own flesh and blood? That would be cruel.

Oh, except Rowan seemed to have no problems with it. If I wasn't so freaking scared of that kid, I would have punched him in the face by now. Multiple times.

But that was all beside the point. I had been sitting in the uncomfortable chair by Kate's bedside for hours, holding her hand and waiting for her to wake up, but I wouldn't be able to wait much longer. They were beginning the first call for trainees, and I would be expected to leave soon to make it to Trial three.

"Get better soon," I whispered to her. "Or I'm going to kick your ass."

When I moved to stand up, I could hear my joints popping and creaking. How long had I been sitting here? Probably wasn't the best idea in hindsight, but I really couldn't be expected to be anywhere else. Brushing the hair out of Kate's eyes, I sighed and walked out of the infirmary, following the crowds to the arena again to meet and greet Death for the second time this week.

The arena was already filled to capacity when I arrived. People crowded around the rail, hoping to get a good spot for the main event (still barbaric in my mind). The faces of my peers were already ashen and frightened under their stoic masks. Even my friends were quieter than usual. Kate's loss and hospital stay was already weighing heavily on our minds. Having this on our plates too couldn't be good for our sanity level.

The wait was worse this time around, too. Instead of posting a roster of names and matches, we had to sit and wait until our names were called. We had no previous knowledge of our opponents and would only know what we were up against when we clashed in the arena.

Luckily, I wasn't first around this time, and had the opportunity to watch the first match. However, fifteen minutes in, I found myself regrettomg it.

The first trainee was dead.

The vampire she had faced stood over her body with a small smile on his face. With a deep chuckle of amusement, he slanted his gaze up to the trainee balcony, where we all stood paralyzed with shock. "She is only the first, puppies." His smiled widened at the edges, tinged with something feral before he turned around and let himself be led out of the arena.

I couldn't bear to watch anymore after that.

Vince went first of our group, but (thank God) he didn't face off against that awful vampire. He wrangled himself a particularly nasty golem that was dumb as dirt (ha ha get it? Dirt? Golem? No? Okay.), but packed a mean right hook.

It was another seven matches before my name was finally called.

This time, I gave each of my friends a tight hug with the full knowledge that it could be the last time I did so.

I felt like I was walking in a dream from the balcony to the arena; everything seemed so surreal, but I had to focus now. At the entrance of the arena, my feet stopped moving, and I had to take a deep breath and force them to walk confidently into the space.

The tension in the room was outstanding, and hushed anticipation could be felt like a physical force gathered around everyone.

It felt as if every single bystander was leaning over the rails of the stands waiting to see the outcome of this would be.

I couldn't blame them.

I was the second human to make it this far in the training and the first human in almost a decade to even enter this space.

With a nod of acknowledgment towards Kate's family again, I moved to the center of the arena and waited some more.

The instant another presence joined me in the arena, I could feel the temperature drop by more than just a few degrees. A piece of my bangs that had slipped free of my tight braid brushed against my face lightly, seemingly of its own accord.

A breeze? In a space like this?

Lifting my chin slightly, I took a delicate whiff of the air with a wolf-enhanced nose. I recoiled almost immediately. The room smelled like death, a scent I would have written off on the trainees who didn't pass, but, unlike normal death, there was no accompanying scent of decay that was *supposed* to be there.

My body registered the threat before I did.

Without another word, I *moved*, drawing on every ounce of speed I could muster to get away from the spot I had been.

It wasn't a second too soon either.

Where I had stood not moments ago, a fist met the ground and caused spider-web cracks to appear on the stone surface.

I went down into a crouch and pivoted to face my attacker, a tall, slim boy who appeared just a few scant years older than me. He was fair-skinned, with long, light blonde hair that curled around his ears and brushed against his neck. His eyes were dark and piercing. To my shock, he was smiling with mirth, and amusement shone clearly in his eyes as he shook out his fist.

"Very good, pup," he praised lightly as if I were his young student rather than his opponent. "You managed to miss the first hit. I am impressed."

Fantastic, of course I would get stuck with a nutcase.

Not only that, but now I recognized him. This was the vampire that had killed that first girl, and issued the threat to the other trainees.

Son of a *bitch*.

My face became a stone mask as I refused to let any emotion whatsoever show on it. My heartbeat and breathing calmed immediately, slowing until they were a smooth and steady rhythm; cold, precise calculation took over my normal thinking process so emotions wouldn't get in the way.

Ladies and gentlemen, it's now time to get down to business.

Seeing his words had not affected me, his lips turned into a small moue of distaste to the point I would say he was actually pouting.

What the- ?

"So serious, for someone as young as you," he admonished teasingly, his smile suddenly returning to his face and somehow becoming sharp, warning me immediately. I didn't have any time to react, though, because out of nowhere he was *there*.

Move, Ria! Get moving!

I called forth my magic as if it were the most natural thing to do in the world, moving with a speed that could by no means rival his, but was fast enough to get away.

His teasing voice followed me, warning me he was right on my tail. "You can't run away every time."

So I didn't. Without warning I stopped in my tracks, turned sharply in time to see his surprised face and kicked with all the force I could manage. It worked. He had not stopped in time, and the momentum had knocked him clear across to the other side of the arena.

This was the time I expected his to lose his cool like Desiree had when she discovered I was holding my own, but he didn't.

His loud, boisterous laugh echoed around the arena, making my hair stand on end.

Making sure my expression was still composed and collected, I stared him down as he slowly stood up, wiping the corner of his grinning mouth, and gazed back at me with warm delight. His voice reflected his expression perfectly and there were no signs of him being angry or indolent in any way. He was calm, loose, and relaxed.

"You keep surprising me, little one." Once more he cocked his head. "How amusing. I haven't had this much fun in *ages*."

And with that he lunged, leaving me completely unaware. I was hit in my stomach, and he appeared behind me again while I was still mid-flight, knocking my back, and throwing me to the ground. I didn't stay down long though. I rolled, scrambled to my feet and turned to face him, focusing with every part of my mind as he flickered through the space between us and searching for the moment to strike.

I stood there waiting patiently for him, he made his mistake in thinking I would fall for the same thing twice. At just the right moment, when he had almost reached me, I ducked down, and then pushed forward with my legs, pivoting to the side to catch his neck with my elbow in a painful blow.

It didn't last long, though. Going on as if the strike had done nothing to him, he gripped my neck and hauled me up until my feet were no longer touching the floor. I fought desperately against his hand, scratching with my nails, but he would not give an inch. I lifted my legs to kick him, but his grip tightened in warning.

And that's when I heard the distinct sound of metal breaking around my neck.

Eyes wide, I watched in slow motion as the silver chain slid gently off my neck, carrying my locket with it, and landed into the open and waiting palm of Lunatic numero uno.

Everything else ceased to exist for a moment except for the fact that he had the only piece of Daimon I had left in the world, and I was helpless to get it back. I watched as he examined it curiously, genuinely puzzled by what was so important about the little locket that I had almost completely lost my composure and started behaving like a caged animal. He continued to hold me easily with one hand as the other turned over the charm every which way.

I noticed distantly that his eyes narrowed and his expression turned serious and contemplative as he found he couldn't open it. Instead, he bent his head down to its level and smelled it.

I wasn't prepared for his reaction.

Immediately, he reeled back with wide, wild eyes, shock and surprise clearly evident on his face. Fisting my locket in his hand tightly, he turned a curious eye back to me, and, with careful slowness, he leaned forward to sniff slowly and deeply at my neck, filling his lungs completely with my scent. I was so close to him, I could *feel* the approving hum that rumbled in his chest. A flinch of surprise nearly escaped me as he once more had a bout of lively, happy laughter that was even louder than before.

"Finally," he practically purred. He stared straight into my eyes and I felt distinctly like a fly that had been trapped in a spider's web. "You are the human."

I stiffened as this and his smile broadened to stretch across his sickly handsome features enough to reveal one of his gleaming, sharp fangs. "I've heard so much about you already, my dear. It's a pleasure to meet you."

He released me, and I fell to the ground heavily, taking deep, gasping breaths and massaging my newly-bruised neck while still trying to keep an eye on him. He opened his hand again and took another whiff of the locket. I didn't bother hiding my confusion. This match was turning out to be much weirder than I had thought, or wanted, it to be.

179

"I'd say the pleasure's all mine, but my mother told me to never lie," I snapped.

"Ah! So you can talk," he crowed happily. Bending down to get in my face, he asked perhaps the most bizarre thing I had heard that day. "Tell me, little one. Are you the one that poor Daimon is searching so desperately for?"

After a few moments of blurred motion, I was reaching down to the body of my opponent (who had somehow ended up on the ground) in order to grip the front of his shirt. It was my turn to get into his face. Every inch of his mocking expression set me on edge, except for the split lip he now boasted, which made me disturbingly pleased.

"What about Daimon?" I bit out.

His smug look warned me he was about to be an ass. "How am I to know? I haven't seen him in weeks. I've been in my cell awaiting the chance to fight with you, love."

I bared my fangs (Oh hey, when did those puppies sneak out?) and snarled at him, slamming his head against the hard stone floor once before bringing him back up. I forced myself to see past the red haze invading my line of sight and think around the blood-chilling, violent voice howling for blood in my head. I needed to think clearly; Daimon could be in danger.

My voice sounded so murderous that the small part of me that was still human cringed in fear and surprise. "I can keep this up until your head cracks like an Easter egg, you murdering, raving lunatic. It would be in your best interest to tell me sooner rather than later. My patience is kinda thin today."

He stared at me for a moment, then opened his idiotic, troublesome mouth and said, "I'm getting chills, I really am. You're really very good at this for being human."

All right buddy, you want to play this game? I enjoyed the feel of the sharp, deadly smirk that pulled at my lips, and the way his eyes instantly became wary when I did so. I mocked his expression by cocking my head like he had done.

I'll play.

And with that I threw that self-absorbed, sadistic jerk at the wall with enough force to crack it.

Which, by the way, felt *really* good.

I ran over to him, and used the grip I had now established on his neck to hold him up against the cracked surface of the wall. I took pride in the fact that his face had been wiped clean of amusement, but when I saw the feral, hungry look in his eyes I nearly regretted it. It suddenly made me very aware of the slow trickling of blood I could feel running down my neck. Must have gotten those when he dropped me.

Mrs. Johnson's rough, barking voice echoed through my head like some kind of twisted Jiminy Cricket.

Girls! There are three things you need to keep in mind when you're fighting a vampire! Listen closely, this could save you one day! Don't let them see blood, don't let them get to your neck, and don't let them get in your head.

Huh, I somehow managed to forget all three of those things within the span of a single fight. Damn.

His dark eyes were practically smoldering as his intense gaze zeroed in at my neck. His voice was husky and rough, making goosebumps prickle at my skin. "It's no wonder he was searching so desperately for you." I watched carefully, tensing as he lifted one of his hands to his face. At the edges of his fingers I saw unmistakable red stains. "You smell so sweet as a wolf; I can't even begin to imagine how you were when you were still all human."

My stomach turned in revulsion and fear as his tongue darted out to catch a falling drop of blood that had almost escaped his fingertips.

That is so freaking disgusting. I could tell he had seen the unmasked abhorrence on my face; he leered amusedly looking down at me with dancing eyes. "You know what this means don't you? According to the laws of my kind?"

I could only assume he meant the fact that he had had a drop of my blood, and I knew perfectly well what he thought it meant. "Can't be your property if you're dead, now can I?"

He smiled maddeningly, eyes gleaming too brightly as his fangs extended to curl wickedly over his bottom lip. "We'll see about that, little one."

And then, so fast I could have thought he whipped it out of thin air, he pulled out a silver dagger from the waistband of his tattered jeans and brought it down to cut my arm.

A cry of alarm and pain broke free of my lips at the searing pain. He fell free of my grasp as I stumbled back, trying to focus past the pain that was so intense it made the whole world blurry. Liquid fire ran through me and white-hot searing agony set every nerve ablaze.

I fell to the ground writhing and twisting, holding back screams that longed to burst free. I vaguely heard people screaming objections, he shouldn't have had a weapon with him, but I knew nothing could be done. No one was to enter the arena once we had begun our match.

They couldn't do anything but watch.

His steps were even and measured as he approached. He paused just by my side before kneeling ever-so-slowly next to me.
I hadn't realized I'd closed my eyes until I fought to see what he was doing. I struggled to open my heavy eyelids, and, when I did, I saw his face closer to mine than I had expected, the knife twirling in his hands absently.

"What will you do now," he mused dispassionately. "You have no weapons, you can barely stand, and you now cannot Transform into your other form for strength. What is left to be done?"

So glad you seem to have the utmost faith in my abilities, just like everyone else around here.

He seemed to think this was over, that I was finished, but I wasn't anywhere near done yet, not even close. People really needed to learn that I'm would not give up until he was done or I was dead.

The entire span of my vision was enveloped in a shadow similar to that of Transforming as I drew strength from my magic and let it out for me to use, for me to finish this.

I felt my fangs lengthen until they were as long as his, my claws followed their lead, and the pain was pushed aside for the sole purpose of taking his ass *down*.

He seemed to be frozen as he watched this transformation from his ensured victory to a change in the play.

Rocking my body swiftly back, I tucked my knees to my chest and *kicked* with all the force of an angry horse.

He went flying through the air, but (in an easy manner that made me so. Damn. Frustrated.) he landed on his feet like a cat.

"That's more like it," he bellowed happily. "Let's see just how good of a wolf a human can be!"

We flickered so fast that human eyes wouldn't have been able to keep up with us. I fought in a way that was governed more by instinct than conscious thought, and it seemed to be working.

I was actually holding my own, but, even as I struck, scratched, and hit him, that infuriating smile was still plain on his features.

"You, my dear, are far too much fun to kill," he announced after a particularly spectacular hit to his jaw. With a pointed look towards the Council, he continued, "Maybe if I'm a good boy, the Council will let me keep you, after I kill more of your classmates, of course."

That. Is. Enough.

Moving so quickly even he widened his eyes, I was suddenly in front of him, taking the knife that had stopped twisting between his fingers and to plunge it hilt-deep into his chest.

Fun fact: silver may be deadly to a werewolf, but, in the heart of a vampire, it's enough to paralyze them, sometimes even permanently.

The world froze on its axis again as he stared disbelievingly first at his chest, and then at me.

There was a fleeting touch at my cheek, cold like ice; I didn't bother flinching away from it. He tensed suddenly as his eyes narrowed. "This is nowhere near over yet."

"It is for now," I returned, throwing him away from me.

He rolled flat on his back on the ground, coughing heavily and reaching for the knife. His hands were shaking so heavily it was a miracle he managed to get a good enough grip of it to pull it out, but he did. He looked at me straight in the eye, mouthed something silently, and then fell all at once, completely paralyzed and no longer my problem.

Completely assured that he was done, I fell to my knees, and picked up the knife gently in my fingertips, faintly surprised when I brushed the silver and it did not burn me. My arm was still burning steadily, a pain that was beginning to grow fuzzier (or was it just me?).

When I held the knife firmly in my hands, I fell to the ground just as he did, my stamina on empty. My whole body ached in a way that wasn't normal and the life seemed to be falling out from me. I didn't know what was happening, but I couldn't find the will to care. Was this what dying felt like?

I hoped not, I still had too much to do before I died. There were people here that I loved and wanted to be with still. That would suck to have just passed the test, and *then* die. I could have at least gone out dramatically when he stabbed me.

As I closed my eyes, and people surrounded me all shouting different things, my mind, without any prompting, put a voice to my nameless opponent's final, soundless words. Those words echoed through my head as the world fell away from me.

We've only just begun, my dear…

I opened my eyes and blinked past the sunlight trying its hardest to blind me. As my vision cleared, I found myself lying in a bed in a familiar room.

One that I had just spent the entire day in.

Sighing at finding myself caught in this situation, I struggled to push myself up to a sitting position, wincing when I put too much weight on my wounded arm. My eyes scanned the room only to see that everyone else was still sleeping in their beds, and there were no nurses in sight.

It must still be early morning.

I looked at my bedside and smiled as I saw Kate, still dressed in her hospital gown, curled into a chair sideways, sleeping contentedly. I didn't trust my legs at the moment. So, I pulled a pen from my bedside table, examined it for a moment, and then threw it lightly at her.

She startled awake, almost throwing herself out of her chair, to my great amusement. There was a scowl on her face as she righted herself, but her expression fell when she heard my rough laugh.

She was out of the chair and sitting on my bed in an instant, taking hold of one of my hands and looking my face over to discern if I was in any pain.

"You know you could just ask if I feel all right," I informed her sardonically.

She didn't seem to hear me, her eyes continued to look me over and over again. I poked her on her forehead and she drew her attention to my face once more. "You're all right." She confirmed shakily.

I shrugged, regretted it when pain sparked in my shoulders and back. "A few bumps and bruises here and there, but I'm fine."

She shook her head distantly, biting her trembling lip hard. "You almost died," she whispered painfully.

I closed my eyes, taking a deep breath and tried to push away the sound of his laughter still ringing clearly in my head. "I know," I stated flatly.

"You idiot!" My eyes flew open in shock hearing her so angry. Her face was twisted with emotion. Tears poured down her cheeks as she yelled as quietly as she could at me through clenched teeth. "You were almost killed!"

My mouth hung open at her outburst. It was strange to see someone normally so composed and calm having an emotional breakdown.

Noting my lack of speech, Kate turned to pull something else off of my bedside table. Light glinted off the metallic surface of the newly-cleaned knife, the same one I had used to finish off my last match. She held it up between our faces.

"Do you have any idea what this is?" Without letting me answer, she continued on fiercely. "It's a weapon made by vampires and human hunters for killing werewolves. It's made to bring the most amount of pain possible in order to render the wolf helpless." She looked down at my arm. "A cut like that would have killed a normal wolf."

I took the knife away from her, setting it back in its place beside me telling her, "Then it really is a good thing I'm not the average wolf, isn't it?"

She only stared flabbergasted at me for a few moments, her mouth working like a fish's, before launching herself at me, pulling me into her arms, and holding on for dear life. I returned the hug, despite how painful it was to move. I heard her muffled voice tell me, "You're supposed to block sharp, pointy things, you dork."

Smiling, I retorted, "I'll try to remember that next time."

"Good, I can't have you dying on me just yet. I've gotten too used to having you around."

I hugged her tighter. "I'm not going anywhere, Kate, not just yet."

"Promise?" she asked me weakly, her voice betraying her fear.

"Together forever, you and me," I promised solemnly.

She laughed at that. "You think? Well, we're too good at this job to die anytime soon. We could so make it to the big leagues."

"We will, Kate. We will."

After a few days of makeup matches and retests, every one of us passed the Trials. A day later we submitted our request to be made into a pack. The request was returned on the same day, approved and ready for our waiting signatures on the contract.

From that day forward, we were no longer just friends. We were a pack, a family closer than any blood relatives.

Our new pack was given a codename just like everyone else's. We were known as the Elite.

A pretty bitchin' name if you ask me.

Within the week, it was time that all trainees took our oaths, one at a time, to the Council; swearing allegiance, and signing away a good portion for a noble cause. It was slightly reminiscent to a graduation day, I observed nostalgically. Parents and siblings were gathered, food and drinks were served, and everyone was laughing and hugging each other while taking pictures and wiping away the occasional tear.

It went without saying, though, that I'd much rather be here then at my high school graduation.

Soon enough, it was my turn to give my oath. I walked into the formal Council room with my head held high and my classmates cheering me on, even the ones that had thought I was the spawn of Satan my first day.

Kate's family was there too, waving enthusiastically and yelling out my name happily (mostly in the case of Aunt Rose, who was not giving up on this whole wave thing).

Then, there were my friends.

My pack, I thought pleasantly. They were acting like their usual crazy selves with Vince whooping loud enough for me to hear him over everyone else and Cindy seated on Austin's broad shoulders once again (how did she keep convincing him to let her up there?), laughing and pumping her arms in the air wildly while Austin held onto her for dear life. Kate was shouting and smiling at me and Carter…

Carter was looking like he was wondering why the hell he was friends with such weirdoes until he turned to me and, as much as his emotionally-constipated self would allow, his expression warmed to one of pride and contentment.

I shook my head disbelievingly at their antics, my smile only growing wider; I was secretly overwhelmed by such a sending-off. I had never imagined in anything beyond my wildest dreams that this was what I was to expect on my graduation day.

With their support bolstering me, I wasn't afraid to stand up in front of the Council anymore, and my oath was perfectly memorized. My voice was strong and sure, resolute in what I was saying and promising.

Giving my word was not something I did very easily, especially in something as important as this, but I felt a weight being lifted off my shoulders as I ended my training and worry with a few measly sentences.

Kate's grandfather shared no emotion on his face as he sat absorbing every word that I spoke. He had heard the same speech countless times already, and would continue to all day. Only when I was done did he stand up and ask, as was customary. "Maria, do you always and forever give you word to follow this oath, and faithfully serve and protect your fellow werewolves?"

Feeling everyone's eyes at my back, I spoke the final, sealing words.

"Until the end of my days, I swear."

PART II:

TO LOVE FOREVER

CHAPTER ONE

"In three words I can sum up everything I've learned about life: it goes on."

-Robert Frost

And that's how our happy little fairy tale began, boys and girls. It seems longer than a year ago, but, then again, so much has happened in the last year.

After the formal ceremony that bound our packs together, we were assigned areas to protect and monitor for the first five years of our service (the duty of every new pack), and then, finally, were sent out into the world.

These first five years were expected to be pretty dull compared to the rest of our careers, but everyone has to start at square one in the beginning of the game; it's only after that we can skip spaces and play the way we want.

Unfortunately for me, square one for the Elite was the region that contained one little town I would have preferred to keep distant from.

Ye olde hometown of Ria: Rochester, New York.

No one else in our little group knew the truth behind the reasons Kate sent others to scout around that area, why I would always be the last to volunteer to take a job there, or avoid any conversation involving it, but I would bet all my beer money that they had guessed. We weren't top in our class for nothing, and I didn't doubt their ability to put two and two together, but they never mentioned it. I was never forced to admit it out loud either, and that made me more than a little grateful towards them.

My brothers and sisters, I thought happily, *my family*. The Elite had proven its name and worth in the single year we were active. There was not a single obstacle the Council sent our way that we had not overcome with only minor property damage.

Together, we were an army of six, and it was proving to be all the army the Council needed, even in a bad area like this.

Who knew my hometown had vampires crawling around every corner? No wonder I was obsessed. I'm surprised the humans can't tell yet.

The thought brought a frown to my face, and made me think of my other family, my first one. A part of me twinged in concern for their safety as it normally did when my thoughts strayed in this particular direction.

I suddenly realized I had been rubbing my bite mark again, the one Kate had so creatively made when she changed me. When the packs had been formed, we were each given a symbol to mark our own identities. That symbol was then tattooed onto us; it was a symbol that packs were forever, even longer than normal families.

For some odd reason, I had chosen to put my tattoo over the harsh scarring of the wound. On a whim, I pulled up the sleeve of my shirt and turned to look at it.

Our symbol was the merged faces of the sun and a moon. The sun took over the left half of the circle, its smiling face surrounded by a myriad of warm colors like yellow, pink and orange. On the right half, the blissful-looking moon returned the sun's attention with a half-lidded gaze. It was a light blue in color with darker blue stars dotting its surface, and green swirls intertwining them.

Overall, in my professional opinion, I'd have to give it an eleven out of ten on the awesomeness scale.

My thoughts were interrupted as I heard someone calling me. "Ria! Get your behind here this instant, or there won't be any dinner left for ya!"

It was one of the great mysteries of the world how someone as small and petite as Cindy could yell all the way from home base so that I could clearly hear her.

Rolling my eyes and laughing, I stood up from my new designated "thinking spot." It was similar to my old one back in training, sharing the same defining feature, a rocky cliff, but, unlike the one grandmother had introduced me to, this one was surrounded by a deep forest. I came here often to meditate and just to ponder the mysteries of life.

Because what kind of adolescent girl doesn't do that?

With one last lingering look at the bright, nearly-full moon behind me, I quickly Transformed and started off through the woods back home.

Every time I did this, it always felt exhilarating, as if I was flying amongst the trees rather than just running. The wind twisted in my hair and burned at my eyes, the ground seemed to disappear under my feet at the speed I was going, and no animal in the forest wanted to get in my way.

All too soon, I was back at our little HQ, a decently-sized house constructed solidly of wood and nestled in the thick of the woods. I Transformed back and ran into the house as fast as I could, making a beeline for the kitchen.

Cindy was waiting at the doorway with a plate, which she discreetly handed to me and advised, "Go ahead and exert your feminine authority, babe."

I saluted her and made a mad dash for the counter where our dinner was always set out like a buffet. The boys were there already, just getting ready to eat. Vincent was first in line practically salivating as he eagerly reached for the closest edible thing within reach.

Oh, snap.

I used my months of excessive stealth and speed training to move just as Vincent picked up the spoon for his mashed potatoes. I smoothly ducked under his raised arm and put my plate over his, making him deposit a healthy-sized amount of potato goodness on my platter rather than his.

His distraught look was the stuff comedy was made of.

I patted his cheek. "Thanks buddy, ladies first! Wouldn't want to be rude now would we?"

Austin was suppressing his laughter to the point where all I could here were mangled snorting sounds; even Carter cracked a small smirk at Vincent's misfortunes.

"She's got a point there, man." Austin said, clapping a hand on his shoulder.

Vince scowled. "Just wait until it happens to you, traitor."

I was whistling a happy tune while I dished out the rest of my dinner and walked to my usual spot at the table. Kate was already sitting to my left at the head of the table, and Cindy moved away from the door to take her spot in front of me, her tinkling laughter, much more girly than mine would *ever* be, reaching my ears as she reached across the table to give me a high-five.

"Nicely done," she complimented.

I smiled wickedly at her as I sat down and waited for everyone else to take their places. Carter was the last to sit in his place next to me, and, when he did, we all began the group inhaling of dinner.

I looked over at Kate, who was being uncharacteristically quiet. She would normally have supplied a few sarcastic comments to our dinner conversation by now, but, instead, she was staring at some random point in space with a distant look in her eye, barely touching her food. Kate was thinking again, and that was enough to make me nervous.

"Yo, Captain Crunch," I called as I poked the side of her head. "Care to share what's goin' on up here?"

Seeing as my finger was on the side of her face, I could feel and see the twitch she was trying in vain to suppress. Everyone in our pack had become just as accustomed as I was to the "annoyed-Kate-twitch." All heads turned and saw as it became more and more pronounced due to my lack of relent.

"What did you do now, Ria?" Vince asked around a mouthful of food, slurping it rudely. I narrowed my eyes at him; his bad manners always annoyed the heck out of me.

When I saw the not-so-innocent look on his face, I knew he was just asking for it. Rolling my eyes, I sent a quick, beseeching look in Cindy's direction.

She nodded gravely and set her fork down. Suddenly, there was a series of bumping noises under the table followed by Vince's short cry of pain.

"Gracias, Cindy."

"Anytime."

I turned back to Kate. "So, are you going to tell me what's up, or am I going to have to keep poking you?"

Twitch, *twitch*.

With a deep, heartfelt sigh, she put all of her utensils on the table and stood up. Staring down the table with hands on either side of her plate was the standard "hey I'm making an announcement" stance.

It was one of those expectations she had picked up as our pack leader.

One by one, we all sobered up and tuned in to listen. Her voice was firm and full of authority. She had the natural voice of a leader – a trait I was beginning to think was hereditary – while still lacking the egotistical derision most of her relatives possessed (cough DOUCHEBAG BROTHER).

"For the past few weeks, a coven of vampires has been closely following our every move and is closing in on our staked territory." She turned to Cindy who nodded her agreement, meaning together they had been keeping tabs on the coven's position with her tracking magic.

I thought about this for a moment; why hadn't anyone else in our pack noticed? Subtly, I looked around the table, and shared similar looks of confusion with the boys.

"Normally, we would have gone gun ho at the first sign of trouble, but sources have concluded that this is no run-of-the-mill, simple-minded coven. It's believed that over the past few years they have followed this pattern with several other packs." She paused for a moment, her expression darkening, warning us immediately of trouble. "When they didn't find whatever they were looking for, the packs were disposed of, and they moved on."

We all stiffened right away. "Disposed of?" Austin questioned with a hint of a growl in his voice.

Kate nodded gravely. "They aren't exactly weak either."

I'll bet, I thought, just barely repressing a shiver. The strength it took to take down a pack was remarkable, but to do it multiple times successfully without being caught? And now they had set their eyes on us...

A thought struck me, and I shifted my gaze in time to see Cindy's dainty little hands gripping the edge of the table so hard her knuckles were bleached white.

Oh, my God. It's gotta be them. The ones who killed her sister.

And we were expected to go after them. Lovely. This couldn't be healthy for Cindy's emotional sanity.

"Well, we're not called the Elite just because it sounds cool," I informed them gruffly.

"Which it does," Vince chipped in.

"And we're sure as heck not going to sit here and play patty-cake while they move in." I looked up at Kate and asked, "When are the piggies coming out to play with the big, bad wolves?"

Her grin was feral as she sat back down and answered calmly, "Tonight, when you're all done eating. So hurry up, would ya? Let's get this show on the road!"

Needless to say, there was an extreme choking hazard with how fast we now downing our food. Kate looked on approvingly, chuckling slightly at the little bit of mayhem she had caused as she stood up to wash her plate. One by one, the rest of us followed her, then went to our rooms to suit up and get our weapons and gear in place.

Cindy, Kate, and I managed to share a room without causing repeated bodily harm to one another, unlike the boys. In a very organized and precise fashion that betrayed the rituality of our actions, we each walked around the room, pulling out supplies, handing them to each other, and helping to strap them on if need be.

Some girls play dress up with makeup and pretty outfits. We play with weapons and armor. Well, to each her own.

I kept my hair in its usual style nowadays of half up, half down with the top half of it pulled back into a braid. Opening the closet, I pulled out my standard hunting outfit to go with it.

I chose to wear a pair of jeans with some pretty hard-core, black leather boots that I was just in love with. They fit like a dream and no longer creaked when I was in sneaky-mode. I topped it off with a black, stretchy t-shirt that was easy to move in and hid bloodstains well enough.

After I had slipped on my elbow-length, fingerless gloves, Kate helped strap on the arm guards that went with them (a graduation present from her parents). I helped her put hers on, then walked over to my bed and attached my knife I had haphazardly thrown there to my hip.

After my third Trial match, I kept the knife close by me at all times. At first, my pack balked at the idea, but I countered that it was much safer to keep a dangerous weapon where I could clearly see it.

It wouldn't kill me anyway. I seemed to be a special case.

Believe it or not, I'm getting a little sick of being a "special case."

I looked up in time to see Kate and Cindy just finishing, and, nodding to one another in contentment, we threw our arms over each other's shoulders and walked out of our room. The yelling coming from the boys' room (courtesy of Austin and Vincent) was audible through their door across the hall.

Kate just rolled her eyes and, seeing as she was between Cindy and me and had no arms to spare, she kicked the door once and shouted, "Five minutes until lift off! Get your butts in gear fellas!"

The distinct sound of swearing was heard at the other end of the door, and we just looked at each other and laughed while walking towards the entrance of the house.

Letting go of each other, we grabbed our long, black standard-issue cloaks that could keep us warm and hidden in the shadows of the forest. Something we found very, very useful at a time like this.

With no small amount of noise, the boys soon came out and joined us, reaching over our smaller heads easily to grab their own things and put them on. Before we knew it, we were armed to the teeth and ready to go, all within the span of ten minutes.

We strolled out the door and fell into our standard formation without even thinking about it, with Kate in the middle and me at her right. Kate looked us over one last time, making sure we were ready to go, and then nodded.

"Shift," she commanded brusquely.

We followed the order and automatically opened our minds for the resident psychic to work her magic on opening up a mind link so that we could talk to one another in our thoughts.

"Lock and load," she said to us before taking off into the trees with us right on her tail.

The hunt was so on.

It only took us ten to fifteen minutes to reach the vampires' campsite, which was disconcerting enough to chill me to the bone. Just how had they gotten so close without the rest of us noticing? And why wouldn't Kate and Cindy have told us when they first discovered their location? Shaking it off as something to worry about later, I focused on the movements of the vampires, and on Kate.

Lucky that I did, too, because in the next instant, Kate Transformed back into her human form.

When she saw our heads snap in her direction, Kate sighed deeply. "Due to the strength of the coven, the Council wishes to see if we can sort this out diplomatically first. That way we can gather a larger force to take them down later, if need be." Her eyes narrowed. "I don't trust diplomacy enough for us all to Change back, though."

I snorted in disbelief, but didn't speak out against the order. What the Council did was their own business and for their own benefit. It wasn't my job to question it; it was just my job to follow what they told me and trust in their opinion.

The thought made me freeze. Since when had I been thinking like that, I wondered dumbly.

"To the tree line," Kate ordered firmly.

As smoothly as the shadows themselves, we moved towards the edge of the woods, taking positions in the trees or on the ground.

Settling into my place behind a rather nice looking shrubbery, I scanned the grassy hill in front of us as well as its occupants, a coven of seven or so vampires. We were only outnumbered by one; nothing we couldn't handle.

"Cindy," Kate murmured quietly enough for only us to hear. "What's the status on the vamps?"

Cindy spent a few moments with her eyes closed, taking deep breaths, discerning the different scents of the vampires. When she opened her eyes again, she looked at Kate and reported, "*Seven. Mostly newbies, they must have come here recruiting. A few of them are senior citizens though. There's only one we really have to worry about; he's ancient.*"

Kate nodded, absorbing all of this. I looked back out towards the coven, but stiffened when I noticed something.

The wind had shifted.

My eyes caught sight of one of the vampires pausing in her tracks. For a moment, I thought she was going to disregard it, but, then, she snapped her head in our direction.

"*Heads up guys,*" I called out. "*They've caught our scent.*"

As soon as the words were out in the open, a soft, feminine voice echoed around us from the top of the hill. "Come out from the trees and play, puppies."

Everyone looked at Kate for orders. When she nodded in confirmation, we moved out from the cover of the shadows into the moonlight.

I jumped out from my place and landed smoothly next to Carter. Casually shifting my weight, I lifted my head and to level a fearsome glare to the nervous looking neophyte directly across from me.

Cindy was right, as always. There were seven vampires, three girls and four boys that stood in a pattern that mimicked ours. I didn't need magic like Cindy's to tell me the age of each one of them. The elder vampires glared down at us or grinned in obvious anticipation for a fight; the younger ones were shaking visibly in their boots at the notion of facing us. The coven had obviously sustained some damage after facing the last pack they decimated; at least three of the vampires were neophytes, maybe more.

Kate made her entrance then, walking between Austin and I and stopping just between us so we could cover her, if need be. Just as Kate was about to speak, though, one of the vampires at the top of the hill rode over her.

The voice came from the vampire in the middle, a super-aged one based on my earlier analysis of the coven. He was the only one who was practically exuding that strange sense of *wrong* that all of the really old vampires shared. This was obviously the one Cindy warned us about. His face was hidden in the shadow of moonlight behind him, making his features indiscernible, but his voice was clear as day.

"Ah, the Elite, you saved us a trip to your home base. We were just now coming to visit you, too."

If I was expecting anything out of this encounter between a werewolf-exterminating coven and the Elite, it was certainly not what this was shaping up to be. The familiarity the voice carried with it made me freeze in place with sudden horror and utter disbelief. I thought I was hearing things, that I was imagining the impossible, or that I was at least going nuts.

It's impossible, I told myself. It's beyond impossible.

Every muscle I possessed in my body froze in shock, and blood roared in my ears as I looked up at the center of the line where the apparent leader of the coven had spoken in a voice that had haunted my nightmares for a solid year now.

But his eyes weren't for me, and for that I was secretly grateful. On the other hand, though, I wanted him to look at me and know just whom he was facing. Maybe if I was lucky, he would just run away now.

Then again, when was I ever lucky?

No, he wasn't looking at me, but rather glaring with all the hatred and bitterness in the world at Kate, who stared back just as ferociously. Confusion filled my mind until he spoke again in that gloriously torturous voice of his.

"*Kari.*" That single word held more malice than every evil name and curse in the world. "You have exactly ten seconds to tell me where she is before I drain all semblance of life from you."

When did he become so angry? I had never heard him speak like that before.

Deceptively innocent, Kate cocked her head with a slight smile on her face, looking up at him and asking sweetly, yet with an edge that tore at the air between them. "Why, whatever could you mean, oh fearsome one?"

His growl displayed just how not amused he was with her sarcastic question. His eyes narrowed and his fangs were bared as he snarled back, "Don't play dumb, dog. You were the last one seen with her all those years ago. I *know* you took her with you."

My eyes widened at the implications. Oh, please don't let him still be looking. Not now, oh please–

"Where. Is. Maria?"

Oh, Daimon...

CHAPTER TWO

"Chance is a word void of sense; nothing can exist without a cause."
–Voltaire

Around me, I felt the other members of my pack tense up in surprise just as I had done. I really couldn't blame them. Thank goodness they all had the sense not to look at me, though. That could have ended badly.

"I don't see how that concerns you, *murderer*," Kate spat angrily. "She doesn't belong to you; she never has. Wherever she is now, she's safely out of your reach."

The air could've frozen over with the glare Daimon was sending Kate at that moment. His voice became calm and collected, but so chilling it made my hair stand on end. "She is *mine*, wolf. She would have been mine forever, but, mere hours before I was going to make it so, you stole her from her home, from *me*!"

I swear to God, my heart stopped beating at the implications of his words. He was going to Turn me. The day we were leaving, our anniversary, he came to the house. He was going to take me and Turn me. A sudden thought made the confusion and inner conflict in my head double.

I would have let him do it.

"Enough of this." Kate must have noticed how it was getting harder for me to listen to this. Funny, I hadn't even realized I was trembling. "You and your coven are responsible for the deaths of packs under the jurisdiction and protection of the Council. This is not acceptable. We are to give you a choice, cease and desist all such murders, or be prepared for your immediate execution. Choose now," she ordered, sounding every inch the Council's wolf.

Choose life, I begged silently. Please, for the sake of my sanity choose life and leave. I can't handle this right now. Everything was going so well!

A murderous smirk appeared on many of the faces looking down at us, and a few chuckles were heard. Daimon himself smiled without mirth and replied dryly, "I think you know our answer. We will not 'cease and desist' anything until Maria is returned safely to me."

As I distinctly felt a little piece of myself shrivel up and die, I looked over at Kate and saw her eyes narrow even more and a flash of a grimace that was more fang than tooth before she spat, "You don't have the authority to give such an order, *vampire*."

The tables were turned, and now he leered amusedly down at her. "You don't have the facts to verify that, *wolf*."

"Enough," she snapped, her control over her frustration fraying at the seams. "This is irrelevant. You have made your choice and, by order of the Council, you are sentenced to death."

Without another word she transformed and immediately sent a thought my way. *"Ria, you are forbidden to fight him. Do you hear me?"* She nearly yelled.

"You don't have to tell me twice," I assured her, though I really wanted to suggest running away all together. I was in no way, shape, or form ready to handle whatever was about to happen.

"We'll keep you safe, Ria," a voice that sounded suspiciously like Carter's growled.

"Fan out," Kate commanded everyone. *"Attack."*

And with that we charged up the hillside and began to fight.

I had been right that one day with Austin. No matter how many times I did this, it never got any easier. I'm just not a fighter at heart, and, though his words gave me enough comfort that I didn't lose my mind, I still agonized over every single death. Even the face of the lunatic in my Trial three fight haunted me at night.

In the end, it was Grandmother that gave me the wisdom I needed to get through my day to day choice of lifestyle.

"Is it really a life, little wolf? Is it a living, breathing soul with a beating heart filled with compassion and feeling?"

"No Grandmother, they are dead."

"Are you planning to become a mindless killer? Filled with no remorse or mercy?"

"No! Of course n—"

"Then you have nothing to worry over."

Another thought had struck my mind. I didn't know where it, nor where the impulse to voice it, came from. "Did she have the same problem? Alessandra, I mean."

Grandmother did not speak for a while, for so long that I didn't think she was even going to answer my question, but then she sighed and said, "Alessandra was more hardened than you, little wolf. She had no qualms with killing vampires."

Since that day, I haven't thought about it much, and, although I'd much rather just sit in a circle and have some major kumbayah time, I'm able to do what I must in order to protect others because that's my job, my duty; and I have to put that before the little voice in my head that's screaming for me to stop, that cringes away from what I'm seeing and doing, and that believes every life is sacred, no matter how tainted it is.

Because in today's world, listening to that voice could get me killed, no matter how right it is.

So, once more, I blocked out that little voice, and met my opponent with a clash of fangs, claws, and eerie battle cries. We were at a disadvantage running up the hill, but some of the new vampires, green in the ways of fighting, had foolishly run down to try and meet us halfway. It allowed us to easily overcome our disadvantage. My opponent was one of those vampires, a boy who only looked to be in his late-teens, just like me.

When he came head-on at me, I ducked down, grabbed his leg between my teeth, and threw him up on top of the hill, where the fight would be on level ground. His shriek of rage was ear-splitting and distinctly inhuman, but I ignored the pain in my ears and continued running towards him. He scrambled to his feet, nearly falling when he tried to put weight on the leg I had bitten, and rushed at me again.

This time, I side-stepped away from him, pivoted, and kicked out with my back feet, sending him flying off somewhere. He was back quickly enough, though, and now he was smarter, waiting instead for me to come to him.

I slashed with a giant paw, but, miraculously, he caught it in his grip, and squeezed until I heard little bones of my wrist groan under the pressure.

With a yelp, I managed to yank it out of his grip and come at him on my hind legs, armed with both sets of claws. It was easy work from there. I overwhelmed him quickly, and drew him to the ground.

His death was as quick and as painless as I could make it, and I prayed it was more peaceful than his life had turned out to be.

I looked around to see how everyone else was fairing, but noticed immediately that someone was missing. Another panicked glance found someone else missing as well.

Worriedly, I called to her in my head, *"Kate! Where are you?"*

Her response was immediate and distracted, she was fighting someone. *"Ria, stay away! Go back to the house and don't you dare leave! Go now!"*

Fat chance in heck that was going to happen.

I lifted my nose and took a whiff of the air around us. I had lived in the same room as Kate for three straight years; I could pick out her scent in a landfill (not willing to take that out for a test drive, though). I caught it quickly. The wind had not changed directions, so it had to be coming from the forest.

Not wasting a moment, I hightailed it in back into the shadows of the woods, consequences be damned. Daimon was furious, and it didn't take a genius to figure out he held Kate responsible for my disappearance. I couldn't blame him, but I wasn't about to let him take it out on her.

Even if I still loved him with every part of my traitorous, wolf heart, Kate was my friend, my sister, my pack mate, my leader.

I wasn't about to let her risk dying for me a second time.

My eyes adjusted to the darker surroundings of the forest even as I weaved in and around trees, following her distinct scent. I wished I could run faster, but in my larger wolf form I had to choose speed to get to her as quickly as possible over the agility to weave between trees.

As I got closer, a new scent reached my nose, and it took me a second to place it before my heart did back flips in my chest.

It was Kate's blood.

Not one moment later, the trees broke to reveal a clearing bathed in silvery moonlight. Without stopping, I took note of the situation, nearly tripping over my own paws in shock.

Kate had been thrown to the ground, her eyes were closed and her mouth hung open slightly in a grimace. She was in pain, even as she was unconscious, and had been wounded enough that she was now in her human form.

Daimon loomed over her, back to me, posture tensed, hand raised in preparation to make a killing blow.

But that was before I plowed his ass over.

No one, no one, no one is going to kill Kate. Not on my watch.

That was the only reason in the world I was now standing in between Kate, and the newly righted, extremely furious Daimon, braced for attack. My heart literally ached in my chest as I saw his beautiful face set into a fearsome scowl towards me. I never thought I would ever see him this way, not in my wildest dreams.

Focus Ria! You have Kate to protect now! Focus!

"Your interference is most irritating, dog. Leave now," he ordered firmly.

I made no move to follow his request; I merely stared him down, and waited for him to make a move. He cocked his head and eyed me from head to toe, trying to weigh if I was any real threat against him, I imagined.

His voice was as blank as his face when he warned me, quietly and detachedly, "I will give you one last chance, pest. Leave now, or be slain with your comrade."

The thought managed to make me furious enough to snarl at him.

His smile was like an icy touch to the back of my neck. "I will take that as answer enough, but maybe you can be more help than that meddlesome fool," he thought aloud as he glanced quickly at Kate, then back to me. "Perhaps *you* know where Maria is?"

Honest to God, I was not expecting him to throw that one at me, even though I probably should have. I couldn't help my reaction. I stiffened and took a step back, my foot just barely brushing Kate's side. Daimon's face immediately lit up.

Oh, shit.

"Oh good, the little wolf is not as ignorant as it seems," he said happily, his smile spreading and his head righting itself to narrow his gaze at me.

If Kate had not been directly behind me, I would have taken another step. His emerald eyes were like live flames, burning with intensity, as if he could draw the answer from me with just a look.

With a jolt of shock, I realized where I had seen that look before. Against my will, I was reminded of the psychotic vampire I had faced during my third Trial match, the one who had regarded me with the same sort of concentrated scrutiny Daimon was now leveling at me.

Ironically enough, it was only then that I remembered that that same vampire had mentioned Daimon during our fight, and only now did I know why.

I had the sudden urge to bludgeon the stupidity out of my own head. How could I have been so damn blind to the truth?

I was brought back to the present as Daimon's voice reached out to me again, logical and persuasive. "If you Transform back now and tell me what I want to know, I will leave you and your infuriating pack in peace," he promised.

It was so tempting; I almost gave in, but was it selfish of me to refuse? My pack was fighting a useless battle. If I just did what he wanted, then it would be over, and they could all go home and sleep soundly, but, then what would happen to me?

I was coward; I knew that much because, in that moment, I found myself afraid of so many stupid things.

I was afraid that Daimon would take me away from my newfound happiness if he knew who I was, or was I more afraid that he would reject me when he discovered just what I was now?

I was afraid that my pack would never accept this part of my past. Even if I hadn't known it at the time, I had fallen in love with a vampire, our sworn enemy.

And, most of all, I was so, so afraid that I would never stop loving him, despite whatever happened. Without a doubt, any path I chose to take regarding my future with him would lead to heartbreak for me.

So, I didn't Transform back. I stood there facing him, stalling the inevitable for as long as I could and steeling my heart for a scar it would definitely bear forever.

When it became obvious I wasn't going to Transform for him, Daimon's expression darkened considerably. His voice was tight and impatient. "If you will not do it willingly, I will have to resort to less-than-appealing measures." He nodded towards Kate again. "I know how your kind works. One hit too many, and you will be human again, where I will get my answer from you, no matter what it takes."

Oh it won't take that much, dude. You have no idea.

I don't know what possessed me to do so, it might have been frustration over this whole situation or simply a lack of understandable communication with him, but I did the most mature and formidable thing possible.

I stuck my tongue out at him.

To my surprise, he actually chuckled. "You have spirit; I will give you that, but come." His voice softened, becoming a cajoling, rough purr. "Wouldn't you rather just tell me?"

Even the best of my memories did not do that voice justice. That was The Voice. The one he used to persuade me to say anything, the one he used to make me blush fiercely, and the one that never failed to make my heart pound crazily.

Figures, he probably had no trouble hearing it.

I would not fall for it this time, though, because I was not the same girl who would simply go weak of the knees and spewing admissions of love and forever. No, I had seen and done so much since that time. I was no longer the same person. My heart might have ached for him, but my mind was still controlled by my logic and willpower, and it refused to let him have any hold over me.

In that moment I came to the sad realization that our time had passed, and with that thought, I almost felt like crying for the first time in a long time.

I released my claws and prepared for the fight, or maybe the beating, of a lifetime.

He understood instantly, but, instead of getting angry like I expected him too, he smiled, a chilling, cold, *murderous* smile that would have had me sweating if I could as a dog. "Have it your way."

And with that he attacked.

It was all I could do to dodge the first hit, but I couldn't run away. I couldn't move and leave him there standing by Kate. I drew on every ounce of speed I possessed, ignoring a spike of pain as he clipped me, and gave him a hard hit to the chest.

It had the desired effect of throwing him to the other side of the clearing. I followed quickly and pounced. He threw a punch that I neatly dodged, causing him to hit a tree behind me instead. The wood of the tree shattered on impact.

That certainly would have hurt in the morning.

I tried to hit him again, but he grabbed my leg just above the paw and bore down on it, just as the other vampire had, but this time, a distinctive, sickening crack sounded between us. He had broken my wrist.

Now officially pissed off, I snarled and kicked him, sending him flying through the trees. It bought me some breathing time as I looked down at my broken leg.

It wasn't a compound fracture, luckily, but I couldn't set it properly when I was in this form. First world problems.

My thoughts were stopped immediately as his form stalked slowly back into my line of vision.

I looked up to see him, my heart catching in my throat and my pulse pounding loudly in my ear, but this time not with anxiety, but rather cold, deathly fear. His face, darkened by shadow, looked more menacing than ever.

I think I succeeded in totally pissing him off. Fantastic.

One moment, he was walking through the shadows; the next he was *there* in front of me, moving with the eerily fast speed of older vampires that I could only match on my best days. I took a hit to the jaw, then one to the ribs that sent me flying until I came into contact with the rough bark of a tree. My skull was ringing from his hit and the tree I had just become acquainted with. Within a second, he was there again, picking me by the scruff of my neck and hauling me into yet another obstacle.

After this hit, I was starting to get a teensy bit irritated. Who needs an arcade, I thought, let's just play pinball in the woods using *Ria's head*! Doesn't that sound like oodles of fun?

God help the next pinball machine I come across.

"You are resilient," he said, his voice considerably calmer than his expression. I frantically fought to get to my feet as I heard him coming nearer, but only fell with a yelp after pushing with my wounded wrist. "Most of your kind would have Transformed back by now. I am impressed. Though, it should not take much longer to break you."

Gee, thanks. Is that supposed to be a compliment? I think I'm blushing.

Just as I made it on my feet, I was kicked in the ribs again. A party favor before I was thrown at yet another freaking tree.

This was really getting old.

Chest heaving with pained gasps, I gently added pressure to the side he had mercilessly kicked. The ribs weren't broken, thank goodness, but they may have been cracked. I was really more worried about my head though; I only had one of those, and I really liked it the way it was. Slowly, I reached up with a shaking, aching arm and felt a particularly sensitive spot, just barely fighting past a wince. Bringing my hand back to eye level I took note of the blood that now coated my fingertips with a grimace. Then it hit me…

Hold up, hand...fingers...when had I Transformed back?

Wait. Then that meant–

Someone seemed to have caught on a bit faster than I did because soon relentless fingers were at my throat drawing me up to hold me against the harsh bark of the tree. My head fell back to hit the tree roughly, and I couldn't hold back the small cry of pain as I opened my eyes and searched for his.

I hadn't expected there to be much of a difference looking at him with human eyes, but I couldn't have been more wrong. For a bare second, it was almost like I had stepped into my seventeen year old self experiencing a part of my life I had never imagined I would lose.

Now that I was up close, I saw things in his face that were so familiar to me, things I had forgotten, but now recognized right away. His pale, flawless skin shone out in the night, brighter than the little trickle of light that poured into the clearing between the breaks in the trees. His handsome features were frozen in an expression of disbelief: his mouth hung slightly parted, his blade of a nose the perfect size and shape for his face, his brown-blonde locks were wildly mussed from our fight; the longest parts of it hung in his face just to his eyebrows, and his eyes, oh God his eyes. They glowed in the night like polished emeralds, glistening with aged wisdom and hidden secrets.

Those same eyes were staring at each part of my face the same way I was staring at his. Only now, his had much more to learn. He had not changed, but I most certainly had.

"It couldn't be..."

His hand moved from its limp position at my neck trailing softly to my cheek, cupping it softly. The caress was so familiar to me that I leaned into it without thinking about it, but when my head tilted just so, my eyes caught sight of something in the clearing.

Kate's limp body.

That's when I stiffened, and reality came flooding back to me all at once. Now was not the time for a touching, heart-filled reunion, no matter how badly I wanted it to be.

There would be no more time for that.

I hardened my heart, detached my emotions from the situation, and forced myself into the mindset of a werewolf staring down a vampire. I was not Maria the human girl who was madly in love with Daimon; I was Ria the werewolf soldier and member of the Elite pack serving the Council.

Schooling my face into a scowl, I ordered him in a low and calm voice, "Get off of me. Now."

His eyes narrowed in confusion, but he didn't make any move away from me.

"I mean it. Get off." Emotions were desperately clawing my throat, hoping to leak into my voice, but I would not let them.

He tilted his chin back, staring down his nose at me, observing. Then, calmly as you please, he answered, "No."

I was pretty close to sputtering incoherently, but, thankfully, the years of training I had gone through simply would not allow it. "You have exactly five seconds before I return your little favors and throw your ass into a tree. Get. Off. Now."

"No," he said with a little more force this time. "I will *not*. I haven't seen you in three years, Maria, three *years*. What else do you want me to do?"

Let us default back to the original request.

He seemed to understand my exasperated glare. "I have traveled all across God's green earth looking for you, and you want me to just let you go the instant I find you? Why should I?"

I was going to have to let him know exactly where he stood as of now, before he made any assumptions. Whatever he thought we had now, whatever there was left of us, it had to end now. Either that or the in-laws would end it permanently, and I didn't even want anyone else to find out about this. It would put him in danger.

Even with my newfound resolve, my voice was barely above a whisper when I told him, "Because it is inappropriate for a vampire to interact with the Council's werewolf in such a way."

It was only after I said it that I looked up at him through my eyelashes. His eyes were narrowed in confusion and pain flickered somewhere deep in their depths. "Have you forgotten me then, Maria?"

Before I could even answer, something at my neck caught his eye. His hand finally fell away from my face, tracing down my neck in a feather-light touch. I steeled myself not to react as he lightly ran his finger down a familiar silver chain and pulled the locket out from behind my shirt. I could hear him skillfully open it with one hand and saw as a genuine, happy smile came to his face, a familiar one that made my breath catch in my throat.

Whispering so gently even I had a hard time hearing it, he spoke my name. This time though, the way he said it, it sounded like his voice was caressing the word and I felt the love and warmth that I had missed from him for *so damn long* poured into it.

"Maria..."

I'm so screwed.

CHAPTER THREE

"Death may indeed be final but the love we share while living is eternal."
–Don Williams Jr.

Knowing I was about two steps away from being completely emotionally compromised, I tried my best to copy Kate's mask, the one she now resorts to using only in the worst of situations. Seeing her wear it over her normally happy expression always gives me the heebie jeebies, and it seemed to be having the same effect on Daimon. After seeing the locket and affirming my identity, he was nearly ecstatic, and, apparently, he expected me to feel the same way, but seeing my closed-off, stoic face made him knit his eyebrows together and actually take a few steps back.

Guess I should have tried that first.

"What have they done to you?" he accused, somewhat subdued. I saw his throat move as he swallowed hard, an uncharacteristic display of apprehension from him. It was an anomaly for me to see him this way. "You've become one of them."

Next I had to copy Kate's empty voice she would use. It was easier than I thought, or liked. "What was your first clue, the lack of excitement or the monstrous form you so kindly beat me out of?"

He didn't have a reply for that, but I saw him clench his fists tightly at his sides and his gaze was practically burning as it met mine head-on. He looked me over, beginning at my toes and slowly climbing up to my face. I wanted to hide from his searching glance, but I forced myself to stand still with my chin held high and just wait it out. When his eyes finally caught and held mine again, he seemed so astounded.

"You've changed so much."

I don't know why, but that made me snap. All of the emotions I was feeling were finally tired of being shunted aside. They burst out all at once, and, before I knew it, I was yelling at him,

"Oh gee, really? I had someone help me with my hair ages ago, and the glasses are *long* gone. I think I may have slimmed down a bit too, been working out a little, and, let's see, what else? Oh wait, *I'm a freaking werewolf!* Of course I've changed!"

A small smirk touched his face. "I've gathered as much."

"Really? Because it doesn't seem to be clicking all that well in your head! Are you finally starting to catch on? Werewolf....vampire....bad combination! *Bad!*"

He shook his head, face suddenly serious as could be. "I don't see in that way, Maria."

"Well you should," I pushed. "Because that's how I see it and that's how everyone else sees it too."

"I *do not care* how anyone else sees it." His voice carried a hint of a growl underneath it, warning me to tread very carefully.

How does one tread carefully in a minefield?

I sighed deeply and stepped away from the tree, not willing to give him an opportunity to corner me again. Looking up into his face from just scant few feet away, I shook my head sadly.

"I know you've just made this very astute observation, but I really have changed. I am not the human girl you were in love with all those years ago; there isn't even the slightest resemblance. So, I suggest you save yourself a lot of effort now and just forget about any plans to relive the past because that is never going to happen. Not even if we wanted it to."

Daimon absorbed this for a moment, his honest curiosity open to me. I was expecting him to leave now, either that or get angry and attack. Actually, I had no idea what to expect anymore.

"Do you love me?"

Well, I knew I wasn't expecting that.

I couldn't think of the right words to answer him with. Everything I was thinking would either make him mad or encourage him even more.

So, instead, I opted for silence as my answer.

He cocked his head and watched me, eyes burning as they trapped my gaze. "The locket," he said quietly. "You would not have kept the locket if you did not care. You would not wear it every day if your heart did not belong to me."

Was it really necessary to voice that thought out loud?

"Don't overanalyze it," I informed him coolly. "It means nothing."

With only a wind shift as a warning, he was suddenly standing right in front of me. He grabbed hold of my elbows with a light, but still firm, grip I knew was capable of breaking bone without any effort (as he had so kindly demonstrated earlier). When he took a small step forward, he was suddenly looming over me. I found myself so panicked, I barely registered him speaking.

His voice was so quiet and fierce. "It means *everything*." Without warning, he used the grip he had on my elbows to jerk me forward into the circle of his embrace. His arms wound tightly around me and held on for all they were worth. "You silly, foolish girl," he whispered into my hair. "It means *everything* to me."

I didn't reciprocate his hug, but my traitorous heart was begging me too. It was now blatantly obvious to me that Daimon's feelings, like my own, had not changed.

The only thing that had was common sense.

"Come away with me," he whispered gently into my ear. "Come and live the life you were supposed to have with me. Come with me and hold my heart for all eternity."

I closed my eyes and took a deep breath. "No," I told him firmly, albeit a little shakily. "Have you heard anything I just said? That time has passed, and that world holds nothing for me now."

In an instant, the embrace became a prison as he pulled back just far enough to level me with an infuriated look. "It holds nothing for you, does it? The 'world' you were born and raised in, where your family continues to live, where you truly belong, means absolutely nothing to you? Do you take me for a fool, Maria? Or have you really been so thoroughly brainwashed by your little friend and the Council of Terror?"

I was two seconds away from snarling in his face I was so affronted by his words.

"I have not been brainwashed by anyone, thank you very much," I contradicted. "Believe it or not, this was a decision I made on my own, despite Kate's efforts to keep me home and human. I knew what I was getting into and chose the path I thought was best for me."

His ironic laugh set my teeth on edge. "You knew what you were getting into. I've never heard anything so foolish in my entire life." His face bent down until it was at my level, and he spoke his next words right in my personal bubble. "You could be a werewolf for another century and not understand what games you are playing into. You have no concept of just how young and easily led you are, or just how much danger that puts you in."

I tilted my head and sent him one of most unpleasant smiles. "So, what? I should just throw my good sense out the window, put all of my trust in you, and be led around by your better judgment? Thank you for putting so much thought into my best interests, Daimon. I would be absolutely lost without you."

"This is no joking matter," he admonished bitingly. "You have not even the slightest idea how much danger you placed yourself in when you chose to recklessly follow your friend to the world of werewolves."

"Recklessly? Excuse me–"

He didn't let me have the anger combustion that was three seconds away from slipping out. "No. You are going to listen very carefully to what I have to tell you, Maria." Leaning forward, he placed his head beside mine and whispered his next words right in my ear. "You are sitting on a game board in the middle of a match that has been underway for centuries upon centuries.

"Your decisions thus far have placed you right in the center of play as the trump card everyone has been waiting ages for. You have neither the experience nor the knowledge to contend with any of the players of this game. So, if you are not careful, you will place yourself right into one of their hands and spend the rest of your life being pushed from square to square."

"You expect me to believe Kate dragged me here just for some *game* she's trying to win?" I challenged disbelievingly. "You must be out of your mind."

"Not her, Maria," he returned. "She is firmly in the Council's hand. There is no escaping that for her. You, on the other hand, still have a chance to escape, to be free of that life."

"I will never allow myself to be controlled by anyone," I warned him fiercely. "Not even you. You don't have the right to run my life just because you think you know best."

I felt rather than saw the grimace that overcame his face and the sigh that touched my cheek. "You leave me no choice, then. You refuse to see reason, and I refuse to lose you even to yourself."

An ice-cold fear gripped me as the breath I felt on my cheek slowly made its way downward. It seemed strange that his vampirism only really hit me when his fangs were an inch from my neck. "You wouldn't dare."

"You have no idea what I would do, what I have done, in order to keep you safe and bring you back to my side, Maria," he hissed. "I suggest you remember that."

I was literally shaking with fear, my tough girl image swept out the door. "You don't know what happens when a vampire bites a werewolf." No one really did, but I could try bluffing. In training, we were only taught that werewolves who were bitten by vampires were lost forever. "I will not *ever* forgive you, and you're not willing to risk that."

"I would rather you were here, angry and betrayed, than dead to me."

I tried to break free, I really did, but I was injured, and he had a good hold on me. The inevitability of the situation hung heavily over my head, but, the moment I felt the slightest brush of a fang against my skin, I couldn't help but struggle even harder and pray for my life.

"*No!*"

My prayer was answered.

Out of nowhere, a menacing growl echoed throughout the clearing.

Before Daimon could even look up to see what was going on, he was knocked away from me by a huge, unstoppable force. I fell to the ground just as Carter Transformed into human form.

Not daring to take his eyes off of Daimon, he stepped backwards to come beside me. Crouching down, he wrapped my good arm around his shoulders, one of his larger, warm arms around my back, and easily lifted me off of the ground. He held his arm in place even after I was rebalanced, and I gratefully accepted his support.

"Boy, am I glad to see you," I told him, relief obvious in my tone.

"I bet you are," he replied evenly without turning his head to look at me. I was stunned to note that his voice was a tad bit strained. I had scared him. "Let's not do this again."

I snorted. "You don't have to tell me twice."

As he opened his mouth to say something else, Daimon reappeared within the clearing looking like the Devil himself in all his fury. His eyes might as well have been spitting sparks, and his fangs were fully-bared and extended from his almost-successful love bite.

Too close. That was way too freaking close.

"Mutt, I will not hesitate to kill you for this transgression. Leave now or you die where you stand," he snapped, his voice barely hiding his chilling fury.

Carter, God bless him, didn't even blink. "Your coven has been downsized. You stand on the losing side of an uneven battle, and you nearly killed two of my pack members," he growled. "Idle threats test my patience."

Daimon's eyes narrowed dangerously. He opened his mouth, obviously about to say something concerning Carter's imminent demise, when a piercing shriek of one of female vampires rang throughout the forest. It was high pitched enough to make my ears ring, but then it was abruptly cut off.

How many are left, I wondered. If Carter was here then that would mean there were at least three down, and that female would make four. We were winning.

The sound of my pack's yips and hurried steps reached my ears. I felt myself sag with relief. Tonight wasn't my night to die, either; we had all survived.

I chanced a look at Daimon and saw his fury had been replaced with cold, precise calculation. He couldn't remain here for long and expect to come out unscathed, but it didn't look like he was ready to leave.

Well I'm sure not going with him, not today.

He sighed angrily, his face set into an irritated scowl. "This fight is over. We will retreat for now, but, mark my words wolves, we will return again."

His eyes traveled over to me as two other vampires who were fleeing the pack ran into the clearing towards the protection of their leader.

My pack ran in just seconds after, assessed the situation, and came to stand by us while Austin's big wolf frame stood protectively over Kate, who was still out cold a good distance away from us.

Daimon raised his voice so everyone could hear him clearly. "I will take back what is rightfully mine, no matter what it takes."

I snarled at him. "I *do not* belong to you. I do not belong to anyone but myself!"

"No," he snapped. "You are the Council's pet, running at their every beck and call. You're playing at being a superhero with a bunch of misfit mongrels, and it does not suit you."

"We will not give up Ria so easily, vampire," Vincent intoned coldly. "You want her? You're going to have to go through each and every one of us to get her."

A roguish smirk touched his face. "I look forward to the day."

And with that, he vanished, the rest of his coven following closely behind, disappearing like smoke in the shadows.

It seemed like ages I just stood there, looking at that little spot of existence that Daimon had last occupied, half-expecting him to just emerge again.

I didn't notice how I was slowly being lowered to the ground, or how people were shouting at me. I forgot about the pain that shot through my entire body and the ache that was now consuming my energy. The shock of the whole experience was just settling in, and my mind refused to register anything going on around me.

Daimon was here. I saw him, I heard him, I fought with him.

Daimon is a vampire. He tried to bite me.

Daimon still loves me. I broke his heart.

It wasn't until warm hands firmly held each side of my face and forced my head to meet depthless black eyes that the endless mantra finally stopped. Somehow, the sight of his familiar, strong gaze brought me back into the present, sitting on the ground, legs folded under me, and good arm supporting my weight.

Not fully registering the action, I lifted my arm to inspect my wrist. My wrist is broken, I noted dumbly. He broke my wrist.

He must have seen the pain cover my face because he let go of me and pulled out his boot knife. With careful precision, he began to cut the end of his shirt into a thin, but substantial bandage.

I felt somebody at my right side and turned just as Vince knelt to examine my head and my rapidly-coloring arm. He grimaced as I flinched slightly when he gently touched the break. "I need to set the bone, Ria," he told me calmly, laying a comforting hand on my shoulder.

Cindy came to my other side, and supported my weight with hers when I took my good arm off the ground. I was secretly thankful when she took my hand in her own and held tightly as Vince lifted the broken arm; I gritted my teeth against the wave of nausea and agony.

"Look away, Ria," he soothed. "This'll only take a second."

Unbeknownst to me, he set it while I was in the process of looking away, when I least expected it. A short cry of pain escaped my lips before Cindy's cooing words and soft touches to my hair calmed my rapid breaths and helped push my thoughts away from the pain. Vince was already splinting my arm, while Carter chose to use his makeshift bandage to start cleaning my head wound.

"Ria?" Austin called from across the clearing.

The situation at hand hit me like a ton of bricks. I even tried to shoot my feet, only to be forced back to the ground with Cindy and Vince holding me firmly there. Knowing I wasn't going anywhere anytime soon, I responded from my spot on the ground, "What's her status, Austin?"

"She's out cold," he reported after a few moments of silence. "We're going to need to carry her back."

"You do it then, big guy," I told him. I looked at Vince. "On my feet, please."

Both Cindy and Vince, each with a hand under my arm, levered me up off the ground. "You're in no shape to move either," Vince informed me. He looked at Carter. "You're the second fattest. You take her."

I still found enough energy to kick him in the leg for that.

Carter didn't respond to the insult, as usual. Instead, he just nodded and Transformed again right in front of us. He lay out on his side on the ground, and Vince helped me onto his back and held me on as Carter stood up straight.

Luckily, this was something that we had taken great care to practice more than once, even though I cannot begin to describe how ridiculous it actually looks. Sometimes, it was just unavoidable.

I kept a careful eye on the others as they loaded Kate onto Austin's back and Transformed themselves. "Let's go," I ordered tiredly, my energy leaving me faster than it should have been able to.

Carter's strides were smooth and even; I was barely jolted at all. I caught myself falling asleep a few times and eventually just laid my pounding head between his moving shoulder blades, resting for as long as I could.

It was only then that I realized no one had asked me anything about Daimon or what had happened.

My pack, always prioritizing; I knew it was only temporary, though. As soon as we got back to the house, I was going to be interrogated like there was no tomorrow.

We all have things that can't be said; we all have things we'd like to hide. Since when has this stopped being common knowledge?

I only noticed that Carter had stopped when he Transformed with me still on his back. Without missing a beat, he held my legs at his sides and carried me into the house piggy-back style.

I love this guy; he's become my personal pack mule without uttering a single word of complaint.

Kate's still-unconscious form was resting in Austin's arms in front of us. The knowledge that Daimon had hurt her so badly, and was prepared to do more made me sick to my stomach. I buried my head in Carter's shoulder breathing in his familiar, soothing scent with ragged breaths as unwonted images of what could have happened if I had arrived just a second later flashed through my head.

"You okay?" His soft voice asked right by my head.

I nodded weakly, and he took that as answer enough. Somehow, even as he was silent, I felt his wordless support and was comforted by it.

He carried me into the girls' bedroom, still following Austin, and set me down on my bed, tucking me under the covers and everything. When I saw Vince walk into the room towards me, I pointed him towards Kate first. "I won't be healed until she's 100% better and awake to see it," I told him firmly.

With a gusty, dramatic sigh, which earned a dangerous glare from me, Vince quickly scurried over to Kate's bedside and worked his magic. I laid my head back against the pillows and relaxed all of my muscles for as long as I could.

I lost track of the time, but it must have been close to an hour when, finally, I felt a gentle touch at my shoulder. Sluggishly opening my eyes, I looked up to see a tired Vince looming over me, looking weary after such a heavy healing.

"I can only heal you one at a time, unfortunately," he said softly. "I'll come back in an hour or two to check on her and then you can have your turn."

"Remember what I said," I warned.

He shrugged and pushed away from my bed, heading for the door. "No worries, she'll be up by then."

He dimmed the lights and closed the door firmly behind him. It was only when I heard his footsteps enter the bedroom across the hall and his door click shut softly that I pulled all of the covers off my bed and gingerly swung my legs over the side – wincing slightly when I stood – and stumbled my way over to Kate.

Looking down at her, I flinched. I had known it was going to be bad if Daimon had managed to knock her back to human form, but it was even worse up close. Ugly-colored bruises mottled her exposed skin (I could only imagine how much more she actually had everywhere else).

Ever so slowly, I fell to my knees beside her, reaching out for her hand and brokenly whispering a thousand apologies while simultaneously making a thousand threats in the case she didn't wake up for me to hug her soon.

How could this have happened? And, perhaps more importantly, what was going to happen next?

With the events of the day catching up to my exhausted body, I fell asleep kneeling on the floor with my head against the mattress and Kate's hand held tightly in mine.

It wasn't until someone was casually combing their fingers through my hair that I was startled awake, reflexively trying to stand up, but failing miserably when I discovered had no feeling left in either of my legs, courtesy of the ridiculous position I had fallen asleep in.

Soft, soothing noises reached me as I began to grow distressed, and I calmed right away when Kate's face came into my line of sight. As I sank back down to the floor, I looked over her face and her injuries, gauging how much she had healed within the past few hours.

She was still covered with bruises on nearly every inch of skin that was exposed, but now she could breathe normally and she was finally awake.

Count your blessings, Ria. They only come one at a time.

"You know, you could just *ask* me how if I'm okay," she teased in a raspy voice, smiling weakly at me. "Been out long?"

"How are you feeling?" I asked worriedly, completely disregarding her question in favor of my own.

She laughed lightly, noticing the worry on my face. "I'm fine; I'm guessing this is Vince's handiwork that's making me feel a whole heck of a lot better?"

I nodded, not knowing what else to do. I couldn't get it out of my head that it was Daimon's hands that fit those bruise marks perfectly, that had broken her bones, and had caused her such pain.

This was all my fault.

"Ria?" she questioned worriedly, taking both of my hands in hers. "Ria, what's wrong?"

"Nothing," I answered quickly, automatically. "You're fine, nothing could be wrong." I tried smiling a little to back up my story, but the look on her face told me she wasn't buying it for a minute.

"Answer denied, please try again."

I laughed a little, weakly and half-hearted at best, feeling closer to tears than I had been in a long time. I closed my eyes and bowed my head so that my forehead lay against our intertwined hands while I attempted to speak over my closing throat.

"I'm sorry," were the only words I could manage to force out. "I'm so sorry, Kate."

She seemed to understand what I couldn't force myself to say. No more words were necessary. Instead, she pulled one of her hands free and rested it on my head, stroking my hair gently as she was doing before. Slowly the tension ebbed away from my over-stressed body at her soothing touch; my muscles relaxed and sleep lingered nearby. If I just shut my eyes for a moment…

"I was scared."

Her voice abruptly brought me out of the tranquil haze I had allowed myself to fall into. I opened my heavy eyelids and concentrated my energy on every word she was saying.

"I've never been one for mental warfare during a confrontation," she mused. "It's been a long time since anyone's been able to get into my head like that."

I immediately sought to assuage her fears. "Don't worry about anything he said," I reassured her. "I didn't buy into what he was saying, and neither should you."

That didn't seem to alleviate her fears. I felt the bed move as she shook her head and laughed without any real humor and turned my head on its side so I could look up and see her face, only to be surprised to see the sad and lonely smile that was there. I hadn't seen Kate like this in a long time.

What really happened in that fight between her and Daimon?

"That's not what I'm afraid of sunshine," she admonished, sighing deeply. "I was afraid...that he was right. I was afraid that I had chosen the wrong path for you. Maybe you really should be with him now, happily in love, rather than with me dragging you through hell and back just for a lifetime of servitude."

My jaw literally dropped. There was airflow and everything; I'm even convinced some drool leaked out unintentionally.

"That is perhaps the stupidest thing I have heard you say since you thought that you could successfully climb a tree in wolf form."

"Honest mistake," she mumbled.

"Regardless, I'm tired of you going around thinking that you've damned me and sentenced me to a life of eternal misery. I'm going to tell you the same thing I told Daimon–"

"*You talked with him?!*"

Completely disregarding the aneurysm Kate was currently having, I chugged along. "And that is that I belong here with my pack, with *you*, as a werewolf. When I was human, I wished for an escape and I got it. You gave it to me, and I will be forever grateful and happy because of that decision."

The tension that had been lingering in every one of Kate's muscles eased. "Thank you," she whispered, gratitude shining from every part of her expression.

I returned her smile happily and turned my head back to face the mattress. "I was scared too," I confided to her.

"Thus the reason you directly disobeyed orders and came running to my rescue?" she asked dangerously.

"Kate, he was going to *kill* you. I saw him; he was ready to do it, and I was almost too late to do anything," I recalled with horror.

She continued to calmly play with my hair, as if she had not been at all shaken by what I had just told her. "A time comes for even the greatest of soldiers and the best of friends, Ria," she whispered gently. "It's something none of us can prevent."

I stilled abruptly and looked up at her. "Don't say things like that," I snapped without meaning to.

I didn't like the philosophical Kate as much as my happy-go-lucky Kate. She talked about things I didn't want to hear.

Her hand paused in my hair for a moment before she let it fall away completely. "You weren't brought up the way we were, Ria. Death is something that is second nature for a wolf. We don't like it, but it's accepted as inevitable, and honorable to the one who falls in the line of duty."

"Why would you even *think* like that," I asked stunned at how she could view death so piteously, like she was just waiting for it to happen. "What's the point of life if all you're concerned with is how you die?"

She sighed again and gave me that look like I was a child who just didn't understand, which made me that much more aggravated. "Like I said, I was raised that way, along with everyone else." She leveled me with an uncharacteristically hard look. "Live your life, follow your orders, and die protecting your brothers and sisters. That is the mantra every young wolf grows up with and lives by. It's how we've become what we are today. It's how we grow even stronger."

"Well it's dumb," I informed her plainly. "As a human and I grew up with: go to school, move out, get married, pop out some kids, and die old and wrinkly with lots of grandbabies. Does it sound like I'm doing that anytime soon? Negatory. Life's too complicated to rely on a set plan, and it's too damn short to be thinking about your tragic and heroic death."

She stared at me for a while, then surprised me by chuckling lightly. "Where were you when all of these ideas were created, huh? We needed you a few hundred years ago."

I scowled. "Ain't that the truth."

"I'm sorry I upset you, but it's something I hope you grasp sooner rather than later. It helps when you look Death in the eye every day of your life."

"I know, Kate, but don't worry about it. I'm fine."

Peace was reestablished between us when, all of a sudden, the door to our room opened. We turned to see Vince, followed dutifully by the others, coming into the room. Doctor Vincent didn't seem too pleased that I had escaped from my gurney.

"What in the hell do you think you're doing?"

Nope. Not happy.

I just sent a cheerful smile his way, determined not to let him spoil my newly-happified mood. "Well, currently, I happen to be stuck. You could help change that if you want though."

His expression was nothing short of exasperated; I couldn't help but laugh as he scowled angrily at me. Since he didn't seem to take the hint, I pulled my hands away from Kate and lifted my arms for him, wiggling my fingers invitingly. Rolling his eyes in response, he made his way over me, effortlessly getting me to my feet and leading me over to my bed with a sturdy arm around my waist.

While he was helping the invalid, the others situated themselves between the two beds, be it on the floor or in a chair. Preparing themselves for the story of a century, I imagined.

I hoped they weren't expecting it from *me*.

Vince prepared to work his magic on me, not bothering to sit down like the others. As he began to unwrap the makeshift splint from my wrist, he asked, "I don't suppose someone would like to explain to the rest of us what's going on here?"

"Can I have a vowel?"

"Shut up, Austin."

I laughed and turned to Kate, wondering where on earth we were going to begin with this one, but she was just smiling at me.

"The floor's all yours, Ria."

I'll remember this, *you damned jerk.*

So, not bothering to put it off for any longer, I began to tell them the story, starting at the very beginning of time.

It was nearly an hour of effort before the story was finished start to finish, with added in commentary, expletives, and surprised outbursts included.

The room had descended into a sort of stunned silence. Vince had long since finished his handiwork and was now sitting at the edge of my bed, staring off at some random point in space, trying to comprehend everything; the others shared similar looks, including Kate.

The silence was growing stifling, even for me. I looked up at Kate. "What is it we're going to do next, fearless leader?"

She was broken from her distraction, turning to look at me blankly. "There's not much else we can do," she sighed. "We never finished the job. How many did we take out?"

"Four," Cindy supplied coolly.

"That means that there are three left that need to be taken care of." She paused for a moment, her face glowing from the light of the sunrise filtering through the window. "We will leave and finish the hunt tonight," she said finally. Then, her gaze shifted back to me. "You will stay here and recuperate.'

Immobile as I was, I couldn't get out of bed and throttle her like I really wanted to. "Like hell I will; this is more my fight than anyone else's, Kate. You know that."

The look she leveled me with wasn't one of an exasperated friend, it was an unmoved leader. "Regardless of that fact, have you noticed what tonight is, Ria?"

I *had* noticed, I thought grinding my teeth together angrily. It was the full moon, the one night that I couldn't go out and hunt with them, of course. There was a simple reason for this. You see, it's a part of the original werewolf curse. The night of the full moon, a werewolf is said to revert to his or her true, undisguised form, unbidden by the wolf in question.

This means that during the night of the full moon there are a lot of wolves just running around, unable to transform back into their human forms. Which, when you think about it, isn't too much of a problem.

However, for someone whose "true, original form" isn't that of a wolf, it's a night of weakness, just another one of those "special cases."

"Fine," I snapped weakly, the exhaustion my unintentional nap hadn't taken care of was making my tongue heavier than usual. "But shouldn't you stay behind too? You aren't exactly at 100% health right now."

She shrugged nonchalantly, brushing the matter away with a wave of her hand. "There are only three of them left. I don't need to be at full strength for us to take them down easily."

"Don't bother arguing with her, Ria." Austin sighed. "She's going whether we like it or not." He was cut off from saying more as a pillow scored a direct hit on his face, suspiciously from Kate's direction.

"She seems fine to me," Cindy laughed.

It was getting harder and harder for me to keep my eyes open, interesting as this conversation was turning out to be. "All right, you guys go ahead and git 'er done. I'm not going anywhere anytime soon." My words were coming out slurred and tired.

Gingerly, Kate stood up from her bed to walk slowly towards mine. There was pity shining in her eyes, and I didn't like it. I tried to ignore the sinking feeling in my stomach and the thoughts of what she was going to be leaving me to do.

I felt her hand searching by my side and wrapped my fingers around it. "I'll take of everything, Ria," she said quietly. "I promise."

I smiled gratefully up at her, and gave her fingers a final squeeze with the last of my strength before letting my heavy eyelids finally have their rest.

I wasn't sure how long I slept, but it seemed like the instant I closed my eyes I was blinking them back open, awake and reenergized. Taking a good look around me, I found myself alone in a room illuminated only by the light of the full moon. Everyone else had gone to finish their hunting.

Lifting my arm, I held my wrist close to my face, inspecting the damage. To my pleasure, there was not even the slightest twinge of pain as I opened and closed my hand, rotating it every which way in the process. Slowly but surely, I levered my body off the bed to a vertical position and tested the rest of the healing. Everything seemed to be in tip top shape.

I didn't care what anyone said, Vince was, and always would be, a miracle worker in my eyes, but he wasn't even here for me to thank.

I felt my lips turn down automatically at the thought. They really had left without me. I could have been fine within a few hours, but they had chosen to leave me behind instead.

No, I corrected myself. Kate left me behind. It was an executive order, and she had been its creator, obviously thinking I couldn't handle myself in this situation.

But who was she to make that decision, I thought angrily. This fight was more than personal, and I had every right to be a part of it. Not to mention the fact that she had been even more injured than me tonight. She was putting the whole pack at risk going out without it being at full strength! Maybe that was just the Council Head's influence rubbing off on her.

I froze where I stood. Where had that come from? I had never, never compared Kate to the Council, nor anyone else I held in any sort of esteem.

What was wrong with me?

Maybe I just had to wake up more. With that thought, I made my way to the bathroom, attempting to get the negative thoughts all out of my head.

Damn that Daimon, coming back into my life and messing with my thoughts. If they didn't take care of him tonight, I was personally going to make sure that not a single word would leave his mouth ever again.

So much for getting the negative thoughts out of my head.

I realized, with great surprise, that I had never been so angry in my life, and not just at one person too. This culmination of events was showcasing the negative qualities of all the people I had grown to love and trust in my life, and it didn't make for a fun time.

There was Kate, who always thought she had to protect me because I was the poor, weak human, and she was my savior.

There was my pack, who followed Kate unquestioningly, who did what they thought was best for me, whether I liked it or not.

There was now Daimon, who was convinced that I had made some grave mistake in choosing to follow Kate, and who had now made it his life mission to liberate me from my choice of lifestyle, no matter the consequences.

And then, behind everything, as always, was the Council, who moved us around with the ease of any professional puppeteer, and who treated us like their purebred pets.

I was grinding my teeth together so hard that I was convinced there would be nothing left but stubs, but that quickly stopped when I tasted blood in my mouth.

Raising my finger to my lip, I flinched when I found that I had somehow split it.

But that wasn't all. The hand by my face wasn't as it should be. It was the new moon outside; I was powerless, stuck completely human for the night.

So, why did I suddenly have claws?

I took the last few steps into the bathroom, wanting to clean the blood off my lips, but stopped in my tracks the instant I caught sight of my reflection out of the corner of my eye.

It was a feral, animalistic creature that stood on the other side of the glass. It couldn't have been me. With wild, red eyes and great, white fangs, this image bore almost no resemblance to what I should have looked like.

But, as I lifted my hand to the mirror, it did the same. My palm came to rest on the glass at the same time and place as the reflection's too. What was going on here?

All of a sudden, the unthinkable happened.

The terrifying reflection actually reached its hand through the mirror, locking it claws in a firm grip around my wrist. It had been a while since I had jumped and screamed like a little girl, but this was beyond anything I was ready to deal with in real life.

But that wasn't all the monster did. Using its newfound grip on my wrist, it hauled me towards the mirror so quickly I was sure I would break the glass with my face. Knowing I couldn't react fast enough to stop it, I closed my eyes and waited for the inevitable to happen.

However, when there was no shattering contact, I found myself opening my eyes, only to find myself on the wrong side of the glass. Lifting my hands, I pushed against the mirror, looking into a bathroom I had been standing in not moments before and where the monster now stood in my place.

Smirking in a manner that turned my blood to ice in my veins, the monster turned away from me and began to walk out of the bathroom, running its claws along the walls as it did so, leaving four perfect lines behind.

I beat my fists against the mirror, but it was no use. The monster had taken my place, and I was stuck in a prison I didn't know how to get out of.

I was thrown back into consciousness abruptly with only a gasp and a painful reminder from my ribcage that it was only newly-healed.

I sat up carefully and looked around my room only to find that I was alone. The full moon was shining brightly outside.

I had slept the whole day off and well into the night. Just like in my dream.

Lifting my hands to my head, I covered my face and tried to comprehend what the hell I had just seen. I had had similar dreams before; the red-eyed figure was a familiar one. Back in the earlier days of my training, it was a constant fear of mine that I would lose control of myself and become that mindlessly violent creature.

But I had overcome that fear years ago, and the dreams had gone with it. So, why had they decided to come back for a visit?

Scared shitless for reasons I couldn't name, I found myself quaking slightly as I got to my feet. Again, just like in the dream, my pack was already gone, most likely to finish the hunt we had started last night.

The thoughts and anger that had polluted my dream hovered in my mind again, waiting to take hold, but I didn't let them. By now, I knew that such mindless anger was not only dangerous, but also useless; if anything, that dream had shown me that quite clearly. Kate and the rest of my pack only had the best of intentions at heart; I knew that they were only trying to spare me the emotional pain that was going hand-in-hand with this mission.

Finding a sort of peace that I had distinctly lacked in my dream, I decided to face that fear head-on. Taking a deep, grounding breath, I walked to the bathroom.

There was no red-eyed monster waiting to greet me in the mirror, but, just to be sure, I hesitantly reached my hand out to the glass, prepared for something to reach back. When it didn't, I breathed a sigh of relief.

It was then that I decided I should just push the memory of the dream from my mind. There was no she-monster hiding in my mirror, and I seemed fully capable of handling my own anger.

Now that I wasn't so afraid of my reflection, I could take a look at myself much more closely. There was a single cut already scabbed-over on my right cheekbone that would probably heal without a scar along with various other similar scratches on my arms and legs. Lifting my shirt slightly, I saw bruises marring the pale skin of my ribcage, but, feeling along the ribs, I could tell that they were all healed. My head was a little sensitive to the touch, but I didn't plan on hitting more trees anytime soon, so I was probably fine with that.

I turned the sink on scalding and waited until the steam started to collect on the mirror to cup my hands in the water and splash it on my face. I felt gross with dried blood and dirt in my hair, but I felt too vulnerable to take a shower while the others weren't here. Nothing was more embarrassing than facing an ambusher alone in the house with only a towel on.

Don't jinx yourself, Ria; the coven isn't finished yet.

When I finished, I twisted the knob on the sink off and toweled my face dry. As I went to wipe the mirror, though, I heard it.

It was the soft click of a door being shut. If everyone else was here with me, I wouldn't have been paranoid enough to have registered it. It could have even been written off on the wind from an open window, but I wasn't willing to risk it.

Lowering myself into an easy defensive crouch was a natural action now, I rested my fingertips against the wood of the floor. Concentrating with every erg of mental energy I could pull at this point, I held myself in complete stillness as I listened and felt for any undesirables.

The pad of a muted footstep vibrated through my finger and ear drums.

My eyes shot open, and I fought the urge to drown myself in the water left in the sink.

No need to worry about Kate and the rest leaving me anymore.

The coven was here.

CHAPTER FOUR

"For you and I are past our dancing days."
-William Shakespeare, *Romeo and Juliet*

I can't believe I jinxed it!

There was no longer any time to think. The coven was *in the house* and I was still defenseless and weak from the last fight I'd had with them. I had to move.

Using every inch of stealth I possessed, I slunk back to my room, automatically grabbing my cloak that someone had thrown over a chair and my knife. It was on my bedside table, thrown carelessly there next to my pair of armguards. I wasted a brief moment of time trying to decide whether or not to bring them too, but then realized it was better to be safe than sorry.

As I tightened the straps on them with shaky hands I looked around the room, judging the best escape route before deciding on using the window. There was no telling whether or not I could get out of my room to use one of the official escape routes. The window was probably the only option I had.

Taking a deep breath, I attached the last arm guard strap and pulled it open slowly. I could hear them clearly now, they were in the kitchen just down the hall.

They would have to go in the boys' room first. It was before the girls' room in the hallway.

I had the window open, but came to the depressing realization that they would hear me when I broke through the screen, even if I cut a hole in it with my knife, their – *stupid, sensitive, obnoxious* – ears would catch it.

The distinct sound of a door being burst open off of its hinges might as well have been an alarm to me; there was officially no time left.

This place wasn't safe anymore, my home away from home away from home. I had no choice but to get the hell out. So, I took a deep breath and mentally prepped myself for what would probably be the run of my life.

With that, I took my foot to the screen and jumped through the window after it.

I had a little advantage over them knowing the woods as well as I did, but that only evened me out with their ridiculous speed. I didn't dare look over my shoulder to see if they had started following me, or even to see if one of them was Daimon. At least I didn't have to worry about three.

It made sense, though. Have one lead the pack away from the house and while they're running around in circles the other two ambush. Daimon had to be the one leading the others away. The pack wouldn't be looking for anyone else. It was the only thing that made sense!

If I could just find someplace where I could hide out and mask my scent, then they would never find me, but, as I stumbled over my own two feet, I realized anxiously that exhaustion was going to set in soon.

I needed to find a place *now*.

Desperately searching my surroundings, I found that they were more familiar than I thought.

They were going to chase me straight into my old town.

Really karma? What did I do to deserve this?

Did Daimon plan this? The thought unnerved me more than it should have.

Then it hit me like one of Austin's slide tackles. I might just have the perfect place to hide in this place.

Smirking at my own genius-ness, I pulled on the last of my energy, picked up the pace even more, hearing my cloak whipping loudly behind me, and ran straight for the heart of the little town's shopping district.

When the backs of old, brick buildings came into my line of vision, I could have laughed with relief if I was not already gasping for breath. Only a little ways more and I would be at my final destination. I scaled a chain-link fence within a few seconds and landed in the alley on the other side in a somersault that became a sprint again.

Just a little farther, Ria. You're almost there.

I skidded around the corner of the building, turning so sharply that I threw my hand to the ground to balance myself. I bolted through the middle of the street, where nothing was in my way. No one would be on the road at this hour. Everyone who lived here would be safely tucked into bed by now, oblivious to the sound of nimble feet thundering down the asphalt. It was another few more blocks before I hit the residential section, and, by then, my two pursuers were just struggling over the fence.

It took little time to find the house; my feet seemed to remember the way with minimal interference. It was the same brick beauty with classic black shutters and window boxes filled with well-groomed flowers. I found myself stopped right in front of it for a moment, taking in the tidal wave of memories that tried to swallow me whole at the sight of it. However, as some part of my mind reminded me, I didn't have the time to stand and stare. I was still being chased.

The plan was all well and good, but now I had to figure out how to get inside.

When I lived here, the door was always locked after ten at night, and so were all the windows. I really didn't want to have to break down the front door. That would be like putting a blaring, neon "she's hiding in here" sign on the house.

How the hell did I sneak into this house before? Think, Ria! You have to *remember*!

And suddenly, I did.

Without wasting any more of the precious time I didn't have, I made a dash to the back of the house. Just as I remembered, a trellis, covered in beautiful, red roses in full bloom, leaned against the wall that held my old window.

The window with the broken lock.

It was quick work up the trellis, just as it was with the fence. When I reached the top, I prayed to any god that was listening that this would work as I laid my hand against the glass pane of the window and applied the correct amount of pressure needed to lever the window open.

It stuck at first, only opening an inch or two. Ice ran through my veins as I desperately pushed it twice more until, finally, it gave, and there was enough room for me to dive into the room and out of sight.

Gaining to my feet, I pivoted to shut the window with a sigh of relief. Now it was just a matter of staying out of sight of the street and anyone who might pass by.

I sat on the floor under the sill, tucking my knees to my chest and wrapping my cloak tightly around me for good measure. Despite the fact that I hadn't been here in years, my old room should still have been infused with enough of my scent to effectively hide me from my pursuers.

I must have been hours that I sat like that and waited. When I looked up again, the sky was lightening to a pale shade of blue that would soon turn pink. The vampires would have to turn tail soon; the older ones would have no choice but to flee from the coming sun. I ignored the pins and needles sensation in my legs in order to get into to a crouch position and, much like a toddler would do, peek out the window to the street and yard.

There was no one there.

Sagging with relief, I leaned back against the wall again, shutting my eyes, relaxing for a moment, and running a hand through my wind-streaked hair. I had escaped; I was safe again, for now.

It was only then that I opened my eyes and allowed myself to look around at the achingly familiar sight that was before me.

Nothing had changed. Nothing had been moved. My bed was still made, some clothes were still slung over my chair, and there was even an open book at my desk, still marked on the same page I had been reading three years ago.

The only thing that was remotely different was the thin layer of dust that coated most of my old belongings. The space was eerily still, and, strangely enough, felt vacant. With the way everything was scattered around the room, it would seem as if someone was living here every day, but somehow it was devoid of any life.

It felt *empty*.

Trying to take my mind off the strangeness of the room, I stopped and listened, trying to discern if there was anyone else in the house with me. However, I found, to my great relief – and only slight disappointment – that I was completely alone in the house of my childhood.

Once again being an advocate of safe rather than sorry, I knew staying put in the house until dawn was probably the best idea, but, then, I would have to high tail it out of here; I couldn't risk being recognized.

While I was here, though, I knew there was no way I could deny the temptation that was bubbling eagerly inside me; this was a once in a lifetime opportunity I now had at my fingertips.

I had to go through the house.

Without wasting a moment, I stepped away from the spot in the center of the room I had frozen in and moved towards the door. It took more courage than I had needed in a long time to turn the knob, and while a – werewolf-trained, vampire-hunting – part of me knew it was utterly ridiculous to be afraid, I was anyway. I was afraid what I might find on the other side of the wall.

I opened it slowly, noting vaguely that the hinges didn't squeak when I did so. Someone was obviously taking better care of the door than they were my room.

Did someone still go in there? Did they sit on my bed, leaf through that book, or maybe just stand in the center of the room like I had done and try to take everything in? Did they really miss me?

The thought made my stomach turn violently. I had undoubtedly caused my family pain; it wasn't fair to them that they were affected by my choice.

Were things really meant to turn out this way?

With a wry laugh, I realized that I hadn't even stepped past the threshold of my room and I was already emotionally compromised.

So, I took that first step and looked up until my gaze landed farther down the hallway on my parents' bedroom door.

Oh God…

I wondered if, even now, three years later, after merciless training, after time in the field of combat, after facing horrors only known in fiction, I could walk into that room and not break down like I did the last time I went in there.

Somehow, I was convinced that if I could do that, I could do anything.

I was prepared to take the next step, when I heard something. At first, I chalked the insignificant noise up to heightened nerves (an insignificant noise was what led me here in the first place), and was completely prepared to disregard it, but…

I heard it again.

I spun toward the bannister I was standing next to. It was undeniable now; I could hear something – or some*one* – moving downstairs.

Apparently, I wasn't as alone as I had thought.

But my parents weren't here. There was no human in the house; I would have easily heard them, even without my heightened werewolf senses.

It hardly mattered, though. Whatever it was, I would have to face it sooner or later, and I would much rather have it on my terms.

I reached over to grip the railing in one hand, swinging my legs over the edge sailing through the air until I landed soundlessly in a crouch on the floor, but stiffening when the sound came from behind me.

Down on the lower level, I recognized it immediately.

The sound of rustling clothing and barely audible footsteps.

It seemed, as I whipped my head around, that all the pieces came together, and, as I took in the sight of the source of the noise, a mixture of horror and anticipation overwhelmed me.

His smile was triumphant, exuding pleasure even as it was partially hidden by the blooming rose he held up to his nose. His back was facing a window with a view of the ever-lightening sky, but his emerald eyes were only more piercing in the dark shadows.

He pulled the rose away from his face. "Scent is not the only way to find someone, Maria."

The rose landed at my feet; I gave it only one dispassionate glance before returning my gaze to the theatric-loving vampire in front of me. I just can't win can I?

Daimon's smile became almost predatory, and I swore I caught a glimpse of a fang as he whispered the single word that pretty much summed up the situation from every angle. "Gotcha."

Not yet you don't, you arrogant jerk.

As if somehow understanding what I was thinking, Daimon hummed in amusement.

Feeling my eyes narrow automatically at his reaction, I growled and barked out, "What in the seven hells are you doing here?"

The venom in my voice seemed to have no effect on his good mood. Calmly as you please, he answered, "Waiting for you, of course. I knew you would come back here."

I felt my eyebrow lifting incredulously. "Oh did you?"

He grinned wolfishly. "It's the only logical place you could have gone to in order to outrun the other two. Well, it was the smartest place, and, now that you have finally decided to join me, you and I are going to have a little chat."

I didn't like where this was going, "I don't think so. We did plenty of 'chatting' in the clearing; nothing else is necessary."

It was his turn to narrow his eyes. The smirk he had on his face fell away as he did so. "It *is* necessary. You and I aren't quite seeing eye to eye yet."

"And what, may I ask, would *ever* make you think we could see eye to eye?"

His gaze seemed to burn right through me as it shifted to stare at my neck, I raised my hand to it as if it would protect me from his thoughts – a natural reflex – but his eyes only narrowed.

"The necklace," he answered simply.

I could feel the locket like a weight around my neck now. The cold of the metal seemed to burn against my fingertips. I made my hand fall back to my side. "A memento of the past, nothing more; don't think anything of it, Daimon." I was trying to make myself sound firm, but the only emotion that found its way to my voice was a heavy sadness.

"I refuse to believe that," he whispered quietly.

"Believe what you will Daimon, but I'm done. Stop having your coven chase me down because my pack will always come for me. Stop following me because nothing you say is ever, ever going to change the fact that you are a vampire and I am a werewolf, and I have no desire to ever change that."

"I will never stop chasing you, Maria," he swore fiercely. "I *love* you."

My heart was tap dancing in my chest at his words; I tried my best to control it, there was no doubt he would be able to hear it, but it just couldn't be helped. I looked to see his expression, and by the soft smile he wore, I knew he *had* heard it.

Aw, shoot.

"You aren't hiding your own feelings very well, Maria. Come." He held out his hand invitingly towards me. "Stop fighting your true feelings. Come live the life that was meant for you. I'll give you freedom from this life you've been pulled into."

"Can you please just get it through your head? What makes you think that I want to leave?" I snapped at him. "What if I was perfectly happy with the life I've been given?"

"You can't be. You *hate* fighting; you always have! What on earth would possess me to think that this could make you happy?"

"Because," I told him calmly, "there is only thing in this world that I hate more than fighting, and that's innocent people getting hurt from it. What you do is *evil*, plain and simple. There's no excuse for it, and now I can fight against it. I can protect those people that need it, and that makes me happy. It makes me proud, much prouder than I would feel being a blood-sucking, life-stealing monster like you!"

243

I regretted the words the instant they left my mouth, but, before I could take them back, he was moving.

With a yelp of surprise I rolled away from the fist that was now halfway through the floor of my parents' foyer. I felt cold fear rolling down my spine as I looked up and saw Daimon's frigid glare directed right at me. Never before had he struck at me while knowing who I really was, *never*.

Without trying, he could, hands down, be the scariest opponent I had ever had to face.

Daimon was visibly trembling with rage as he stared me down. His breath was ragged, and his fangs were curling over his lower lip, bared for me to see.

After a few moments, though, something changed. He looked into my eyes and his expression softened once more. Never taking his eyes off of me, he pulled his wrist and hand away from the floor and stood up slowly.

His voice was ragged and guttural, straining through the anger he was trying to suppress. "Please. Please, Maria," he begged. "For centuries, I have been hunted, cursed, reviled, and countless worse things. I've been hated by werewolves and feared by humans. I can take all of that in stride, but you...I can't." He actually stumbled back two steps. "*Please*, I can't have you hate me. I can't have you stand there, and pretend to be like them, forgetting everything we had...that's unbearable."

I had no response for that. It was heart-breaking, as he stood there and bared his soul out for me to see; there were no words I could say.

He took a single step towards me and I stiffened automatically, ready to bolt if need be. Seeing this, he paused mid-stride.

"Maria," he whispered, trying to sound as soothing as possible. "Please, don't be frightened."

"I am *not* afraid," I told him fiercely. "I'm not afraid of anything anymore."

He shook his head, smiling sadly. "That is far from the truth. You're afraid of a lot of things."

I reacted without thinking to the slight.

Straightening up to stand tall on my feet, I took a few steps towards him until I was only a few feet away. "See? Not afraid." I could have slapped myself with how squeaky my voice sounded. It made his smile grow into a full-blown smirk.

"Mhmm, I can see that." He reached out to me and traced his fingertip down my cheek to the line of my jaw. "But I know a few more things you are afraid of."

I steeled myself not to react outwardly, knowing it would only give him fodder. "Oh really? Like what?"

His gaze centered on me, "You're afraid to love me."

Okay, so there's that one little thing.

As I found myself immersed in the emotion filling his gaze, I felt a sudden weariness weighing more than just my body down. We had just argued ourselves into a never-ending circle. He was too stubborn to give up, and I could never let our relationship continue knowing it would only bring him danger. I refused to be stuck in this circle with him forever, though. I was just going to have to be the mature one and own up to my fears.

"You're right," I admitted softly.

If I thought I had his unwavering attention before, it was nothing compared to the way he stared at me now. I could not hold his gaze after his awareness honed in on every little nuance of my words and expressions.

Staring at a point beyond his shoulder, I continued. "I'm afraid to love you, and you should be just as afraid to love me."

The touch of a single finger to my cheek was replaced by his entire hand cupping my jaw so that he could gently raise my head to meet his eyes once more. "Tell me why," he bid me calmly.

I was already seeing this conversation as ten times more constructive than all of the previous ones combined.

"If … if my superiors, if *anyone*, found out about this – about what we once had – you would without a doubt be killed, or worse."

"And you?" he asked again, in a quiet whisper, almost too quiet for me to hear.

"I would undoubtedly be tried for treason, and then imprisoned. They don't like me that much to begin with," I answered simply enough. "But I would never be able to stand the idea that you were killed because I was too stupid to say 'no.' I won't let you be hurt because of me, Daimon."

"Why?" I hadn't noticed how close he had gotten until the word was a breath on my lips.

"Because even now...I love you too."

The words slipped out on their own, as all higher thought was currently at a standstill. As soon as they were in the open, though, the hand at my jaw wrapped around the back of my neck in order to pull me forward just as he leaned down and pressed his lips to mine.

It was by no means overly-passionate, but it was heartfelt. I felt the kiss burn all the way through me, from my head to my toes, like nothing ever had, from the feel of his lips, achingly soft against mine, to his warm hand, firm against the back of my neck.

He made no move to deepen it, but, rather, pulled away after only a few moments. I could feel my heart pounding frantically in my chest as I looked up to meet his gaze.

Thanks to the hand at the back of my neck, personal space was a faraway dream, as was fleeing from this situation. He leaned forward again, but this time it was merely to rest his forehead against my own.

I was beyond surprised when he chuckled happily, huge smile firmly in place. "I knew they hadn't changed you. I knew you were still my Maria." His eyes found mine and his smile grew even larger. "You still love me."

There was no taking back the words now. "Did I ever deny that part?" I asked breathlessly.

"No, I don't suppose you did," he relented. "It's just that other part we have to work on."

I let out a heartfelt sigh. "I'm not getting anywhere with you, am I?"

"No, not at all. In fact, I do believe you just lost ground."

And that was my cue to take matters into my own hands.

Daimon was never going to see my point because he was never going to give me up. As happy as that idea made me, I also knew something that he did not.

I was already lost to him.

And while I wanted the same thing, the only way I was ever going to be able to keep him close to my heart was by keeping him alive, and that started with me doing what had to be done.

Ignoring the happiness swelling in my heart, I reached up to Daimon's face tracing the line of his cheekbones and his jawbone. When he felt my fingers, soft and soothing on his face, he let his eyes fall shut. His blatant trust in me nearly made me gasp in shock, but, instead, I cradled his face in my hands and leaned up to kiss him again.

He stiffened in surprise, but relaxed quickly, reaching with his other arm to wrap around my waist as the hand at my neck wound in my hair.

I allowed myself to enjoy it for as long as I could, feeling the warmth of his love and his embrace. Committing this moment to memory, and the feeling of being loved that came with it, I pulled away first and rested my forehead on his shoulder, strengthening my resolve even as his fingers played softly with my hair.

As I noted the first rays of true sunlight filtering into the window, I felt the strength of the werewolf curse returning to me and whispered the words that I needed to say to him, feeling my lips brush against his neck as I did so.

"Remember the last date we had together, Romeo?"

I felt the happy hum deep in his chest and imagined the smile lighting up his face. "I would never be able to forget it, not even in the next life, Juliet."

"I'm sorry, but I refuse to have their same ending, Daimon."

He registered the words too late.

As he stiffened beneath me in surprise, I scraped the bottom of the barrel for the strength to push him away. It was enough force to knock him out of the foyer and into the wall of the next room, where he landed with a painful crash.

Refusing to turn back or to break down in tears I hadn't felt the need to cry in years, I high-tailed it out of the house and into the safety of the coming sunrise.

CHAPTER FIVE

"Letting go doesn't mean that you don't care about someone anymore. It's just realizing that the only person you really have control over is yourself."
— Deborah Reber

I didn't have the stamina to last much longer. Even as I ran, I could feel my muscles cramping and becoming dead weight, but I had to get out of there.

For one, Daimon was there waiting for me to frolic off somewhere to live 'happily ever after' with him (possibly to his own death).

Secondly, this was an early-to-rise community. It would be hell on wheels if someone managed to spot me out in the open and recognize me. Plus, who knew if anyone had actually heard Daimon's impact with my parents' living room wall?

I retraced the path I had taken to the house only a few hours earlier, running through the middle of the street until I reached the familiar, little shop with the narrow alley next to it. The fence seemed harder to get over this time. The climb was slower, filled with slips and cuts from the metal, and I didn't land in a graceful somersault either. I jumped from the top, only to land painfully on the other side. A few moments were spent sprawled out on the ground trying to catch my breath, but luck wasn't on my side. Over the sound of my heavy panting, there was another sound.

The sound of feet beating swiftly down the pavement of the street.

I looked up at the sky and saw that Rochester's reputation of bipolar weather was as true as ever. The majestic sunrise that I had counted on for my salvation was being covered by a black storm cloud of death, bathing the city in shadows once more.

Perfect for a vampire chasing down a poor, weakened werewolf.

Thinking a string of more profanities than I had ever used in my entire life, I fought to my feet and took off once more. I would have no choice but to take the short cut through the woods, it would only give him more shadows, but I wasn't going to make it much longer.

I toyed with the idea of Changing into a wolf now that I was in the cover of the woods, but quickly discarded it. That would only take up more of my energy.

All thoughts went out the door, though, as I looked ahead of me and saw glorious, wonderful sunlight filtering into a clearing in the trees. If I could just make it there, he wouldn't be able to get me. Then, I could wait there for my pack to come and sniff me out, or, at the very least, I could rest for a moment and come up with a better idea.

Hope seemed to make my feet lighter as I made my final dash for the clearing. There was the distinct sound of leaves crunching from behind me; I had no doubt that Daimon had caught up. Desperately, when I was within the last ten feet of the clearing, I leapt, feeling the sunlight warm more than just my face.

That is, until I felt an unyielding grip on my ankle halted my progression in its tracks.

Pain spiked across my shoulders and head as they hit the ground, and, for a single, terrifying moment, I thought that my head wound had opened up again. I felt the bruised spot with my fingertips, but, except for being overly-tender, it seemed to be fine. That being affirmed, I looked back over my shoulder and let my gaze travel down past my leg to the edge of the clearing, where a definite line of shadow was drawn just past my calf. Just past that was a very pale hand, holding onto my ankle for dear life.

His face was a contorted mask of weariness and pain. "When," he questioned breathlessly. "Are you going to stop running away from me?"

"When do you plan to stop following me," I retorted childishly.

"Never."

The word was spoken so fiercely it actually startled me. Maybe it was that look in his eyes, or just the way his grip tightened on my ankle, but I knew that he really wasn't going to ever give up.

What was worse was that there was a part of me was casually suggesting that maybe it wasn't meant to be like this. Maybe, it was pointless to run away from something we both wanted.

"Daimon," I said in the calmest big kid voice I could muster up. "This is getting really old, really fast. Get it through your head: I cannot go with you. Why can't you see that I'm trying to protect you?"

"Why can't you see that I'm trying to protect *you*?" He returned immediately. "Why is it you would go back to a life of being tied up like a dog on a leash? You aren't free there, how could you be? You're at the mercy of a Council of power-hungry tyrants, whose solution for anything that goes wrong is to kill more innocent vampires."

"There is no such thing as an innocent vampire. You defy the very coarse of nature. You are the dead amongst the living, taking life from others just so that you can escape your own deaths!"

"You talk haughtily for being another monster that 'defies the very coarse of nature,'" he snapped. "We do what we must to survive. No more, no less. It has been that way for everyone – man, vampire, werewolf – for centuries, and it will continue to be that way for many more. Don't throw stones at my kind when yours isn't as innocent as you would paint it out to be. Heroes aren't born as a race; they are born as individuals. Not every werewolf is a saint just because they kill a vampire in the name of 'protecting the innocent.' Widespread murder hardly constitutes as heroism."

251

"Nonetheless, I made a vow when I finished my training, Daimon. I swore that I would always and forever protect serve those who followed the Council until the end of my days, and I never break a promise. *Ever*."

"So, you've sold your soul to a group of decrepit sadists who would have no qualms in sending you off to your own death in order to fulfill their self-interested whims?"

I couldn't even yell at him for that, could I? I would have said the same thing a few years ago. I still didn't even like them all that much.

I took a deep breath and responded calmly, "That's the idea."

"That's the most idiotic, asinine, and unintelligent thing I have ever heard you say in our entire acquaintance, Maria," he told me plainly. "I've been around for a long, long time, and *never* have I seen more corrupted and self-serving men. I find it hard to believe that you could ever follow anyone remotely similar."

He was hitting the proverbial nail on the head. Three years away from this guy and he still knew me better than I did. Story of my life.

"It is for the best," I responded quietly.

He shook his head. "You could never believe that. Not you, never you. I see that look in your eye. There must still be some human part of you that refuses to give in and submissively tie yourself down."

His eyes seemed to spark with realization in a way that made me more than a little nervous. "That's why they don't like you, isn't it? The Council. They see that you're different from the others, that you have a mind of your own. You are not a piece they can just put on their chessboard to push about and do their dirty work. You're a wildcard."

"So I won't be the one to march out to my own death," I responded blankly. "Therefore, your worries should be assuaged, and you should feel free to let me go."

Based on the way his hand tightened even more around my ankle, I think it was safe to say that he wasn't taking the hint. I didn't pull back, though. I had lost the game of tag; I wasn't willing to give tug of war a go.

"You cannot go back," he gasped through clenched teeth. "You don't understand; you are in danger if you do."

"I get it, I get it. You are under the impression I'm an ignorant baby immortal, and I have no hope of contending with great and mighty minds like yours when it comes to scheming evil plots. Well, news flash, buddy, I'm still not stupid enough to fall for your little word games."

"How many times do I have to tell you, Maria? It isn't a game to me, and, despite how strongly you reject it, you cannot change the fact that there are enemies around you that have had centuries more time to make their way in the world."

I found myself smirking. "They'll need that time and more to contend with me."

"You may not think that after you meet them," he warned. "I have been living amongst these vipers. I know who poses a threat to you and who I must keep you away from completely." His voice dropped to an undertone, as if there were bystanders in the woods he didn't want hearing us. "I also know when it's dangerous to be a werewolf, when other creatures are threatened enough to threaten back."

That didn't sound promising.

I stiffened in his grip. "Explain," I ordered tonelessly.

He emerald eyes locked with mine for some time, as if assessing the situation, deciding whether or not to tell me, I assumed. I sent him my most unrelenting stare back. Finally, though, he sighed, and I knew he had given in.

"There is going to be an attack on the Council's main headquarters before the end of the month. Several covens of vampires have decided to band together in the hopes of removing the merciless hold the Council has on every mythical creature in their territory."

I honestly didn't hear anything past "attack on the Council." I also interpreted that this not only meant the Council, but also my friends, neighbors, and countless other loved ones.

Daimon wasn't quite done with his piece, though, and I was still too shocked to interrupt. "If you go back now, you may be caught in the crossfire, or at least called to give support. I cannot let you go when there is a chance you may be killed...or worse."

"What exactly do you think I've been doing for the past four years? Playing patty cake with my wolf buddies in the midst of extensive lessons in knitting and cat's cradle?" I asked, exasperated. "Give me a break! I can hold my own in a fight now."

He gave me a dubious look. "Says the girl who's not fully healed from the last time she fought me."

"That doesn't count."

"When *does* it start counting then, Maria? *After* you're struck down in the name of your precious Council?"

"Listen up, Daimon, because I think you'll find this quite interesting." Despite every instinct telling me I should keep as far away from him as possible, I scooted closer under our face were on the same level. I kept my voice low and serious as I said, "I see how you think it's really noble and heroic to try and save me just because I'm the weak and fragile female in this relationship, but you couldn't be more wrong. I hate to break it to you, but I am not the girl you fell in love with all those years ago. As you've pointed out yourself, I am quite different now. I have the strength, the skill, and the motivation to stay here and protect my friends and family." I shook my head without looking away from him. "I won't ever leave them behind. I love them."

He tried to mask the overwhelming sadness in his eyes with more anger, but it was still enough to take my breath away. "You won't leave your friends now, but you were just fine leaving me back then." I immediately fell silent as the grave, not moving, barely even breathing at his words. "Was I wrong, then? Is there really no love for me in your heart?"

I should have said no. If I lied and told him that, then it would have all been over. I wouldn't have to worry about him following me relentlessly or about the Council's reaction or even keeping my friends safe.

But after everything we had been through, I knew he didn't deserve that.

Even with this realization, I wasn't sure of what to do. Spurn him and save him from the Council's wrath? Accept him and put us both in danger? What was the right answer?

I noted that, ironically, the last time I had asked myself that question, I had been deciding whether or not to leave with Kate and embark on this whole crazy adventure. I remembered thinking of it not as a question of what was right or what was wrong, but, rather, who needed me the most.

So, who was it now?

I didn't mean to think out loud, but the words just slipped out into the space between us. "Who needs me more?"

Instead of being taken aback like I assumed he would be, he became thoughtful. Tilting his head to the side, he studied me curiously. "You would base your decisions on the whims of others? Is that how you want to live your life? No, Maria." Reaching out, he brushed his fingers across the part of my hand that escaped the sunlight, and then said something that I would never forget. "What do *you* need more?"

It hit me. Had I ever once asked myself that? Had I ever once considered that what the people around me needed wasn't what I really needed?

He seemed to understand the flabbergasted expression painted across my face. "Maria, you are allowed to consider the needs of those you love, but, the first part of being selfless is to have a sense of self. What is it you want? What is it you need?"

I honestly didn't know the answer to that, and that was quite a frightening prospect.

"I think I want both, but I know that can never happen," I said sadly. "I may be awesome, but world peace is a little beyond my reach at the moment."

The corners of his lips turned up in a sardonic smirk. "Glad to see you know where to start."

I took a chance. "Will you let me think about it?"

Again, he fell silent, looking over my expression and mulling something over in his mind. "This isn't a ruse? An excuse to simply escape me?"

"I may have changed, but not that much," I informed him. "You're going to have to trust me. Let me go; let me think, and then I will give you my answer."

He paused for a moment. Then, miracle upon miracles, his grip on my ankle loosened before falling away completely. "There is a saying. 'If you love something, let it go. If it comes back to you, it's your forever. If it doesn't, then it was never meant to be.'"

I nodded "I know it."

He reached out his hand between us and held it open for me. "I had to let you go once, but here you are again. I just have to believe it can happen again."

How could I ever have hated him, even for the slightest moment? Here was someone who had fought so hard, so long for the chance right before him, and he was throwing it away to give the time and space I needed. Sure, he was pigheaded and stubborn and a tad bit uncompromising, but it was his turn to give *me* what I needed most.

So, I took his hand and gave him my warmest smile. "I will came back to tell you my answer. I give you my word."

The return trip through the woods was slow, but it was also proving to be the least stressful trek of the day. I took my time walking, deep in thought the whole trip. After all, I was past overdue for an inner, existential debate.

Despite Daimon's words of wisdom, I still found myself asking who really needed me more. Was it Kate and my pack? The Council? Grandmother? Was it Daimon? Or even my own family?

I really had no way of answering that question. So, I moved onto the next one.

What did *I* need more?

However, just as I finally allowed myself to consider the thought, the sight of my pack's headquarters came into view. I saw my pack too, but they had their backs turned to me. In fact, they looked like they were just about to leave, most likely to go on a manhunt for me.

Well, they weren't going to have to go very far.

"Guys! *Guys!*" I called out to them.

Whirling around in surprise, they broke formation one-by-one to run to me. Surprise, surprise, Kate got to be first.

Barreling towards me at Mach 5, she threw herself into my arms, buried her head into my shoulder, and held me tightly.

"Whoa, Kate, I'm fine! Calm down!" I couldn't help but notice she was shaking slightly.

Pulling her head up, she looked me straight in the eye. "You're okay? Are you sure?"

I nodded, smiling. "Perfectly fine now."

"Good."

That's when the throttling started.

"HOW COULD YOU BE SO STUPID? DID YOU REALLY THINK NOW WAS THE BEST TIME FOR A LITTLE STROLL IN THE WOODS? I THOUGHT THEY TOOK YOU, YOU LITTLE SHIT. I JUST HAD LIKE FIVE CONSECUTIVE HEART ATTACKS."

Past the screaming, I vaguely heard what sounded like Austin's voice. "Um, Kate…"

"I'LL REMEMBER THIS THE NEXT FULL MOON. APPARENTLY, JUST BECAUSE YOU'RE HUMAN DOESN'T MEAN YOU CAN'T GET INTO TROUBLE. I AM LOCKING YOU IN A CELL NEXT TIME. DO YOU HEAR? A GODDAMN CELL."

"*Kate,*" Austin insisted, pulling her away from me and giving me a moment to recover. I was already seeing stars. "Calm down. Let her explain herself first."

"Yeah," Vincent joined in, "let her explain herself, but, if her answer is unsatisfactory, we can all kill her."

I swallowed hard seeing the looks on my packmates' faces. And I had thought explaining how I knew Daimon was hard.

"Rest assured, I did not just randomly decide to go for a walk in the woods." Insert pointed look at the harpy here. "The coven came for me."

My pack sobered up even more. "We were chasing Daimon's scent," Cindy explained quietly, "but it led us in a circle, right back here. They must have had something to leave a false trail."

"I tried running, but I knew I wouldn't be able to make it far as a human. So, I hid."

Vincent gave me a dubious look. "You hid. You just hunkered down and hid from two lethal hunters like an adult version of hide and seek."

"They're not the only ones who can play with a scent trail," I explained quietly, looking up at Kate again.

She didn't get it at first. Shaking her head, she said, "But you were human. Your scent is totally different that way. You'd have to–" I immediately knew when she guessed what I had done. "You didn't."

"I had no choice," I told her. "It was the only place I could go."

"What are you talking about?" Carter interrupted.

Cindy realized it next. That wasn't really surprising, though, seeing as she was the expert on tracking. "Did it work? Were you caught by…anybody?"

"No, I got in and kept myself hidden until daybreak–"

"WOULD SOMEONE PLEASE TELL ME WHAT IS GOING ON?" Vincent bellowed loud enough that I found the urge to hit him over the head. Luckily, Austin did it for me.

I was surprised at how easily the words escaped my mouth, at how natural they felt even after all this time. "I went home."

I couldn't tell if the strange looks were from my phrasing or my action, but, in any case, Kate had overcome her shock and felt the need to continue her little interview. "So, if we were chasing down a false trail, and you were running away from the coven, where was Daimon?"

Turning my head to face her once more, I tried to keep my voice as calm as possible. "He was waiting for me at the house."

Everyone sucked in a large breath. Vincent's eyes were so wide I thought they would pop right out of his head.

"He was waiting? In the house?"

"That's what I just said."

"Ria," Carter asked, "how did you escape?"

"He wanted to talk to me, and then he tried taking me away, thinking that I wasn't suited for this kind of life." I couldn't help the small smile that came to my face. "In the end, though, he let me go."

"He just...let you go." Kate sounded skeptical.

"I know it sounds strange–"

"It doesn't sound strange," Vince cut in, "it sounds downright impossible."

I was attempting to think of some way to explain this whole debacle when it hit me. To be perfectly honest, I really should have thought of it sooner, but, at that moment, I found myself recalling just why Daimon wanted to take me away in the first place. The attack.

"This doesn't matter right now," I told them firmly. "We have to go."

"Have to go? Ria, are you out of your mind?" Kate asked. "You just got back, and go where exactly?"

I grabbed her shoulders in a white-knuckled grip, and she shut up pretty quickly. "Listen, Kate, the reason he was trying his damndest to take me away was because he had heard something. There's going to be an attack on the Council headquarters before the end of the month. We have to warn them. Now."

Now Kate was looking pretty bright-eyed and bushy-tailed. "Pack your bags. *Now*," she ordered as she spun around with me and ran to the house. "We have to warn the Council what's coming."

The coordination of our pack was something truly admirable. Within fifteen minutes, we packed everything we needed to in one large bag and were ready to go once more. Because I was still tuckered out from my day's adventure, they each took turns carrying the bag and me. It wasn't quite as fast as the train could travel, but we made good time nonetheless.

Kate was a woman on a mission. I noticed out of the corner of my eye as I rode on Austin's back that she hadn't asked any more questions after learning about the attack. She was the first one ready and the first one out of the gate when it was time to go.

It's that damn loyalty, I thought to myself. They may be self-centered and controlling, but she's grown up listening to the Council. She would do anything for them.

When we did reach the headquarters, I expected her to set us loose so that she could find the best time to talk to them. Instead, she ran the whole way down the driveway, Transformed mid-run, and bolted for the doors of the building. Naturally, we followed behind her, despite our conclusion. Kate wasn't usually one to bust in unannounced. She was normally too docile when it came to the Council to do such a thing.

But she went all the way. Bypassing a completely baffled Aunt Rose, she didn't stop until she reached the doors of the Council's main chambers.

"Let me in," she ordered in a voice that made her sound more like her grandfather than I'd ever heard her.

The two door guards exchanged glances. "Kari, the Council is currently engaged at the moment. Go find Rose and make–"

"This cannot wait," she insisted. "Open the doors. Now."

I don't think the Council Head himself would have refused that order. The door guards looked at each other again, then finally gave in, opening the heavy doors and letting Kate inside.

She strode in without pause and made her way to the dais where her grandfather sat. However, when we started to file in behind her, I noticed that someone was occupying Kate's usual spot in front of the Council.

Rowan looked over his shoulder at us, his disdainful expression made worse by his narrowing eyes. He didn't bother acknowledging the rest of us.

"Kari," the voice of the Council Head resonated threateningly throughout the entire hall. I could swear I saw the rest of the pack flinch. "What is the meaning of this?"

"Forgive me, Council Head," she answered, only slightly out of breath, "but this could not wait. I have urgent news."

"We have distinct methods of contact for news, Kari. Perhaps, it would have been better to use one of those rather than to barge into our meeting? Especially after leaving the last assignment I gave you incomplete."

His tone nearly made me shiver in my boots, but I had decided a long time ago that I wasn't going to be afraid of the Council Head.

Kate took a deep breath and continued anyway. "The coven you had us hunting provided grave intel. You are in danger."

Everyone was really quick to stop and listen after that. I knew that once Kate managed to spit it out that the Council would be more concerned with saving their own hides than meeting formalities. The instant the words left Kate's mouth, eleven of the Council members began questioning Kate's knowledge or squabbling amongst themselves. Stoic Rowan even widened his eyes a little bit, one of the most obvious shows of emotion I'd ever seen from him.

There was one man, though, who handled the situation with a calm that was almost unnatural. The Council Head appeared to be made of stone as he sat quietly, head resting on folded hands. His gaze centered directly on Kate, and a quick glance told me she was looking right back at him. There was some kind of wordless communication there that, I assumed, was helped along by their telepathic abilities.

After a few hair-raising moments, the Council Head finally sat up fully. That alone was enough to shut up the rest of the members. As he looked up and down the table, those who had stood up in outrage suddenly found themselves slowly sitting down.

My heartbeat kicked up ten notches as the he centered his full attention right on me. At that moment, I knew, without a doubt, that the Council Head was aware that I had told Kate about this so-called intel, but had absolutely no idea what he was going to do about it.

"Thank you, Maria, for bravely bringing this information to Kate's attention," he told me coolly, instantly making me nervous. "Perhaps it would be best if you explain the situation to us in detail."

A gentle hand at my back nudged me forward so that I was standing in front of the group, almost right next to Rowan, who gave me the same look I would give to a cockroach, not that I gave a shit anymore. My focus was on the Council Head.

This was quite different than the last time I had stood in this room, speaking to the Council. I was cool, confident, and collected, and my voice was more self-assured than it had ever been years ago.

"Our last assignment given to us by the Council was to exterminate a coven of vampires that posed a threat to every pack in the general area. Amidst our best attempt to complete this task, the leader of this coven, and perhaps the most dangerous vampire amongst those ranks, imparted some information to me. He told me that vampires were tired of being hunted, and were gathering together in order to overthrow the Council, as well as those who followed you."

Miraculously, it seemed like the Council was actually taking me seriously. "Did they say when this attack would be?"

"Not specifically, but before the end of the month."

"Then we must act quickly." For a moment, the members of the Council talked amongst themselves, sparing us glances every so often. We stood by quietly, knowing that any future action would be decided by them. Our part here was done.

Or maybe not. When they seemed to come to some agreement, the Council Head beckoned the rest of my pack forward.

"We have no reason to initiate any major attack against the vampires," he said calmly. "However, we will not simply sit back and wait for this to happen. We will prepare our forces to meet the vampires when they come for us. For now, though, we will hunt down anyone that comes too close. I would like you six to lead the scouting missions that we will conduct in the coming days, as you are familiar with several covens from your time out in the field. You will be notified when we have assembled a team for each of you."

Satisfied with our marching orders, our pack began moseying out the door, except for Kate, who took a step forward once more. "Honored Council Head, I have a request."

I watched as he raised his eyebrows and many of the members looked at Kate with a bit of surprise on their wrinkly faces. Even I was beginning to get a little worried; Kate was taking a lot of liberties with her position as Council's favorite today.

"Though she will not bring any attention to it, Maria risked herself to bring this information to us. The dangerous leader she spoke of took a particular interest in her, and attempted to hunt her down."

What was she doing? I could practically feel the burning stares of everyone in the room looking right at little ole me; the weight of everyone's attention was stifling to say the least.

"Is this true, Maria?" The Council Head asked me.

"Yes, however–"

But Kate wouldn't let me finish, though. "I would ask that you assign Maria a task here rather than send her out to the field. She could be of great use to you here without having to risk her safety should the vampire come for her again."

Why was she doing this? Hadn't I clearly told her that Daimon had willingly let me go? However, to be perfectly fair, I hadn't had the chance to explain the whole situation to her yet. She was just trying to keep me safe, in her own twisted manner, and I couldn't really get angry at her for that. "Council Head, I do not need–"

"No, Maria, if what Kari says is true, then we will keep you here. Rowan will take up your duties out in the field."

As frustrated as I was, I had to bite my lip to fight the urge to stick my tongue out him. That's right Council bitch. Get my scraps.

"Instead, we will include Maria as a part of our assembled war council. You will help us strategize and prepare for the coming times with your knowledge and experience."

My mouth wanted to drop open. The Council, the misogynist, human-hating, stick-up-the-ass Council, wanted to include (female, human, fun-loving) me, on their elite war council? Was the universe unraveling at the seams?

Gathering some semblance of composure, I bowed to the Council Head without any prompting from anyone else for the first time ever. "Thank you, Honored Council Head. I will put all of my effort into this task."

He nodded once. "You are dismissed. All of you."

It wasn't long before the whole campus knew of the coming attack. Everyone seemed to be running in ten different directions at once, including me. I felt like someone had effectively lit a fire under my ass. It wasn't enough that I had been appointed to a very prestigious and, therefore, busy group of people, but, since I was the baby, I had a lot of catching up to do. I spent most of my time ensconced in the library, several piles of great tomes detailing war tactics, mythology, and vampire history surrounding me like a fortress of smelly paper and knowledge.

In fact, that was an apt description of my current position. Hiding in the far reaches of the research department, I took up my place between the stacks and buried myself in words and stories. However, I wasn't simply playing the role of the model student.

I was really just sulking.

I know, shocking behavior for someone as mature and adult-like as me, but I had bad days too, and today was most definitely one of them. What put me in such a foul mood? It wasn't the General who sent me all over God's green earth doing his little errands, it wasn't the trainee who spilled his coffee all over my tediously done research, and it definitely wasn't the way Rowan had deliberately shut the door behind him (in my God. Damn. Face) when we were walking into the Council's main chamber.

No, it was Kate.

Considering everything that had been happening around us, it was only days after our arrival back on the campus that I had been able to come clean.

I had felt terrible leaving her lost and confused in regards to what had happened between Daimon and I, but there was simply no time to talk it out, and there were way too many prying ears to have our conversation over a nice breakfast date.

However, I did eventually tell her everything, and I mean *everything*; it was practically required of me as her best friend. From start to finish, I told her about finding him in the house, to running away from him in the coming dawn, to the promise to see him again.

She sat quietly on the edge of my bed, absorbing everything with a straight face. At first I assumed her silence was due to attentiveness, but, as my story went on, it became thicker, full of tension, until the last sentence of my tale was imparted nervously with shifty eyes and wringing hands.

She still said nothing, even when it was obvious that I was done. "Kate," I begged, "please say something."

But she didn't. She simply sighed and held her face in her hands, shaking her head back and forth and leaving me in absolute suspense.

I tried again. "Kate…"

"Just what do you think you're doing, Ria?"

I was a little taken aback, but only a little. Kate and Daimon, for as little time as they had spent together, had quite the volatile relationship. I tried another tactic. "Kate, I haven't done anything wrong."

"Really?" she asked me, getting up off of the bed and stepping towards me. "Is that how you think the Council will see it? Ria, you are consorting with the enemy!"

I should have been more concerned about the volume of our conversation, but that wasn't the prominent issue on my mind.

"Whose enemy, Kate? Huh? Certainly not mine."

"He became your enemy the day you swore your allegiance to the Council. No, not even that. He became your enemy when you became a werewolf."

"Not that I knew that at the time," I bit out. If Kate was going to get mean, then so was I.

She shook her head at me. "Regardless, he is a vampire and you are a werewolf. He is the enemy and you are the hunter." Getting right in my face, she narrowed her eyes and said, "That is the thing that threatened to wipe out your whole pack, that murdered Cindy's sister, and that selfishly tried to steal you away. Is that really who you want to fight so fiercely for?"

She certainly knew how to make me feel terrible about myself.

"I still love him, Kate. I haven't learned how not to yet. It's going to take time."

"Well, start thinking about it because if the Council ever catches wind of this you are going to regret ever knowing that boy." Lowering her voice, she almost spat in my face, "Do you think that they would ever entertain you becoming another Alessandra?"

Shit. I hadn't even thought of her. Just my luck to follow in the footsteps of the vampire-sympathetic, human werewolf before me.

"The Council does not control my emotions, Kate, they don't own me," I argued fiercely.

She snorted. "Is that what you really think? They have control over everyone here, every wolf and every citizen. They hold power over everything that *breathes* around them, and you're much too valuable to them to be let go without a fight. You're one of a kind, even amongst the werewolves. You are already bound to them for life."

Just as Daimon thought, I recalled chillingly.

"Rest assured, Kate," I told her calmly, "the Council has my loyalty, but they will never have my life. It's mine to do with what I will."

But she was shaking her head again. "I don't have time for this." Grabbing her cloak off the bed, she began to head for the door. "I have to go do a run on the south side, but, when I get back, we are going to finish this conversation."

I said nothing as she gathered her things. I didn't make any move to help or to follow her either; I never even looked up from the floor.

On her way out, though, she stopped, her back facing me, and asked, "Do you regret it now? Is this still the life you were looking for all those years ago?"

Knowing I needed to say it as much as she needed to hear it, I answered, "I will never regret the decision that kept me by your side, and I will always be grateful for the new life you have given me, even if you don't approve of the path I decide to take."

The click of the door handle was the only response I got.

And now, here I was, sulking in the library, not even able to concentrate on any of the words swimming across the page in front of me.

Frustrated at my lack of progress, I shut the book in front of me and placed it on one of the growing walls of my fortress. Knowing I needed to get my mind off of Kate, Daimon, and the Council before any more work could be done, I carefully stepped free of my paper stronghold and walked out of the library towards the one place where I could clear my thoughts.

The path to the cliffs was not as well-worn as it was when I was still in training. In the year I had been gone, some brambles and weeds had grown across the beaten path, making for a harder trip than I was accustomed to.

Some stress was relieved by slashing all of the barriers to pieces.

It was well worth it, though, when the trees parted and the flora finally cleared to reveal the breathtaking view of the waxing moon. It shone brightly down on the landscape around me, as well as on the sagely Native American woman who sat on a rock just to my left, looking down upon the same scene with ever-wise and ancient eyes.

God, I hope I'm near half as insightful as she is when I grow up.

Without looking away from the sight before her, Grandmother called out to me, "Are you going to stand there and collect bugs in your mouth, or are you going to come and talk with your grandmother, little wolf?"

I felt a smirk pulling at my lips as I walked over to her occupied rock and sat on the ground near her feet. Leaning my head back against the stone surface, I let the feel of the small breeze touching my face and the comfort of her presence wash over me and allowed myself to quit worrying over my problems, if only for a moment.

There was a comforting touch to the top of my head; I opened my eyes and looked up to see Grandmother staring down at me contemplatively, albeit a little uneasily. "You have that look again, little wolf. Like the heavy weight of the world is sitting on your shoulders, and you want nothing more than to push it off."

I smiled up at her feebly, and she must have seen the truth to her own words in it because she frowned and sat up straight with both hands on her staff. Looking more like the Chief she was than ever, she demanded imperiously, "Tell me everything."

Who was I to refuse a command like that?

I answered by telling her everything that had transpired between Daimon and me, then followed up with the conversation I had had with Kate not too long ago. Sometimes she would stop me to ask a quick, curt question, and then she would have me continue with my story, until I finally reached the end of it sometime later.

She sighed greatly when I finished my tragic narrative, and I waited patiently for her response. I knew she would never judge me as harshly as Kate had. Well, she might, but it would never be in such a hurtful, scathing manner. She was more like my mother than my grandmother really. No matter what I did, or how idiotic I may be, she would always love me. There were times Grandmother acted so much like a parent that I forgot she was not actually related to me.

By the way she took me under her wing and treated me like her own, she might as well be.

"Your heart is in the right place," she told me sadly, wistfully. "And so is most of your head, but your young friend is, to some extent, right. I do not believe the Council will let you go, little wolf. I truly don't. They are the most power-hungry men that have ever come into my acquaintance in the same sitting."

"If only you were in charge, Grandmother," I mused jokingly.

She chuckled lightly at that. "This place would be very much different if I was, little wolf, and," she paused once and then looked down at me again with sadness glistening in her eyes, "I would have let you go without another word if I was."

Chapter Six

"If the people we love are stolen from us, the way to have them live on is to never stop loving them. Buildings burn, people die, but real love is forever."

–Voltaire

It was late when I finally finished talking to Grandmother. If it was a standard run, then Kate would be expected to return soon. Now, with Grandmother's words and support under my belt, I was ready to face her. I was not going to let her walk all over me again. No, this time, I was going to tell her *exactly* what I thought of the situation, and where *exactly* she could put her own opinions on the matter, but only because I loved her.

I walked back through the doors into the lobby of the main Council building, where I was staying in the esteemed guests' wing. Miserably, I came to the realization that I had to pass directly by the main assembly room doors to get there, which, I was sure, would do nothing for my already chaotic thoughts.

The two standard guards stood at their post, one at each door. The first was the poster child, scary-as-hell, steroid-induced door man that the Council felt was sufficient to protect them well. He did not nod politely to me as I passed, but rather stood completely stock-straight in his spot next to the door, not even deigning to look at me as I went by.

The next man, though built in a way similar to the first, did not share the same frightening, merciless-muscle qualities as the other man. My sharp, well-trained gaze didn't miss this guard's shifty, frightened eyes, his hands clenching and unclenching at his sides or the sweat dotting his brow.

Now there's something you don't see every day.

Normally, I wouldn't think twice about interacting in any way with a door guard to the Council. They took their job super seriously and didn't appreciate distractions throughout the day, but this guard looked genuinely troubled by something, like he would feel more comfortable standing on the edge of a cliff.

Well, unless an alien beamed him up within the next two seconds, I was going to have to do my good deed of the week.

Damn my soft heart.

Unfortunately, there were no aliens (a fact that made me sorely disappointed). So, I walked over to the anxious guard's side of the door.

When he saw me approaching, he almost looked *relieved*, which nearly made me stop in shock. Just what was going on here?

"Maria," he greeted. I had been a rather frequent visitor these past few days, it was no surprise he knew my name, but to say it in such a comforted and reassured manner really threw me for a loop.

"Hello Brutus," I returned with a casual, friendly smile. "How long have you two been standing here, potty breaks not included?"

"Close to three hours now, I suppose."

"Well then," I said, surprised he was still able to *stand* in one place for so long. "I think you deserve a well-earned break." I pointed with my thumb over my shoulder behind me. "Why don't you go run around and enjoy freedom for an hour or two and I'll take your place here."

I was not stalling my next meeting with Kate. I was just doing my civic duty. You know, helping out my fellow man.

He looked genuinely astounded by my offer, a far cry from the standard emotionless façade you'd usually see around here. Composing himself after a few moments, he said, "Half an hour, nothing more, and then I'll come back and relieve you."

I nodded. "Go have some fun and regain some brain cells. This can't be healthy for three hours straight."

He laughed and walked away from his designated place. When he came close to passing me, he stopped for a moment, placed a heavy hand on my shoulder, and said, "Thank you," in a very solemn and grave manner.

Confused and not knowing what else to do, I nodded; he stared at me for a moment longer before taking his hand back and walking away swiftly. Reassuring myself that there was nothing wrong, I looked at the other guard who had been watching me carefully.

I smiled at him too. "I think I can handle door duty after a year in the field if you want to go too." I would have said "have fun" but it seemed like a stretch for this guy.

Mister Silent-but-Deadly said nothing, but, after a time, nodded once briskly before following the path of the other guard. I was taken aback he even listened to me, much less actually left his spot as well.

Something had to be going on here.

Don't panic, I told myself. If something was wrong, you would have heard about it by now.

Pfft, yeah right.

I didn't *feel* comforted by my thoughts, just more confused, but I couldn't think about this now; I actually had to do a job. The other guards would get upset if they saw me standing in the same spot they left me in with my head in the clouds.

The doors loomed greatly ahead of me, tall and somber, same as they did the first day I ever saw them. It was almost nostalgic to stand in front of them. I felt so much older now, so much wiser, but there were also days I only felt more like a child than ever, kept in the dark and always relying on other people.

So much had changed since that time, especially me.

The dark wood was smooth and cool against my calloused hand as I traced the intricate design of the twelve wolves that had so enraptured me the first time I saw them. I followed the pattern all the way to the end of the door.

That is, until the tip of my finger caught against a hard, cornered edge.

I thought I was seeing things at first. Why would there be such a thing along the smooth, wood of the door? I felt along the edge with my fingers and discovered, low and behold, a door within a door. It was perfectly level with my head and small, only about six by six inches, made of the same dark wood and carrying part of the same design on its surface.

Hello, what's this? A door to Narnia, perhaps?

I looked over my shoulder and made sure no one was watching me sketchily standing by the doors, alone without any guards. I had a reputation to maintain.

When I didn't see any passerbys, I attempted to pry open the little door with my fingers, and, to my surprise, it gave way quite easily.

Someone had been putting this to good use lately.

I peered through the small opening and had to concentrate to keep from falling over on my butt when I found myself with a perfect front row view of the Council's table, with all twelve members present.

Holy Crow, have the guards been spying on the Council, or was this just a safety measure I didn't know about?

Their voices were raised enough that I could hear them through the door, which immediately caught my attention. They were *arguing*? Was that even possible?

I always pictured the Council as a stoic group of hardened, yet united, individuals who found joy in stealing souls and taking candy from small children together, but to hear them squabbling amongst each other like old women was nearly unfathomable.

My curiosity had officially been peaked.

So, as not to be caught by surprise when someone walked by, I turned around, leaned my back against the door, and lined myself up so that my ear was against the frame and my shoulder rested just under it. Keeping my eyes up and even with the wall ahead of me, I crossed my arms in the standard guard position, casually sharpened my hearing, and listened.

"–idea is absolutely preposterous! Absurd! To even think something of this nature…"

"What has you thinking like this? She is a valued member of the ranks, one of the best in her class, with unbelievable leadership skills–"

"You cannot replace her! She is unique in more ways than one, and will only come once in a generation, maybe even less than that."

"Yes," I recognized this calm and deep voice. It was Kate's grandfather everyone was fighting against, the Head of the entire Council himself. I would have been much happier to hear everyone arguing against him had the whole situation not been so strange. "There has been one like her in the generation before and will probably be more in the generations to come."

"But such drastic measures! Is this really necessary?"

"I hear the Council's demands and understand the concerns it has brought up," their leader said firmly, "but such a thing is truly necessary. The benefits of this decision outweigh the loss of a single person..."

My stomach lurched into my throat. I didn't like the sound of any of this. This person was sounding a little too familiar, and for even the Council to be arguing over a "drastic measure" was unheard of. I didn't think they even knew the meaning of drastic.

"This Council has been assembled for over half a century," he began solemnly. "We have done what we must in order to ensure our legacy and methods will survive our time, and have been largely successful. However, it is obvious that our time on this Council is drawing to a close. Our faces are aged ones and this new generation is young and restless. Their minds are filled with new ideas and outrageous visions. If we wish to carry on with this ideal way of life, then we must make it clear to the coming generation that sacrifice is necessary in order to preserve the peace we have fought so hard for.

"We have never had any such fear of this initiative, and, if we are successful, this will be the sacrifice they will come to know as the greatest of all we've had to make these fifty years. It will be the key to victory over *every single* vampire in the area, and it will ensure that the ultimate game piece is entirely devoted to our side."

And with that he dropped the final bombshell and the idea that would shape the way I thought about this Council, and the world in general, forever.

"With our staged murder of Kari by a coven of vampires, the human wolf will disregard her feelings for her vampire mate and form a vendetta against his kind that will help us in finally overcoming the surrounding enemy covens."

I didn't hear what the others said after that; I fell to my knees the moment the words left his mouth, but there was no doubt in my mind they would all agree to it. What he had said was true. The Council had sacrificed countless wolves in the name of honor and peace over the years. Why should they worry over one more?

Maybe because it's his granddaughter!

It was just as Daimon had said. He had been right all along. The Council didn't care about its soldiers. It cared about the game, and we were nothing but pawns to them, pawns that were used and discarded, if need be.

It was always so great to read about in the textbooks, the tale of the fallen hero.

Now, I was finally seeing how it from the other side. There was nothing noble about throwing a life away for a small victory. There couldn't be.

They wouldn't get away with this. They couldn't. Not while I could say anything about it.

Not while I was still the wildcard.

And with that, I pushed myself up from the ground, turned around to face the door, and took my foot to the damn thing with an angry cry worthy of a banshee.

The doors flew open, hitting the walls around them and filling the room with a thunderous crash and the distinct crack of marble as I strode into the room, the fury of all of hell behind me, and faced the Council.

A few were standing, startled by the noise; others were snarling viciously in my direction, but there was only one man who sat completely composed, only one man who didn't have the distinct look of panic shining in his eyes.

The man seated in the middle of the table, in the place of honor; the man staring me down with absolute derision and cold, precise calculation, just as he did every time he looked at me;

The man heartless enough to send his own granddaughter – his flesh and blood – to her death.

As if all were normal and wonderful in the world of Ria, he looked down at me with raised eyebrows and the beginnings a sneer, his standard happy face. "Maria, your entrance can hardly be considered acceptable. Would you care to explain yourself?"

Oh, I'll explain something all right.

"My deepest apologies to the most *honorable* Council," I spat in my most magnanimous voice, adding a bow just for good measure, "but I find I am the last person here who needs to *explain* myself under the current circumstances."

If the others looked panicked before, it was nothing compared to how they looked now.

The leader straightened himself in his tall-backed chair, and appraised me like I've seen an enemy do so many times before. "I cannot recall what you would be referring to," he stated calmly.

*Bull*shit.

I snorted derisively, "Yeah, I'm sure you can't. Either that's your old age come knockin' or you're a bigger idiot than I've just naturally assumed."

Now he was sneering completely, "You overstep yourself, *pup*."

"Like hell I do, it's about time someone put you in your place!" I yelled up at him.

He lifted his chin a fraction of an inch, a typical look on him. "And what charges would you have put against me?"

There was a part of me – a growing one at that – that was warning me that this was *dangerous*. The Council was not to be messed around with.

But I hardly cared anymore.

I glared with all the hatred I possessed in me. "For planning to fabricate the murder of one of your finest soldiers for your own selfish reasons."

In the years I had come to know him, I had thought that there was nothing more terrifying than the glare you would receive from Kate's grandfather when you displeased him enough. I was definitely wrong.

Goosebumps covered the skin of my arms as his booming laughter echoed around the room, eerily bouncing off the stone walls in a way that made it sound like he was everywhere in the room at once, laughing at me.That couldn't be good.

It was the most grade-A, perfect evil cackle I'd ever heard in my entire life, and the smirk that followed it up was just as nightmare-inducing. "I was wondering why you strolled in here in the first place, now I see." Leaning forward in his chair, he placed his elbows on the table in front of him and rested his chin on his coupled hands. "Tell me, Maria. Where is Kari *right now*?"

The meaning of his words wasn't clear after a few seconds, but, then, it sank in, slowly but surely, and my world seemed to unravel at the seams.

His smile grew more pronounced as he studied my look of horror. "You have come too late to save your friend, human. You now have no choice but to follow along with our plan, for the sake of your pack and other friends."

It was my turn to laugh this time, making the smile on his face disappear immediately. "You still don't have me figured out, do you? To think that for one moment I would follow any order you gave after learning of this; you must be out of your mind." Taking a step back, I declared boldly, "I refuse to believe it's too late."

"Then I suggest," he advised mockingly, "That you run very quickly, human, for Kari's sake."

It was the only time in my life that I would ever take that man's advice.

I turned on my heel and bolted out of the room without sparing them another glance. The marble floor was so slick and clean that I nearly slipped more than once. When I made it to the door, I reached out and grabbed the side of the opening and swung myself out into the hallway just in time to hit one of the guards that I had replaced.

It turned out to be Brutus, and, instead of questioning my suspicious behavior, he grabbed me by the shoulders and pushed me past him and the other guard standing beside him. "Go!" he yelled behind me.

Following his order without question, I bolted down the hallway, not at all wondering why he would let me go so easily. Quite honestly, I could care less at this point. Nothing else mattered besides getting to Kate as soon as possible. Before it was too late.

I made it through the hallways in record time and turned the corner only to be met with the sight of my pack walking through the main doors. They were in their usual splendor, all mud-streaked and sweaty from their own runs. Laughing loudly and shoving each other around jokingly, they were the picture of happiness, the same picture we had been ever since we had been made a pack, ever since we had become friends. With a heavy heart, I knew that it was going to be a long time before we were all that carefree again.

But I couldn't tell them now; it would only take up more time. Their peace would last a little bit longer. I tried to just blow past them, but it was kind of hard to ignore someone running like a bat out of hell through a serene lobby. Maybe it was his oversized peripheral vision over everyone, but Austin noticed me first.

"Hey, Ria! *Ria*! Where's the fire?" he laughed, obviously not comprehending my sheer panic.

Others seemed to easily enough, though. "Ria," Carter's quiet, but firm voice called. "What's wrong?"

They continued to call out to me, but I didn't answer them. I had to keep running. Their hands reached out to grab me and pull me back, demanding answers and time, but I couldn't *do* that! I nimbly avoided everyone's searching fingers and kept going.

Feeling only a little guilty, I managed to call back to them over my shoulder, "It's *Kate*," before bursting through the doors and into the night.

I had thrown on my cloak before going to the cliffs and hadn't taken it off since then. It flapped and fluttered in the wind and gave me cover from the night that was becoming colder and colder as time went on.

I'm not sure that had much to do with the weather, though.

Okay, think, Ria! Where did Kate say that she was going? The answer came to me quickly: the south side, the farthest border from the compound; the farthest part of the Council's staked territory.

I wanted to scream at the utter unfairness of it all. Of course the Council would send her far, far away to let their dirty work be done. God forbid they had been caught doing anything wrong! Why were they allowed to get away with all they had in the past fifty years? Why had everyone made it so easy for them?

But I had, too; I'd followed along with their every whim until today, but now? Now, I was finally going to do the right thing even if it was harder, even if everyone hated me for it, even if it got me killed in the end.

'Thank you.' She whispered blearily into my shoulder. 'Thank you for not leaving me.'

It was with that one little memory that all the other ones followed. As I ran to her rescue as fast as my legs would take me, Kate's voice filled my head in the form of my memories and kept me going forward.

'This is my best friend in the whole, wide world Maria'

'I'd be willing to do whatever it takes to get you to stay with me.'

'You weren't brought up the way we were, Ria. Death is something that is second nature for a wolf. We don't like it, but it's accepted as inevitable, and honorable to the one who falls in the line of duty.'

I don't want to remember that one, I thought as I neared the southern border. I don't want to think about death or anything like that right now.

Frantically, I searched everywhere around me for any sign of Kate, or at least a coven of vampires, but there was nothing. I couldn't smell her or hear her anywhere, either. So, I used the only thing I had left.

I reached out with my mind just like Kate did when she used her power. My thoughts screamed out into the air around me *"Kate! Kate! I'm here, Kate! I'm here; where are you?"*

When it didn't work, I felt utterly ridiculous, but, even so, I tried it again…and again….and again…

Until, finally, I got a response.

"*Ria?*" I couldn't even tell it was her at first. Her voice was so feeble, so small. I ran faster in the direction I could feel the connection strongest.

"*I'm coming to help you, Kate! Just hold on a little longer!*"

"*Ria.*" Even with her voice so weak, the command was unmistakable. "*Go back, Ria. Go home.*"

Fat chance in heck that was going to happen.

I followed the voice as best as I could until my other senses caught up. The sounds and smells of a fight reached me and made me sick to my stomach in a way they never had before.

But when the sight of it reached me, I nearly fell over.

I felt like my whole body was running through water; time had slowed down to move in freeze frames.

And I had come at just the wrong picture.

'*I was raised that way, along with everyone else.*'

There was Kate, and there was the coven, just as was promised, but, instead of Kate fighting valiantly through her enemies, she was down on her knees.

Even I could see that she had given up; she was breathless and barely able to hold herself up. The vampires around her shot vicious jeers and insults at her, but she didn't seem to care.

Her eyes were searching, searching, until they caught sight of me running so madly towards her.

'*Live your life*'

She relaxed visibly, earning more jeers from the others. I was so close now, *so damn close*. She was less than two hundred feet away from me, and I was gaining.

"*Come on, come on, I'm almost there! Kate! Get up! Fight, damn it! Fight!*"

But she didn't.

She didn't see the knife that the vampire pulled out behind her, either, but I did. I saw it all.

Like a chain of pre-destined events, I saw it all unfold in front of me, and became painfully aware that I was not only too late to stop it, but destined to see it all from start to finish.

'Follow your orders'

Kate's face was so terribly sad as she looked up at my helpless form.

"I'm so sorry, Ria. Live your life for yourself, not someone else."

Kate was smiling when the vampire stabbed her in the back.

'And die protecting your brothers and sisters'

"I will always love you."

"KATE!

CHAPTER SEVEN

"Heaven knows we need never be ashamed of our tears, for they are rain upon the blinding dust of earth, overlying our hard hearts. I was better after I had cried, than before – more sorry, more aware of my own ingratitude, more gentle."

-Charles Dickens

I watched as Kate's eyes widened, and she gasped for breath. Clutching at her chest, she saw the silver of the knife and whispered, "No..."

As Kate fell limply to the ground at their feet, the vampires turned their attention to me. The younger ones threw Kate's insults in my face and laughed at me.

They were *laughing.*

The older vampires, with faces set in stone, simply stood in the background, impatient to get going now that they had finished what they were supposed to do.

I shoved them all aside, not caring that they were probably just waiting to finish me off next. "Get out of my way! *Get out!*"

A hand caught me on my shoulder blade and pushed me roughly to the ground, just in front of Kate. Feeling something warm on my hand, I lifted it to find that it was coated in blood.

Kate's blood.

My stomach rolled violently, but I forced myself to forget about it as I lifted Kate's shoulders and pulled her towards me protectively. She looked up at me with eyes that couldn't see. "Kill me, Ria. Kill me, please."

I didn't have the heart to tell her she was already dying.

But then her eyes fluttered shut and I was suddenly the one in denial.

"Kate! *Kate!*" I yelled in her face. "Open your eyes, Kate! I have to get you back to Vince!" A dry sob gripped the words I wanted to say.

Kate wasn't waking up.

I pushed against the wound on her back, where a sickening red stain was growing, but was surprised to see that there was another wound on her neck.

Two pinpricks. Like vampire fangs.

"Oh God, no," I whispered.

"Look at her, boys. Have you seen a sadder sight?" I looked up around my armful of Kate to see the younger vampires had assembled in front of me, all of their faces in the mocking and amused spectrum. The one who was speaking stood in the front. Obviously, he was the ring leader. "This is what the fearsome Council has to offer us?" They laughed again as the vampire leaned down to get in my face. "What's the matter, dog? Never seen death before?"

Anger, white-hot and strong, welled to the surface adding acid to the words, "Shut. Up."

"Oh! Look boys! Kitty's got claws!" More laughter.

That's when I felt myself snap. With my vision covered in a crimson haze, I felt the beginnings of a murderous smile that rivaled Trial three Lunatic's crazed grin stretch across my face. Casually lifting my hand for inspection, I turned to Ring Leader and inquired madly, "Wanna see 'em?"

Before he could answer, the claws that had extended from my hand slashed four deep scratches right over that pretty smile of his.

Funny, I didn't remember calling on my magic. This seemed to be something else entirely.

He fell back into his little flock shrieking and grabbing at his face.

"That is enough." The deep, resonant voice came from one of the elders, obviously done dallying around with an emotionally unstable werewolf and her dead comrade. "This is the one that is to be left alive. We are done."

"Oh, I don't think so," I growled out, not recognizing my own voice. Every head snapped in my direction. "I'm not quite finished yet."

I gently lowered Kate to the ground and stood up slowly. It was strange, but I could swear there was a darkness settling over my thoughts and emotions, something that was distinctly inhuman and like nothing I had ever felt before.

Kill them all, whispered the dark thoughts in my ear in a voice that I immediately paired with the red-eyed monster I had seen in my dreams. *Numb my heart, feel no more pain and kill those responsible for Kate's death.*

So, I let the ice cover my heart. I let myself become that monster so I didn't have to face that pain. I turned my face away from the world as something else, like an entirely new person rose within me, and took care of the mess around me.

When the last of the screams died down and the final vampire dropped dead, I hardly felt any better. It had been too easy for the monster and too empty for me. Kate was still dead. No matter how many of them I killed, she wasn't coming back.

I fell to my knees by her body again and placed her head in my lap, gently stroking her tangled, blood-crusted hair just as she always did for me. My claws caught in the knots; I hardly noticed. I was at a point where I was beyond tears.

I felt dead.

Tears won't bring her back either. Grieving won't make me feel better. Kill the vampires. Kill the werewolves. They are all responsible for her murder. Everyone.

The awful truth was I believed it. I was so angry, so confused that I would have believed anything anyone told me to take the hurt away. The feeling of betrayal was so overwhelming that it seemed like, somehow, the world was responsible.

It was close. On the brink of madness, I was prepared to give away my soul to this evil inside of me, until the sounds of howling wolves echoed through the clearing and caught my attention.

With horror, I realized that I recognized those howls. I knew who was coming.

My pack had followed me out.

Not fast enough. They didn't come fast enough. And because of it she is DEAD.

And suddenly I didn't agree with that violent whisper.

I knew they weren't guilty; they had been on patrol when the order went out. They were innocent; they had loved Kate just as much as I did. I couldn't let this *thing* kill my pack just because it wanted to. Even if it drove me mad with fury, I wouldn't let it hurt them. I would kill myself before I let that happen.

No one is innocent. Not anymore. Not even me.

The howls came closer, and I knew I had to move. I couldn't control this thing inside of me. If anyone came too close to me, I would probably end up killing them too.

But it wouldn't be able to hurt anyone if I kept myself away from everyone.

Looking down at Kate's pale and lifeless face, I prepared myself to do the hardest thing I had ever done in my entire life. I touched her face one last time, brushed my fingers gently over her lifeless, pale cheeks, and laid a final kiss to her forehead.

Gently, I moved her head from my lap and placed it on the ground. The howls echoed again, closer this time; they were closing in. I fought against every possessed nerve in my body screaming for me to stay with her and *fight* for her death and ran away as fast as I could.

A wolf is taught early on to recognize the different kinds of howls our comrades use in a variety of situations, even when not in wolf form. It's crucial to be able to respond immediately despite circumstances surrounding us.

So, it made it twice as hard when I heard the sound of despairing cries that equated to the call for a fallen friend.

When they called after me, I forced myself to keep running.

And when they called for the chase, I ran even harder.

I should have known it wouldn't be that easy. With one of the best trackers in my generation coming after me along with the rest of my pack, and a voice lusting for violence inside my head it was impossible to keep moving.

Without warning, I felt as if all of my muscles were locked together, and would no longer move for me. I fell to the ground hard, writhing every which way and trying to get back to my feet. I really wasn't surprised. The monster now had free rein in my thoughts, thoughts control actions, and it was my actions it wanted to have full control of next.

"Ria?!" four voices seemed to shout at once.

No, no, no!

When they came within my line of sight, the monster used the opportunity to slash out with an opened clawed hand, but they pulled back in time. Shock and hurt etched deeply into their expressions as I forced myself to roll onto my arms so I couldn't attack them again.

Someone else, someone I didn't know, spoke up. "This one is beyond our help."

"Her eyes," Cindy breathed disbelievingly. "Her eyes are red."

"She is mid-transformation. Soon enough she will be a wendigo and completely unable to control herself." He paused for a moment before casually supplying, "She must have been the one to kill those vampires."

Abruptly, the wendigo inside me (that's what it had to be) decided it had a voice of its own, even if it had to use my vocal cords to voice it out loud. "*Step closer and you could be next, traitors!*"

"Ria, snap out of it! Don't let this thing control you!"

"Come on, Ria. We're here now; you don't have to do this!"

I looked out of the corner of my eye to see that they were being held back by others who had come with them. Everyone but Carter had tears shining in their eyes, but even he had two spots of color high on his cheekbones. Carter wasn't letting his grief rule him, but if he got any angrier, he would end up like me.

And then, suddenly, their attention wasn't on me. Everyone stiffened and looked past me, beyond my curled up body into the shadows at my back.

My eyes may have tricked me, but I could have sworn I saw Carter's eyes flash crimson for only a moment before returning to normal and he snapped, "What are you doing here? What could you possibly want from her now?"

Oh no.

"Maria?"

Please, God, no.

An enraged snarl left my mouth as I turned to lunge at the vampire I could smell behind me.

Another one, another vampire. Kill him too, he is just like them. He's guilty too.

But then I saw his face. I saw Daimon's face, and I stopped.

No. Not him either. It wasn't allowed kill him either.

"Maria," he called to me worriedly. "Maria, what's wrong? What have they done to you?"

"What have *we* done?" Cindy shrieked in outrage. "Why don't you ask your little friends, you filthy murderer?"

He was not listening to her though. His entire focus was on me. "Maria," he whispered taking a tentative step towards me.

KILL HIM.

One of my hands reached out to strike him, but I pulled it back. Wrapping my arms around my waist, I backpedaled straight into the trunk of a tree.

"Surely, even you can see, vampire," the other werewolf who had spoken before said. "The death of her friend has affected her so greatly that her heart has frozen, and she is becoming a wendigo. She must be executed immediately or else she will kill all of us."

Daimon's head snapped towards the wolf, and, with a voice made of ice, he announced clearly, "You make any move towards her, wolf, and you will die where you stand." He turned to face me again. "Are you too blinded by your rules of your kind to see that she is fighting it?"

It renewed its efforts, and it was unimaginable pain every instant I fought against it. Somehow, I was on the ground again, screaming and snarling enough to make me sound feral.

"Suit yourself, vampire, we will leave you to deal with this one. When she finally decides to kill you, we will simply come back for her later." I could hear my pack struggling to stay, to help him, but orders were orders, and they were dragged from the clearing. "Know this, though, she cannot fight it. No wolf has ever broken free from this curse, why should she be any different?"

"You would be wise not to underestimate Maria, werewolf," Daimon warned him in a voice that sounded calm, but I knew it was anything but.

The werewolf's footsteps filed out of the clearing, leaving just Daimon and I behind.

"Maria..." his voice was much softer now. "Maria, please."

His voice, which had always seemed so soothing and pleasant to me before, was agonizing. Now that we were alone, all of my new, murderous instincts were centered on him, making it all the harder to fight it.

"Leave," I somehow ground out. "Get out."

He shook his head. "We've been over this before; I will not leave you, Maria."

With a cry of fury, I launched myself at him, claws reaching for his face. He managed to dodge in time, and I threw myself against a tree, holding myself to the trunk. By now, I was snarling incoherently. Each passing moment I felt more of myself disappear into the darkness overtaking my mind. Soon, I wouldn't even be able to recognize myself.

"Maria, this is not you. Don't let your grief turn you into something you're not!"

Again, I attacked him. This time, though, I felt my claws against the skin of his face, and saw the scratches they left behind. Not losing focus for a second, Daimon grabbed hold of my wrists and turned me so that I was pinned against him, not able to move in any direction. I struggled without any success.

"Don't listen to what they tell you, Maria. You can break free from this. I know you can."

But how? Just how was I supposed to do that? I was under the curse of the wendigo, in the middle of an irreversible transformation. No werewolf in history had ever been able to break free from it. So, why should I be anything special?

I can't do it. I can't handle my grief any other way. I don't have the strength to do it. My emotions are too weak, too human.

And, for once, I let my rational thoughts listen to that crazed monster inside my head because it was right.

For so long, I had fought against the label of "human," trying to prove to everyone that I was a true werewolf, through and through, but I wasn't, not really.

I was human, too, and maybe that was the only chance I had to break this curse.

A werewolf becomes a wendigo when they experience too many strong emotions. In other words, when they lose their balance and feel more human than wolf, their bodies tip the scale in the other direction, and, in the process, they just become a monster with no emotions at all.

I just had to find my balance again.

Gathering up all of my strength, I threw myself away from Daimon and landed hard on the ground, crawling away from him as quickly as I could until he wasn't too distracting. It was difficult, ignoring my clamoring instincts, but, with a superhuman effort, I pushed them aside. I felt my teeth grind together and my nails cut the palms of my hands as I forced myself to think, to focus.

I am human, I thought to myself, not just a werewolf. I can handle all of these emotions. I've done it before.

I did it in my parent's bedroom when I was preparing myself to leave the only home I had ever known.

I did it when I confessed to Cindy that I would miss my brother, that I would always love him, no matter what.

I did it every morning when I felt Daimon's locket around my neck and remembered a night long ago under a starry sky.

I did it every day when I did my damndest to prove to Desiree, to Rowan, to the Council that I was worth something.

And I did it every night when the world came crashing down around me, and I fell asleep knowing that the next morning I had to wake up and do it all over again.

There was a strength that I had been carrying all these years that I didn't even know about because I assumed a human heart was a weak and fragile heart. I assumed to be human was to be weak, but now, now I knew it was just the opposite.

And, with that, I let myself do the most human thing I had done in years.

"Maria?" His voice was so hesitant compared to before, and, yet, there was something hopeful in the sound.

Taking a deep breath, I felt the monster in me temper just the slightest. Ever so slowly, I let myself turn to face him until I looked up at him with crimson eyes and tears streaking down my face for the first time in a long time.

His eyes softened, and, even though he had been told to abandon all hope, even though the cut I had left on his face was still bleeding, and even though he was staring down into eyes I knew were still filled with madness and violence, he held out his hand for me to take.

I examined the hand held out to me in wonder. Didn't he know what was happening to me? Wasn't he afraid I would hurt him? Shifting my gaze to his emerald ones, I immediately got my answer.

No, he wasn't afraid at all.

Unashamedly, he stared right into my frightening gaze as if he could see right past the evil that was trying its damndest to swallow me whole and see into the place where I had retreated. I felt like he was looking past that madness and seeing the part of me that was caught in a cage of my own grief and despair.

He saw where I really was and was reaching out to me.

"It is all right, Maria," he whispered gently. "I am here."

With those words, I felt the last of the ice that had swallowed my heart melt and heard the mad ravings quiet.

Tentatively, I touched my feral-looking clawed fingertips to his and let him hold them tightly, just to see if he really meant it.

Without another word, he pulled with a grip so strong that I was vaulted right off of the ground and into his embrace. It was with undeniable surety that he wrapped his arms around me and pulled me so close I thought we were one person.

I felt his breath at my ear and heard his voice not a second after. "She would not have wanted this for you, Maria. You may grieve, but do not lose yourself in your sadness."

"Kate. She's gone," I whispered, feeling more tears slipping free.

"It's okay, Maria. You can cry now." Impossibly, his arms held me even more tightly. "I won't let you fall again."

That was when I let the sobs I could feel clawing at my throat burst free. Burying my head into his shoulder, I clung to him as I let myself mourn the right way.

I don't know how much time I spent in his arms, but, when I finally emerged from his shoulder, I noted that we had somehow come to sit on the ground. He leaned back away from me so that he could look me in the eye.

With a feather-light touch, he traced the skin around my eye. "You know, blue was never my favorite color until I met you. It was the first thing I noticed, actually. You have the most astounding blue eyes." Coming closer, I closed my eyes as he laid soft kisses against my eyelids. "I can't tell you how happy it makes me to see them again."

My voice was husky and gravelly from all the crying I had done. "I thought I was a goner." I lifted my fingers to the cheek where a line of blood still lingered. "I'm sorry."

"Don't be. What matters most is that you are back to your old self."

I watched as my fingertips began to quiver. "Kate..." I whispered as my eyes began to water once more.

"Yes," he said sadly, "I heard what was to be done and rushed here as quickly as I could." He held my face in his hands. "I truly am sorry, Maria."

Now that I had had my crying fit, I was left with a hollowness that hadn't been there before. "I don't know what to do, Daimon." Looking up into his eyes, I held his shirt in my fisted hands and told him as firmly as I could, "They can't get away with this; I won't let them, but I can't take on the Council alone."

"And you won't," he reassured me. Letting go of my face, he extricated my hands from his shirt and used the grip to bring me to my feet. "It's past time the Council paid for their crimes." He seemed to ponder over something for a moment, but, then, he brought my hands together and lifted them to his face, laying a soft kiss against my knuckles. "I think I know what must be done. There is someone I'm sure can help you. Listen to me Maria, just before dawn, go to the edge of the forest around 20 miles west of here. Someone will be waiting there for you."

My grip tightened spastically on his hands. "What about you? Where are you going?"

Ever so softly, he kissed my forehead. "Don't worry, Maria, I must go assemble your troops. You, however, must lay low. You are the only one who knows the whole truth, which makes your position especially dangerous. Hide until dawn. I will see you not long after that."

I somehow could feel it in my veins: there was a war coming. Pulling myself together, I wiped at my eyes with my sleeve. "Yes, thank you. I'll hide here until then and try to come up with some kind of plan."

He graced me with a small smile. "We're going to get through this, Maria. You have my word."

And, somehow, I believed it.

Saying our goodbyes, he disappeared into the shadows of the forest, and I went on the move. I knew the Council would send a search party after me now that they thought I was a wendigo. I had to get away from this place.

The time for crying was over. It was time to put on my big girl pants and get shit done. I could feel sad again later, but, if I wanted the vengeance that Kate deserved, I was going to need my wits about me, especially if my enemy was the Council.

So, I danced around the landscape for the rest of the night, not letting myself stay in one place for too long. Occasionally, I heard the sounds of other wolves in the distance, but I was always one step ahead of them.

When I finally deemed it safe to move to Daimon's appointed spot, the sun was just beginning to peek over the horizon, bathing the forest in a golden glow.

Breaking free from the forest I had spent the whole night hiding in, I found myself in a clearing at the bottom of a hill. The birds were starting to sing softly, and a soft breeze made its way to me. Closing my eyes, I took a deep breath and let myself relax for the first time in hours.

That is, until I heard a sharp voice and suddenly became aware I wasn't alone.

"Yo, kid! You lookin' for something?"

CHAPTER EIGHT

"I will love the light, for it shows me the way. Yet, I will endure the darkness, for it shows me the stars."

-Og Mandino

My head snapped around to face the unfamiliar voice with the speed of a rattlesnake. A little ways from where I was standing, I could see an entirely new character in my midst. She stood in the direction of the rising sun that was threatening to blind me.

Well, if I couldn't see her...taking a deep breath, my eyes widened at the realization that she was not a vampire, but, rather, something else entirely.

"Daimon sent me a werewolf," I asked dubiously. "What, are you here to giftwrap me for the Council?"

A distinctly female snort reached me followed by a drawl, bored tone. "Sweetie, if I gave a rat's ass about anything the Council did I wouldn't even be here right now. I gained some common sense a hell of a long time ago."

"All right, I'm stumped," I said lightly, but still no less wary. "Who the hell are you supposed to be? The Easter Bunny?"

A warm, and somehow familiar, chuckle reached my ears. "Not quite," she said as she took a step forward.

I could see her clearly now. She stood a little taller than me, and had clear, olive-toned skin and bright green eyes to match. Her hair was left unbound, a great brown mess, and she was definitely older than I was, probably just shy of her thirties.

"I've been waiting one hell of a long time to meet you, Maria."

I was still no closer to an answer. "And you are..."

Amazingly, she laughed. "Sorry, sorry. I've heard so much about you, I feel like we already know each other." Holding out her hand, she finally introduced herself. "I'm Alessandra, maybe you've heard of me before?"

I may or may not have been this stunned if Lady Gaga had introduced herself the same way. I was still debating; it really depended on what she was wearing.

Seeing my expression, Alessandra's lips twitched with mirth. "Close your mouth, kid. You're catching bugs."

My mouth snapped shut, and I hurriedly reached to shake her hand in the human manner. "What are you doing here?"

"A little birdy told me you wanted some Council-flavored payback," she said lightly. "I want in. In fact, a lot of people do."

I very nearly gasped in surprise. I hadn't been expecting anything like this. "Enough people to take on a werewolf army?"

Her head tilted slightly to the side in a way I was so used to seeing and a smirk spread across her face. "You could say that we have an army of our own."

Then it hit me. "You're talking about the vampires."

She seemed to catch the skepticism in my voice. "I know it's going to be hard for you, fresh off the Council bandwagon and all, but, believe me when I say, they have just as much at stake as you do here."

"I'm sure they do." I could have punched myself in the face. Here I was, judging the reinforcements that Daimon himself had sent me, just because the word "vampire" was attached to it. On top of that, here was the only other human-werewolf in existence, someone I had been waiting *years* to meet in person, and I was almost sticking my nose up at her.

What was wrong with me?

But it seemed Alessandra could decipher the look on my face well enough. Sending me a sympathetic look, she walked beside and wrapped her arm around my shoulder, bringing me along with her.

"I know it's heard, kid, believe me, I do. People who have a history with the Council tend to have trust issues. It's only natural."

She stopped for a moment and looked me in the eye, her face carefully composed. "I heard about what happened to your friend. I can't tell you how sorry I am."

It took a physical effort to quash the tears and sadness that wanted to rise to the surface at her words, but I noticed something in Alessandra's eyes as she spoke. There was a deep, lingering sadness there, too, something I had seen plenty of times before.

"You know," I said softly.

She didn't even have to ask what I was talking about. Nodding, she said, "I do, and, just like with you, the Council's to blame here." Alessandra started walking again. "I'm going to tell you a little story, Maria. Hopefully that will help you believe me a little more, or, at least, it'll convince you that you're not alone out here."

Looking up into the lightening sky, she started her story with a small smile on her face. "As you probably know, I was born a human, just like you, but we can't exactly compare childhoods. I was born into a family of vampire hunters, part of an ancient line that dated back centuries with a long-lasting family business to boot. We had a somewhat close liaison with the Council for years. We killed vampires...they killed vampires...We were all happy." Darkness and grief clouded her eyes over for a second, but when I blinked, it was gone. "But then, one day, we were attacked.

"An overwhelming amount of vampires attacked the compound where we lived. We fought hard, but, in the end, I was the only survivor. I even thought I was going to die when the search party of werewolves found me and brought me back to the Council with them. Feeling pity, and honoring the truce between my family and the werewolves, they took me in, made me one of them, and allowed me to train and be given the chance to go out and fight against the scourge that had claimed the lives of my family."

Pity like I'd never felt before rushed through me and reached out to the hurting woman in front of me. Her story was already so much sadder than my own, and I had a feeling it was only going to get worse.

I was right....and wrong.

"But then, years later, I came across a vampire while doing a run on my own. He didn't want to fight, and easily overpowered me when *I* did. Surprisingly though, he made no move to kill me. Even after I taunted and insulted him with jabs about my own family and how one more death from a vampire would be nothing...he didn't do it. It was then that he made some cryptic comment about how things didn't always appear as they seemed, and then just vanished. Poof. Nothing. Leaving me confused as hell."

"Been there before," I told her dryly.

She smirked quickly in shared exasperation. "And then, after that, I just kept *seeing* him. Every time I went out alone or was separated from my pack for two seconds, he showed up. Like a good and loyal wolf, I fought him, but when he shut me down quickly enough to make my pride hurt more than a little, he never mocked me. Not once. He would just talk to me; make conversation as if I hadn't been trying to remove his spleen moments before.

"It was with his outside influence and knowledge that I began to see just how corrupted the Council was, and just what they were capable of. It made me sick. Until, one day, he dropped the bombshell on me." her eyes met mine and burned with an anger that I recognized – the deep pain of betrayal.

"The Council *ordered* the massacre of my *entire* family."

My eyes closed on their own accord. I didn't want to see the look on her face. I'd had my own fair share of anger lately. Truth be told, I wasn't even close to being over it yet either. The whispers lingered, even now.

"So what did you do?"

"I left and my vampire helped me," she said calmly. "He brought me to a safe place and let me vent my anger and revisit my grief over my family all over again. Every old wound and abandoned demon had resurfaced. I would have been driven mad if he wasn't always there."

Visions of a hazy crimson world filled with nothing but thoughts of revenge nearly overcame me. However, I could hear the smile in her voice now, and it was only because of that that I was able to resurface and open my eyes to see if it was really there. The smile was small and private, but heartwarming all the same.

"It wasn't love at first, like everyone says. He was too annoyingly quiet and stoic, always hovering over me as if he expected me to explode any minute, but he *healed* me; held me together, piece by piece, until I could sleep again at night...or day really, and it *became* love. It's only because of that love that I'm here today."

I thought of Daimon, of his soft words and warm embrace, pulling me back when I had already resigned myself to madness.

Cindy, promising something no one else would dare for my happiness.

Vincent, who did his damndest to get me the truth.

Carter, standing guard over me, not willing to let anything hurt me, not even myself.

Austin, who reminded me that the strength of my heart would always overcome the strength of my fists.

"Yeah," I whispered, a small smile lighting my face. "I know the feeling." I stopped walking and turned to face her. "I'm sorry I doubted you for even a second. I know I'm going to need your help if I want some semblance of a chance of facing the Council."

"It goes both ways, kid," she returned. "You see, I think with your help we could even get some of the werewolves on our side."

I nodded, beginning to understand. "That's why Daimon wants us to work together."

"It's not just that, though." Her face suddenly became more serious. "The situation has escalated. Because of recent events, the counterattack that the werewolves had planned has become an all-out war." She turned me and placed both hands on my shoulders. "Tonight, the opposing forces will confront one another."

"You can't be serious. I was on the war council. They had no intentions of turning this into a war." It was only after I said it that I realized how ridiculous that sounded. Even so, I thought back to all of the meetings I had attended, but couldn't think of a single time when someone had suggested initiating the attack. "The casualties would outweigh any benefits–"

"Even an appointed war council can't ignore orders from higher up. If the Council Head had no qualms assassinating his own granddaughter, your entire generation is in trouble."

I wanted to rip out my hair in frustration. "And without me there, they all think they're dying for a just cause. We have to somehow come up with a plan before tonight."

She nodded. "I can easily get the vampires to rally around you because you are working against the Council, but you have to decide a few things first."

I swallowed. Hard. I wasn't sure how I felt holding the reins. "Like what?"

She held up a finger. "One, you have to decide what you are going to tell the werewolves so that they have a chance to see the truth before they consider you a traitor, and, two," Another finger, "you have to decide just what it means to depose the Council."

CHAPTER NINE

"Your time is limited, so don't waste it living someone else's life. Don't be trapped by dogma - which is living with the results of other people's thinking. Don't let the noise of other's opinions drown out your own inner voice. And most important, have the courage to follow your heart and intuition. They somehow already know what you truly want to become. Everything else is secondary."

–Steve Jobs

After she dropped those bombshells, everything else seemed to pass by in a blur. Despite her confidence, it took more than a tea party for the vampires to have any sort of faith in me.

I mean, I didn't really blame them; I had spent a solid year hunting them down coven by coven for the Council, and then just massacred a group of them the night before in a fit of rage.

I would be a little skeptical too.

However, it seemed Alessandra held a lot of influence over them. A little convincing and a few threats later, we were all coordinating and plotting like one, big happy family. We even managed to scrape up some kind of plan before the clock struck twelve and we had to make our way to the edge of the Council's territory.

My heart was pounding the whole way there. I was safely ensconced in the middle of the vampire horde with Alessandra and several of the Elder vampires, busting my ass just to keep up with the rest of them. As we got closer, I was beginning to pick up the sounds and smells of a huge mass of werewolves waiting for us on the other side of the line in the sand.

My heartbeat went double time.

I heard the piercing howl of the first werewolf who caught sight of us, as well as the others who were quick to join in. I tried my best not to think about how some of those howls sounded familiar.

As was customary, both sides came to a stop a respectable distance away from each other so that appointed leaders from both sides could speak with one another. It seemed pretty damn pointless to me, seeing as the game plan at this point was to fight until there was only one species standing, but, it seemed, even in war we couldn't leave out the niceties.

"Are you ready," Alessandra quietly murmured beside me.

"No one is ever ready for something like this," I told her seriously, sparing her a side glance.

She nodded understandingly, and turned just as I did to pay attention to the delegation in front of us.

"Vampires," I recognized the arrogant tone of one of the Generals on the war council, "by order of the Council, you are to be executed this night for the assassinations of several werewolves that occurred last night. We are here to carry out that order."

"And we are here to spare you from such a burden." I considered myself pretty tough, but just hearing the sound of an Elder vampire's voice was enough to give me a serious case of the willies.

"Are you now," the General asked skeptically, "and why, pray tell would we want to be freed from such?"

"Because you have been lied to." I didn't even notice Alessandra had disappeared from next to me. She parted the sea of vampires and moved to stand in front of the group.

Call me crazy, but the werewolves didn't look too pleased to see her.

"What are you doing here, *traitor*," the General spat menacingly.

Alessandra didn't react to the animosity. Instead, she simply bypassed him to address the crowd of werewolves. "Your intentions are noble, you are fighting for a fallen friend, but you've been lied to, and, thus, find yourself fighting for a lost cause."

The reaction was immediate and the backlash furious. My opinion of Alessandra rose more than a few notches as I watch her stand there quietly as werewolves shouted things that were borderline cruel at her.

I couldn't stand it very long. Rushing out past the vampires in a much less impressive fashion than Alessandra had, I stood beside her and hollered at the crowed at the top of my lungs.

"HEY, shut the hell up and listen when someone's trying to help you, you ungrateful little shits!"

The shock etched deeply into everyone's faces told me immediately that my "undeserving and wretched" death was probably one of the selling points the Council used to get everyone out here in the first place.

Even the General, bigheaded and stubborn as he had been when I had worked with him, seemed to be shitting his pants.

"That's impossible," he spoke, shaking his head slowly. "You were pronounced dead."

"Oh, is that what they told you," I crossed my arms over my chest and gave him a look, "and just who did they blame for my murder?"

He was quietly assessing the situation, but, behind him, several werewolves pointed fingers towards the vampires like frightened first graders.

"Mmm, and, yet, I'm standing over here, and you thought I was dead. Curious, isn't it?"

"Enough with the games, Maria," the General snapped, clearly out of his comfort zone. "What is going on?"

But I didn't even get a chance to start my story. All of a sudden, in the middle of the werewolf army, I heard the sound of four voices yelling for me at once.

"*Ria!*"

My heart clenched in my chest. I wanted nothing more than to go and group hug the hell out of all of them as they burst through the ranks, but I stood right where I was.

Vincent was the first to notice my unmoved stance. "Ria, why are you on their side?"

"It's not a matter of sides anymore, Vince. It's about who's kept in the dark, and who's finally seen enough to step out of it."

"What happened, Ria?" Carter's quiet, but firm, voice asked me.

"What *really* happened," Austin clarified.

I took a deep breath. "It's just as Alessandra says; you've all been lied to."

There were fewer outbursts from the crowd this time at the mention of Alessandra, but people objected nonetheless.

"HEY, if you have a problem to share with the class, then find the kahunas to get up here and say it to my face." They fell silent at that. I didn't blame them; I was a woman on the edge. "No one? Good.

"Honestly people, you'd think I'd be the last one standing up here. My pack leader, *my best friend*, has just been murdered. I've seen things in the last 24 hours that would drive any good person insane, and you better believe I'm gonna do something about it, even if it means going against the Council itself."

"You promise us knowledge, yet you yourself leave your comrades in the dark," the General growled threateningly. "You were set against the Council before you even set out tonight, you harlot."

Well, I didn't see that one coming. "I beg your pardon?"

"I was at least warned of this possible outcome before your supposed 'death.' The Council told me of your vampire lover. You would have all of us," he gestured to the werewolf army, "turn against the Council just to protect your precious bloodsucker!"

"Cover up the lies with inconvenient truths," I marveled angrily. "The deviousness of the Council is unparalleled."

"So, you won't even try denying it," the General demanded.

"Not deny, defend. It's true that I've had a past relationship with a vampire. Oh, and BTW, the harlot part is completely unappreciated. I ran into him on our last mission out in the field, seeing him for the first time in three years, and not knowing until then that he was even a vampire."

Fantastic. I approached this with the idea that I would explain why the Council is the seed of evil and ended up delving into my past relationships. Great.

I was surprised to hear Cindy's little voice rise over everyone's renewed mutterings. "It's completely true! We were there with her when it happened. She fought tooth and nail to get away from him once she found out and shared her story with us." The boys were quick to confirm this, too.

"The Council must have learned about it somehow," I continued, trying to figure out what must have happened while explaining it to them. "They saw any relationship with a vampire as a threat to their control over me and feared the past repeating itself."

Insert pointed look at Alessandra here.

"So, without consulting me, they devised a plan to assure themselves of my allegiance." I had to swallow past the lump in my throat as guilt threatened to overwhelm me.

"You're saying that the Council is responsible for everything that has transpired."

It's people like the General that made stress balls such a big hit.

"Yes, General, that's exactly what I'm saying."

"How would you have even learned of all this?"

"Because, unfortunately General, I saw everything, from start to finish." Sick of his condescending attitude, I stalked closer towards him with every word I spoke. "I was there standing guard at the doors to the Council's chamber as they discussed, loudly and in great detail, their plan to have Kate killed in action, the subsequent benefits of said plan, and the lie they had devised to cover it all up, and I was there at the end, too late to stop it as the vampires they had hired to do the job murdered her."

I was all up in his face now, and, despite a height difference of several inches, I felt like we were on equal ground, even when he leaned down to talk right in my face. "And just what, pray tell, do you think the Council Head gained in killing his own granddaughter?"

"They gained *me*."

It was a jaw-dropped moment all around. I saw as werewolves shifted nervously on their feet and whispered to one another. Good. They were beginning to suspect something was amiss.

The General's beady eyes narrowed dangerously. "Why on earth would they need to do that? You have given your oath to serve the Council, they shouldn't have needed to kill Kari for *you*. Your logic is faulty."

Regardless of my conviction, my voice was still quiet when I talked about Kate's death. "They sent Kate out on a routine patrol, followed by a coven of vampires to execute her. With her...gone, they planned to place the blame on Daimon's, my vampire's, coven, knowing that my anger over her death and his betrayal would be just what they needed for me to throw away any prior relationship and go on a vampire-killing spree." I paused for a moment, thinking that over. "They were right. Luckily, I relieved the guards stationed outside the Council's chamber just as they were discussing their plans, and managed to hear what they were going to do."

"I will swear by that!" Everyone turned to face the huge hunk of werewolf that stepped out of the shell-shocked crowd. To my delight, I realized that it was a familiar face.

"I was one of the guards Maria relieved," Brutus announced as he walked towards me. "I heard the beginnings of the Council's plans just as Maria was walking by." He now stood right next to the General in front of me. I literally had to strain my neck to look up at him. "I knew that she would have the courage to stand up to them, maybe even the wit to survive it."

I was flattered. "Thank you, Brutus. If not for you, I'd be a part of that army, and Kate would have died without purpose."

"You've already done more than I ever could have."

Nodding gratefully, I turned to the General. By the look on his face, I could tell he was having second thoughts. A quick glance at the rest of the werewolves told me that others still needed a little push, too.

"I may have been too late to stop their plan, but I refuse to be deceived by the Council anymore. I have now heard countless stories about similar acts of betrayal conducted by the Council for the purpose of solidifying their own power at the expense of innocents, and, more often than not, they have vampires, those same people they have us relentlessly hunt down, do their dirty work for them."

"It is true." I almost blew my tough girl cover and jumped when the scary Elder next to me spoke up. "The Council has hired vampires for years to take care of political and strategic executions. It keeps them from getting their hands dirty." He spit on the ground, a surprising act for someone so refined.

"And you don't refuse them," someone blatantly accused from the werewolf side.

The Elder raised his chin and glared at the one who spoke out. "I would assume that it is universally understood that the Council is something no one wants to make an enemy out of. Not even *you* would speak out against them when they did things you *knew* were wrong."

Wise old man: 1. Ignorant arrogant whippersnapper: 0.

As silence reined once more, I silently thanked the Elder for the doubt he had fed them on a silver spoon.

"The Council has literally been teaching you for years that you are to live for an honorable death in their name. All those teachings have done is make it easier for them to send wolves out on suicide runs that serve their needs. No more! *No more*," I bellowed, fed up just at the thought of it. "The Council has for too long ruled and repressed the werewolves that have served them faithfully and has only rewarded them by throwing them away when they ran out of usefulness. *No more.* The time has come for new faces to stand in their stead, people who have judgment that is not marred by selfishness and cruelty. It will be people who *we* believe are best suited to lead us; people who will appreciate us for the soldiers we have become and the loyalty we have to give!"

And then, by some miracle, a cheer rose up from the army of werewolves in front of me. I tried not to let the shock show on my face as they yelled out encouragement, agreement, and praise. Even while brainstorming, I had only the lowest expectations as to what their reaction would be, and now could breathe my first sigh of relief for the night.

The General, though it seemed he was mostly convinced, still had a look of skepticism firmly embedded on his face. "So, how do you plan on handling this, young General? A political execution of all the Council members."

"No," I said firmly, much to the surprise of many different people. When Alessandra told me to decide what it meant to depose the Council, I knew this is what she had meant. "I refuse to handle this the way they would. No more cloak and dagger plotting in the shadows." Addressing the two crowds, I raised my voice and yelled, "We are going to storm the Council's main headquarters and force the current members to step down. Imprison them in the Kennel to await a fair trial."

People seemed to agree with this, as there was no enraged protest of any kind, but the skepticism still lingered.

The General, for once, seemed to be on the same page as me. However, his voice was cautious as he said, "There will be those who will not step down without a fight."

Without a doubt, I knew exactly who he was thinking about. Seeing the sudden fear on the expressions of many of the wolves, I knew they were thinking the same thing.

"Fight if you have to and only as much as you need to," I looked right up into the General's eyes, "and leave the Council Head to me."

Squaring a firm gaze on me, he stared me down for a moment before nodding. "It won't be easy, but, after hearing your story, I, like many others, cannot live under the rule of such people."

I gave him a sharp smile. "Easy ain't any fun."

He seemed wary of little ole me. Good, he really should be. "I see." Turning so that he stood next to me, he observed the werewolf army. "It won't be easy pitting werewolf against werewolf. Differentiating between the two sides will be near-impossible."

I thought on this for a moment. "Transform," I ordered, "and roll around in the dirt a little. Be able to recognize the smell of this place. If you see a werewolf attack a vampire, automatically assume it's a Council werewolf."

As they began Transforming and following my orders, Alessandra came to stand at my shoulder and cautioned, "Maria, notice that the numbers on the side of the werewolves have dwindled slightly."

My eyes widened at the implications, and, with a newfound urgency, I addressed everyone. "We have deserters! We need to move out *now*!" As the troops reassembled themselves into their neat rows and companies, I couldn't resist calling out, "You know the way; *haul ass*. If anyone needs me, I will be throwing the Council Head a kickass retirement party."

As they laughed and whooped in delight, Alessandra, the General, and I Transformed and ran through the ranks so that we could position ourselves in front, ready to lead. I looked over my shoulder to make sure everyone was assembled, and, satisfied that they were, I lifted my head to moon shining overhead and howled a war cry that was echoed by many werewolves and mimicked jokingly by many vampires.

Ready or not, here we come.

The army at my back was less like a large group of disgruntled citizens, and more like a full force of nature. The effect of having such an impressive and powerful army at my back was indescribable. To merely call it exhilaration would be putting it to absolute shame.

It was an absolute euphoria.

But as the sight of the Council's compound became clearer in my vision, those feelings suddenly became grim.

Fear flickered in my heart before the hardened warrior inside of me clamped down on it. Sure, I had been fighting for years now. I was well used to confrontations of all kinds, but this wasn't just some standard run I was going out on.

This was war.

The light of the moon was the only thing that was guiding us. Every light in the compound was darkened. Not that it mattered when your entire army was made up of creatures that made the shadows their home, but the effect was a sense of wariness rather than an actual disability.

Oh yeah, staring down an entire battalion of raging werewolves was scary enough, but having only the flash of white teeth and the gleaming of their eyes clear to see was a tad bit disconcerting.

300 feet.

We were so close I could see the wolves extending their claws, and see the dirt that was casually torn away by them. Suddenly, my heart was pounding from more than just the run.

200 feet.

However, even with their attempts at intimidation, I felt the growing growl of the army behind me in my feet rather than in my ears. Unbelievably, it became louder and louder, building up as we got closer.

150 feet.

The image of a powerful wave suddenly conjured itself in my head. Not the lame ass "let's play in the surf" waves either. No, I'm talking tsunami-size forces at work, and if we were the wave, then they were the rock.

100 feet.

The sound bolstered my courage until I found that I was anything but frightened of what was to come. I had a job I needed to do. I had a duty to protect my friends.

50 feet.

I had a debt; a debt I needed to pay to the dead.

0 feet.

By the end of the night, Kate would be avenged.

Chapter Ten

"Our strength grows out of our weaknesses."
-Ralph Waldo Emerson

The sound made when a wave meets a solid wall of rock is powerful, but the sound that was made when our force attacked the Council's was one that I will never forget for the rest of my life.

Gut-wrenching, ear-splitting, and hair-raising howls, shrieks, and battlecries rose around us and filled the air with the sound of war.

Throwing myself over the first line of defense, I collided with a wolf from the second barrier who, braced for my attack as he was, was not ready for the force behind it. He was on the ground within a few short moments, and I made sure to head butt him hard enough that he was unconscious.

If he stayed that way, he may survive the night.

Not stopping for anything, I tore my way through the coming onslaught with all the drive of a woman on a mission. This was nothing like anything I'd faced before, not even in my Trials. There was no exchange of "You traitor!" "You liar!" "Blah I'm going to fight you while simultaneously insulting your lineage!"

This was pure instinct. I threw myself around the battlefield with a flurry of kicks, swipes, and occasionally a bite or two (though I hated doing it because it was actually really gross and messy).

As engrossed as I was in the fight, though, I knew that this was not the place that I needed to be right now.

There was someone else just calling for my immediate and personal attention.

Others seemed to realize this too because, for the first time in my life, I saw wolf and vampire working together in order to create a path for me into the building itself. I wasted no time running full tilt, lending a hand (paw?) when I saw someone in need.

The main doors to the building were already knocked off their hinges, and the windows on either side were shattered, shards of glass littering the ground around me. There was minimal fighting inside the building itself, and none of it was in the lobby where I was now.

There was nothing standing in my way.

My single-minded focus on reaching the chamber was interrupted, though, by a familiar prodding. No, there was no one standing behind me poking incessantly. It was a mental prodding.

Like Kate's psychic magic.

Curious, but naturally wary, I opened up my mind was met with a storm of emotions and words.

"MARIA! Oh, thank God. I've been trying to get to you forever!"

"Rose?"

"Yes, yes! Now hurry! Come to the desk!"

My eyes shot to the ruins of what was once Rose's main command station. Heart sinking, I hurried to clear the rubble, worried on what I would find, but, miracle upon miracles, she was all right. She had found a small cranny of space between fallen pieces of wood, and was tucked in there tightly, curled desperately around something in her hands.

Her glasses were hopelessly broken, enough that she would be able to see more clearly without them. A small head wound (probably administered when the desk had fallen) had dribbled blood onto the glass as well. Desperate to help her, I Transformed back and used my strength to lift heavy pieces of twisted metal and wood off of her and pulled her free of the wreckage. I tried to bring her somewhere safer, but she was having none of that.

With enough force to knock the breath from my lungs, she shoved the large object into my stomach, entrusting it to me. It was large and circular, covered with some kind of rough, rustic fabric.

Knowing it was probably something I didn't want to drop, I rushed to wrap my own hands around it and held it firmly.

"You will need that," she gasped. "To get to him. He is alone in the chamber."

Stunned beyond words, I tried to ask 342 questions at once, but the only thing that managed to escape my mouth was, "But why? He's your..."

She shook her head gravely. "I know my father, and I have seen that man. They are not the same person. Not anymore." Her eyes began to glint suspiciously, but she blinked past the tears. "Do what you have to, and do it quickly."

My grip on the package tightened until the edges dug into my hands dangerously. "Get somewhere safe," I implored her. "I will find you when it's over."

The piercing note of shattering glass reached us in time to see that wolves had fallen back to protect the Council.

"Run! Go! There's no time left!" She was pushing me away from her, urging me down the hall. "I can take care of myself."

And with that, Rose was a beautiful red wolf lunging forward to meet the others and to protect me.

I would not waste the time she had given me, but it was all I could do not to turn back and help her.

The sound of my footsteps echoed eerily in the halls as I skidded around corners and worked my way through the maze of architecture.

Was it really only hours ago that I had been running the other way? Was it really only hours ago that this had all started?

No. I couldn't think like that. This was something that was of the Council's making, not my own, in the works for years and years.

I was just the catalyst.

There was a noise coming ahead of me, towards the place where I was heading, the incredible boom of a collision. It would pause for a moment and then repeat itself, growing louder and faster each time.

Like a battering ram.

When I finally rounded the corner, I found quite the opposite. Instead, the sight of a single person, in human form, running at the door and attacking it frantically with her fists and feet greeted me.

She must have heard me coming and knew who I was without bothering to turn around. "They're locked," she ground out brokenly, slamming a fist against the wood by her head for good measure. "He's protected by magic, and I can't get past it."

Upon closer inspection of the door itself, I was taken aback to find that the doors that I had so reverently wondered at were different than the ones that stood before us now. The proud, intricate carvings of the wolves that I had traced lightly with my fingers were gone, and 12 men stood in their places. There was also something else missing.

The large, ivory moon that had safeguarded over them at the top of the door was gone. Looking down at the bundle in my hands for the first time, I hurriedly unwrapped it to find that moon in my grasp.

Rose had given me the keys to the castle.

Alessandra's eyes met mine over her shoulder and widened when she understood what I had.

"How did you...?"

"That's not important now," I told her gently, but firmly. The cloth that had covered the moon was dropped, forgotten on the floor, as I moved to stand beside Alessandra. "Can I have a lift?"

She smirked sharply. "You most certainly can."

She knelt on the ground next to me, hands upturned over her shoulders. Securing the disk under my arm, I leapt onto her waiting hands, and kept myself balanced as she curled them around them around the arches of my feet and stood. There was a groove on the door just in front of my face, circular and well-worn. The moon had been here a long time.

It was time to return it to its proper place.

As I slid the moon neatly into place and gave it the final push it needed to be firmly imbedded in the wood, a powerful force came from the door and nearly knocked Alessandra off of her feet.

Not wanting to unbalance her anymore, I jumped down next to her and watched, mouth agape, as the figures on the surface of the door *moved*. Like any other werewolf, they shifted, in slow motion, and became the wolf carvings I was so familiar with.

The one in the middle of the door seemed to look straight at us for a moment, before lifting his head and howling silently (I mean, it was still a carving, people) towards the restored moon. The others followed suit, and, when they did so, a rumbling click was heard.

On their own, the doors opened slowly in front of us. I turned my head towards Alessandra, nodding when she did, and walked together with her into the chamber.

The marble made our feet echo around us, like we were surrounded by hundreds of others. It was even darker in here, such a pitch black that even I had trouble seeing anything.

As if hearing my thoughts, though, the torches that were fitted to the side walls between the statues suddenly burst into flame. The room was engulfed in light once more, making my eyes (that I had just spent hours getting used to the dark) tear up.

I swiped my arm across my eyes, blinking them furiously to dispel the pain. I would need them pretty soon here. By the time I could see clearly again, someone had joined us in the Chamber.

I nearly reeled back in surprise when I saw the Council Head standing, facing away from us, arms folded over his chest, staring at the banner that hung behind his place of honor. There was no tension in him, no wariness, and certainly no worry about his back being exposed to us. His confidence was almost as insulting as it was terrifying.

It meant his strength was something to be confident about.

"Alessandra. Maria," he greeted calmly, like he didn't know what we had come to do. We didn't grace him with a response. "What happened to you," he mused to himself. "You two had all of the potential in the world, all of the strength and brilliance I needed for you- to be of use to me." His head turned to the side, not quite facing us, but enough that we could see the profile of his features. "What is it about you humans that gives me such grief?"

"Our moral dignity, perhaps?" Alessandra casually suggested beside me.

"Or maybe our refusal to manipulate our loved ones for self-serving purposes," I added.

Amazingly enough, the Council Head chuckled softly. "Ah, yes. It is your blindness to reality that makes you so weak. That and your unfathomable affection for vampires."

"I would prefer being blinded to reality over twisting the one around me by any means necessary for the sole purpose of power," I assured him quietly.

It was my words that finally made him turn to face us. His usual stoic mask was in place, but curiosity lit the corner of his eyes. "I did what had to be done, nothing more."

"Is nothing sacred to you? You *murdered* your own granddaughter," I accused harshly.

"You massacred an entire family of your closest allies," Alessandra ground out.

He watched us for a moment, completely unruffled by our tones. "I did what had to be done," he repeated monotonously.

It was then I knew that there was no hope for this man. He would see nothing else but his own ideals, and he would see nothing wrong in his actions.

'I know my father, and I have seen that man. They are not the same person. Not anymore.'

I wondered if he had always been like this, or if, rather, he had once been a father to Rose and Samson; a good one at that. Not someone who would callously order his granddaughter to be killed in order to gain something stronger.

'Do what you have to.'

He seemed to sense the change in the atmosphere around us. "Do you really think you stand a chance against me? Or are you simply under the illusion that I will just allow you to kill me?"

"Where would the fun in that be," Alessandra told him.

His eyes widened and I saw the white in them turning into a murky black. "You stand on your own graves," he warned dispassionately.

"As long as we're buried beside you tonight, it hardly matters."

He did not deign any more time speaking to her. His Transformation was smooth and frightening, especially because the wolf that stood before us was nearly two times the size we were in wolf form. Alessandra and I turned to one another, sharing a moment of wordless communication, before facing him together and beginning the fight of our lives.

Fighting against the Council Head was like fighting the war outside this room. It was like he was everywhere at once, always ready with an attack that would send me sprawling if I didn't dodge it in time. Regardless of the fact he was facing two people at once, it was everything we could do just to stay even with him.

I knew his magic centered on his psychic abilities. I knew that he was capable of what Rose and Kate could do, that if I opened my mind to him I would hear his voice.

I was not aware of the fact that he could rip apart my mental barriers as he pleased and rummage through my thoughts like a stack of magazines. Not only that, but it hurt like *hell*.

The feeling of him fingering through my head was enough to throw me for a loop and lose my focus. It gave him an opening. Claws fully bared, his enormous paw slashed across my back and sent me flying, with four open gashes making my back burn.

My stomach hit the floor first, skidding backwards farther away from the fight. Knowing that I was back in human form, I set my feet and hands against the hard floor, wincing slightly when my palms began to burn. Finally, the momentum from the hit fell flat, and I stopped again. A hiss escaped me as I shifted and the four gashes on my back burst with agony. I forced myself to lift my head to see how Alessandra was faring only to freeze in surprise.

There she was, on the ground below the Council Head, weakly trying to get her feet as he raised his paw for the attack that would end her life.

For a moment, their images shifted into to other figures, and I relived the moment where Daimon attempted to kill Kate the same way before I stopped him.

But I had been a wolf then, and Daimon wasn't nearly as powerful as this man.

It hardly mattered to me though.

All thoughts of pain were shunned from my mind as I kicked myself off the ground and ran towards the Council Head. With a cry that would have befitted a falcon rather than a wolf, I launched myself onto his back and slashed at his face with clawed hands.

His roar of pain was nearly soundless in all its fury as he twisted and struggled to get me off of his back, bull riding style. I refused to let go, though. Refused. I slashed at every piece of skin that was close to me while somehow still holding on for dear life. Eventually, he let himself fall onto his back, crushing me between his awesome weight and the floor (the fatty).

Crying out as the pressure on my back wounds grew to be too much, I gripped the blood-stained fur of his coat in my hands and *pushed*. His large form was catapulted off of me and into a bay of statues, breaking the exquisite marble without even trying.

I bolted towards Alessandra, who was still weakly trying to get up. She was still in wolf form, but I could see the contorted way her leg was sitting. Cursing at my lack of Vince-knowledge, I bent over her leg.

"Don't you dare bite me for this," I warned her. I snapped the bone back into place with sheer force and her yelp of pain abruptly cut off. "Can you stand up? That won't stop him for long."

She tried again, and this time made it to her feet. Valiantly, she was on all four legs, albeit with a little less pressure on her left front one.

The rumble of marble moving alerted me that this wasn't over yet. Snapping my head in the direction I had thrown him, I suddenly saw a hand burst through the rubble. The rest of him soon followed. He glared ferociously at me.

"Your impudence and refusal to die is most trying, human." Straight out of a nightmare, he started Transforming again, though it should have been impossible. Hadn't that injured him at all? "There will be no more mercy for you."

317

Well, if he could do it again buried under a motherload of marble, then I could too with four petty scratches on my back. Gritting my teeth against the pain, I followed suit and opened my eyes again as a wolf.

But it wasn't me he came for first. Again, he viciously attacked Alessandra, and, with an already-damaged leg, she went down quickly, her unconscious human body colliding with the Council table, cracking it slightly, before falling at its base.

Satisfied with his work, he tilted his head so that he could slant glinting silver eyes at me. I tensed, and waited for him to come at me, but his next attack was anything but physical.

A canine cry escaped me as he once again dove into my thoughts and scavenged them.

"You have no idea what I'm capable of, child. Do you?"

I shook my head frantically, as if that would dispel it at all, and tried pushing him away; trying to force him out, but my efforts were useless. He hadn't even moved any closer to me.

"My granddaughter's powers were mediocre, at best, compared to mine. You asked me what I considered sacred? Nothing in your mind is. I control everything. The pain..."

The pain that was centered at my back suddenly increased tenfold, like it had burst into flames. I thought my jaw would break at the force I was using to keep myself silent. This was the kind of pain that could break a person.

"Your memories...."

The chamber had vanished from my line of vision, and, suddenly, things I had already seen and lived before played out in front of me. I relived them like some kind of twisted 3D movie. I saw the faces of my family (my biological one), I saw Desiree mocking me, I saw my pack fighting for their lives, I saw the single tear that had fallen down Daimon's face,

I relived Kate's death.

Suddenly, the force in my mind not so much flinched, but paused, as if interested in what I was seeing. I could hear her words too, the ones she had whispered in my head before she died.

This was when I realized that I had no idea how to actually defeat this enemy. He was stronger than I was, faster, merciless, and he now had control over my mind, memories, and body.

I felt so completely and utterly helpless like I hadn't in such a long time.

The next memory played out, of my near-transformation into a wendigo. A ghostlike chill tried to overcome me as I recalled the ice surrounding my heart.

Even that was easier to defeat than this. All I had to do was just be human.

It was all I could ever do, and it was all that this man mocked me for. I would always choose being human over becoming someone like him, always, even if it made him so much stronger than me.

Strong enough to kill me.

As the memory of Kate's voice began to filter in my thoughts, the force paused again, listening intently to the memory, and was distracted enough to miss my train of thought as I considered everything I had learned during training, all of the lessons and spells I had under my belt.

But what about what I had learned outside of my training.

It was impossible, it was gutsy, and it was something I had never tried before, but, God help me, it was the only thing I had left.

Kate had always been super strict about the Council rules (stemming from the fact that the tyrant not only ruled the Council, but her as well), but the day Grandmother had finally told me about the powers of human werewolves, and the other members of my pack helped with tidbits about their own powers, I had come back to the room and Kate had imparted some of her families secrets to me.

Unlike the others, though, Kate didn't give me a strength, but rather a weakness.

The strength of her power was the ability to overcome the weak minded, she told me, and it was something that I could probably never learn how to do myself, but she wanted to give me advice in case I ever faced a fellow psychic from her family.

When she tried to overcome someone's mind, read their thoughts, or set up a link between multiple people, she wasn't just extending her own powers…

She was connecting her mind to someone else's.

Even this man, as sharply as he had defined his magic, as strong as he had made his power, was bound to this one weakness, the Achilles' tendon of his family.

And I was going to take great pleasure in using it against him.

Pair this with one handy dandy, forbidden, and *super*-secret ancient spell Grandmother entrusted me with that same night, and we were in business.

'This is best in your hands, little wolf. If there is anyone who will benefit from this spell and use it wisely, it is you. Use it only when all else fails.'

All the knowledge was in my head, all the instructions and mechanics of the idea. Now it was time to put it all to the test.

Time to pull out the big guns.

Instead of pushing away the Council Head's presence in my mind, I gripped it tightly and held on for dear life, like I was swinging on his back again.

Using that kryptonite connection, I whispered the words of the spell in my thoughts and let the magic spread over my mind and then extended it to his. Realizing something was amiss, he tried to let go, but I refused to let him. Failing to get free, he tried instead to do the most damage he could in my mind while I was busy being stubborn. Feelings, thoughts, emotions burst with an intensity that nearly made me black out.

He was not going to get me. Not this time.

I felt myself Transforming back, and let the transition happen, accepting it gratefully. Suddenly, the chamber had returned to my vision and I saw that what was happening to me was also happening to him. He was returning to his human form.

On my hands and knees, I gasped for air and finally let go of his mind. Amazingly, he stumbled back a few steps and stared at his hands in shock, letting the stoic mask slip from his face.

"What have you done to me?" His voice was thunderous.

"You should have taken more care in knowing what it was exactly that your students studied," I informed him.

Grunting in effort, I noticed the sheen of sweat at his brow as he attempted to Transform back and found himself unable.

"I've Transformed you back to a human, honored Council Head."

He froze in horror before lashing out with brutal obscenities and threats.

I ignored him quite easily. "There is something that I want you to realize before you die. Something that I am going to tell you now." Looking him in the eye while gaining my feet I enunciated clearly, "You were right."

I watched as fury gave way to confusion before finally settling on wariness. "Oh?"

"Yes." I lifted my chin proudly. "I am human and I am werewolf, but I will always, *always* be human first. Because of that I will always be a better human that you will ever be."

"I have no desire to emulate your human qualities," he snarled. "Spell or not, this form is a temporary one and one that I will not be bound by."

"And that will forever be your greatest weakness."

"What exactly?"

My eyes sharpened as I extended my claws and fangs once more. "Your unwillingness in allowing yourself to *just be human*."

I knew he had never given this form much of a chance. With his wolf side so much more powerful and terrifying, he never needed to rely on his human one. The animalistic nature of his more wolf side was what had driven him over the edge. It was the oldest mantra of werewolf training:

A werewolf is a balance between a human and a wolf.

He had lost his balance. His human side was weak, and it never stood a chance.

My speed rivaled a vampire's as I rushed at him. He knew what was coming and tried to defend himself, but he was too weak like this.

He was vulnerable.

The strike went right through him, through his chest.

Where his heart should have been, if he had one.

Disbelief so strong it was almost denial consumed him as he fell to his knees in front me shifting his gaze from my hand, to his chest, to me. I pulled my claws from him and flung the blood from my fingertips, disgusted.

Silver eyes that were so similar to hers, and yet so different, gazed up at me, and, in an instant, childish fear filled them. He then whispered the most human thing I had ever heard him say in our entire acquaintance.

"What if I see her?"

It took me a moment to understand whom he was talking about, and, when I did, the tears rose unbidden to my eyes.

"Ask for forgiveness," I whispered gently, feeling wetness falling down my cheeks. "For both of us. It's all you can do."

A thousand more questions lingered on his tongue, but I watched as, slowly, the light winked out of his eye, and all life faded from him.

The Council Head fell to the floor, finally dead.

And all I could do was cry stand and cry for him.

Chapter Eleven

"I wanted a perfect ending. Now I've learned, the hard way, that some poems don't rhyme, and some stories don't have a clear beginning, middle, and end. Life is about not knowing, having to change, taking the moment and making the best of it, without knowing what's going to happen next."
-Gilda Radner

The sight of the Council Head's fallen body on the floor below me was strangely blurred. Lifting a hand to my face, I pulled it away only to be shocked to find tears were still silently tracking down my cheeks.

This was the man who took my best friend away from me and devised a plan to keep me under his control. I had hated this him more than anything else in the world.

So, why was I still crying?

My attention was pulled back to him, unable to be centered anywhere else. He looked so different now, so less terrifying. He was sprawled across the floor in such an indignant manner, and the fear that had filled his last moments of life still lingered in the expression his face was frozen into.

It looked so…wrong.

The gentle weight of a hand settling onto my shoulder would have startled me out of my skin had I not been so engrossed in the fallen figure at my feet. Alessandra's voice was strained, tired (it was a miracle she had even made it over to me), but somehow was soothing, calming nerves I didn't realize were still wired.

"It's over now," she said softly. I could tell she was staring down at him with the same sense of incredulity. This man who had caused both of us so much misery was dead. "We should go…"

"Wait."

Bending over, I knelt beside his body and looked into his face again. Decision made, I reached over his face and, with fingers that were stained with his blood, gently closed his eyelids and hid his frightened look from view. I would at least allow him his dignity in death.

That done, I stood again, swiftly wiping the remaining tears away from my face.

"Maria?"

"I'm coming," I called out to her, finding the courage to turn away from that man and face her.

Strength was beginning to slip through my fingers as I worked to follow her to the door. Alessandra seemed to be in the same shape I was. Breathing deeply to dispel the pain that sparked every time I moved, I drew her arm over my shoulders and supported some of her weight.

Her look was nothing short of grateful as she did the same for me. Together, we managed to make to the door.

"Well, Maria," she laughed tiredly. "Think we're up for this?"

"Oh yeah, but, Alessandra?"

"Yeah, kid?"

I smiled at her. "My friends call me Ria."

She turned that over in her head for a moment before returning my smile and squeezing my shoulders lightly. "All right then, Ria. Let's blow this popsicle stand."

Mustering up all of the energy we had left, we pushed the doors as hard as we could, not knowing what we were going to find on the other side.

I was expecting to find anything but this.

The instant we stepped over the threshold between the chamber and the hallway, a tremendous ovation hit our ears.

Hardly believing my eyes, I looked up to see the congregation that had gathered was a mix of werewolf and vampire.

At the sight of Alessandra and me, joyous cheers and applause rang out. I saw them raise their arms, hug their neighbors, and…were people crying?

I faced Alessandra, my confusion clearly written everywhere on my face because she shook her head and told me, "They're cheering for *you*, Ria. You did it."

Hearing what she had said, the sounds of approval swelled up again in the crowd, and I could hear people chanting my name. The tears I had wiped away moments ago were suddenly dangerously close to resurfacing, and a feeling that I had never experienced filled me with pride and a sense of completion.

I felt accepted. This was truly where I belonged.

Alessandra, again sensing my emotional upheaval, removed her arm from across my shoulders in order to grab my hand and lift it high into the air, like I had just won some kind of wrestling match, and, finally feeling like I had survived the night, a happy, free laughter broke free of my chest.

I lifted my other hand into the air, and responded with my own cheer.

"Alessandra," a voice called out to her, quiet and calm, but also full of love and relief.

She turned the same time I did and ran with a speed I had no idea she was capable of to the embrace of a vampire. She tucked her head into his chest, as if to assure herself that he was really there with her. He helped by firmly wrapping his arms around her waist and resting his chin on her head.

With one arm wrapped around Alessandra's waist and the other combing his fingers through her hair, he turned his eyes to me. I was astonished by the sheer age and power that I could see in their depths. I had no doubts that Alessandra had manage to rope herself an Elder vampire.

"Knowing how reckless my mate is." He was swat on the arm for that. "I believe thanks are due to you for keeping her alive thus far." The look that he sent down to her was so beautiful that I suddenly longed for my own vampire. "You have my thanks, wolf. I am forever in your debt."

A debt from an Elder vampire was nothing to sneeze at, mind you. They took that kind of thing seriously. Acknowledging what he had just offered me, I responded appropriately by nodding my head.

"Thank y-"

"RIA!"

Hardly caring that I was in the middle of paying respects to undoubtedly one of the most powerful people I would ever meet, I whipped around on my heel, trying to find the source of the call.

Oh, please. Oh, please. Oh please...

Mid-turn, Cindy was the first to collide with me, sending me two steps back. I couldn't wrap my arms around her fast enough, and suddenly the tears I worked so hard to hold back flowed freely down my face. Vince was the second one to reach me. Sweeping in beside me and not even bothering to try to get Cindy to let go, he wrapped his strong hand around the back of my head and moved it forward so that his forehead lay against mine. Our faces were so close that I could see each tear that trickled down his cheeks.

Seeing Carter rushing towards us, the other two let me break away slightly and go to him. He had been so close to falling over the edge like me. I had been so worried that his temper would snap, and I wouldn't be there to help *him* for once.

Hardly containing myself, I reached up to hold his face in my hands and run my hands over his cheeks and (my favorite) hair. Realizing too late that Carter might not appreciate all this overemotional touchy-feely crap I hesitantly pulled my hands away from him, three seconds away from mumbling an apology.

That was when he reached over and lifted my off of my feet, pulling me into a fierce hug that I would not soon forget.

Unwilling to waste any moment of closeness with him, I wrapped my arms around his shoulders, and forgot how the strength of his arms was causing my back to scream with pain.

"Thank you," he whispered raggedly into my hair. "Thank you for doing what none of us could have."

A choked sob was all I could manage as I nodded into his shoulder.

Two, strong arms were suddenly lifting us both up into the air. "Stop hogging her, Carter! It's my turn to greet the hero!"

Carter slipped out of Austin's hold with a dexterity that I would ponder over some other time, and Austin took this opportunity to spin me around in the air. "You did it!"

He set me down again, and we all gathered around connected by various limbs. Holding our heads close together, there was a small silence between us that greatly differed from the commotion that rang out around us. We were all here and alive and whole.

My family was back at my side, even if someone was missing.

"Maria."

His voice, hushed and serene as it was, was louder than any of the boisterous shouts in the building around us.

The circle of familial love parted, each of them with a knowing smile lighting up their face. The rest of the crowd parted too, sensing the dramatics involved with the moment. Automatically, my eyes found him in the crowd, standing alone at its center. The small, warm smile that stretched to his eyes was reserved only for me as he reached out his hand and called my name again.

I understood now where Alessandra got her strength to run.

I threw myself into his arms and held onto him for all I was worth, brushing his hair, his cheeks, his lips with fingers that shook. Relief flooded my senses seeing him here and alive in front of me.

"You're okay," I assured myself as I held my forehead against his like I had with Vince. "You're okay."

"More than okay," he promised. He tucked a strand of hair that had come undone from my braid behind my ear and stroked my cheek softly with the back of his fingers. "I am so proud of you."

He painstakingly kissed away every one of the tears that fell, moving down my face until he finally pressed his lips to mine, and the entire world, and everything that had happened this night, fell away.

He was here, too. Daimon was safe.

A giddy laugh escaped my lips when we broke apart, and the smile that widened on his face sent my stomach to my knees.

"All right, kids." Vincent's arm somehow found its way over Daimon's shoulders in a companionable fashion. "That's enough PDA for one night."

Seeing danger in my raised eyebrow, Austin came to Vincent's rescue, ducking under me so that, in one moment, I was standing on the ground and, in the next, I was observing the world from Austin's shoulders in Cindy's usual place of honor. I let myself be paraded around by the giant and stared out into the crowd, noting the friendliness that was forming between the wolves and vampires.

There was peace finally within our reach.

That made me happier than anything else had tonight.

"It's all over, Ria." I could hear Austin's voice from below me. "This war is finally over."

"Almost," I promised him, ruffling his hair a little bit. "But, yes, the fighting is over with, Austin."

We're done fighting.

Two days later, when the darkest part of the night covered the landscape, the procession followed the path that had already been tread so many times over the past few days.

I followed the person in front of me silently, lit candle held firmly between still hands. It had taken some time for the shakes to finally go away. Sometimes, I could still feel an occasional tremor from my hand and was reminded of what I had done, but it was quick to vanish.

Our solemn group gathered around the pyre, standing close enough that our cloaks brushed together. I watched the wax drip down from the stick, unable to look up and see.

There was a gentle brush of fingers at the back of my hand, and I looked up into the face of Kate's mother.

"Come stand with us, dear," she implored softly. "It's only right."

I peered around at my pack mates and felt an insistent push from behind me, urging me to go stand with the family. I nodded to her, and she reached out her hand again to hold one of mine and lead me to the section of the clearing closest to the actual pyre.

Samson held his arm out for me and I settled at his side with an easy familiarity, his mate's hand still tightly grasped in my own.

I had told them personally the truth only days ago; how their only daughter's death had truly transpired, and, more importantly, the last words of the Council Head. I'm glad I hadn't left that particular detail out because it had given them a sense of peace that I could just barely relate to.

I could hardly imagine just what they themselves were going through.

"You were closer to her than any sister would have been," her mother said gently next to me.

"She would have wanted you here with us."

I nodded, biting my lip. Over the past few days, trusting my voice was increasingly difficult.

Grandmother moved forward and did her part, saying the funeral rite for Kate and lighting the pyre, sending her soul to some serene place, where she could rest in peace.

"Ria...."

I didn't turn this time and look for where it was coming from. The wind that swept over my face and ran through my hair was so familiar I didn't need to look to see who it was.

All of the candles in the clearing suddenly blew out, and the pyre's flame rose twice as high as it had been.

"Thank you..."

You're welcome, Kate.

Daimon had elected to stay behind from the funeral, feeling it was hardly appropriate for him to attend.

'The only things we shared were our enmity and our love of you. Though I regret her death, I was not her friend in life.'

329

Anyone else would have been furious to hear such, but, nowadays, truth was something I was coming to appreciate more and more.

After the funeral was over, I stayed for a few moments of sad meet and greet before realizing that that was probably not the best idea for my emotionally fried self.

So, bidding one last goodbye to Kate's family and to my pack, I fled to the place I needed to be most right now.

The moon always seemed to bathe this place in such a breathtaking glow. The beauty here was so disconnected from the horror of the outside world, and, luckily, this place had been untouched by the events of the past week.

My spot was the same it had always been: calm, peaceful, and safe.

She was already waiting for me (had she really fled the funeral faster than I had?) sitting on her customary throne, watching the stars twinkling overhead.

"Has it really been four years, little wolf?" She did not turn around and no greeting was necessary. "It feels like yesterday we stood here for the first time."

"I think it's been more like an eternity, Grandmother."

She did turn then, and her only greeting was a nostalgic smile that was tinged with sadness. "You have grown so much," she whispered. Whipping her head away from me, I saw her take a few deep breaths before asking, "You are leaving so soon?"

I shrugged, regardless of the fact she couldn't see it. "I only stayed for the funeral. There are other things that I have to go take care of. Pressing issues."

"It never ends," she added quietly.

The day after Kate's and the Council Head's deaths, I sat in the makeshift hospital tent with Daimon and my pack. They told me about what had happened on their side of the events and how they thought I'd gone mad with sadness.

As a group, we came to a mutual agreement never to speak of my almost-wendigo transformation. It would raise too many questions.

Noticing their suddenly shifty eyes and uncomfortable shifting, I knew there was something they weren't telling me. When I accused them of such, Carter took up the duty of handing me a familiar and appalling sight.

Handle-first, he handed me a silver dagger that I would have mistaken for my own had it not been digging into my hip.

'This was how the Council convinced everyone that you were guilty. They all thought it was your dagger. It's the same as the one you kept from your Trial, right?'

Which meant that Lunatic was somehow involved in this. Seeing the desire to run to his cell and interrogate him until he told me the answers to all of life's questions, Carter shook his head.

'His cell has already been searched. He somehow managed to escape the Kennel before we could get to him, though. We think he must have had help.'

So, somewhere out in the world, a lunatic that may have helped kill Kate was running lose, and had answers that I really wanted to hear about. Sooner rather than later.

Immediately after learning this, I made it clear that I would go out to find him and make him talk. Either that or bring him back here to that he could rot in his cell for the rest of his miserable existence.

My pack sprang at the idea, but knew as well as I did that they were needed here more, and that this trip was more than just a search for Lunatic.I needed to get away for a little while, regain some sanity and brain cells.

That was not enough to get Daimon to stay home too, though. He insisted, and I put up little to no defense. Knowing that I wanted out as soon as possible, he told me he owned a property near here we could stay at while we concocted our search and destroy plans.

Speaking of the devil, the soft crunch of grass marked his presence. He was clearly doing it for our benefit, as he could be completely soundproof when he wanted to. Resting a hand politely at my waist, he gave me a chaste kiss on the cheek in greeting and then nodded to Grandmother.

"Chief."

"Prince Charming."

Lolz. Too much.

Her eyes narrowed in on the hand that was touching her precious granddaughter's waist. "So this is the one you were pining over, little wolf?"

"He's the one," I affirmed, elbowing him lightly when he chuckled.

"You watch yourself around my granddaughter, boy," she warned lightly. "She cries, I beat you with my staff. Do we have an understanding?"

"Grandmother…"

"Do not worry, Chief." Daimon pulled me lightly so that I fit into the curve of his waist. "I won't let anything happen to her."

"Good. Then I have no need to remind you that I am old and very creative with my spells."

"*Grandmother!*"

Some things would never change, but, you know what?

I wouldn't have it any other way.

ACKNOWLEDGMENTS

When I was a little girl, I dreamed of writing a book that would change someone's life, but I never even considered that life would be my own. However, this story would still be gathering dust in my computer's hard drive if it weren't for the efforts of some very patient and persistent individuals, individuals that I would like to take the time to thank.

First of all, to the great and all-knowing Meghan Barrett, who was there for me from the very first drafts, who always has an honest opinion, and who heartily threatened me when I told her I couldn't publish a book. Joke's on me.

Kelly Davis, whose late night correspondences would keep me relatively sane if we weren't crazy to begin with. Our friendship started over a book and grew as we discovered that we were actually the same person. I couldn't live without my Kellson.

To the friends I'm blessed to have and the classmates I just finished four unbelievable years with. You reminded me that the world is mine for the taking. I laugh at impossible because of you ladies.

And, finally, to my family, the base of my entire life, for being utterly and wholly abnormal. To Parker, who read chapters over my shoulder even when I told him not to; to Jack, for reading the first draft and telling me it was something worth continuing; to Daddy, who gave me my love of stories and rhymes until I finally found my own; and to Mom, yes, it's finally done.

ABOUT THE AUTHOR

MACAIRE O'GRADY has, much like her heroine, lived in Rochester, NY for most of her life. She has written for her own enjoyment for several years and is now venturing out to share her first book in the world of publishing. When not working on Ria's sequel, she enjoys sailing, horseback riding, and pursuing her degree in engineering.

www.ingramcontent.com/pod-product-compliance
Lightning Source LLC
Chambersburg PA
CBHW021445240626
47153CB00001B/301